sierra

taylor dean

TAYLOR DEAN

this book is dedicated to all the j's in my life

. . . and the s.

(and the newest s, too)

prologue

"EVERY ADAM NEEDS his Eve," Pa said as his eyes scanned the rest stop, quickly calculating their chances at success. The newly acquired truck they were driving sputtered and coughed as if it objected to its unexpected occupants. "We'll be findin' her, Boy. I can feel it in my bones. Wur close, very close."

The plans were laid. Everything was ready and waiting for their return. They were only missing one more thing to complete their goal. Then they were home free. *Boy's* eyes darted around wildly as he hit the door of the car—slowly, rhythmically—with his fist several times to combat his nerves. He'd never been able to control his emotions. Stupid Boy.

"Knock it off," Pa warned and Boy obeyed immediately. He always did.

Weary travelers were usually in and out of rest stops quickly. In a hurry to get to their destinations, they were rarely very observant. He'd hit the jackpot at places like this in the past. They'd often served his purposes. *Unsuspecting fools.*

"This truck is as old as me," Pa muttered, as they rumbled into the parking lot, hoping they weren't calling attention to themselves. He pulled his bedraggled hat down low over his forehead, keeping himself unrecognizable—unmemorable.

"How 'bout that one, Pa?" Boy suggested. "She's purty."

"No, I told ya the requirements and she don't fit." Boy had pointed out a young girl of about twelve, walking with several family members. He really was rather dense—which had also served Pa's purposes.

"I is tired of waitin'. This is takin' sooo long . . ." Boy whined.

They'd been searching for a couple of days for just the right one. Pa enjoyed making Boy wait. The anticipation was making him squirm like a fish on a hook. His frustration was palpable.

"Look there to yur left," Pa interrupted. "Now that is mighty fine."

Slowly, they crept passed a family of three playing on the grass, oblivious to danger. Pa parked and simply watched them for awhile. It was just the three of them, no one else joined them. Perfect.

"Ya like her, Boy?"

"Nice hair," he said. "Cute kid."

"That's it, she's the one," Pa said determinedly. He turned off the ignition, wondering if the jalopy would ever start again. Didn't matter. If all worked out as they planned, they were about to abandon it.

"Now listen ta me, Boy, from now on yur name is Adam, got that?"

"Adam" nodded his head vigorously. "I'm not 'Boy' anymore. I got a name." Adam wrung his gloved hands with excitement as nervous laughter erupted . . .

-1-

"ALYSSA, WAKE UP, sweetheart."

Alyssa awoke with a jolt as Sam parked the car.

"Where are we?"

"A rest stop," Sam answered.

"Wow."

"I know, right?"

It looked like a setting for a mountain home, and hardly resembled the usual public restroom motif. They'd just left Tahoe and were taking Highway Eighty into Sacramento. The drive was scenic, to say the least. It was a beautiful June day in the Sierra Nevada Mountains. The sun was beating down from a blue sky and a light breeze wafted through the air. The smell of pine trees permeated every deep, glorious breath.

"How much further do we have to go?" Alyssa asked.

Sam laughed. "An adult's way of saying, *are we there yet?*"

"Shut up and go pee," Alyssa said while Sam continued to laugh as he left the car.

They'd been driving for several hours—taking the scenic route—and she knew Sam must be tired. Typically, his fatigue didn't dispel his cheerfulness. She decided she'd take a turn driving next.

Alyssa turned to check on Clay. He was sound asleep. A smile automatically appeared as she spent the next few minutes watching her precious son in peaceful slumber. He was so adorable in repose, nothing like the active two-year old she knew and loved.

The picturesque setting once again caught her attention. An ocean of pine trees surrounded her, making her feel slightly claustrophobic in spite of the beauty. Arizona, their current home state, boasted wide open spaces and was what she'd become accustomed to. This, however, was a sight for sore eyes.

"Excuse me, ma'am, I believe it's illegal to look as beautiful as you do in public," a ridiculously deep voice said from the driver's window.

Alyssa rolled her eyes at Sam's imitation. "Is that your best line?"

"Only one of many, ma'am. Would you like to hear another? I happen to have an arsenal."

"Sir, I'm a happily married woman and a mother, at that. Please leave me alone."

"I can't do that, ma'am. It's your hair, I've never seen anything like it and I'd like to run my fingers through it."

Alyssa hid a giggle. While Sam was trying to do a *Randy Travis* deep voice, instead he sounded more like *Pee Wee Herman* on steroids. "If I let you touch it, will you leave me alone?"

"I'd be much obliged, ma'am."

They both laughed at their silly banter. Her heart skipped a beat at the sight of her handsome husband. With blond hair, blue eyes, and six-foot-two frame, he stood out in the crowd. Clay had inherited most of his father's features and looked like a little rosy cheeked cherub. His blond locks sat atop his head in a mass of curls. Other than his large brown eyes, it was the only evidence he was her child. Clay had inherited her curly—bane of her existence—hair. Since elementary school her dark brown mane had been unmanageable. As an adult, the unruliness had finally left. With age, she'd let it grow down to her waist, leaving only gentle waves. The weight and length tended to tame the twisted strands. Sam always joked he'd fallen in love with her hair first and the rest of her second. But that was Sam. He was rarely ever serious.

"Why don't we stretch our legs for a bit?" Sam suggested, his voice normal. His gaze turned towards Clay. "Hey, little man. Let's boogie."

Alyssa noticed Clay had awoken. He smiled at his Dad

with a mischievous grin, holding out his arms. "Booooogie!" he squealed.

Sam grabbed Clay and began to dance with him in the parking lot as Clay laughed with delight. Clay and Sam shared a bond Alyssa knew would always be a mystery to her. She chalked it up to "a guy thing."

"Stop it, you two. People are staring."

"Let them look," Sam said, continuing to dance with Clay.

Alyssa shook her head. Sam was anything but reserved. The pine-scented mountain air hit her nostrils, reminding her of their honeymoon. They'd spent a wonderful week in Tahoe and they'd always wanted to come back.

This time they brought their son. Clay had loved playing on the shore of Lake Tahoe and they'd laughed uproariously when he tiptoed to the edge of the water and dipped his foot in. His eyes had widened and he shivered, a whole body shiver, like a dog when he shakes the water off after a bath.

Lake Tahoe was cold even in the summer.

Alyssa continued to watch Sam and Clay's antics. She'd been married to Sam for five years, but it felt so much shorter than that.

She'd married him against her father's wishes. He'd deemed Sam 'not good enough' from the moment he'd met him. Her father was mortified by the fact that Sam simply taught high school English and coached the baseball team for a living. Sam was content with being a teacher and this irritated her father to no end.

"He has no ambition," he'd often bellow.

They owned a modest three bedroom home and her father couldn't understand why that was enough for her.

But she didn't want the life she'd enjoyed as she'd grown up. She'd never told her father, but Alyssa thought of her childhood as rather cold. Her father was always working to provide the big house, fancy cars, nice clothing—it seemed so important to him.

The sad part was, all she really wanted was him.

She liked the life she had now with Sam and Clay. Sam loved and doted on his family. They were more important to him than his job and although he provided well for them, Alyssa loved that his family was his number one priority.

"You don't match," her father told her, as if they had to look alike to be compatible.

Alyssa's olive complexion was as dark as Sam's was light. She tanned easily making her constantly a shade darker than Sam. Alyssa stood at five-foot-six and she was often told that she and Sam made a striking couple.

Her father thought differently. He always did.

"C'mon, Mom, let's take a walk," Sam invited with a smile.

"C'mon, Mom," Clay imitated.

Sam had a brilliant smile. He could brighten up the dullest of rooms with his mere presence. Alyssa had always found him irresistible.

The three of them strolled the meandering sidewalks, enjoying the exquisite beauty of the mountains. Clay and Sam played a game of tag. Alyssa thought it was the cutest thing she'd ever seen—watching a grown man pretend he was running as fast as he could to let his two year old tag him and think he'd won.

Clayton laughed with delight as Sam tried and tried but couldn't run fast enough to get away from his son. As Clay tagged his dad, Sam picked him up and twirled him around in the air. A soft smile crossed Alyssa's face.

The men in my life.

It was now early afternoon and Sam was expected at a teacher's seminar in Sacramento by tomorrow morning. This was a vacation/business trip for them. Sam grew up in Phoenix and he loved it there, but his heart held a passion for the mountains. He'd traveled to many beautiful places, but he always told her the Sierra

Nevada's were something else altogether. She agreed. Alyssa had grown up on the East Coast, but loved this area of the country with the same enthusiasm as Sam.

"We'd better get going. I'll take a glance at the map," Sam gave her a quick kiss and started to walk off. Alyssa held onto his arm and didn't let him go.

"Hey, come back here, Samuel Fontaine, and give your wife a proper kiss," she said a little mischievously. While always affectionate with her in the privacy of their home, he was embarrassed by public displays of affection.

Still, he kissed her, willingly—if not a little shamelessly. Must be the vacation mood.

Clay interrupted their kiss. "Kiss me too, Mommy."

Alyssa gave Clay a big kiss and they all laughed.

"I'm gonna run to the restroom before we take off."

"Okay, meet you back at the car, baby," Sam said, holding Clay in his arms and dancing down the sidewalk.

"Booooogie!" Clay yelled.

Alyssa grinned broadly. She adored her family, even if they were a little silly.

≈

"PURFECT, ADAM, SHE is just purfect."

Adam fidgeted on the bench. "Hurry up, Pa, I can't sit still no longer."

Pa sat quietly and continued to watch. Adam hated when he did that. He could sit and watch people for hours. Sometimes he called himself the 'people watcher.' He said people don't pay no attention to their surroundings, that they were blind. He didn't know what Pa meant by that.

Pa let out a sigh and said, "We have found our Eve."

≈

ALYSSA STROLLED BACK to their SUV where Sam and Clay waited, taking several more deep breaths of the fresh mountain air. A lady in the restroom had engaged her in conversation, going on and on about the scenery and she was sure Sam was wondering where she was by now. Sam sat in the passenger seat, more than ready for her to take a turn at driving. Alyssa climbed into the driver's seat and as she adjusted her seat belt said, "Sorry I took so long, Sam, I . . ." Her voice trailed as she noticed Sam's unusually pained expression. Alyssa was startled as she realized an older man sat in the backseat. An involuntary gasp escaped as she saw he held a gun in his hand, pointed right at the back of Sam's neck. Alyssa started to scream and suddenly from behind her another man wrapped his arm around her neck. She felt the pressure of something cold and sharp against her throat.

"Drive!" the man said.

Alyssa glanced around them, hoping someone had noticed the two men in their backseat. Parked at the edge of the parking lot, the area was practically deserted. She looked to Sam.

"Just drive, everything will be all right." His normally sunny disposition was nowhere to be seen. Sensing the tension in the car, Clay started to cry.

"Shut that kid up or I'll do it for you," the older man yelled.

Sam, moving slowly, handed Clay his favorite blanket and stuffed bear. "Hey little man, you go to sleep now, okay," Sam said with forced cheerfulness. Clay promptly began to clutch his favorite things and suck his thumb.

"Look, take the car, take my wallet, you can have them. Just leave us here," Sam pleaded with gritted teeth.

"That ain't what wur here for," the old man said. "Now, drive!!" he yelled, making Alyssa jump.

With a gun at Sam's head, and a knife at her throat, Alyssa began to drive, not knowing what else to do. Clay was in the backseat with these men. What would they do if he started to cry in fear? The thought left her cold. The older man kept barking out directions and she was so scared, she didn't think, she just complied, feeling as though she was on autopilot. He guided them back to the main highway with decisiveness, clearly having a destination in mind. The men smelled of stale beer, day-old campfire, and dirt. The arm around her became moist with sweat, the blade of the knife resting on her shoulder. His breathing was heavy, his hot breath fanning her neck, making her feel as though she was going to be sick. The man was jittery with nerves and hardly able to sit still, which only increased Alyssa's tension. Sam tried to engage the two men in conversation, but they refused to participate.

"What do you want from us?" Sam demanded, losing his patience.

"Shut up and face forward!" the old man yelled.

Alyssa knew the situation was volatile. Her life memories began to pass through her mind. She remembered hearing this sometimes happens to people just before they die.

Her wedding day was the happiest day of her life. She remembered walking down the aisle toward Sam. He smiled and her heart melted. He cried during the ceremony and his three brothers had ribbed him about it endlessly.

She thought about the birth of Clay. It was a long labor, leaving her exhausted. She knew it was worth every moment when they handed her a beautiful baby boy. She'd never forget the look on Sam's face, tears of happiness streaming down his cheeks. He was so overcome with emotion—he didn't even try to rein it in. That was Sam. He wore his emotions on his sleeve. Alyssa loved that about him. He'd been voted the senior class favorite teacher for the last two years. He loved the kids he taught at school and they adored him. He was easy going and always had a big smile on his face. Alyssa loved that smile. It was the first thing she'd fallen in love with.

She stole a glance at Sam. The smile she loved was nowhere to be seen. His eyebrows knit and his fingers tapped nervously — typical of him when he was worried.

We'll get out of this, I know we will. They probably just need a ride somewhere. They probably committed some crime and the police are after them. That had to be it. Alyssa concentrated on her driving and let her thoughts wander back to happier times.

A whisper of a smile formed on her face as she thought of another time when Sam's eyebrow's knit and his fingers tapped. It was when they were dating and he'd taken her to an elegant restaurant. They were enjoying their meal when she looked up to find him frowning. She wondered if he'd brought her there to break up with her. As the evening wore on, she was sure of it, he was acting so strangely. But then, to her surprise, he produced a ring and asked her to marry him. When she said yes, the smile she loved appeared again. He leaned over the table and kissed her, right there in the restaurant, a long, slow, tender kiss that had everyone staring by the time it was over.

She longed for that now.

Alyssa's smile faded as she wished they were anywhere but where they were right now. She stole another glance at Sam. He caught her gaze this time and they shared a worried look between them. He nodded at her, trying to reassure her.

"Eyes forward," the old man commanded, stabbing the point of the gun into Sam's neck.

A vein in Sam's neck protruded angrily, revealing his tension. She hoped he wasn't going to try anything rash. *Stay calm, Sam. Please stay calm. We'll get out of this.*

Sam was wearing a light blue polo she'd given him last Christmas. It made his blue eyes look even bluer. He was so dear to her and she longed to feel his arms around her. Her thoughts drifted back to last Christmas Eve as they'd sat by the fire, opening their presents to one another. The glowing lights from the Christmas tree had illuminated the room, giving it a magical feel. A sudden fear gripped her as she wondered if they would enjoy another Christmas together. All she wanted was her husband and son. She knew she'd give these men anything they wanted, as long as she had her family.

Alyssa's thoughts wandered to last night. Clay fell asleep early, exhausted from his day of frolicking on the shore of the lake. Sam ordered pizza and they ate by candlelight on the porch of the rented cabin, leaving the front door ajar so they could hear Clay if he needed them. They had a gorgeous view of the moonlit lake. Sam held her hand across the table.

"Can you believe we've been married for five years, Alyssa?"

"Five happy years," she added.

"I've been thinking about something a lot lately. I think we should consider having another child." He smiled his huge smile, showing his gleaming white teeth. "I want a daughter who looks just like you." His blond hair was tousled from his day on the lake and her heart skipped a beat. He was 'golden boy' good looking and he had the charm to match his looks.

"I've been thinking about it too. There's nothing I would like more."

"No time like the present," he said with his boyish grin.

"I guess we should get started," she teased back.

He took her in his arms and they spent a romantic night together, their dinner on the porch forgotten. It was one of those nights you don't soon forget. She wished they could start the day over, that it was last night again.

A bump in the road brought her back to reality. This is ridiculous. My life with Sam and Clay is not over. Why would they hurt us? Why would they kill us? Her mind whirled with possibilities. Surely they just want to steal our car and take our money. They'll leave us out here in the middle of nowhere so they can make a clean get away.

Briefly, she wondered if she would soon wish that was

all they wanted.

≈

SAM NOTED THE worried look on Alyssa's face, his mind going a thousand miles a minute. Alyssa was a very beautiful woman. Part of her charm was she seemed completely unaware of her stunning looks and never noticed the appreciative stares from members of the opposite sex. Her skin always held a golden hue and a man could get lost in her large brown eyes. He most definitely had. He remembered the first time they'd met, when her eyes met his and he'd stared at her, dumbfounded. Her beauty left him speechless and he'd stumbled over his words like an idiot.

Still, to his surprise, she said yes when he'd asked her out. He was still in awe that she loved him and had married him. She'd kept her slim figure after the birth of Clay and hardly looked her twenty-seven years.

With these thoughts running through Sam's mind, he asked himself the question, if they didn't want money or their car, then what did they want? He was scared for her. He would die to save her or his son. He had a sick feeling in his stomach at the thought of these two taking his precious Alyssa.

Before Alyssa had come to the car, he'd started to defend himself, but then the older man held the gun on Clay. There was no way he would risk his son's life. Sam was completely helpless and he hated the feeling. The further they drove into the mountains, the deeper his worry became. Was it better to fight now, even if they were killed? Should they wait and see what the men wanted? If there was a chance he could save Alyssa and Clay, he'd do it. No question. Perhaps it was best to bide his time.

≈

HER STOMACH IN knots, Alyssa took a deep breath

and tried to calm herself down. Clay slept and for that she was thankful. She had no idea what they would do if he cried uncontrollably. He'd only turned two last week. Her thoughts floated to that day.

They'd held a barbeque/birthday party at their home and invited several of their close friends and a few of Clay's little friends from the neighborhood. Sam, who was quite the sportsman, donned his hockey gear and in all of his padded glory let the kids throw water balloons at him. He feigned fear at each throw and fell over with each hit as if they'd knocked him over with the blow. The kids squealed with delight and giggled at Sam's antics. Alyssa was sure he'd had more fun than any of the kids. Sam was just a big kid himself. The thought made her smile.

Her smile quickly faded as unqualified fear settled in the pit of her stomach. They'd been driving north on the highway in silence for nearly an hour when the older man barked out, "Turn left at the next road," making her jump, and the car swerve dangerously. "Watch it, watch it!" the old man yelled. The sweaty arm tightened around her neck till she gained control of the car again.

The thought had crossed her mind to crash the car on purpose from the beginning. That was one way of getting the attention of the authorities quickly and ending this nightmare. In the end, she decided not to risk it. Sam or Clay could be seriously injured and that would defeat the whole purpose, wouldn't it? She also feared her neck would be slit and Sam would be shot before the car ever came to a screeching halt. It just wasn't worth it. Right? Obviously she wasn't thinking clearly, in fact, she was numb with dread. Reluctantly, she guided the car onto a smaller paved road leading directly up into the mountains.

Off the highway. Away from civilization. Far from help.

Alyssa's stomach clenched. Soon the road changed to gravel, then dirt. Periodically, the older man gruffly shouted out directions.

After a couple of grueling hours, they were deep into the backwoods. Her nerves were at their breaking point. If her family was safe, nothing else mattered. She didn't care if they had to hike out of here, as long as she had Sam and Clay at her side, everything would be okay. A little voice was niggling in the back of her thoughts. She wasn't naïve. She knew how vulnerable she was. When a woman is taken by men it's usually only for one thing. Surely, if that was what they wanted they wouldn't have taken Sam and Clay too. They would've simply taken her. Her eyebrows furrowed at the thought and she pushed it away. It was unbearable to consider. She knew Sam wouldn't let them hurt her. He'd grown up with three brothers and they were a rough and tumble crowd. They grew up roughhousing and trips to the emergency room were the norm. Even now that they were all grown up and married, they could be caught at family dinners elbowing each other or poking at one another. It drove her absolutely crazy. She and the other wives would often make them take it outside. And they did. They would wrestle on the lawn like they did when they were twelve. As frustrating as it was, all Sam had to do was flash his huge grin and all was forgiven. He was adorable in a huge teddy bear kind of way and she loved him. He was one of those people who smiled his way through life. He had an uncanny ability to make others around him smile too. She loved him for it.

"Pull over," the old man demanded, effectively taking her out of her reverie. There was a small lake in the distance. It was now dusk and the sun was beginning to set. Alyssa was sure their ordeal was almost over.

"Get out of the car!" the older one demanded, gruffly. "Leave it running!"

Evidently they wouldn't be staying here long. She wasn't sure if that was good or bad news. They let Sam retrieve Clay from his car seat. Clay began to cry softly, his grip on his dad, fierce. He had, for the most part, stayed quiet during the car ride, other than an occasional whimper as he dozed in and out of sleep. Free from the grasp of the sweaty man, Alyssa fell into Sam's arms as they huddled together. Sam kissed the top of her head while holding onto her and Clay tightly, revealing his tension. The older one held them at gunpoint while the younger one removed an unfamiliar rolled up blanket from the back of their SUV. Alyssa was puzzled as to its contents. They ordered them to walk to the rocky edge of the small lake.

Alyssa was able to get a good look at the men in the fading light. They were dirty and scruffy, as if they'd been camping and living outdoors their entire lives. Their clothes were smudged with dirt and torn in various places. They were unshaven and their teeth were crooked, yellowed, and some were missing. They both wore hats and what she could see of their overlong hair was greasy. Both looked as if it had been a while since they'd seen a comb, much less a shower. They wore hiking boots caked with dried dirt and faded old coats of a long forgotten color, even though it had been a beautiful day out. The older one was heavily bearded, big and bulky. The younger one was tall and too-skinny. They looked like mountain men who had never entered civilization. They were so out of place in the human race, they may as well have been aliens coming down to earth. The only time you saw men like them was at an entry to a highway. They always held a sign that said, 'Starving, need money.' They were the ones you never made eye contact with. They were the ones who made you quickly check to be sure your doors were securely locked.

And now they were at their mercy.

"Lady, come on over here now!" the younger one demanded.

Alarmed, Alyssa held onto Sam and Clay. She and Sam exchanged a frightened look as Sam's arms tightened around her.

"No, just take our car, take our money, and leave us!" Sam yelled.

"Pa . . ." the young one whined, "She's not doin' what I say."

A father and son duo? Alyssa suddenly felt like they'd been kidnapped by the cast of Deliverance.

A smile did not cross her features at her levity. The man called Pa stormed over, grabbed Alyssa's arm and yanked on her, making her feel as if her shoulder had dislocated itself right out of its socket. Sam immediately swung at Pa with his free arm and his fist connected with his jaw. Stunned, the older man staggered, his gun dropping to the ground—and he almost fell to the ground with it. Sam was about to make a mad dash for the gun but was stopped by the sudden actions of the younger one.

"You let yur lady come with me or I'll shoot the kid," the younger one growled as he pointed a short, fat shotgun at the toddler's head, the now unrolled blanket lying at his feet. During the commotion he had acted fast.

Pa, recovering from the blow, with blood trickling down his chin, now held his gun on Sam. Several seconds passed in dead silence. Sam held tightly to Alyssa while shaking his head in the negative. "No . . . no . . ."

Alyssa was frozen with fear as the two men held their guns on the people she loved the most in this world. The ball was in her court and she knew it. She knew what she had to do.

Alyssa's eyes met Sam's and she knew that he knew what she was going to do without her saying a word.

"Alyssa . . . no," Sam protested, his grip brutal.

"Okay," Alyssa said. "I'll come with you. Just don't hurt them."

Her eyes never left Sam's. "When Clay is safe, come for me," she whispered.

"I will," Sam breathed. "I swear it," he promised as

Alyssa kissed him on the lips and Clay on the forehead. She held onto Sam's hand, not wanting to let go. Pa once again grabbed her by the arm and dragged her away. Alyssa felt herself panic as her grasp on Sam's hand was broken. Clay was crying and screamed for her, breaking her heart.

Sam shook his head back and forth. "No . . . Alyssa . . . no."

They slowly backed her away from her family.

"Hold onta hur, Boy!" Pa yelled as he handed Alyssa over to the younger one, at the same time holstering his small gun. "Give it to me," he said as he took the shotgun for himself.

The young one wrapped his arm around her neck and once again, Alyssa felt the cold, sharp blade at her throat.

"Okay Pa, do it now!" He laughed nervously with excitement. "Do it, Pa, do it!!"

Clay started to cry even harder and Sam looked confused. "What do you want?" he yelled.

Pa put the shotgun to his shoulder. A look of understanding passed onto Sam's face as Alyssa screamed, "No . . . wait . . . what are you doing?"

Sam held Clay closer as his gaze locked with hers. "I love you, Alyssa."

The sun was setting. Sam and Clay's silhouettes moved into the shadow.

"I love you, Sam, I love you, Clay!" Alyssa said, still not understanding what was happening. The man holding her grabbed at her hair painfully, preventing her from looking away from her husband and son.

"Pay good attention, now," he whispered in her ear, eerily.

This can't be happening. This moment cannot be my life.

And then there was a deafening roar and Sam fell to the ground and Clay's crying abruptly stopped.

"Let's get outta here!" she heard the old man yell as if from a great distance.

Darkness closed in on Alyssa as she collapsed to her knees in shock, a scream escaping from her lips that sounded more like the wail of a wounded animal. It took her a minute to realize the sound had come from herself. The sweaty man let her fall to the ground as she slipped into oblivion.

This moment *was* her life.

-2-

THE LOW HUM of the car's engine was the first thing that registered as Alyssa became conscious again. She couldn't quite remember where she was. *Oh yeah, I'm on a trip with Sam and Clay. All I have to do is open my eyes and I'll see Sam sitting next to me, he'll smile that huge smile I love so much . . .*

Her memory came crashing down on her at that moment and a scream ripped out of her chest. She struggled, not just at becoming conscious again, but also against ropes that were tied on her wrists and ankles. She began to scream and writhe and wriggle to be free of the ropes that bound her, becoming more hysterical by the moment. The men in the front seat began yelling at her to shut up. She kept on screaming. They'd taken her life from her and she wanted to die too. The butt of the shotgun came down hard on her head and blessed blackness once again overtook her.

The next time she awoke, the men were forcing her to get up. Her head pounded with pain, she could barely open her eyes, and she felt nauseated. She heard the old man yell, "You done concussed her, you idiot!" She winced at the sound. They carried her into an old rusty truck with torn seats. The sweaty man held her head up painfully by her hair and said, "Say goodbye to yur car." She held her eyes open long enough to see their SUV—lit up by the headlights of the truck—being pushed over a cliff, disappearing into the darkness. She heard the crash of the car as metal hit dirt and rock. Briefly, she wondered how anyone would ever find her and then passed out, welcoming the darkness that overtook her.

She next awoke to her body being violently shaken.

"Wake up, wur not gonna carry ya."

The chill of brisk mountain air engulfed her. It was morning. They'd driven all night. Huge pine trees surrounded them and the sound of rushing water seemed close by. Her head throbbed with pain and her mouth felt stuffed with cotton. It took great effort to stay upright. She felt as though she was in a nightmare, watching the scene before her, not living it. The sweaty man untied the rope on her ankles and re-tied it around her neck.

"Fur safekeepin'," he said.

In essence, she now wore a leash. Like an animal. Roughly, he pulled her over to a brooding Pa, who stared sullenly at a teeming river. The remains of a bridge lay splintered at each water's edge. "The bridge is out," Pa muttered. "Wur gonna have ta walk the rest of the way," he announced decisively.

"It's too far, Pa," the younger one whined. "At least twenty miles."

"Hide the truck in the trees, Boy," Pa commanded, ignoring him. "Pack the backpacks. It'll only take us a couple of days. We'll come back fur the rest later."

They placed her back in the truck and Alyssa welcomed the reprieve as she collapsed into the black void of unconsciousness. It seemed only seconds later that they were pulling her up by the leash. An agonized wail escaped her tight throat.

"C'mon, get up, woman. You best snap out of it. We have some walking to do," the young one scolded.

The two men now wore huge packs on their backs. They set off walking, the young one tugging on her leash as she stumbled and lagged behind. Her neck burned with pain. She felt reduced to nothing more than a piece of property. They hiked through the mountain terrain for the next several hours. Alyssa was unsure how she managed to put one foot in front of the other. She felt numb, as if in a fog, and she couldn't think straight. Tears streamed down her face.

They gave her a canteen of water and she drank from it

thirstily, feeling sick to her stomach almost immediately. She refused the granola bar they offered her during a short break.

Although the day had been hot, early evening hit bringing chilly night air along with it. Alyssa was wearing jeans and tennis shoes, but only a light t-shirt covered her upper torso. She began to shiver, not just from cold, but with fear. They walked into the darkness and she had no idea where she was going . . . or what awaited her at their destination.

Finally, they pushed her down next to a tree, securing her tightly to the trunk with a rope around her torso. They threw a scratchy blanket at her and the two men lay down on their bedrolls. Her hands tied in front of her, she pulled the blanket up close to her chest and curled into a ball. In shock, her head dangled to one side as she literally passed out from exhaustion.

Alyssa awoke abruptly to the sound of a crackling fire and yet she was chilled to the bone, every joint in her body aching. When she came to her senses, her eyes darted frantically as she took in her surroundings. The one called Pa sat by the fire. The younger one sat next to him and they were both staring at her eerily, looking like lions preparing to eat their prey. She couldn't help herself, she immediately began to struggle against the ropes holding her captive. The desire to flee coursed through her like an adrenalin rush.

"Give it up, lady. It's no use."

She stilled, her breathing ragged, staring at her captors with wide, blinking eyes. Pa had a cold, calculating gaze, as if he didn't miss a thing. He was a big bear of a man with labored breathing and a bushy beard. The young one had wild eyes that darted about and he was constantly wringing his hands as if very nervous. He was tall and scrawny looking, reminding her of an emaciated scarecrow.

"What do you want from me?" she asked, her tone

laced with despair. She hadn't been raped and she wasn't dead yet. Alyssa knew most kidnapping victims were sexually assaulted and dead within hours of being taken. She didn't understand what they wanted with her.

"Yur name is now Eve, and you belong ta us. Yur part of our family now," the one called Pa told her bluntly.

"Eve? My name is Alyssa," she blurted, feeling perplexed.

Pa stood quickly for a man of his size and thundered, "EVE!! Don't let me be hearin' any different. Understand?"

Startled at the outburst, Alyssa simply nodded.

"You have a new life now. The old one is over," he continued brusquely. "That's why we made ya watch, so you would know they're gone and you wouldn't be off pining for 'em all the time."

Alyssa sat in stunned silence, feeling utterly numb, almost anesthetized to life.

Sam . . . Clay . . .

A paralyzing pain gripped her. She drew in a ragged breath, unable to breathe at the thought of her husband and son. It was too much, she was overwhelmed and on overload as she buried her face in her hands, not wanting the sight of these two men to greet her.

Dear God, is this really happening?

"No time for talkin', we have a long walk today."

They left her wondering at their enigmatic comments. *Family? Eve? New life?*

She couldn't choke down the so-called breakfast, her emotional pain was too great to notice the physical pain of hunger. The morning meal consisted of beef jerky they hastily chomped on before putting out the fire, packing up, and continuing on.

"Let's go. We have ta put more distance between us and our truck," Pa demanded. Then he added, "Just in case." He was clearly the one in charge. The young one seemed scared of him. He wasn't the only one.

They walked deeper and deeper into the woods, hiking

through a long draw to access a large mountain face. "It's on the other side of this here mountain, Boy. We ought ta be there by ta-night."

The hike was grueling, the terrain rocky and uneven. Alyssa stumbled along, hardly able to think. Her head pulsated with pain and her vision was blurry. They seemed to be in a hurry and didn't stop for lunch. The young one handed her pieces of beef jerky from his pocket throughout the day. Pieces of lint stuck to the leathery bits of dried beef and she couldn't bring herself to eat them. When he wasn't looking, she tucked them into her pocket, wondering if she would soon be desperate enough to consume them. He seemed to be chewing on the jerky all day, like a cow with its cud. During breaks, she gingerly sipped from her canteen, letting her stomach settle in between gulps. The water had a nasty metallic taste which activated her gag reflex. She hadn't eaten in nearly forty-eight hours and her hands shook from weakness. The only thought consuming her befuddled brain was taking the next step, thus preventing a painful tug on her leash.

They didn't make it to their destination that night. When Alyssa collapsed to her knees three times in only half an hour, staring at her captors blankly as if she couldn't understand English, Pa declared they were stopping for the night.

"The lady needs food or we'll never make it. Stupid boy, you hit her too hard!" he yelled at the young one. "She's the walkin' dead."

Alyssa buckled to the ground, knowing she didn't have the strength to walk another step. She let the darkness overtake her as she collapsed, stomach-side-down, onto the ground. She was done.

It was pitch black when she awoke to movement. Pa and the young one had grabbed her by the underarms and were dragging her across the dirt. They sat her up, leaning her against a tree. The young one secured her to the tree as Pa splashed cold water onto her face. He handed her a can of beans and commanded her to eat. "If you don't eat, we'll stuff it down yur throat. Got it?"

It was a rude awakening. It took great effort to keep her eyes open long enough to consume the food. Alyssa balanced the can between her knees and clumsily spooned beans into her mouth while her ears rang and her head throbbed. Eating with her hands tied together was no easy feat, but she managed. When she was done, Pa unwrapped a granola bar and handed it to her. "Every last speck," he warned.

She ate quickly, then gulped from her canteen, the water suddenly tasting good. The young one tucked a blanket around her and she flinched at his familiarity. Feeling as though she'd be sick at any moment, she watched them stoke the fire and settle into their sleeping bags, her eyes wide.

Sam and Clay are fine, of course they are. Sam will come after me. He'll be here soon. They aren't dead. I know they're not. The bullet didn't hit them in a life threatening manner. Sam is staking out our campsite right now, this very minute. He's placed Clay someplace safe and warm. And now he's coming for me. I'll awaken and he'll be here, untying my ropes and holding me in his arms. Yes, he'll be here tonight and he'll save me. He'll smile that huge smile I love so much and everything will be all right . . .

Alyssa let her thoughts continue on in this vain as she wondered how she was supposed to sleep while sitting up with her head against the knotty bark of the tree. However, sleep still claimed her, whether or not she wanted it to.

She awoke filled with the ache of sore muscles, but the pain in her heart made her gasp for air. A sob escaped as memories washed over her. Tears poured down her cheeks as she felt panic overwhelm her.

Sam hadn't come for her in the night.

Sam and Clay were gone from her life forever. In her heart she knew it was true. She couldn't continue to delude herself. It had happened so fast, she wasn't expecting it. She'd gone with them willingly, why did they have to shoot them? Why?

Her breathing turned ragged as she became aware of her situation. She longed for sleep to take over again. The skin on her neck was raw from the leash, the muscles stiff from sleeping while sitting up. Her feet ached from walking. Her shoes and socks were still wet from walking through shallow creek beds and the skin on her feet felt inflamed.

However, the pain in her head had lessened to a dull ache. She felt as though she could think again and to prove it, her eyes guardedly darted around the area. A fire burned in a pit close by, yet her captors were nowhere to be seen. Her hands clutched at the rope around her waist. Tugging at it, she tried to get to the knot and as she did so, Pa and the young one walked back into camp, tossing firewood into the fire. Frozen with trepidation as she surveyed her captors, Alyssa considered feigning sleep, but knew it was useless. She had to face them. Wiping at her tears, she tried to remain calm.

Pa sat down by the fire and said, "Look who's awake. We was just fixin' to throw water on ya. We thought ya was dead fur awhile there."

Alyssa wished she was. A bluish tinge graced the side of Pa's cheekbone and she was glad Sam had caused him pain.

His last act on this earth.

The thought caused her actual physical pain.

"Guess ya want to know why yur here," Pa said coldly. "This here is my son. His name is Adam. We've got a piece of land in these here mountains. We're startin' a new community, our own community, away from the confines of society folk. And you're going to be helpin' us start that community," Pa stated as if the whole idea wasn't crazy at all . . . perfectly logical.

Adam nodded his head vigorously.

Alyssa stared back at them, not knowing what on earth they were talking about.

Pa continued, "We've been searching for the right one. Yur decent enough, and yur son was fine lookin' . . ."

Alyssa flinched at that remark, hating the word *was*.

"Must mean yur fer-tile. You can make more. That's why yur here. You'll be the mother of our community. Yur name is now Eve, and Adam will be yur husband. When we get to the community, you'll be married to Adam and have yur weddin' night, right an' proper. I expect a baby nine months later," Pa told her. "A son."

Adam and Eve. Alyssa shook her head back and forth. "No . . . no . . ."

"The bearing of children will be yur job," Pa said callously, a hard glint in his eyes. "Adam will see to it yur with child. I predict many babies, a posterity to be proud of."

Alyssa stared in shock, her heart filled with horror, looking between them, waiting for one of them to laugh and say, just kidding.

It didn't happen. They were serious.

"Are you kidding me?" she yelled.

Pa stormed over in two short strides, leaning towards her, his nose almost touching hers. He could move quickly for being such a burly man. He grabbed her by the shirt and lifted her slightly off the ground. "This is an honor above all others that we have chose you. You will be our Eve, the mother of all living." Pa stared into her eyes and then smiled a wicked smile. Roughly, he let her fall back down to the ground, then took his place by the fire.

Adam was smiling at her, which looked more like a sneer. And then in his whiny voice, thick with a southern accent he said, "We is goin' to be real happy together. Pa will marry us and then we, ya know, gets to have a weddin' night."

Of any scenario she could imagine in her mind, this never occurred to her. The whole idea was beyond ludicrous. The thought of Adam impregnating her made her blood run cold. An icy sensation descended on her as the reality of her situation hit her. Despite Adam's simple and boyish ways he had a mean glint in his eyes. It was clear anger hid just beneath the surface. She needed to tread carefully. She didn't know who scared her the most, the wild-eyed Adam who was clearly not all there, or Pa, who was.

Alyssa knew in that moment she had a choice to make. Go with the flow and accept her fate or fight them to the death. She chose the latter. Spending one second in Adam's arms would be far worse than death. She shuddered. Anger took over and became her primary emotion, making her feel so much stronger, almost empowered. She vowed to make them pay for what they'd done to Sam and Clay.

An intense feeling of claustrophobia took over. Alyssa desperately tugged on the ropes binding her hands. When she realized it was futile, she began to scream at the top of her lungs, getting louder and more hysterical with every scream. She kicked her feet and shrieked as loud as she possibly could, "Help! Help me!" Maybe a hunter — or hikers — would hear her.

Someone. Anyone.

Pa slapped her across the face. Hard. Stunned, stars danced in front of her eyes and blood trickled down from her cracked lip.

"Silence or a gag. Yur choice, lady."

"I hate you! I hate you!" she screamed, not really caring what the payback would be for those words.

Pa said cruelly, "We don't care if ya hate us or not, we only need ya ta make babies."

≈

LATER THAT MORNING, after she'd fallen into a sullen silence, they handed her a can of cold soup for breakfast and — knowing she had to keep up her strength—she made fast work of it. It was better than lint jerky. She gulped down another stale tasting granola bar followed by half of her canteen. There had to be a way out of this situation. The alternative was not an option. Undoubtedly, she hadn't been kidnapped by the sharpest men in the world. Still, her fear of them was completely justified after what they'd done to Sam and Clay without any hesitation or remorse on their part. A sharp pain radiated in her chest at the thought and threatened to overwhelm her, but she held it at bay. Breaking down and crying her eyes out was not one of her choices right now. As they hiked the morning away, she kept thoughts of revenge and escape foremost in her mind. It kept her from completely losing it.

At lunch, compass in hand, Pa wandered off to survey the land, muttering under his breath that they should have found their land by now. She was alone with Adam.

This was her chance.

Adam sat next to her, so close their hips and thighs were touching. They were on a mountainside with a breathtaking view. A steep slope tapered off just to the right of them. As she looked out upon the landscape, she couldn't see a single sign of life. Alyssa suddenly felt very alone. Adam released her leash, opened a can of beans and offered her bites from the same spoon. She refused.

"Aren't ya hungry?"

Starving, actually. But the thought of sharing with Adam made her skin crawl.

"I could tell ya were a right fine ma."

His hot breath slithered against her cheek as he spoke. She almost retched from the smell. Alyssa stared straight ahead and tried to pretend he wasn't there.

"We were watchin' ya, we liked ya from the first." He reached up and touched her cheek. Alyssa tried not to show the revulsion she felt.

"I've always wanted a woman, but Pa says women is evil. They is only good for havin' babies. Pa says there ain't no other purpose fur ya." He began to run his fingers through her hair. Her heart was beating fast with fear, but she gave him no response.

"I never knew my ma, but Pa says she was no good. But, yur good, I can tell. Pa says men are meant to rule the earth. I don't want no girl babies, only boys. Pa says we'll drown the girls in the river. If we need more girls, we'll just go get 'em. Just like we got you."

Alyssa felt horrified at his words, her mind whirling at the thought. She took a deep breath and challenged, "Do you always do everything your Pa says?"

This made him angry and his hand grabbed at her hair painfully. He turned her head forcefully and made her look at him.

"Of course and you will too," he said through thin lips.

His fingers tightly wound through her strands of hair, painfully, making her a prisoner. When she realized his intentions—the very thing she most dreaded—she dodged his mouth the best she could. His lips landed on her cheeks, her nose, her chin—everywhere, but on her lips.

Please don't let his lips touch mine, please, please . . .

This made him mad. "Hold still," he grunted, using his other hand to grab her chin. His open mouth landed on hers clumsily. It was wet and disgusting, the taste making her feel as though she was going to be sick. With her wrists tied together, her only weapon was a strategically placed elbow. She brought it up as hard as she could and it hit Adam's chin with a thump. He let out a loud yelp and slapped her across the cheek, the force making her fall sideways to the ground. Quickly recovering, she turned onto her back to see Adam advancing on her. Alyssa bent her knees to her chest. He leaned towards her and her feet landed directly on his chest as she heaved with all her might. Adam stumbled backwards, lost his footing, and tumbled down the slope behind him—a startled look glued on his face.

Alyssa was more surprised than Adam that she'd

overpowered him, but she didn't hesitate. She took off running without looking behind her, moving as fast as the terrain would allow, branches catching her in the face, whipping against her arms, causing angry gashes. Desperately trying to control her gag reflex, she spit the taste of Adam from her mouth. Tears of happiness streamed down her cheeks. Nervous laughter, akin to hysteria, erupted from somewhere deep inside of her. She jumped over rocks as if she was a hurdler in a race, only in this race she was running for her life and she knew it. She changed directions several times just to be sure the way she went wouldn't be obvious to anyone. Her hair flew behind her like a flag in the wind. The simple act of moving in any way she wanted felt exhilarating. There was no plan, no direction. Her only goal was to put as much distance as possible between herself and Adam and Pa. She ran till her legs were like spaghetti noodles and her lungs wheezed in rebellion. In the end, the only thing that stopped her frantic escape was the bushes that tangled around her ankles and tripped her. She landed on the ground in an undignified heap, buried her face in her hands and let out a few sobs while attempting to catch her breath at the same time. When she regained control, she stopped and listened to the sounds of the mountains. Wind rustling in the leaves. Birds chirping. A stream gurgling.

Water.

She needed water. The sounds of Adam or Pa in hot pursuit did not meet her ears. But she couldn't stop. She had to keep going. Being lost in the mountains was preferable to a life with Adam. Worry about survival could wait for later. Right now, escape was critical. Alyssa followed the sound of the water and came across a small stream. After finding the fastest running spot, she filled her canteen. It would have to do.

Now, which way? Wasn't following the path of water supposed to eventually lead to a larger body of water? In the mountains, water meant life. Maybe she'd find people close to that water. The water was rushing downhill. Downhill had to be a good choice. Downhill would lead her out of the mountains. Choice made, she walked at a brisk pace, following the path of the stream for the next several hours. She stumbled upon a wild raspberry bush and gulped down the luscious fruit quickly. At least she had something in her stomach now. When dusk was imminent, she decided the first order of business was to get the ropes off. Her eyes scanned the area till she found a sharp looking rock, jutting out from the earth. Stable, yet jagged. Perfect.

Perfect was not the word she had in mind when an hour later she was still rubbing her wrist rope against the pointy surface. Only a few more strands to go and she'd be free. Sweat dripped down her forehead in rivulets. The thought of finding shelter before dark made her almost give up, but at last, her hard work paid off as the last strands of rope broke free. She pulled the offending ropes from her hands, then worked the knot at her neck till she was free.

Free.

After hiding the ropes in a bush, Alyssa then went to the stream's edge and washed her face, neck, and wrists. The water was cold, but felt good on her raw skin. Shivering, she chose a tree surrounded with waist high bushes. The thought of creepy crawlies made her hesitate, but she plunged in anyway. She removed her socks and shoes and hung them out to dry. Nestled in her hideaway, she cried—deep, gut wrenching sobs that made her lose her breath. The loss of Sam and Clay was a pain the likes of which she'd never felt before. It was inexplicable.

Nothing mattered anymore. Nothing. She had nothing. Sam and Clay were gone from her life. Why was she fighting for hers?

She knew why. Alyssa was a fighter. She'd been told so all of her life. She huddled into a ball as her mind drifted to a happier time and place. One of the favorite themes of conversation on holidays with her grandmas, grandpas, aunts and uncles, was to always tell the story of her birth. She'd been premature. When she was born she didn't have the usual healthy pink skin color of a newborn. She was a light shade of blue. One of her lungs had collapsed. She was suffering from a disease common to premature babies called Hyaline Membrane. The doctor had gone into her mother's room and told her Alyssa would not make it through the night.

To the surprise of everyone, she did. The next morning the doctor came in and said, "She's a fighter. She made it through the night."

Then her relatives would all look at her with a sparkle in their eyes and smile as if she was a miracle. She loved hearing that story. She needed it now.

"I'm a fighter, I'm a fighter," she told herself over and over.

-3-

ALEX STOOD ON the highest mountain peak in the area. He loved to ascend the giant mass and survey the surrounding beauty. He took a deep breath and released it. Up here, he knew he was just a speck, a dot, in this huge universe. It was humbling to say the least. He didn't know why so much tragedy had occurred in his life. But when he looked at the majestic beauty of the mountains, he knew there was a God in his Heaven who was in charge of it all.

He was at peace now. Here in the mountains with no civilization around to bother him, he'd found complete and utter peace and calm. He loved the life he'd made for himself. It was at least a six day hike out of these mountains before you could reach any form of civilization. And he liked it that way. He'd lived this way for three years now. It had taken that long to get rid of the ghosts from his past.

He'd been named after his great-grandfather, Alexander James Kendrick. He knew he'd been born with the proverbial silver spoon in his mouth, never wanting for anything. His early childhood was happy, his parents and grandparents, devoted. The thought brought a smile to his face. His grandparents had lived with him all of his life. He remembered being surprised in kindergarten when he realized not everyone's grandparents lived with them. He remembered feeling sorry for the other children.

An only child, he knew he'd been doted on and yet they'd taught him well. He'd attended the best schools and experienced a great family life. Whatever money could buy was his. Still, he wondered how he was somehow not a spoiled child. Maybe he was and didn't know it.

That, again, brought a smile to his face.

In spite of his inherited wealth, he came from a family of doctors. They didn't have to work, but he had a work ethic that had been ingrained in him since he was born. The thought of just lazing around and enjoying his money had never occurred to him. Although he supposed that's what he was doing now. He, again, smiled to himself.

His grandfather and father were doctors and he followed in their footsteps. They'd been dedicated to making a difference in people's lives and he'd caught on to their vision.

Alex had wonderful memories up until the age of twelve. That was when everything changed for him. His smile slowly faded as his thoughts took another turn.

He didn't want to think about the losses he'd suffered in his life. It was due to those losses that Alex had inherited a fortune—and had become an extremely wealthy man.

He would've given it all away just to have his family back.

He loved living up here in his cabin, away from everyone. His good friend and colleague, Jerry, was always trying to get him to talk about what had happened, as if talking would somehow make it better. Alex shook his head. Jerry was a true friend—persistent little fellow—but a true friend all the same. Jerry oversaw the management of his estate and he had complete trust in him. Jerry also managed the delivery of supplies to Alex once a year. He knew he could count on Jerry to not forget about him. Once a year, a helicopter delivered all the ongoing supplies Alex needed for the year from a master list. Usually it took as many as four or five trips to get all he required. It was his only contact with civilization—he thought of it as a necessary evil. Getting settled up here had taken so many trips, he lost count. And every trip was filled with Jerry trying to convince him not to do it. Of course, as he unpacked his supplies, he found Jerry had added all kinds of things Alex hadn't wanted. When he found himself using those things he thanked God for a great friend.

The delivery workers as well as the pilots were interviewed and handpicked by Alex. They were confidential and discreet. Alex had paid dearly for his privacy. Each agency, each company involved in getting him settled was paid handsomely for their silence. He knew he'd paid them more than any newshound would ever pay for his whereabouts. While he lived in civilization, he was big news, but he wasn't so important that they would spend time and money looking for him. As far as anyone knew at home, he'd disappeared off the face of the earth. The location of his cabin was kept as highly confidential information, as was the fact that he was even in the mountains in a cabin.

After the first year passed, Jerry came to visit him. He agreed Alex had made himself a paradise. Alex joked that for the bargain basement price of two million dollars, he now had a five-hundred square foot cabin and an outhouse.

Yet, everything had worked out for the best. He was happy living in his mountain retreat, as happy as he could be in this life anyway.

It was enough.

-4-

ALYSSA OPENED HER eyes and stared at the beauty surrounding her. Vibrant green colors met her eyes. Fresh mountain air greeted her lungs. Still, no joy entered her soul. She hadn't slept well. Every part of her body ached, especially her heart. She longed to hold her baby in her arms and to feel his little arms hold on tight in return. She longed to see Sam's big smile and to feel her hand in his. A tear fell and she dashed it away angrily. Chilled, she huddled into a tight ball. Her arms burned with the all consuming itch of mosquito bites.

She ignored it. There were more pressing issues demanding her attention. Was anyone looking for her? Surely her father had realized something was wrong when she didn't call him on his birthday. It was the day after she'd been abducted and she never missed calling him. Sam's parents always expected a phone call to let them know they'd made it safely to their destination. Someone must have called law enforcement by now. Maybe the police were hot on her trail, she thought hopefully as she strained her ears, wishing to hear the sounds of search and rescue dogs barking excitedly as they led help straight to her.

She didn't see how. Letting out a deep breath, she admitted to herself she was on her own. They might find the wreckage of their car, but it wouldn't lead to where she was, not after driving for hours on end before finally getting out and walking. These mountains are deserted. There were no witnesses at the rest stop. Foolishly, they hadn't put up a fight. They should have, she realized that now. But how could they have predicted the outcome? They did what they thought was best at the time.

It was up to her to get herself out of this nightmare.

Alyssa arose, knowing she had to keep moving. She continued to follow the stream as it gurgled downhill. Once down, however, she found herself in a small, dry ravine, surrounded by tall mountains on every side. So much for the water leading to water theory. It seemed as though there was no way out, except up. Telling herself she needed to think logistically, she walked across the ravine, and headed for the opposite mountain. If she could get to the top of the next mountain, she'd be able to survey her surroundings. Maybe she'd be able to see civilization from this mountain top. Maybe a small town is just over the horizon. She had to try. After hiking through a long draw, she was faced with a steep mountainside. She'd never been mountain climbing in her life, not once, even for fun at one of those amusement park climbing walls. But if she went this way, the odds of Adam and Pa following were slim. They wouldn't expect her to go the hard way. She was positive they weren't on her trail, but decided to play it safe. The climb was grueling and several times she wasn't sure she'd find footholds strong enough to hold her. Taking her time, she painstakingly made it to the top. It was worth it. The view of the valley below was fantastic. Alyssa decided to continue up, follow the ridgeline, and see what was on the other side. Eventually she'd find a road. Eventually she'd run into someone.

She came across a wild grape bush and ate so many she felt sick. They weren't like cultivated grapes, but when you were starving they were like manna from heaven.

By the time she reached the desired ridgeline, the sun was high in the sky. She walked along the highest edge, assessing the surroundings.

Still no sign of life, of roads, of people — of anything.

Discouraged, she slept in a stand of trees that night, with a pile of leaves as bedding. She swallowed the impulse to cry like a baby and told herself to stay strong.

The next morning, she wondered, now what? There was only one way down off the ridgeline, without backtracking. It was a deep draw, rocky, with unstable ground beneath her feet. She literally slid down portions and by the time she was down she was dusty and thirsty. Finding water was the next priority. *You'll make it, Alyssa. Keep going. It's the only way back.*

Miserably, she thought, back to what? She had nothing to go home to anymore. Nothing and no one. The thought left her gasping.

"Hello, Eve."

They found me.

Alyssa whirled around at the sound of the all too familiar whiny voice. Adam stood about five feet behind her, a satisfied smile on his face. Alyssa turned to run, only to find Pa a few feet in front of her.

"First rule of concealment. Never walk along the ridge. You make a beautiful silhouette, Eve. Did you know this draw is the only way down from that ridge?" Pa laughed as if something was hilariously funny, sure of his victory.

Alyssa was frozen in place for at least a full thirty seconds before she took off running with Adam hot on her heels. She pushed herself harder than she ever had in her life. Her breath came in short spurts, sweat beaded her face, and her muscles burned from the exertion. She ran as if her life depended on it—because it did. The tips of Adam's fingers grasped at her hair and her clothing—and she tried to run even faster. When Adam tackled her to the ground, she screamed with frustration, fighting him with every ounce of strength she possessed. But she was weak, and he knew it. Before she could grasp what was happening, he was on top of her, holding down her arms.

"I knew you'd show up sooner or later. All I was havin' to do was bide my time. It's the first rule of hunting. Just sit real silent like and wait. A scared animal will always take flight when they think it's safe, it's just the nature of things. Even if ya'd stayed hidden, I'd a found ya, I'd a waited forever if I'd had ta. Yur mine now and I don't take kindly to losin' things that are mine." His hot breath fanned her face with every word making her want to retch. His forehead boasted a golf ball sized bluish lump on it and she wondered if it was the result of his fall down the slope. She hoped so.

"Get off me," she grumbled through gritted teeth.

"If you ever escape, I will hunt you down and kill you. Do you hear me? You are mine, no one else can have you, ever!" And with that he slapped her hard across the face, momentarily disorienting her.

All at once, his countenance altered. His entire demeanor changed. Alyssa struggled even harder to get free. He began to kiss her face and neck, leaving a trail of sticky saliva in his wake. Even though he seemed to like it when she struggled, she absolutely could not lay there and let him do what he wanted. Freedom had almost been hers. If only she'd had the strength to run faster. She'd always suffered from a bit of claustrophobia. With Adam's full body weight on top of her and her hands being held down by him, she panicked, unable to stand his touch or the feel of his lips on her. Screaming and struggling to be free, she felt hysteria overtake her—a feeling of panic so strong, she lost control of any reasonable thought. She began to scream wildly, and squirm beneath him with all the strength she could muster.

"Get off me! I hate you!" she screamed.

When Pa, gasping for breath, entered the clearing where they lay, she was actually relieved to see him.

"Adam," he said in between breaths, "Get the ropes on her. Quit messin' around."

Adam gave his Pa a nasty look, but did as he said. As the ropes were placed on her wrists and neck once again, Adam told her, "This better not be how ya behave on our weddin' night. I might get mad and you don't want to make me mad."

A chill went up her spine. *Not going to happen. I'll die before I share a wedding night with you, buddy.* "You will never have me willingly," she spat. "Never!"

His face turned red and he slapped her again. "But I will have you," he said ominously, his accent suddenly non-existent.

The afternoon was miserable for Alyssa. The feel of the ropes on her tender skin made her want to scream and never stop until they killed her and ended this nightmare. Tears slipped down her cheeks as they hiked and she didn't try to hide them. Her failed escape weighed heavily on her. After facing the exhilaration of freedom, capture was a hard pill to swallow. She cursed herself for making foolish decisions and allowing herself to be captured again.

When they tied her to a tree, she felt like an animal being secured for the night. It was the smallest she'd ever felt in her life. They gave her no dinner for running away. She was becoming accustomed to the raw ache of hunger in the pit of her stomach. It was the least of her pain. As she tried to fall asleep, she contemplated her predicament. Alyssa had at first thought they'd done the worst thing they could possibly do to her. They'd taken her husband and son from her. And yet, here she was, alive. Somehow she should be appreciative of that fact.

But some things were much worse than death and she realized she was facing that now with Adam.

How long would it be before Adam tried to have his way with her? Why was he waiting for the fake wedding night? The thought of him on top of her sent ripples of fear up and down her spine, making her feel physically sick. She didn't know or understand what moral code they lived by that made it okay to murder her husband and son, and yet, they had to wait for a 'wedding night' to rape her. She was glad for it though and would not question it.

That night, tied to a tree, cold and ever so alone, she looked up into the heavens and stared at the stars in the night sky. It was so beautiful. Alyssa wondered how she could behold such beauty while in a terrifying, ugly situation. Everything around her should be drab and gray to match her life. The very stars in their heaven should fall to the earth in sorrow at the cruelty of these two men. The trees should wither at the sight of them, the grass, die under their feet.

Gazing up at the stars, she prayed to God in Heaven to please save her. As she drifted in and out of sleep, she repeated the prayer over and over.

It was a night spent in prayer.

When she finally drifted into a deep sleep, she dreamt of Sam and Clay. They were together, laughing and hugging. She dreamt of family dinner and watching Clay's expression as he tried new foods. The thought of his little face as it shivered with distaste at some new food he'd trustfully taken into his mouth made her smile in her sleep. She dreamt of being snuggled up on the couch, watching TV together. She dreamt of running races with Clay in the backyard and always letting him win.

In the early morning hours, just before she awoke, she dreamt Sam held her in his arms. He was whispering in her ear, *"Alyssa, don't give up, stay strong, everything will be all right. Great happiness awaits you, great happiness awaits you . . ."*

Startled, Alyssa awoke with her face wet with tears. The dream seemed so real. It was as if Sam had really been there with her. It gave her the boost she needed to endure her captors. With the memory of the dream fresh in her thoughts to sustain her, she knew she could get through the day.

If only Sam's words could be true.

-5-

STERLING McCALL SAT on the Reno-bound plane staring morosely out the window, deeply worried about his daughter. The investigator better have some news for him. He'd never liked Sam. He wasn't good enough for Alyssa. Not a very ambitious man, but he was sorry to hear he was dead. And what they'd done to Clay, his only grandson, he could hardly think about it.

Sterling let anger override his emotions. It felt good to be angry. It was either that or cry like a baby. That was not an option. He did not allow himself to cry. When his wife passed, he didn't cry and he wouldn't cry now. He hadn't made it in business by being a baby. He was known for being a hard man and he liked it that way.

His thoughts went back to his daughter. He'd never told her, but the house—and even his life—have seemed so empty since she left for college. Then she never came home again. Up and married. His life was his work now. Really it always had been. He wished he'd told her how much he missed her.

Where are you, Alyssa, where are you?

≈

HOMICIDE DETECTIVE MICHAEL Pitaro hated this part of his job—family coming to identify their loved ones. When Sterling McCall walked into the building, he knew it was going to be a tough one. He had a granite exterior and it was impossible to read his emotions. He had a full head of silver hair and sharp gray eyes that reminded him of an eagle. He suddenly felt like a small mouse about to fall victim and become his prey. He was tall and trim and moved about the room with complete control of every muscle he owned. He had a formidable air about him. This wasn't going to be easy. Of course, it never was.

He took him down to the morgue in silence. It was obvious to him the man was seething. When he identified the body of Samuel Fontaine, he ran out of the room and was violently ill.

Michael joined him in the bathroom and asked if he was okay. Mr. McCall was cleaning up and wiping the sweat from his face. He was clearly embarrassed by his human weakness.

Mr. McCall was suddenly all over him. "What are you doing to find my daughter? What leads do you have? I want her found."

"Mr. McCall, at this time, quite frankly the trail is cold. There are no witnesses. We haven't even found her car as yet. Mr. Fontaine's wallet and all of his money and credit cards were on his person. We don't even know the motive. We did find an old truck abandoned at a rest stop in the area where they were last seen. Upon further investigation, we found it'd been stolen the week before. No unidentifiable fingerprints were found. We believe they were, more than likely, abducted in their own car and whoever took them arrived in that truck. We're looking for witnesses who saw the passengers in the truck." He cleared his throat. "So far, no one remembers anything. People on vacation are never as observant as usual," he added and then wished he hadn't. It was a hopeless comment. "There is something I need to discuss with you."

Detective Pitaro explained the forensic evidence found at the scene and what it meant. At least that caused Mr. McCall to pause. His eyes even got a little watery.

But then he blustered on. "This is ridiculous. How hard can it be to find one woman and her car? I've hired a private investigator to find my daughter. Here is his card."

Mr. McCall threw a business card at him and then continued. "If you will work with him, between the two of you, maybe something will get done around here. If there are any new developments, I want to be the first to know," he almost yelled as he stormed out.

Michael let out a deep breath. Where are you Alyssa Fontaine? Michael would never tell this to the grieving father of the victim, but he feared the worst for the lovely Mrs. Fontaine. It was obvious to him that the woman had been kidnapped. They disposed of the husband and son and took her. When they take a woman, there's only one reason for it. Who knows what she has endured at this point. As cold as it sounded, it would almost be better if they found her dead.

-6-

PA STUDIED BOY carefully the next morning. Adam was besotted with the girl and completely blind to the fact that she could hardly stand the sight of him. Pa hid a smile. He loved to taunt the boy. He could always get a rise out of him. He was the only boy he'd been able to truly control. Making him wait for a wedding night has been a hoot. The boy can hardly control himself. *What a riot! I'm having the time of my life. I'm not going to let this long hike get to me. I love watching Adam squirm.*

Women did not like Adam. It had almost gotten him arrested in the last town they'd passed through. Pa gave him a good beating for that. Stupid boy.

≈

"AT OUR COMMUNITY, we got plenty of supplies stored up. Mostly canned foods. Pa and I have been gettin' it ready fur a whole year now. There's a tent fur Pa and a tent fur us. And lots of wood and nails ta build our new home." Adam chomped on his beans sloppily as he spoke. "We got seeds to plant and that's how we'll live when the cans ur gone. I's a good hunter too. Pa taught me."

He probably likes killing small creatures, Alyssa thought sarcastically. She finished off her can of beans, even though her stomach revolted at having beans for breakfast.

The never ending hike continued. Alyssa began to suspect they were lost. It was her fault since she'd made them wander off and track her down. As far as she was concerned, the longer they were lost, the better. *Destination: Community* meant *Wedding Night: Adam.* She shivered violently even though it was blazing hot.

They stopped at a fairly fast flowing river's edge to cool themselves. They allowed her to scoop handfuls of water onto her face. Adam walked into the tree line to relieve himself, she assumed, and Pa held her leash.

"Enough already," he growled impatiently.

Alyssa sat at the water's edge as Pa began to wash his face with the refreshing water, tucking her leash under his foot. He was distracted and Alyssa soon realized this was the chance she'd been waiting for. Slowly, she stood.

Pa didn't notice.

She gave the leash a tug and it easily came free from under his foot. She looked around wildly as she gathered the leash in her hands. Adam was nowhere in sight. Using all of her body weight, she pushed Pa and, with a yelp, he easily fell head first into the flowing river, his backpack making him top heavy.

Alyssa ran as fast as she could, heading for the coverage of the trees. She was weak, but running felt so good, so free. The wind on her face was exhilarating. Once at the tree line, she stopped to catch her breath, the sound of Pa yelling and cursing in the distance ringing in her ears. A rustling of leaves caused her to dash behind a tree. Adam rushed past her, calling out to Pa. He'd be back to look for her in no time. Frantically running from tree to tree, she paused every few seconds, listening for someone in pursuit. Feeling disoriented and unsure of which way to go, she ducked into a thick row of bushes and huddled inside of them, willing herself to calm down and not breathe so heavily. Holding herself as still as she could, she gave herself a pep talk. *This is your second chance, Alyssa. Don't mess this up.* Soon she heard footsteps approaching. Her heart began to race riotously. She covered her mouth tightly with her hands as if it would stop Adam from hearing her very breath.

"Eve, I know yur here. Come on out and I won't beat ya fur runnin' away."

Alyssa, my name is Alyssa. She wanted to scream the words at him. By the sound of his voice, she knew he was only a few feet away from where she hid. *You're hot, Adam, boiling hot*, she thought to herself, remembering the childhood game. As he moved through the area, getting farther away from her, his voice became softer and softer as he called her name and said things he evidently thought would coax her out of hiding.

"C'mon, Eve, I'll let ya get extra food fur dinner tanight, just come out now."

Cold, freezing cold – iceberg – keep going, Adam, keep going. Does he really think more beans will get me to come out? I'd starve to death before returning to be with him. No contest.

After a few minutes he was hot again and so was his temper. Pa must've seen what area of the woods she'd entered. He knew she was somewhere in this vicinity. Suddenly, he screamed her name over and over like a crazy man. He sounded like a child having a temper tantrum. The sounds of branches breaking and rocks being thrown met her ears as Adam acted out in a fit of rage. Fear helped her to remain frozen in place.

And then utter silence . . . eerie silence.

Alyssa waited in the bushes for a long time, straining her ears for any sound. How much time had passed? Fifteen, maybe twenty minutes? It seemed like an eternity. She had two choices. Stay where she was and risk them returning to the area to find her or making a run for it.

She decided to make a run for it. She had to do something, if she didn't act now she may not get another chance. Flying through the woods as fast as her legs would carry her, she tried to not let her spirits soar too high at the feeling – knowing she wasn't home free yet.

Just as she decided to find another spot to hide . . . she ran straight into Adam's bony chest.

Alyssa screamed with frustration, swinging her arms at him wildly, hitting him high on the right cheekbone, making him cry out in pain. They struggled as she desperately fought to be free of his grasp. For a man, he was weak, but still stronger than her. Then he grabbed at her leash and pulled it tight, till they were face to face. Her raw skin burned as if on fire, leaving her breathless. She couldn't fight against the leash.

He had her.

"Why, Eve, so nice ta see ya again. I warned you, I don't take kindly ta losing the things that are mine. And you are mine. What have ya done to Pa?"

Pa was yelling in the distance, as if he was throwing a temper tantrum akin to Adam's earlier display of anger and aggravation. The thought of facing Pa left her terrified. Her breath came in short gasps and her heart raced madly as she blurted, "Leave him, Adam. It will be just us. Won't that be nice? No one to tell us what to do. You're a grown man. Why do you do everything he says?" Alyssa cringed inside at the thought of being alone with Adam, but the odds were in her favor when she only had one captor to deal with.

He cast her an incredulous look and slapped her across the face. Hard.

She had underestimated his loyalty to Pa.

He grabbed her by the hair and ran back to the river. She screamed in protest, sure that fistfuls of hair were soon going to be lying on the ground next to her.

Pa was wet, sputtering, and fuming mad as he took items, one by one, out of his backpack to dry them in the sun. It was a sight to see and under other circumstances she would've laughed. Instead, fear washed over her, knowing she was in trouble now. Her plan had backfired. Pa approached with rage in his eyes.

"Took ya long enough ta find hur!" he yelled as he shoved Adam to one side.

He pressed his face close to hers and screamed a loud roar as if he was a wild animal. Of anything he'd done to her this was the most frightening. He was an unstable man. His arm reared back and she knew he was going to strike her, but she was unprepared for the force of his blow. He hit her across the face, causing her to lose her balance and fall onto the ground. Once she was down, he kicked her in the stomach, knocking the wind out of her. Finished with her, he left while grumbling under his breath.

Alyssa gasped for air. Huddled into a small ball, she held her stomach, trying to recover from the blow. Her lungs wanted nothing more than another breath of precious air. Blackness began to overtake her vision and she thought maybe she was going to die.

Finally, laboriously, she inhaled air into her oxygen starved lungs, taking in several deep breaths. Feeling inordinately weak, like she'd just run a mile, she lay there catching her breath. Adam stood there staring at her with wide eyes.

"Don't ever mess with Pa, Eve. He'll hurt ya real bad." He pulled her up by the leash and she nearly passed out from the pain. "I'm real happy ya want ta be with me. I won't tell Pa what ya said, but don't ever say it again."

Slimy, squirmy, little coward.

Alyssa didn't think she was going to make it through the next few hours of hiking. Her side ached and her cheek throbbed. Just putting one foot in front of the other was a chore. Blackness threatened at the corners of her vision.

That night Pa was still in a temper and Alyssa thought maybe he would kill her and get someone new. If only. Pa directed cold, hard looks her way as he and Adam ate dinner. He was waiting for her to ask for food and she knew, instinctively, it would just be denied her, so she didn't give him the pleasure.

Before they turned in for the night Pa approached, falling to his knees in front of her, his breathing more labored than usual. He took the silver gun from his belt, cocked it, and held it to her forehead.

Somehow she'd known it wasn't over yet. Pa couldn't let it go so easily.

"Try anythin' like that again and you'll be dead before ya know what hit ya. Do ya understand?"

Alyssa nodded, while tempted to spit in his face. He

ran the tip of the gun along her cheek, tantalizingly, as if he was imagining the damage he could do.

"Do it!" she screamed. "Why don't you just do it?"

"Too much trouble ta get a new girl. Guess you'll have ta do." His expression pure evil, he added, "Have a death wish do ya?" He placed the gun in her hands, pointed at her at an awkward angle. He held his hands over hers firmly.

The gun could only be pointed at her.

Her finger was free to pull the trigger.

"Shoot yurself if ya want ta. It'll make my life easier. I don't need no woman. It's Adam that wants ya." The glare of his eyes held a wild look. "This is yur chance for escape. Take it."

Her breath came in quick spurts, her heart racing. There was no life in his eyes — as if he was hollow inside. His rancid breath blew in her face. Her hands trembled. She was tempted, wanting out of this situation more than she'd ever wanted anything in her life.

The coward's way out.

I don't care. Under the circumstances, it's totally understandable.

Alyssa slowly stretched out her index finger and rested it on the trigger.

Pa pushed the barrel onto her lips. His huge form leaned into her, paralyzing her. "Do it," he said roughly.

It could all be over in a matter of seconds. No more looming wedding night with Adam. She'd be with Sam and Clay.

It was the thought of Sam and Clay that stopped her. If she pulled the trigger, then Pa won. She wanted revenge. She wanted him to pay for what he'd done to her family. Curling her fingers into a ball, she said through clenched teeth, "Get off me."

He backed away. "I knew ya couldn't do it. Ya can't say I didn't give ya a way out of this. Now yur here of yur own choice." Pa walked off into the woods, pleased with himself, laughing all the way, as if he'd just heard a particularly funny joke.

Alyssa covered her face with her hands and willed herself to calm down. Her heart felt as though it would pound right out of her chest. She wished she'd done it, but she didn't have it in her. If they killed her, then they killed her, but she couldn't do it herself. It was completely against her nature. At the same time, she vowed to herself that when the time came for the 'wedding night,' she would fight Adam till death took her. She wasn't scared of dying, but the thought of being taken by Adam scared her beyond anything she'd ever imagined. The revulsion she felt towards Adam was so strong, she thought it would surely overcome her and she would die. She wished she could die of revulsion, if only it were possible.

While Pa and Adam slept, she gave in and ate a few of the pieces of jerky hidden in her pocket, after carefully cleaning off the lint. It was awful. She thought of it as her last meal. Surely, she'd be dead soon. Or maybe she hoped she would be. Either way, she'd be dead.

Alyssa didn't sleep that night. Her stomach ached from the blow she'd received. She sipped water from her canteen ever so slowly and let that settle. Pain was something she was becoming accustomed to. Shivering, she brought her legs up close to her chest, curling into a ball.

Resting her head on her knees, she made not one single sound as silent tears rolled down her face.

It was either Adam or death.

She longed for death.

≈

ALYSSA AWOKE THE next morning, shivering and teeth chattering, her heart filled with complete and utter despair. They hadn't given her a blanket last night—further punishment. A thick fog covered the area this morning. She rubbed her arms, attempting to warm herself. Two blanket covered lumps lay by the fire and she knew Adam and Pa still slept. Thinking back, she tried to figure out what day it was. She thought it'd been five days, but she wasn't positive. As far as she was concerned this whole ordeal was simply one big, long nightmare.

Her head fell back against the tree until a wave of nausea passed. Her strength and her drive were diminishing. Would she make it to the community alive? She'd never faced such cruelty in her life.

Alyssa felt like the walking dead as they hiked that day. The ropes had rubbed her skin raw and each movement of her head caused the fibrous material to rub against her neck with a piercing, stinging, radiating burn that took her breath away. When Adam tugged on her leash, it was simply excruciating and several minutes would pass before she could see straight. She felt like an animal, the lowest of the low. Her wrists were a constant, throbbing source of agony. Her feet felt as though they were on fire and each step brought a lightning bolt of pain that shot up her legs. A huge bluish bruise cast a shadow across her stomach where she'd been kicked by Pa. A deep breath was pure torture. There was a huge lump on her head, her lip was swollen and cracked and the right side of her face ached. She'd never endured pain like this. Hunger and thirst gnawed at her. She was literally dying a slow, painful death. Tears fell unabashedly and she didn't care if they saw her crying.

Her heart ached for Sam and Clay. Above all, this caused her the most severe anguish.

She was broken.

At lunch, she sat under a tree with Adam close by keeping a lazy watch over her. Even they sensed she didn't have the strength to run anymore. She tried to eat the can of beans they gave her, but felt sick almost immediately. Resting her head on the tree, she drifted off to sleep, knowing she was getting weaker by the day. A rude awakening came when Adam began to shake her roughly.

"Time ta go, no sleeping." He pulled her up by the leash. He was painfully unaware of the agony she was in. Or maybe he knew and liked it, reveled in it. Adam pulled her close till they were face to face. His eyes were sunken into his sockets, giving him a skull like appearance. His voice held that whiny quality even as he said to her firmly, "I suggest ya start trying ta be nice ta me, Eve. We'll soon be husband and wife. I don't want no woman who fights me all the time. But if that's how it is, then that's how it is. The choice is yurs. This can be real good or real bad. Either way, I get what I want."

She didn't respond to his words, hoping she would have the strength to fight him like a tiger when the time came.

As they hiked that day, Adam and Pa began to argue about which way to go.

"I don't think you know the way, Pa," Adam accused.

"Shut up, Boy," he yelled.

Clearly, her little escapade had made them lose their bearings. Secretly, she was glad. She didn't want to arrive at the community. They hiked for a long time that day, even into the night hours. Pa thought they were close, but when nothing looked familiar, they stopped for the night.

Alyssa hardly slept. Staring up at the stars, with tears rolling down her face, she continued to pray to be saved from this predicament she found herself in. She missed Sam and Clay and longed for them. The thought that they were gone from her life — forever — had hardly registered. Surviving the present was all encompassing, leaving her no time or opportunity to truly mourn them. She needed it, but couldn't allow herself that luxury. Her hands felt tingly and numb, her body, sapped of energy. *Stay strong, Alyssa. Another opportunity for escape will come, you just have to wait for it.* And yet, she wondered if she would live through the next day.

It wasn't a matter of being lost in the woods, it was a

matter of being totally, and utterly, *lost*.

≈

"WE HAVE TA find our community today. We're out of food," Pa said at lunch as they ate the last of the granola bars. "I know wur close."

As they hiked, Adam walked behind her and pushed her every time she slowed down. They were all slow today. He never walked behind her. The trip was getting to all of them.

Alyssa felt as though she could simply lie down and die. Her pain, which had been significant, seemed to have diminished into a dull, anesthetized feeling that enveloped her. Maybe this is what death feels like — a sluggish, agonizing death, that is, she thought numbly.

As they hiked down the mountain through a heavily wooded area, a deluge of rain descended upon them. They did not stop or seek any shelter, they hiked right through it. The noise of the storm hid the fact that Alyssa sobbed out loud. The moisture hid her tears. She didn't even try to rein it in — she just let it out and was glad for the cover of the storm. Lightning and thunder roared around them and still they walked. Pa was sure the community was just below them.

Alyssa knew that life — as she knew it — was over.

Her fate was to be with Adam.

The thought set in and her heart sank. She couldn't remember ever being so terrified in her entire life.

It soon became obvious they were nowhere near their precious community, however. Pa cursed and yelled in a fit of temper. They were all hungry and tired. When they stopped for breaks, Alyssa fell asleep each time, hardly able to hold herself in an upright position.

That evening as they walked through an area dense with pine trees and foliage, to their surprise, they came across a cabin in the woods. Pa and Adam stood in the trees staring at it. It was obviously occupied. Smoke wafted out of the chimney, the smell of fresh bread was in the air, and the tinkle of music could be heard if you strained your ear.

As Alyssa's eyes alighted upon the cabin for the first time, she thought perhaps she was dreaming. It was like seeing a mirage in the desert. It couldn't be real—the sight, the sound, the smell. It was . . . charming. She was seeing things. It must be her imagination. After all, who lived up here in the middle of nowhere? But if she was seeing things that weren't really there, then so were Adam and Pa.

They decided to pay the occupant a visit and cautiously began the walk up to the door of the cabin. Alyssa suddenly felt like Dorothy along with *two* cowardly lions approaching the wizard. The cautious music from the movie played in her befuddled brain.

Yep, she was losing it.

Puffs of smoke shot out of the chimney and she wondered if Adam would turn around and run.

Maybe the wizard would grant her deepest wish.

Freedom.

-7-

ALEX SAT AT the table preparing to eat his supper, his eyes scanning his surroundings with a satisfied sigh. He loved his cabin. It had taken him six months of non-stop, bone breaking work to build it. He didn't want to live in a tent for the winter, so he'd had motivation. It was an A-frame design with several windows to allow light in. Once the cabin was finished, he'd taken his time on the furnishings. The craftsmanship was his true love in working with wood. The cabin was simple, but well built. It consisted of two large rooms. The main part of the cabin held the kitchen, dining area, huge stone fireplace with a large couch and a rug, and a large four poster bed with a patchwork quilt. The quilt was handmade by his grandmother. The bed was covered with an eclectic assortment of pillows. Shelves lined one wall, housing all of his books. All in all it was quite homey. For his convenience, an outhouse was only a brisk walk away. Adding to his comfort, the second room was a large storeroom for all of his supplies. Not connected to the cabin was a workshop where he spent most of his days woodworking, his favorite way to pass the time. Alex sat and surveyed the setting, pleased with what he saw.

A noise outside his cabin startled him out of his reverie. Probably just an animal. His initial year here, he'd been armed at all times. After three years and never being bothered by anyone, two or four-legged, he just didn't worry about it anymore.

Therefore, when the door burst open suddenly, Alex was taken by great surprise. He stood up so fast the chair behind him fell to the floor. There were three of them. One of the intruders was holding a short, double-barreled shotgun and the other a stainless steel revolver. Both were pointed directly at him. Although he didn't feel it inside, outwardly he appeared calm. He couldn't help but think of his .357 revolver hanging uselessly on the bedpost on the other side of the cabin.

"Look, we just want a place to lay our heads for the night, buddy, and wur real hungry. So how's about sharing sum of that there dinner with some hungry travelers," the young one said.

"Are you alone here?" The older one questioned with urgency in his voice as his eyes darted around the room.

Alex considered his words, but then realized they would know soon enough anyway. "Yeah, I'm alone."

"We need the use of yur cabin fur the night. How 'bout showin' sum hospitality?"

Polite talk, considering their weapons were aimed at his head. The peaceful classical music he'd selected earlier wafted through the air from his CD player and made a mockery of the situation.

Alex kept his calm. It was then that he turned his attention on the third person in the group. It was a woman. She was dirty from head to toe. Her long brown hair was matted with dried blood on one side of her head. Her clothes were ripped in various places. Her hands were tied together and her wrists had been rubbed raw by the rope. She kept her head down. It was more than obvious she was there against her will, he realized as a surge of anger swept through him. These men had taken a woman captive. He knew, at that moment, he had to do something to help her.

Hiding his emotions he said, "All right. Have a seat, I have plenty." *Unintelligent criminals. The worst kind. You can't predict what they'll do – they don't behave rationally.* He had no choice but to cooperate. At least for now.

≈

ALYSSA SLOWLY LIFTED her head to see the man with the kind voice. He was wearing loafers and a clean pair of jeans. His hands hung at his side, his nails, manicured and clean. Her eyes continued upwards to see he wore a short-sleeved Henley. He was tall, at least six-foot-four. He had jet black hair, looked as though he was freshly shaven, and he smelled good. After being with Adam and Pa, he was a sight. Then her eyes met his shockingly blue eyes.

They were sympathetic eyes and she knew she'd just found her salvation.

This was the man who would save her. She knew it. Silently, she pleaded with her expression.

Help me, please help me, you're my only hope.

≈

ALEX STARED INTO the eyes of the young lady. Even though she was dirty and beaten, he could see she was beautiful underneath it all. He was appalled at her condition. Now that her head was up, he could see she had another rope tied around her neck, the skin also bloody, raw, and bruised. Her lip was swollen and cracked from the force of a blow, no doubt. An ugly, bluish tone covered her right cheekbone, again from being hit. Small scratches and bruises covered her from neglect and abuse. Feeling her pain, he wanted to reach out and take her in his arms. He stared right back into the desperate brown eyes. A chill went up his spine as they seemed to communicate without words.

When the young one noticed their eyes were fixated upon each other, he yanked the rope around her neck possessively and pulled her close. "I'm Adam and this here lady is my Eve."

The girl winced, but did not break eye contact with him. Alex let the kid's statement sink in with all it implied. His eyebrows knit at the thought.

"I'm Alex," he said simply. *A couple of sorry excuses for men – beating on a woman – the lowest of the low.*

Alex placed the large batch of cornbread he'd made

earlier on the table. He also took the simmering pot of beef stew from the stove top and placed it on the table. He wasn't about to serve them. They sat at the table with Alex at the head. The girl sat to his right with Adam sitting closely next to her, as if expressing ownership. The older man sat across from Adam. Their guns were balanced on their laps. They were well armed. He wished he was.

"Alyssa," the young lady suddenly said softly. "My name is Alyssa Fontaine."

The old man and Adam were eating ravenously. The sounds were disgusting. They slurped and slobbered their food down like dogs. At her outburst, Adam reached out and thumped her on the top of her head. He didn't miss a beat of filling his face. He yelled, "Eve!" and cornbread spewed out of his mouth along with the word. The brown eyed beauty once again kept her head down, not touching the food placed in front of her. The outburst had been directed at Alex and she had looked at him pleadingly.

Although Alex was seething at the intrusion of these men into his cabin, he was preoccupied by the woman. Her physical state worried him. She looked as though she was about to collapse. He wondered what she had endured at the hands of these two men. He knew it wasn't good. Clearly the men had treated her roughly and he wondered just what he was dealing with. His heart went out to her. One thing was certain, he wasn't going to let them get away with kidnapping. Alex decided to let the woman know he was on her side.

"Don't you like your food, *Alyssa*?" Alyssa's head shot up with a surprised look as their eyes met. Her eyes were begging him for help and he wasn't about to ignore her plea. Adam couldn't be bothered to be taken away from his food. He pounded his fist on the table and once again yelled, "Eve!"

Alyssa jumped. She obviously knew the force of that hand.

Alex's anger simmered. "*Gentlemen*, your lady does not

appear to be eating. Perhaps we could untie her wrists."

Adam didn't look up. With his mouth full, he muttered, "She can eat with 'em tied. Can't trust her, tries to get away."

Good girl, Alex thought. He hoped she'd given them hell. Presently, however, she was clearly done in. She was someone who needed him and he wouldn't let her down. "We're all gentlemen, here," he said, knowing he used the term *gentlemen* loosely, "and we know how to treat a lady. Let's allow her to eat with some dignity."

Adam's face turned red and he burst out with, "I know how ta take care of my lady. She's mine and she'll do anythin' I say. I'll feed her." Adam picked up the spoon and scooped up some stew. With his other hand, he grabbed at her hair and forced her head up painfully. "Eat!" he yelled. Alyssa kept her mouth shut and refused to eat. "Open yur mouth!" Adam hit the spoon full of stew onto her closed mouth, vegetables spilling everywhere and the broth drizzling down her chin.

Loud laughter escaped from the old man. "Boy, yur gonna have to do better than that. Let our friend here show ya how to be a gentleman."

"Pa . . ." Adam whined.

"Aw, let him, you could learn a thin' or two."

Adam's shoulders hunched and he sat with a sullen look on his face.

Alex was still reeling from Adam's rough attempt to feed Alyssa. If this was the way they treated her, then it was no wonder she kept her head down. She was in survival mode. He reached over and softly placed his hand on Alyssa's cheek. He gently moved his hand to her chin and lifted her face till her soulful eyes met his. A silent scream for help met his ears. He picked up a napkin and took his time to clean her face.

"You must eat, you've got to keep your strength up. Do you understand what I'm saying?" he said with a pointed look.

Alyssa nodded in response. She knew what he meant. If she was ever to escape, she needed to be strong.

He took a piece of cornbread, dotted it with honey, and slowly lifted it to her lips. With their eyes never leaving each others, she took it into her mouth, trustingly.

Alex fed her one more bite and with a hard smile directed at Adam and the man called Pa, said, "That, gentlemen, is the way to treat a lady."

Pa laughed heartily and Adam exploded. He pushed Alyssa off her chair and she fell to the floor with a thud. With her hands tied she had no way of breaking her fall. Alex quickly stood to go to her aid and then froze as Adam pointed his shotgun directly at him.

Pa intervened. "Adam, sit down and finish yur dinner. Enough of this messin' around. Quit bein' a poor loser. Now pick up yur woman."

Shocked, Alex looked down upon Alyssa. A small sob escaped from her that broke his heart. Roughly, Adam jerked Alyssa back onto the chair, pulling her up by the rope around her neck. Her hands held onto the rope to keep it from strangling her.

Alex watched her with a worried expression, stunned at their callous abuse. One glance at the rigid tension of her jaw line told him she was gritting her teeth together to hide the pain she was experiencing. He hadn't expected Adam to take his anger out on Alyssa in quite that fashion. She'd paid the price for his taunting and he felt terrible. When a drizzle of blood wandered down the side of her neck from the damage the rope had done to her skin, he cringed.

The group went on eating. Alex pretended to eat, but really was observing his intruders, his mind going a mile a minute. He had to force himself to not look longingly at the bedpost.

"Whereabouts are you headed?" Alex inquired nonchalantly.

Pa hesitated over his food, looking at Alex with

calculating eyes. "Bout two days walk from here, I'd guess. We're startin' a new community there. Eve, here, will be Adam's wife and she'll be the mother of our community. It's a great honor we chose her, ya know. She makes beautiful babies. Wish ya could have seen hur son. He *was* a right cute little fellow."

The words were not lost on Alex. "Was?" he asked, with a sick feeling in his stomach.

"Aw . . ." Adam put in. "We, ya know, had ta take care of the husband and son."

Alex went very still. "What?" he said dangerously soft.

"We killed 'em," Pa said loudly. "And we made her watch so's she would know they's gone and won't spend her time thinkin' she can go back. She can't, they's gone. No reason to be hankerin' for them. This is hur life now."

Alex felt his blood run cold. A tear slipped down Alyssa's cheek and fell onto her lap. Not only had they kidnapped this poor girl—and who knows what else she's endured at their hands—they'd also killed her husband and son and made her watch. And now they want her to have babies with them? Alex tried not to visibly shudder. The whole idea was too awful to contemplate. No wonder she kept her head down in such a defeated manner. Not only was she in fear of her own life every second of every day, she had witnessed the unthinkable. He had underestimated these two. They meant business. No more playing around. The stakes just changed. They had now nonchalantly told him they'd committed murder, as if it had been the logical thing for them to do. He wondered what fate they had in mind for him. He didn't need anything to be spelled out. When they were done with his 'hospitality,' it was over and he knew it. People don't admit to murder without covering their tracks.

"Why do ya live up here by yurself in the middle of nowhere?" Pa asked him with a look of intense curiosity.

None of your damned business. "I like being alone," Alex replied instead. His mind whirled with ways to get out of this situation. He didn't want to cause further harm to Alyssa or, of course, to himself. He knew he had the upper hand. The trick was to not let them know it.

And then he had an idea. He could hardly stand to see the young lady in the condition she was in.

"Look, I'm a doctor and your lady is in need of some serious medical attention." He gave Adam a nasty look. "Why don't you let me tend to her? I can tell you right now, she won't be able to give you children in the state she's in," he added and hoped they would take the bait.

Adam blurted out, "I don't want you touchin' her."

"Now that is a right fine idea. Think about it, Boy. We need her in good health."

"You can sit here by the fire, relax on the couch and put your feet up. You'll be able to see everything I do. I won't let her escape," Alex stated, trying not to appear over eager.

They turned the couch to face Alex and Alyssa. Then the two men settled themselves onto the deep cushions. Pa kept his revolver pointed at them.

"You clean her up real good now. She's a nasty sight. Smells too," Pa said.

Adam let out a breath of disgust. "I'm watchin' yur every move, Doc," he grumbled with his shotgun aimed at Alex.

The CD player, on repeat, continued to bring beauty into an ugly evening. It was one of his favorites, *Samuel Barber's Adagio for Strings*. Alex wanted to turn it off. He didn't want this memory to go with this music. But he couldn't take the time. If he dallied, they might change their minds. The doctor in him took over. He mentally gave her the once over. So far, all of her injuries were relatively minor from an emergency stand point. He was sure, if asked, she would disagree and if he'd suffered what she had he would've also. But he knew he could clean her up, dress her wounds, and she would eventually be fine. Her mental condition was another story altogether. There are some things a doctor cannot heal. The psychological wounds they had inflicted upon her were beyond horrific. He shook his head. *One thing at a time.*

"Please sit," he whispered. Her eyes were drawing him in. She didn't seem to be scared of him, she seemed to know he wanted to help her. First, he filled a glass with water and held it to her lips. She drank thirstily, but then shook her head negatively when he wanted her to finish all of it. At the sink, he filled a small plastic tub with warm water, grabbed shampoo, and went back to Alyssa. The kitchen sink doubled as his bathroom sink. He had all he needed to clean her up, to include a small first aid kit. He knelt in front of her. Once again, he gently touched her chin and lifted her face to his. Her eyes were bright with unshed tears. She had the biggest brown eyes he'd ever seen.

"Just relax and let me take care of you, Alyssa," he whispered softly.

She responded with a slight nod. Sitting in the kitchen chair, he had her slowly lean her head back till it was resting just above the tub. He gently began to wash her hair, first getting it wet and then massaging the shampoo into her scalp. She winced when he touched the spot where dried blood matted her hair, so he was extra gentle there. Her long hair was tangled and filled with dirt and bits of dried leaves. It took some time to get it clean and several refills of warm water in the tub as he rinsed. Alyssa closed her eyes and relaxed for probably the first time in days. He worked conditioner into the long locks and then had her sit up as he gently combed through it, removing all of the snarls. He then parted the hair where the wound on the scalp was located and took a look at the gash. It was angry and red, and it needed stitches, but would have to wait till he could retrieve his medical supplies from the supply room. He disinfected it with alcohol and moved on.

He again knelt in front of Alyssa. Her eyes opened and stared deeply into his, desperately trying to communicate without words. A lone tear fell, drizzling down her cheek. He brushed it away with his fingertips. This was harder than he thought. He knew this was the first gentle touch she'd felt in days. The abuse she had suffered was obvious to him as he noticed her many bruises. He grabbed his kitchen stool and sat before her. Using a washcloth, he began to wipe her face clean. As he worked, their eyes met and held. Ever so gently he wiped the dirt and grime away from days spent outdoors. And with it he wiped away tears and pain.

"Please help me," Alyssa whispered.

Alex stole a glance at Pa and Adam. Pa's eyes were closed and a soft snore emanated from him. Adam was wide awake, his shotgun pointed at Alex, but he stared into the fire sullenly. Alex leaned forward to grab the tube of anti-biotic ointment on the table. With his lips to her ear as he brushed past, he whispered, "Everything's going to be all right, Alyssa. I won't let them take you, I promise."

Alex then applied the salve to the small cuts on her face and lips. Each and every one of his ministrations clearly brought relief to her. Every time Alex looked her in the eyes, she met him with eyes that spoke volumes. He refilled the tub and washed her arms and hands and then took his time cleaning her fingernails, occasionally massaging her hand as he looked into her eyes. He also applied cortisone cream to her numerous mosquito bites. Next, he decided to tend to her neck and wrists. He cringed inside at the raw, bloody skin underneath the ropes. The first thing he'd wanted to do was cut the ropes, but he didn't want to push his luck. However, now it was time. He went to the kitchen counter and unsheathed a kitchen knife. The sound of the knife being unsheathed brought Adam to his feet immediately.

Shotgun aimed at Alex, he yelled, "Put it down, Doc."

Alex faced him without flinching. "I'm cutting the

ropes. They've rubbed her skin raw and it's going to get infected," he said with steel in his voice. "You can have the knife when I'm done."

Pa awoke from his snooze in the commotion. "Sit down, Adam. Doc's right. Let 'em fix her up," he growled.

Adam continued to stand, anxiously waiting while Alex cut the rope on her neck and freed Alyssa from her leash. He then cut the other ropes and freed her wrists. She closed her eyes and Alex could see the relief on her face. He wondered just how long she had been bound. He handed the knife to Adam roughly and stared him in the face. "Satisfied?"

"Won't do any good, I'll just be puttin' the ropes back on ya know," Adam taunted.

Not if I have anything to say about it, thought Alex.

Alex turned his attention back to Alyssa. She looked ready to flee. Her eyes darted to the door. With Alex and Adam's attention diverted for those few moments, she'd considered running. He again sat on the stool in front of her. He rested his hand on her knee and slowly shook his head in the negative as Adam settled himself back on the couch. She closed her eyes in response and took a deep breath. He took her hand in his and felt her tremble.

"Not yet," he whispered.

He knew she was almost dead on her feet tired. After refilling the tub with clean water, he began to cleanse and disinfect her neck and wrists.

"I'm sorry, I know this stings," he whispered.

He knew it was painful by the look on her face. She endured it well. When he applied the salve to the raw skin he knew it eased her pain considerably. He bandaged her neck and wrists and then moved down to take a look at her feet. He slowly and carefully removed her shoes. Her feet were probably in the worst condition of all. The socks were dirty and bloody. He removed them ever so carefully. Still, she gasped as he did so. Her feet had several blood blisters on them. Many had burst and looked infected. The skin was raw and cracked. He wondered how she'd continued walking. He refilled the tub and soaked her feet in warm water. Alyssa rested her head on the back of the chair and closed her eyes. After carefully drying her feet, he lanced the blisters that had not yet burst and then applied antibiotic ointment to all of the blisters and cracks and wrapped her feet in bandages.

Alex looked up to find she was now watching his every move as he worked. There was no way he was letting these monsters walk out of this cabin with her. He'd die first. Taking her hands in his, he squeezed them gently, trying to reassure her without words. If Adam heard them talking, who knows what he would do. He was a loose cannon.

She gazed upon him like a drowning woman grasping onto the only person who could save her and give her breath. "Thank you," she said simply, but her expression said it all.

Suddenly a shot rang out, interrupting the soft, unspoken exchange between Alex and Alyssa. The beautiful music of the CD player abruptly came to an end as the device blew into fragments.

"I'm sick of that music," Adam exploded. "Enough of this. Move away from her," he yelled.

Alex and Alyssa stood and faced their captors. Alex wrapped his arm around Alyssa protectively and she immediately clung to him, wrapping both of her arms around his waist tightly, surprising him. Her grip on him was fierce. Alex stared down Adam and Pa, daring them to try and take her away from him.

"Get yur hands off hur," Adam yelled with a wild look in his eyes.

This only made Alyssa bury her head in Alex's chest. Alex wrapped his other arm around her, hugging her close.

Adam screamed a cry of frustration in response, sounding like an injured animal. He approached quickly, pointing his shotgun at Alex's head, point blank.

"Going with you will not save anyone's life," Alyssa told him bravely. "I've already learned that lesson."

"Calm down, Boy. Get the rope. I'm tired as all get up and it's time for us ta get sum sleep. Tie them together and we'll take turns watchin' and sleepin'."

Adam whirled towards his father angrily. "I won't have them be together, Pa."

Pa slapped Adam across his cheek and growled, "You'll do as yur told, Boy. I'm too tired ta deal with ya, now do it."

Their behavior made Alex wonder at their father and son relationship.

Pa aimed his revolver at them as Adam roughly put them in a corner of the cabin and tied their hands and feet. Alex heard Alyssa gasp as the rope's were once again tied on her tender wrists, making him burn with anger at their rough treatment of her. Pa told them to sit back to back and Adam tied their two torsos together. Adam was so angry he was foaming at the mouth. He mumbled under his breath the whole time he worked. As he tied the last knot, he leaned in close towards Alyssa.

"Tonight, you are mine," Alex heard him hiss through clenched teeth, for once enunciating each word.

He physically felt Alyssa shudder at the thought. Alex knew Adam was not going to be ruled by his father for much longer. He appeared to be losing his mental balance, if he'd ever had any to begin with.

Hours passed. Pa slept and Adam stared into nothingness, lost in his own crazed thoughts, his shotgun at the ready. Alex waited for him to drift, he knew it was coming. The blinking of his eyes was becoming more and more pronounced. Alex reached into his pant leg and carefully and slowly pulled out the small hunting knife he kept sheathed to his ankle. He worked for the next thirty minutes at his ropes finally breaking through first the ankle ropes, then the wrist ropes. Adam's eyes were now closed, his breathing unhurried and even.

It was time.

≈

A SMALL THUMP startled Alyssa from her sleep. She was half awake, half asleep, scared to death and yet thankful to be back to back with Alex. The human contact was comforting as she felt every breath he took. Not being alone anymore was soothing. She looked to her left and saw the source of the noise. A knife sat beside her.

"Cut your ropes," Alex whispered. "Make it look like they're still tied."

Alyssa worked and struggled and was finally able to cut through her ropes, but left them wrapped around her wrists and ankles, making it look as though they were still tied, as Alex had told her. The only thing holding them now was the rope around their torsos. Alyssa pushed the knife back to Alex.

"I'll get the rope around us now. Hold very still," he said in an almost inaudible whisper.

Suddenly Pa awoke, noticing Adam was asleep. He stormed to Adam's side and pushed him off his chair, effectively awakening him. Then with a loud roar said, "Ya always wur stupid, Boy. Do ya want to lose yur woman?" Pa stared suspiciously for a long time at Alex and Alyssa. He didn't seem to think anything was amiss. With his face only inches from Adam's he roared, "I'm goin' out fur the call of nature. Ya think ya can handle things while I'm gone? I'll keep watch next, only I'll stay awake and show ya how it's done."

After Pa left, Adam sat eerily still with a sneer on his face, his eyes wild. His breathing became labored and he suddenly stood and began throwing a tantrum, carelessly leaving the shotgun on the floor. He threw objects around the room and turned over furniture. He then whirled around to face Alyssa, a fierce look on his face. In two steps he was at her side roughly using his knife to cut her free of the ropes. In a rage, he didn't notice how easily the wrist and ankle ropes came free. He pushed Alex to one side, assuming his wrist and ankle ropes were still tied. Adam picked up Alyssa by her shirt and held her close to his face, "Yur mine now."

Alyssa struggled to be free as he threw her to the ground. Adam dropped roughly on top of her, ripping at her shirt. She pummeled at him with her hands, screaming. He caught her hands, securing them above her head while lying down fully on top of her, smiling a lecherous smile. He buried his face in her neck, licking, kissing and writhing on top of her. Alyssa struggled with all her might, screaming at the top of her lungs.

"Alyssa," she heard Alex say above the commotion, his voice a beacon in a sea of misery.

She turned her head towards Alex and their eyes met. He slid the knife straight to her hands and she caught it perfectly by the handle.

And then everything seemed to happen all at once and yet, in slow motion. Alex stood and in two short strides grabbed the shotgun Adam had carelessly discarded in his rage. Pa, hearing the upheaval, burst into the cabin. Alex shot him at once, the force of the shot knocking him right back out the door.

Adam sat up and, Alyssa, with strength she didn't know she had, stabbed Adam with the knife. It landed in his right shoulder. He howled in pain and shock as he got to his feet and stumbled backwards. He pulled the knife out of his shoulder, screaming like a wounded animal, and threw it on the ground.

Alyssa scrambled to her feet and before she knew what was happening, Adam took out a pistol from the waistband of his pants and clumsily shot at her. It hit her in the leg just above her knee. The pain was excruciating, and she collapsed to the floor in agony, writhing in anguish. It wasn't a fatal shot and in her heart, she wished it had been. She was ready to join Sam and Clay.

Then, mercifully, the world faded to black.

≈

ALEX PROCEEDED TO fire the shotgun at Adam.

Nothing happened.

It was jammed. Thinking quickly, Alex threw the shotgun at Adam, hitting him full in the chest. A whooshing sound escaped Adam's lips as the force of the blow knocked the wind out of him. Alex immediately sprinted for the bed as Adam started firing his pistol wildly in his footsteps.

Finally, with the much longed for .357 in his hand, Alex returned fire. The shot hit Adam in the right arm, the impact knocking the pistol out of his hand. Adam fled out the door before Alex could get another shot. He ran after him, but couldn't see anything as Adam escaped into the darkness of the night, an injured and crazy man.

Alex stared down at Pa. He was obviously dead. His revolver, still safely tucked in his pants, gleamed in the moonlight. Alex immediately collected the weapon and roughly shoved Pa out of his cabin. He closed the door the best he could, it would need repair. He wedged a chair against it and made a mental note to add a lock in the very near future. Maybe even a barricade.

Alex ran to Alyssa. He fell to his knees, picking her up into his arms. "It's over, Alyssa, it's over."

-8-

ALYSSA DIDN'T RESPOND. As a matter of fact, she was dead weight in his arms. It was then Alex noticed the puddle of blood forming under her.

Adam hadn't missed his mark.

He knew he needed to act fast. She was cold, her breathing shallow and thin. Her skin had turned a pasty white and he knew he'd lose her if he didn't immediately take action. He picked her up into his arms and laid her gently on the bed. Quickly, he grabbed a towel and tied it around her leg. He held her face in his hands. "Alyssa, Alyssa! I need you to stay with me."

There was no response. He thought through what he needed to do. First things first. He would not be caught unarmed again. The thought of Adam returning made him grab the gun belt off the bedpost and holster his revolver. Next he quickly moved to the supply room and collected his medical supplies, mentally thanking Jerry as he did so. As a doctor, Jerry had felt it was important he have these items while living in the middle of nowhere—just in case of an emergency medical situation. He'd added them unbeknownst to Alex. Alex hadn't wanted them. At the time he didn't care if he lived or died.

He was glad to have them now.

Alex dashed to the sink, washed, and was back at Alyssa's side within minutes. He checked her pulse. It was dangerously slow. He started an IV and began pumping anti-biotics and morphine into her. The morphine should put her out sufficiently enough for him to perform the impromptu operation. Hopefully, she would feel nothing.

It took over an hour to cleanse and disinfect the wound, painstakingly remove the bullet, and suture the opening. Now that the bleeding was under control, he could slow down and evaluate the situation. The force of the bullet hitting her leg had broken the bone. He set the bone as best he could under the circumstances, threw some odds and ends off a small shelf and used the wood as a splint, meticulously attaching it to her leg. He removed her filthy clothing, cutting them off with scissors, cleansed her of dirt and grime, and placed some of his clean clothing on her. It didn't fit her, but it would have to do. He then tended to the wound on her head which was in desperate need of stitches.

Alyssa lay there still and lifeless. She hadn't made a sound or moved through the whole ordeal. Alex glanced at his watch and took a deep breath. Three hours had passed. It was now four in the morning and he was exhausted, his shirt covered in blood, and his cabin in chaos. He covered Alyssa with a blanket and added fluids to her IV. She was severely dehydrated and finding a vein for the IV had been difficult at best.

Alex observed the beautiful creature lying on his bed. She'd been through so much and had clearly fought every step of the way. Now it was up to him. A surge of love overwhelmed him. He wanted to take care of her and protect her. He wasn't going to let anything happen to her. Unable to stop himself, he caressed her cheek and smoothed her hair back from her face. He sat in a chair next to the bed for the next two hours, willing her to live. She, of course, could have no idea what it meant to him to save her life. Somehow, the fact that he had the ability to save her redeemed himself, in his own eyes, in a way only he would ever understand. His past demons would always haunt him, but saving her made up for so much.

"Keep fighting, Alyssa," he said aloud. "Don't give up now."

Something new and unexpected had entered his quiet existence. He wondered what it meant and how this was going to change his life. One thing was certain, after tonight, nothing would ever be the same again. Sitting in the chair next to the bed, he fell into an exhausted sleep.

When Alex next awoke it was early afternoon. Alyssa was stable and slept peacefully. His limited morphine supply would only last about four days and he worried about keeping her comfortable after that.

The first order of business was to take care of the dead body on his doorstep. He didn't want to leave Alyssa alone, yet he couldn't put this off either.

After placing Pa in a wheelbarrow, he hiked about a mile, dug out a shallow grave and buried him. He was in a hurry and wanted to get back to Alyssa. Surely Adam wouldn't be back, if he was even still alive, but he couldn't take any chances either. Alex paused for a moment at the graveside. He didn't feel sorry for what he'd done. This man was a monster. But he'd never taken a life before and he didn't like the feeling.

Yeah right, Alex. Keep telling yourself that and maybe it will be true.

Telling his conscience to shut up, he hurried back to the cabin and to his relief everything was okay, no sign of Adam, and Alyssa continued to sleep. He showered, dressed, and cleaned up the cabin. Adam's fit of rage had really made a mess of things. Repairing his door took a couple of hours and it was dark by the time he was done. He installed two planks of wood to bar his front door. Over the top? Maybe. But he couldn't stop thinking about Adam and wondering if it was possible he would be back. For the first time, uncertainty had marred his paradise. He tried to eat dinner, but couldn't choke any down. Finally, he settled himself in the chair by Alyssa and read out loud to her until sleep claimed him.

The next few days were more of the same. He redressed Alyssa's wounds and fussed over her. He knew she would heal physically, but her leg, without corrective surgery would never be the same. She would walk with a limp and it would be painful. He changed the splint to a more suitable piece of wood he had out in the workshop and secured her leg so she would not cause further damage with movement. Alex wished he could cast it, but that was out of the question. She wasn't going to be able to put any weight on it for at least six weeks as it was.

Of course, mentally, she was going to be in mourning. The experience Pa and Adam had put her through was not something you ever got over. But time would dull the pain. He knew that all too well.

Much too well.

After the fourth day, he was out of morphine and he knew she would soon be conscious again. However, by the seventh day, she still slept, albeit fitfully. She tossed and turned and sometimes mumbled incoherently, but she didn't fully awaken. Her body was healing from the trauma it'd been through. He was out of IV fluids too, so he began to wake her up just enough to get a mug of broth down her or even just a glass of water. He propped her head up with one hand and held the cup to her lips with the other. He talked her through it and made her keep her eyes open and focus on him as she drank. Her eyes had a wild look to them, like she didn't quite know what was going on. But she drank and for that he was grateful. She would then immediately collapse back down onto her pillow, as if the simple act of drinking exhausted her. He'd planned to crush a couple of pain pills and mix them into the broth, not knowing how else to get them down her. But she didn't appear to be in pain. She seemed confused, as if she didn't know where she was. Her mind wasn't ready to deal with what she'd been through. It was as if she couldn't face reality and she let the sleep her body needed to heal claim her.

Alex had begun to sleep in the bed after the second night, mainly so he could keep a close watch over her. She never woke but, to his surprise, she wrapped her arms around him in her sleep and he knew loving human contact was what she needed.

Presently, however, he hovered at her bedside

uncertainly. He wanted to sleep in the bed with her again, but now that she was coming out of it, he didn't think he should. He didn't think she would welcome the physical contact anymore. He settled himself onto the couch and fell asleep as the fire died in the fireplace.

≈

I MUST HAVE overslept. Sam is making breakfast and it smells good. Clay will be getting up soon. I'd better get up and help Sam.

Alyssa tried to move and when she did, pain shot up her right leg. Her eyes flew open. An unfamiliar room opened up before her and unwanted memories came flooding back. She closed her eyes, willing it to be a nightmare.

She dozed again and then woke, this time knowing exactly where she was. Feeling weak as a newborn kitten, simply lifting her arm seemed a monumental task. Watching the man in the kitchen, she lay very still, taking everything in. He walked back and forth from the sink, to the stove, and to the table, cooking something that smelled delicious. This man had saved her life. How long had she been asleep? He'd continued to take care of her. A rush of gratitude swept over her as she remembered how he'd tended to her wounds, so softly, so gently. His compassion and tenderness after days of cruelty had touched her like nothing she'd ever experienced before. She remembered the way he'd gently fed her a piece of cornbread. Nothing had ever tasted so good to her in her life. This man had saved her from her captors. She was free again. Relief overwhelmed her. Suddenly she realized he was standing there looking at her.

"Sleeping beauty has awoken. Welcome back," he said with a smile. His smile slowly faded as he waited for a response.

Alyssa felt a rush of panic, after all, he was a total stranger to her. She stared back at him and didn't know what to say.

He slowly approached, sat down at her side, and with a familiarity that surprised her, took her hand in his. Concern was written all over his face. He didn't say anything for several moments as they shared a concentrated look.

"Do you remember everything that has happened to you, Alyssa?" His voice was soft.

Memories played through her mind — things she'd rather not recall. Nodding her head in the affirmative, she said, "I remember everything."

The blink of her eyes was long and heavy as sorrow weighed her down. He reached out and caressed her cheek ever so gently. He must've seen the panic in her eyes because he stood up quickly, breaking the physical contact at once.

"I have some chicken broth ready. It'll help you get your strength back."

She nodded again, still not knowing what to say. Solicitously, he helped her to sit up, propping pillows behind her back. He spoon fed her the broth, wiping her chin with a napkin in between mouthfuls.

"How long have I been here?"

"Eight days."

"I've been asleep for eight days?"

"Your sleep was morphine induced for the first four days. The next few days you were in and out. You've been through a lot. It's not unusual for you to have slept for so long. Your body needed to recover from the trauma it had been through."

Alyssa studied him thoughtfully and then said, "Thank you." She knew she could trust this man. He'd saved her and taken care of her. He could have washed his hands of her and left her in the woods to die. No one would've been the wiser. For that matter, he could've done whatever he'd wanted to do to her. She was completely helpless. But he hadn't. He was good and kind. He was the answer to her prayers.

"Pa?" she asked.

"He's dead. I buried him."

"And Adam?"

"He was hurt, but he got away. I'm sorry. I don't know if he'll survive up here with his injuries. It's a long walk to any kind of help." He didn't say more, even though Alyssa knew it was on the tip of his tongue, the elephant in the room. He didn't try to console her with useless niceties or try to tell her everything was going to be all right. It wasn't all right, and it wouldn't be for a long time.

She was able to get down a bowl of broth before she was too exhausted to have anymore and she fell back into a fitful sleep, thankful for the blissful unawareness of slumber.

When Alyssa awoke again it was pitch black, she was covered in sweat, tears were streaming down her face and she didn't know where she was and she began to scream. She knew something was terribly wrong, she just couldn't remember what it was.

Suddenly, the room was illuminated by a lantern and she could see the lit-up face of Alex, the man who'd saved her. He was at her bedside in seconds and held her while she sobbed. He laid her back down, went to the sink, brought back a cool washcloth and wiped her face, arms and chest till she felt cool again.

"Better?" he whispered.

Alyssa nodded. Without saying another word, he turned off the lantern, climbed into bed, and wrapped his arms around her.

Alyssa didn't protest, in fact, clung to him. She felt safe. "Alex," she whispered as she fell into a peaceful sleep.

When she next awoke, he was already up and dressed, preparing food in the kitchen. She again was able to watch him, unnoticed. He was tall, yet well muscled, and not too skinny. Unlike her kidnappers, he kept himself well groomed. She supposed he could become a scruffy mountain man if he wanted to, but that obviously didn't appeal to him. What was his background and why did he live up here alone? *I like being alone*, was his answer to Pa, but she wondered if it was the simple truth. She doubted it.

"Good morning," Alex said with a smile. "Hungry?"

Her eyebrows knit as she continued to look at him and wonder about him. "Yes," she replied, feeling slightly awkward. She'd slept while clinging to him like a frightened child, yet she hardly knew him at all. One thing was certain, he was a decent man. His actions were above reproach.

"What would you like, let's see, there's chicken broth or . . . chicken broth, what'll it be?" She didn't answer so he went on. "Sorry, we've got to start out slow with food or it'll be too much of a shock to your system."

He sounded just like a doctor with that remark. "You know what I really want?"

"What?" he responded with a small smile. "Taco Bell?"

"Well, yes, but since that's not an option, I'm really craving . . . chicken broth," she said decisively.

He laughed at her response. It was the first time she'd heard someone laugh in a long while.

"Chicken broth it is. An excellent choice, madam," he answered as if they were in a five star restaurant. She knew he was trying to be cheerful and she appreciated the effort. But her heart was heavy and she didn't think she would ever be happy again.

After the broth, he encouraged her to eat a few saltine crackers. 'It's a good sign that you want to eat. Just take it slow."

Alyssa ate leisurely, allowing her stomach to settle in between bites. With a little food in her stomach, she felt surprisingly better, and ended up eating the entire packet of crackers. Alex stayed at her bedside as she lay back down. They observed each other in silence for a few minutes.

"Thank you for saving me and taking care of me," she said softly.

"I wasn't about to let them leave this cabin with you," he said fiercely, making her feel safe and protected.

After a deep breath, she asked, "What's wrong with my leg?"

Alex explained everything he'd done in more detail than she cared to know. "The force of the bullet broke the bone. I set the bone the best I could. Unfortunately, without an x-ray, it's not a proper set. I have it well splinted to achieve the best mend possible. However, you can't put any weight on it for at least six weeks. I'll make you some crutches and we'll get you up and walking when you get your strength back. Until you can get back to civilization and have corrective surgery done, I'm afraid you'll need a cane and it's more than likely you'll have a limp. But you're alive and you will walk again."

Undoubtedly, he added the last statement as encouragement, but she wasn't sure how she felt about it. She knew her face clouded over with the news. It was all completely overwhelming.

"Tell me about it," he prompted.

Alyssa hesitated, unsure how to answer. But then in a quiet whisper, she told him her story.

"We were at a rest stop, on our way from Tahoe to Sacramento. I came back to the car and they were in the backseat. I didn't see them until it was too late. We drove for a long time. Adam held a knife at my throat and Pa held a gun on Sam for the entire drive. I thought they just wanted to take our car and our money. It never occurred to me . . . we stopped . . . and they shot Sam and Clay . . . it happened so fast . . . and Clay's crying stopped and Sam fell to the ground . . ."

Alex held her hand and gently squeezed it, giving her strength. Tears streamed down her face as she attempted to regain her composure.

"Everything went black. When I awoke I was in the

backseat and my hands and feet were tied. I wouldn't stop screaming so they hit me in the head with the butt of the shotgun. After that, things are a blur. I think I had a concussion. We switched cars and I remember seeing our car pushed over a cliff. I remember being cold and walking for a long time. I couldn't feel my hands or my feet, they were numb. It was a day or two before I could think straight."

"You were in shock, Alyssa, and it's more than likely you suffered a concussion."

She looked him in the eyes. "When they told me what they wanted, I became angry. I promised myself I would make them pay for what they'd done to Sam and Clay."

"I'm impressed. You fought well."

"I got away twice, but they caught me. Adam . . . he was always touching me and trying to kiss me and . . ."

"You don't need to speak of it, Alyssa," he responded quietly. "We'll face it later."

She liked that he said, we. It made her feel as if she wasn't alone anymore. "They didn't give me much food and I was so weak . . ." She trailed off, feeling disappointed in herself.

"You don't have to make excuses, you did amazingly well, you held up under impossible circumstances." He thought for a moment. "I'm curious. How long did it take you to hike up here?"

"The days are a blur, but I think it was six days. They were lost and they'd run out of food."

Alex nodded. "May I ask, what was the cause of the bruise on your stomach? I noticed it after the makeshift surgery."

His familiarity didn't freak her out. He'd proven himself to her one-hundred percent. "Pa kicked me in the stomach. It knocked the wind out of me."

Anger washed over his expression. "May I check it?"

She nodded, mentally noting the difference between this man and Adam. Adam took liberties with her and

Alex politely asked before touching her. He lifted up her shirt a little to reveal the bruise. It was looking better. He felt around her abdomen checking for any sign of injury to internal organs, watching for her reaction to the pressure of his hands.

She was uncomfortable with being touched in such a manner, yet knew she could trust this man. He had gentle hands, the hands of a doctor. She flinched when he was closest to the center of the bruise.

"Do you have any pain in this area?" he asked.

"Only when you press on it."

He smiled. "Then let's not do that anymore," he said as he pulled her shirt back down. "There don't seem to be any complications from the blow."

Alyssa watched him smooth her shirt into place feeling thankful to be in the hands of a respectable man. She decided to tell him the whole story. "I pushed him into the river."

"What?"

"Pa . . . I saw the chance . . . so I took it. I pushed him into the river. He yelped like a little girl," she added a little mischievously, with a small smile. He smiled back. Then her face grew serious. "It was the aftermath that wasn't so funny. I thought he was going to kill me."

It was obvious he was disturbed by her story as his smile faded. "I'm glad you're okay." He paused. "I would give anything to have witnessed you pushing Pa into the river, though. It would've been priceless," he added, lightening the mood.

"It was."

"You did well, Alyssa," he repeated again. "You were very brave."

Alex wiped the tears from her face and tucked the covers around her. He held her hand and said, "Sleep now, Alyssa. You're safe."

She liked how he said that. It reassured her and she did feel safe with him. He stayed by her side as she drifted off to sleep. Before sleep claimed her, she added, "I wasn't raped."

Relief was evident in his features. "Thank God for that. When you couldn't speak of it, I wondered. Adam was a disturbing young man. I can't imagine the repercussions of such an experience."

"My plan was to fight him until I died. There was no way I was going to allow it to happen," Alyssa shivered with distaste. "I wasn't sure I could stop it though."

"You needn't worry about it anymore. I'll keep you safe, Alyssa," he reiterated.

Alyssa fell asleep, his words drifting through her subconscious.

-9-

ALEX SAT BY the bed reading a book when he noticed Alyssa was awake. He closed the book and leaned forward with his elbows on his knees.

Alyssa's voice was hushed as she said, "Whenever I wake up, you're always here. I feel like I have a bodyguard. It means a lot to me, thank you."

"You're welcome." After presenting her with chicken noodle soup and crackers, Alex somberly went straight to business. "I won't leave you. I don't think Adam will be back. He could be dead from his injuries. But I can't take that chance. At least until you're stronger and can fend for yourself."

It wouldn't be wise to mention it, but the more Alex thought about it, the more he feared Adam's wounds were survivable. He'd shot him with a lead hard cast hunting bullet, designed to penetrate an animal and go straight through it and immobilize, if not kill it. He'd hit Adam in the arm, causing a clean hole, hence much easier to heal from.

However, he was in the middle of nowhere with no food and no way of tending to his wounds. He'd gone over this in his mind a million times. There was simply no way of knowing.

Once she finished eating, Alyssa blurted, "When can I go home?"

Alex hesitated, dreading this conversation. "I'm sorry, Alyssa. It's not possible. It's at least a six day walk to the nearest town. With the injury to your leg, it's out of the question to walk out of here. I have no form of communication with the outside world, by choice. I have supplies delivered once a year by helicopter and they'd just come two weeks before you arrived." He paused, wondering how she was going to react to this news. "It looks as if we're stuck with each other for the next year." Alex smiled, trying to make light of it. He'd been thinking this through for the past few days and he saw no other option. After all she'd been through, he hated to break it to her.

She thought for a moment. "I'll stay here and you can hike out and bring back help."

There was a slight tremor to her voice as she suggested the idea and he knew the concept scared her. But Alex had already considered all of the options. "I can't do that, Alyssa. I won't leave you here alone with the chance of Adam returning."

She stared off into space with a look of desperation.

He sat on the edge of the bed. "I'm sorry, I don't see any alternative." He reached up to smooth her hair and with a look of panic, she flinched.

Embarrassed, she covered her face with her hands. "I'm sorry. I know you won't hurt me . . ." She began to cry and then sob.

Alex took her into his arms. He knew by the bruises he'd tended to, she'd been hit by her kidnappers many times. It had been a natural reaction to flinch. It was common among women and children who'd been abused. It angered him that she'd been treated so abominably.

"It's okay, Alyssa, let it out."

She held onto him tightly and cried so hard, it alarmed him. Alex let her cry herself out. He knew it'd been coming, in fact, was overdue, but he didn't expect it to be so heart wrenching. She clung to him until she finally fell into a fitful sleep.

≈

"I'M STARVING," ALYSSA announced,   surprising Alex with her words. He was working in the kitchen hoping to get her to eat something more tonight. The smells had awoken her. It looked as though his plan had worked.

"That's a good sign. It's time for something more than your favorite chicken broth."

He was rewarded with a small smile. He was worried about her. It was good that she had let her emotions out and had a decent cry, but since then she had slept for almost twenty-four hours straight. He kept checking on her and she was fine, she simply didn't want to wake up. She'd cried so hard, her eyes were red and swollen. Regardless, physically she was recovering well. His next goal was to try his best to not let her fall into a deep depression. She needed time to mourn, but he didn't want her to become despondent. Soon it will be time to get her up and moving about. He served chicken and potato soup, with cornbread, and it was the first time she ate really well. She sat up in bed and ate on her own. He joined her, sitting in the chair next to the bed.

"That was good. Thank you, Alex."

"The epitome of fine dining."

They smiled at one another for just a moment and Alex felt his heart skip a beat. He ignored it and kept his thoughts on the matters at hand.

She'd been very dehydrated when she arrived on his doorstep, not to mention suffering from malnutrition. He felt relieved that she was showing an interest in eating. "You've been in bed for nearly two weeks now. It's time to get you up and walking again."

She took a deep breath and lay her head back on the pillow, obviously feeling defeated. Her thoughts were miles away. "I'm sorry about the other night."

"Perfectly understandable, please don't apologize. After all you've been through, it's to be expected." He wasn't sure what to say. There were no words sufficient to alleviate her pain. Maybe talking about them would help. "Tell me about your husband and son."

Tears trickled down her cheeks as she told him about Sam and Clay. She told him of their life together and how happy they were.

"How did you meet?" Even though she cried, talking about them made her come to life in a way he'd not seen in her as yet.

"College. We both earned degrees in Education. We had that in common."

"Where did you grow up?"

"East coast, Connecticut. A stuffy little town called East Bay."

"I know it. I grew up not forty-five minutes from there in Ashbury."

"My father conducts a lot of his business there." She paused and he marveled at the coincidence. "And yet life has brought us both here, funny how that works, isn't it?"

Alex felt uneasy. "Yeah, small world," he replied. Suddenly this conversation was a little too close for comfort.

≈

"WHAT DO YOU think of them?" Alex stood before Alyssa holding crutches he'd made in his workshop. "It's time for you to get up and start walking again, Alyssa." He wasn't giving in. It was time for her to move forward.

Alyssa rolled onto her side away from him. "I don't want to get up. My leg hurts. Everything hurts."

Lately, all she wanted to do was cry and he knew movement would improve her mental state. Alex rolled her over to face him. "You hurt because you need exercise. You can't stay in bed anymore. Exercise will help you heal physically and mentally. I promise you, if you'd been in the hospital, they'd of had you up and walking a week ago. They're merciless. Time to get up, Alyssa."

Placing his hands on either side of her face, he made her look at him. "Look, I know you've been through hell and I know you've needed time to heal. I know you miss your husband and son. You always will. They will always be here . . ." he pointed to her heart, ". . . and here," he pointed to her head. "No one can take that away from you. But you are alive, Alyssa, and you have to go on living."

Tears rolled down her cheeks. "I don't know how to go on," she whispered.

I know the feeling. "You take it one day at a time. And if that doesn't work, you take it one hour at a time or even one minute at a time—until you can get up in the morning and feel happy you're alive."

Alyssa studied him with a furrowed brow. "I know you're right."

"Let's just take it slow, okay? First, let's get you walking."

"Okay," she agreed reluctantly.

Alex helped her up to a sitting position. When dizziness overwhelmed her, they sat on the edge of the bed until it passed.

"The clothes you arrived in were ruined. I threw them away. I'm sorry." The only thing he'd salvaged was her shoes. They were not in good condition. He'd washed them and put them in the sun to dry. Otherwise she would have no shoes and that would be a problem living up here.

≈

ALYSSA FELT HERSELF blush. "Thank you," she said simply. She was wearing one of his t-shirts and sweat pants that cinched at the waist. He had cut them into shorts so he could tend to her leg easily. Alex had become her caregiver in every way. Now that she was coming out of it and getting to know him, she felt a little embarrassed. He didn't seem flustered at all. He was a doctor and used to that sort of thing, she guessed. "I didn't want them. Okay, I'm ready."

Alex then taught her how to get up using the crutches without bending her leg and without putting any weight on it. This was a feat in and of itself

"Remember, don't put any weight on that leg," Alex reminded her as she began to slowly walk around the cabin with the crutches. Alex stayed right by her side in case she lost her balance. She soon mastered it, but was exhausted. They sat down and took a break

"How long does this splint have to be on?"

"Six weeks. I don't have the materials needed for casting. The splint will hold the bones in place as they mend. It won't be a proper mend, but the best we can do under the circumstances. Once the bones mend, we can concentrate on building up the muscles. But like I said before, you'll need to have corrective surgery. I'm afraid your leg won't be the same until then. I'm confident we can get you up and walking with a cane in the meantime."

"I guess this means I have to take myself to the outhouse." He'd been faithfully carrying her to and from the outhouse whenever needed.

"I'll still accompany you if you'd like. You don't need to go out alone."

It was as if he could read her mind. "All right, let's try this again." She got to her feet on her own and hobbled around the cabin a few more times. Now that she was up, she was determined to master walking. In spite of her fears, it gave her the freedom she needed—freedom to leave if she chose to do so.

After walking around the cabin several times, she leaned against the wall, out of breath and weak from staying in bed for so long.

"Are you okay?" Alex questioned, standing close. "Do you feel faint? I don't want you to fall."

"Just give me a sec." Another dizzy spell overcame her and she slowly lowered herself down to the ground, her back sliding down the wall, her legs sprawled out in front of her. Alex grabbed the crutches and grasped one of her hands to slow her descent. She rested her head on the wall and closed her eyes, taking several deep breaths.

Alex sat down next to her, his back against the wall also. "Don't be discouraged. Perhaps we overdid it for today."

She didn't respond. This wasn't the way her life was supposed to happen. It wasn't in the script. This wasn't a predicament she wanted to be in. Above all, she missed Sam and Clay with an ache so fierce, it often overwhelmed her. Would this nightmare ever end?

"You did really well. It's rare to master it so quickly."

A tear rolled down her cheek. While she appreciated his words, she just couldn't accept that this was her life now. Opening her eyes, Alyssa turned her head and looked at him. He turned his head and met her gaze. With their heads resting on the wall, they studied each other for a few moments. "Thank you for helping me," she said softly.

"Things will get better with time. I know it doesn't seem that way now, but it will," he whispered.

"You saved my life. I'll never forget that."

"There was no way I would've let them take you."

"Do you really think Adam will come back?"

"I don't know. There's always that chance. I'll be ready for him if he does. I won't let him hurt you."

"He's crazy, completely unstable."

"I could see that."

She studied his face for a moment, knowing he was her only connection to sanity right now. Without him, she'd be lost. "I feel like my life is over and I'm wondering why I'm still here."

"You can't change the past. A chapter in your life is over, whether you want it to be or not and now a new one is beginning. You close the book and put it on a shelf. When you want to remember, you take it down and let the memories come. They'll always be there, waiting for you. Everything that happens to us in life becomes a part of us and makes us who we are."

Alyssa contemplated his words. He was right, she just wasn't ready to accept it yet. She, again, wondered what he was doing living up here alone. He was so . . . normal. Isn't living alone in the middle of nowhere something only crazy people do? "Why do you live up here alone?" she asked. They both continued to speak in a whisper, making the moment feel intimate.

"I love it up here. I like being alone."

The statement was obviously his pat answer and not the real reason at all. Clearly, he didn't want to talk about it. "Whatever the reason, I'm glad you're here. I don't know what I would've done without you. I wanted to die. I had the opportunity. I didn't take it."

"What do you mean?"

"Pa . . . he placed his gun in my hands, pointed at me, with his hands over mine. I was free to pull the trigger if I wanted to. I think he wanted me to do it. He said his life would be easier without me, that it was Adam who wanted me." Alyssa paused to compose herself. Thinking of that horrible moment brought it all back again. "I almost did it. I can't tell you how much I wanted to do it. I didn't want to face a life with Adam."

Alex visibly paled. "It took a lot of courage to *not* do it."

"I guess deep down I really wanted to live."

"Human nature," he replied. After a few moments of silence, he said, "I lost some people I cared about, that's why I live up here. It's my way of dealing with life, it's my way of dealing with the fact that I'm still living, that I want to live."

She didn't ask for more details. Instead, she looked in his eyes and knew he knew how she felt. Whoever he had lost, he'd experienced similar emotions. They were kindred souls.

"C'mon, let's get you back in bed. I think you've had enough for one day." He helped her up and tucked her back into bed. "You're doing great, Alyssa. Don't expect to feel normal for awhile. It's part of grieving. Give yourself a break."

Alyssa nodded and quickly fell sound asleep.

≈

ALEX INVITED HER to come to the table for dinner that night. "C'mon, you'll feel better if you get up," he coaxed.

Alyssa was reluctant, but at his insistence she grabbed her crutches and clumsily made it to the table, feeling proud of herself for making the transition on her own. Alex helped her to settle in the kitchen chair, propping her leg up on another chair with a pillow underneath her foot. A fire roared in the fireplace. It was still a little chilly in the cabin, so he gave her a light blanket for her lap and tucked it around her. Her eyes wide, she watched his every move as he put the finishing touches on dinner and brought their plates to the table. When he sat down to join her, her eyes continued to search his face.

"I'm not much of a cook. I hope you like it."

He had served mashed potatoes with gravy, canned beef, corn, and biscuits. It looked delicious. Alyssa didn't know how to respond to such kindness. She'd just endured cruelty beyond anything she'd ever imagined. And now here she was with this man who doted on her, making sure she was comfortable and warm, fed her, hoping she would like her food and encouraged her when she was down. It was such a stark difference and he had no idea how touched she was at his kindness.

Alyssa continued to stare. He began eating, perhaps hoping she would follow his lead. The meal consisted of comfort food, not by chance, she was sure. It was clear he was trying to help her feel relaxed. Of their own volition, her eyes wandered to various spots around the cabin. Alex had made his cabin homey and cozy. The huge stone fireplace was a work of art. It commanded the attention in the room and its very appearance invited you to come and sit on the couch to enjoy its warmth. She could tell he liked to read as one wall was stuffed with books. The huge four poster bed with the patchwork quilt looked charming from this point of view. He had definitely made the cabin into a home.

It made her long to be in her own home. *What am I doing here? I don't belong here. I want to be home with Sam and Clay and . . .*

Unable to hide her distress, her eyes flew to his. Not knowing what else to do, she covered her face with her hands and, to her horror, burst into tears.

"Alyssa," Alex said, with a hand on her shoulder. She opened her eyes to find him kneeling next to her.

"I'm sorry," she said through a loud sob.

Alex took her hands and pulled her up to her feet, hugging her tightly. Alyssa accepted the comfort, needing a shoulder to cry on. He held her until she was spent. All at once, he picked her up, cradling her in his arms like a baby. He tucked her back into the bed.

"You know what? I feel like eating dinner in bed tonight, how 'bout you?" Alex said with a raise of his eyebrows.

She smiled at him, feeling cosseted by the shelter of his compassion. It was exactly what she needed.

"That's the first real smile I've seen on that beautiful face," Alex commented.

He retrieved their plates and they ate dinner sitting in the big bed, balancing their plates on their laps. They ate in silence, lost in their own thoughts and yet it was comfortable. Alyssa felt herself relax for the first time in days.

They were friends.

≈

ALEX WAS WORRIED about Alyssa. The next week was a blur. Every day seemed the same. Alex tried to entice Alyssa's appetite with his limited culinary skills. She was getting stronger every day. He made her walk around the inside of the cabin at least five times a day. But he knew she had fallen into a deep depression. He also knew this was normal after what she'd been through and she just needed time to mourn.

She spent most of her time staring out the window, distant and non-communicative. Alex gave her the space she needed. Physically, she was healing, but mentally she was a mess. She cried a lot and Alex pretended not to notice. He read to her and hardly left her side. He insisted she sit at the table for their meals. She was beginning to be up and around more and more. He washed her hair for her in the same way he had the night she'd arrived — and enjoyed doing it too.

It was a given now that he would sleep with her in his arms. It was purely platonic, like a frightened child sleeping with a parent on a stormy night. He didn't think she could sleep without him. She had nightmares on a regular basis, but he was always there to soothe her.

Alex knew as he sat and watched her nap during the day that he was in trouble. He could so easily fall in love with her. He realized he'd been smitten the day she showed up at his door. The moment her brown eyes met his blue eyes, he knew. When someone needs you as much as she needed him, you can't help but love them.

But it was more than that and he knew it. After three years of being alone up here, he realized he was lonely. He'd always thought he loved his solitude — and he did — but now he realized what he was missing.

He missed having someone to love and to love him in return. He didn't think he would ever want another relationship in his life, losing one more person would be more than he could bear.

Now, however, he found himself rethinking that decision.

Conversely, Alyssa was lost in a world of her own misery. And he was positive her thoughts were miles away from his.

≈

ALEX READ THE same sentence four times in a row as he sat by Alyssa's bedside and let out a deep breath. Three weeks had passed since the fateful night of her arrival and she was doing as well as could be expected. He let out another deep breath. The soft music emanating from the CD player was making him feel sleepy.

"Are you bored?" Alyssa asked.

He looked up to find her watching him. He closed his book and said, "Why do you ask?"

"Because I keep hearing you let out your breath and you can't hold still."

"Sorry," he said with a sheepish grin.

"Alex, you don't have to stay here every second anymore. I'll be okay, really. I feel guilty. You're always here at my beckon call. To be honest, no one has ever done anything like this for me. Thank you for helping me through a rough time. Nothing I do or say can ever convey how thankful I am to you."

He nodded, knowing she didn't suspect his feelings for her had grown out of proportion. It would've scared her and he knew it. She still mourned her husband and son, significantly. "You're doing well, Alyssa."

"The CD player? The one Adam shot couldn't have possibly been repaired."

"I brought this one in from my workshop. If it breaks we're out of luck."

"You like classical music?"

"Yes, although today it's putting me to sleep."

"It's very relaxing. Tell me about you, Alex. I need something to distract me from . . . me."

"What do you want to know?" he asked casually, hoping his expression hadn't become guarded. The last thing he wanted to do was talk about his life.

"Everything. I seem to have a lot of time on my hands."

He smiled at her subtle humor, yet, he hesitated, not really knowing where to start. Then he realized there was a lot to say without getting into forbidden territory.

"You grew up in Ashbury, Connecticut . . ." she coerced.

"Yes."

"Happy childhood." It was a statement, not a question. That got him going. This, he could talk about without apprehension.

"Very happy childhood. We had a large home and my grandparents lived with us. I was an only child, but never lonely. Someone was always home to spend time with me, walks in the park, playing ball, going out for ice cream . . . every day was an adventure. We always had family dinner together, that was one of my mother's rules. My mom really was the one who made the house a home. A big house like that can seem cold and lonely, but she made it warm and inviting. At Christmas it was decorated to the hilt . . . but it all changed after she died," Alex said, suddenly lost in a myriad of memories.

"When did she die?"

"She died when I was twelve. My mother was unable to have more children, so all of her attention was lavished on me. We were in the city on a shopping excursion. It was a perfect day. We stopped and had lunch at a sidewalk café. She bought me this huge ice cream sundae. She told me she would be right back. She just wanted to run to the corner drug store. She hesitated over leaving me alone. I was twelve and assured her I was quite old enough to be left alone. She kissed me goodbye and I was totally embarrassed at being kissed by my mother in public. When she crossed the street, a car ran a red light, and she was hit and I saw it all happen. I ran to her and held her, I cradled her head in my lap. She died in my arms before the ambulance even arrived. It was the worst day of my life." His eyes rested on hers. "I'd give anything for one more kiss from her."

"I'm so sorry, Alex. How awful." Alyssa was clearly shocked at the story.

"I've never spoken of it. I don't know what made me

tell you now. Maybe because—after all you've been through—I know you'll understand." He scoffed. "Maybe I needed to talk about it, after all." On his own terms, it wasn't so bad, but being told he needed to talk about the events of his life drove him crazy.

Alyssa took his hand into hers, caressing his skin softly. It was the first time she had initiated physical contact with him. He glanced down at their entwined hands, something stirring within him.

"My mom died when I was a baby. I don't remember her."

Alex let that sink in. For the first time in his life, he wanted, no needed, to talk about his past with someone else. Alyssa would understand, he knew she would. He continued slowly.

"Then my father passed when I was fifteen . . . pancreatic cancer. It happened so fast, he woke up one morning and couldn't move his legs. He was dead in sixteen days. It was so unexpected. He went into the hospital and never left." He paused. "I still had my grandfather, though. He's the one who taught me everything I know about woodworking. It was his hobby. I spent all my free time with him. He was my salvation. He passed when I was in college. A heart attack. Without him, my grandmother opted to live in a nursing home with her friends. She died several years ago." Their eyes met and he wondered what she was thinking. "It seems as though death follows me, doesn't it?"

"No, please don't say that. You brought life to me," she reminded him. "I'll never forget it."

She had no idea what those words meant to him. "I've never told that to anyone before," he admitted.

"Thank you for telling me. I'm sorry you've had so much loss in your life," she said softly. "I guess that's why you're so good at comforting me, you know how I feel."

If she only knew.

"What made you decide to become a doctor?" she

asked.

This was fairly neutral ground. "My father and grandfather were both doctors and I had this crazy idea I could save the world. It gave me power over death."

"I can certainly understand the desire for that kind of power. Did you enjoy being a doctor?"

"Yes, I found I had a passion for it."

"So, despite your losses, you did find happiness in life? It's suddenly important to me to know your life hasn't been all bad."

His thoughts wandered to another time and place. "Yes, I found happiness in life. I eventually married, I had two daughters, and life was good. Things don't always work out as we think they will, though . . . really, that's enough about me . . ."

"Wait, I'm missing something. You became a doctor, you married, had children, and now you live up here alone . . . I don't understand. I was kinda hoping you'd get to the part where you explained why you live up here by yourself," she said bluntly.

He appreciated her candor even if he didn't want to talk about it. "I became a surgeon. Things started to not go well for me. I lost my family. I took some vacation time and went on a backpacking trip. I needed some time alone. I fell in love with this area. I found I liked the solitude. Things happened fast from there on out. I resigned from my position at the hospital, made all the arrangements to live up here, and here I am."

"Lost your family? To divorce, to a custody battle? What does that mean?" Then she immediately backtracked. "I'm sorry, I can see how uncomfortable you are. You don't have to answer that, I'm sure it's a painful subject. I'm sorry for being nosy. Just tell me to mind my own business."

"I won't say that, but thank you for understanding."

"How long have you lived up here?" she asked, changing the subject.

"Three years."

"Three years?" she repeated, stunned. "Living alone for that long would have driven me crazy."

"Last time I checked, I think I still had my sanity," he said with a chuckle. "Will you let me know if I behave strangely?"

Alyssa giggled. "I apologize again. I'm a direct person, sometimes far too frank for my own good."

He shrugged. "It's refreshing."

"How do you live up here legally? Isn't this National Forest Land?"

"Good question. We're surrounded by National Forest. This particular section of land is private property owned by a mining company. I leased it from them for ninety-nine years."

"How are your supplies delivered once a year?"

"Heavy lifting helicopters. I can't even tell you how many trips it took to get everything up here, I lost count. But here I am in my humble abode, and I love it," he added with finality. He was done talking about himself.

"And that's your life in a nutshell, Alex Kendrick?" she said, noticeably trying to lighten the mood.

He studied her for a moment. He liked the sound of his name coming from her lips and the teasing way in which she'd said it. It was a glimpse of the real Alyssa.

"Yes, Alyssa Fontaine, that's my life."

At least that was all he was prepared to talk about.

-10-

ALYSSA SAT AT the table, her leg propped up on a chair. They'd just finished with dinner and Alex was cleaning up. It had now been four weeks since she'd arrived at Alex's cabin. Every day she felt stronger and became more adept at moving about. An idea had taken hold in her mind and she just couldn't let it go. Her eyes wandered the cabin, seeing nothing, as she thought it through. She was sure she could do it.

Her gaze rested on Alex. He had become a treasured friend and was so good to her. He was kind and he was a gentleman. She would miss him, she had to admit. The last four weeks had been hard on her, but he was always there, making her get up and walk, and tending to her every need. He sat by her bed and talked to her or read to her, keeping her mind off her woes. He'd helped her mentally as well as physically.

But she couldn't stay here an entire year, surely he would understand that. She'd walked all the way here and she was sure she could walk all the way out if she just took it slow. At least, she had to try. The urgency to go now overwhelmed her. There was no way she could put off leaving till she was walking with the cane. The thought of being outside alone scared her to death. But the walls of the cabin were closing in on her. It was time to leave. She wanted to go home. More than anything else in the world, she wanted the comfort of her home, her own bed, her own things. Besides, everyone must be so worried. They don't know where she is or even if she's still alive. What if no one has found Sam and Clay yet? They deserve a proper burial. It was time to go home. Sam and Clay needed her to do this.

Alex had started to go out to his workshop everyday

for a couple of hours. He was still nervous about leaving her alone. He taught her how to load and unload a small handgun and showed her where it was kept. "Just point and shoot, don't even hesitate for a second," he told her. She assured him she was fine, even though they both knew she wasn't.

Tomorrow would be the day, she couldn't wait any longer. The gun would make the journey with her. It would be her protection.

Alex left for the workshop just after breakfast. The minute he left, Alyssa went to work, grabbing a backpack, filling it with snacks, bottled water, water purification tablets, and a light blanket. She took the gun, along with extra bullets, and put them in a pocket of the backpack. Would she run into Adam? She'd shoot him if she did. Without hesitation. They didn't talk about it much, but she lived in fear of Adam returning. She knew Alex worried about it too.

Alyssa opened the door to the cabin and trepidation swallowed her whole. The sounds of Alex working in the workshop met her ears. How could she leave without saying anything to him? He might think Adam had returned. She decided to leave a note.

Dear Alex,
Thank you for everything you've done for me. I will never forget your kindness. Please understand, I have to go.
Alyssa

She hobbled off. The rough terrain made the trek slow going. It was nearly impossible to walk through vegetation and rocky landscape with crutches. Alyssa changed direction several times, having no idea which way to go. In the end, she decided on the path she could manage with the crutches.

After only an hour, she was dripping with sweat and her leg was aching. The extra weight of the backpack and the rough terrain made her lose her balance. She'd put weight on her leg a few times to prevent herself from falling over. Eventually, she stopped and took a break for about ten minutes, but then kept going. Several more times she put weight on her leg to keep herself upright. Sharp pain began to radiate up and down her leg from her thigh to her ankle. The pain left her breathless and she began to feel as if she would pass out. Determined, she kept going. Another hour passed. Her vision began to blur, and still she persevered. After making it through a particularly rough spot, there was suddenly nowhere to go.

Alyssa found herself at a cliff edge.

The sight caused all of her optimism to come crashing down around her. From the cliff, she could see for miles in several directions. Her breathing labored, she observed the great expanse. The foolishness of her undertaking besieged her. She felt small and insignificant, one little inconsequential life in the middle of a great universe. Pine trees covered the landscape as far as the eye could see. Mountains jutted out in the distance. Their majestic beauty was lost on her as she stared with wide eyes at the endless ocean of land. There was no way she could walk out of here. Even with the help of Alex. He was right. She stood there for a long time, a spectator to the land that went on for miles, the land that led to nowhere. No sign of life, no civilization. Her hopes of going home were dashed. It made her feel as though Adam had won. Here she was, still stuck in the mountains just where he wanted her.

But she wasn't with Adam. She was with Alex.

Alyssa turned. None of the paths were crossable with crutches. Even the one she'd just covered looked daunting. A fallen tree blocked one way, bushes another way, and boulders another. Discouragement washed over her. Slowly, she lowered herself down, her back against a tree, and started to cry.

What am I doing? This is such a stupid thing to do. What

made me think I could do this? She cried even harder, letting it all out.

When she finally calmed down, she began to think, pondering on her situation and thinking clearly for the first time since this ordeal began. She thought about her life with Sam and Clay, mentally reviewing her most precious memories.

That part of her life was over now. It'd been cruelly taken away. Her thoughts turned to Alex as she took several deep breaths of the fresh mountain air. She thought about him finding her note and knew he would be terribly worried.

In her heart she knew he would find her. The doctor in him would never let her go off like this. It was certain death, she knew that now. Just walking up here had nearly killed her. It was just a matter of time before he came for her. She settled herself against the tree.

An hour had passed and she was deep in thought when he finally came walking into the small clearing where she was sitting. He didn't look mad, but he didn't look happy either. Concern, as well as relief, was evident on his face. Alyssa knew she must be a sight. She felt defeated as she looked upon him with a grave expression, her eyebrows furrowed. Hopefully, he wouldn't be angry with her.

≈

I FOUND HER. Alex let out his breath and closed his eyes. A helpless feeling had overcome him when he found the note. How could he possibly know which way to go to find her? It was like finding a needle in the proverbial haystack. Impossible. He was determined, however. The thought of her out in the mountains — alone, facing the elements — scared him to death. She'd never survive. Instead of blindly running out of the cabin and yelling her name, which was his first frantic instinct, he paused and took a few minutes to think clearly. She must've taken the path of least resistance. Walking with the crutches would be out of the question in certain areas. Secondly, the crutches would have left deep tracks for him to follow. With these two thoughts in mind, he set out to find her. He followed a few different paths before he'd stumbled upon her. The tracks left by the crutches were only occasional, depending upon the groundcover. He'd moved slowly through the woods, watching for any evidence she'd walked through the area. It may have taken him some time but, in the end, it hadn't been that hard.

Alyssa didn't look well. Her cheeks were flushed and tear stained. There was a disappointed and yet resigned air to her. Her head rested on the tree and she didn't move as he sat down next to her, his back against the tree also. They didn't talk for a long time, he just sat there with her, letting her know she wasn't alone.

≈

THANK GOODNESS, THERE were no angry words or any kind of reprimand from Alex. They had a perfect view of the great expanse before them. Finally, Alyssa broke the silence. "It takes your breath away, doesn't it?"

He didn't answer.

"I thought it was really important for me to get home. Sam and Clay need me. No one knows where they are. I need to be home." She paused, knowing she hadn't been thinking rationally. "The thing is, I just realized I have nothing to go home to. I have no one to go home to. Maybe I don't even have a home anymore. Maybe everyone thinks I'm dead."

They sat in silence for awhile longer.

"Why did they have to kill them? Why?" She started to cry again. He held her hand and waited until she was spent.

"I knew you'd come for me, Alex, I wasn't scared."

He turned to her and spoke for the first time. He

simply said, "Ready to go home?"

She looked him in the eyes. Alex was her life now or at least for the next year. The cabin was her home now. He was good and kind and he took care of her.

"Yes," she whispered, wondering if he knew how much those simple words meant to her. She had a home with him.

He stood, holding his hand out to her.

"Alex, I don't think I can walk."

He scooped her up into his arms and carried her all the way back to the cabin. Her arms wrapped around the back of his neck as she rested her head on his shoulder and buried her face in the folds of his shirt. He'd carried her to and from the outhouse many times while she recovered. But at this moment, she was particularly grateful for him and held on tighter than usual. What would she do without him? It took about twenty minutes to get back. As it turned out, they weren't really all that far away. She must've walked in circles.

He went back for the backpack and crutches. She was sound asleep on the bed when he returned. He removed her shoes and began to readjust the splint on her leg, his ministrations awakening her. "Did I cause damage to my leg?"

"Probably," he answered solemnly.

"I'm sorry."

"What's done is done."

She nodded. "Do you like living here alone, Alex?"

"Yes," he answered as he continued to secure the splint to its proper position.

"I'm sorry I've ruined your solitude," she told him as she winced from the movement adjusting the splint caused. Her leg ached fiercely and sharp pains continued to radiate up and down the length of it. Ignoring the pain, she thought about him for the first time and what an inconvenience she must be to him.

He didn't say anything as he finished securing the

splint. She watched him as he worked, his hands moving quickly and deftly until the job was done to his satisfaction. He had the hands of a surgeon, gentle hands. He went to the kitchen and returned with a glass of water and a pain killer. He held her head up as she gulped it down and then sat next to her on the bed.

"You haven't ruined my solitude." He took her hand in his. "I like having you here, Alyssa. I wish it could be under different circumstances. I'm sorry you're not happy living here. I'd change things if I could."

"You make me happy, Alex. I was sad to leave you, you've been so good to me. Please don't take it personally. It was something I had to do. Thank you for coming to find me. I knew you'd come. I knew in my heart you'd never leave me out there alone. This is my home, I know that now. Thank you for opening your home to me." Alyssa averted her eyes, embarrassed at her effusive outburst of words. They had gushed out of her and she suddenly felt like a silly school girl.

"Don't apologize. In your position, I would've done the same. Sometimes you have to see and know for yourself how impossible something really is. It's human nature. To be honest, I was surprised at how far you got." He paused, looking a little uncertain. "Look, I love my solitude, but the cabin felt empty when I arrived home to find you gone. Honestly, I love having you here." He covered her with a blanket and tucked it around her. "Sleep now, Alyssa. You're safe."

His favorite words. And hers too.

≈

THE NEXT DAY Alex sat at the table having dinner with Alyssa. He finished his meal long before her.

"I'm sorry, I'm a slow eater."

"Really, I hadn't noticed," he said in a serious tone, till Alyssa caught him grinning.

"Shut up," she responded playfully and threw her

crumpled napkin at him.

"We'll be living here together for almost a year, we may as well get used to each other's bad habits," Alex said jokingly, enjoying this side of Alyssa. She'd been so serious all day. He liked the sparkle in her eyes when she smiled.

"Oh, really? And what, may I ask, are your bad habits, Mr. Perfect?"

It was refreshing to see her sense of humor come to life. "My bad habits, hmmmm, let's see, I track mud into the cabin when I'm too lazy to take my boots off. I sometimes leave the lights on when I go to bed, I'm sure it bothers my neighbors." Alyssa giggled at that. "I never eat all of my vegetables. I like to eat peanut butter crackers at midnight—in bed—and every once in awhile I spend the whole day reading and never even get out of bed."

"Scandalous."

"Some days I don't even make my bed."

"Slob."

"I know, huh? Let's see, I love slippers. I'd wear them every day and everywhere if I could." He shrugged. "I guess I can. And . . ." he looked into her eyes, "Even when I'm unprepared, I love unexpected house guests." He winked at her.

Alyssa laughed out loud, her eyes crinkling at the corners. He liked the sound. "Your turn."

"My turn?"

"Yes, I told my bad habits, now let's hear yours."

"You don't want to know."

"Yes I do, now fess up."

Alyssa thought for a moment. "Okay . . . I love flannel pajamas, even when it's hot outside."

"Romantic," Alex said with a raise of his eyebrows.

"Cold pizza is the best breakfast food ever."

A fake look of disgust crossed his face.

"It takes me fifteen minutes to complete the routine of brushing my teeth at night."

"Seriously?"

"Yep. I love new socks, I wish I had a new pair of socks for everyday of my life, and secretly, just between you and me, I'm an obsessive organizer, even my spices. Oh, and I'm addicted to Chap Stick." She frowned. "Or at least I was. Guess I'm cured," she said with a shrug.

Alex threw his head back and laughed, liking this side of Alyssa.

"Will you still like me as a houseguest?"

"I think I'll manage, Alyssa."

≈

"WOULD YOU LIKE to go outside today?" Alex invited one morning after breakfast. "I'll be chopping firewood. You'll be able to see me from where you sit. C'mon, the fresh air will do you good."

"I had plenty of fresh air the other day," she countered, feeling downcast.

"That doesn't count."

"Why not?"

"It was a stressful day, so the fresh air went to waste."

"Oh really, doctor, is this based on medical fact?"

"Yes, from the Book of Alex."

Unable to keep from smiling, she capitulated. "Okay, I'll come outside. Do you chop wood every day?"

"Yes, everyday. If I do a little each day, it's not such an overwhelming job. We'll be especially thankful for it in the winter."

"Is the winter horribly cold?"

"We'll be snowed in for about four months, give or take a few weeks."

"Oh." The thought ruminated in her head. They'd be alone and trapped in the cabin during the winter. How awkward. Alex finished getting dressed—pulling on his socks, putting on his shoes, lacing his boots, tying them, tucking in his shirt, buckling his belt. He caught her eye and smiled at her. "Ready?"

"Yeah." The thing is—she didn't feel awkward around him—not at all.

He settled her just outside the door of the cabin in a wooden Adirondack style chair and told her he liked to sit there at night and watch the sun go down. He propped her legs up on his kitchen stool and gave her a book to read.

"I own all the classics. How 'bout Wuthering Heights? Have you read it?"

"No, I've only seen the movie. I liked it. That sounds good, thank you. This is a comfortable chair."

He sat down on the stool in front of her, replacing her legs on his lap. "Thanks, I made it."

"Did you make all of the furniture in the cabin?"

"Yes. I had the cushions for the chairs and couches made, though. I draw the line at sewing. The first year I had couches with no cushions. That was a priority at delivery time."

He began to massage her good leg. "You do excellent work. I'm impressed. You built this cabin also?"

"Yep, lived in a tent till it was done. That motivated me."

He grinned broadly. A light breeze picked up his hair and it gently wafted about. His black hair was thick and shiny. His blue eyes looked even bluer outside in the sunlight. "Wow, the amount of supplies you had delivered, it must've taken so many trips, so much planning."

He seemed to like that she was showing an interest in things around her. "It was quite an undertaking. But I've loved every minute of it. Have you ever seen large metal storage containers, similar to what a semi-truck would carry? Only on a much smaller scale."

"Yes." She watched his hands as they massaged her leg.

"We packed everything in those and had them delivered. That way my supplies were protected from the weather till I could get to them. They're in a clearing about a mile from here. I'll show you sometime. They take back the empty ones on the return trip. It works."

"Very clever."

"I was determined. I'd better get to work. I'm stalling."

He walked off to get busy with the chore of chopping wood. She was impressed with his skill at woodworking. The cabin and its furniture were amazing. And the area around the cabin was beautiful. Alyssa took a deep breath and realized he was right, she did feel better being outside. The confines of the cabin were getting to her. The heat of the July summer was dulled by the soft breeze that rustled through the trees. It was neither too hot nor too cold. She opened the book and began to read. When she read the same page at least three times, she gave up and watched Alex for awhile. He'd taken off his shirt, displaying a tanned and muscular torso with abs of steel. She buried her nose in the book, feeling like she shouldn't be watching him. The thing was, he made her feel again—he made her feel happy and he made her want to live. After awhile, she couldn't resist, her eyes drifted up to watch Alex. He looked good, she had to admit as she watched him unabashedly. He was sweating and his tanned skin gleamed in the sunlight. She watched as his arms swung the axe up and down, his muscles rippling with each movement.

We'll be snowed in for four months . . .

His words echoed in her head. A little flutter in her stomach caught her off guard.

Suddenly, Alex looked up and caught her staring at him. He smiled and waved. Her eyes skittered downwards, embarrassed and ashamed to be caught watching him. She pretended as if she was intensely interested in her book, feeling like a teenager with her first crush. Ridiculous.

Alyssa stared at the book, not really in the mood for reading. Resting her head on the back of the chair, she closed her eyes and drifted off. She dreamt of Sam, she dreamt of Alex, confusion gripping her. *Great happiness awaits you, Alyssa.*

Suddenly, Adam was before her eyes saying, "It's time for our wedding night, Eve," and he laughed hysterically. She woke very suddenly and looked about her in a panic, Adam's laugh still echoing in her head. Alex was nowhere to be seen.

"Alex . . ." she yelled with desperation in her voice. "Alex . . ." she yelled again, this time louder. "Alex!"

Alex exited the open door of the cabin, concern in his expression, a dishtowel slung over his shoulder. "I'm right here, Alyssa. Are you okay?" he said as he snacked on a cracker.

Relieved, her head fell back onto the chair. The quick rise and fall of her chest told Alex she was alarmed, there was no use trying to hide it. Willing her hands to stop shaking, she said, "It's nothing, it's stupid. I'm fine. I just panicked, that's all."

He sat down on the stool in front of her and held her legs again. "It's to be expected. I promise the farthest I'll be from you is the workshop. I won't go anywhere without telling you, okay?"

He held the half eaten cracker towards her, she opened her mouth, and he popped it in. She nodded and looked into his eyes, liking what she saw. His eyes were clear and bright, filled with honesty and concern. There was no guile in him, no hidden agenda.

"You were sleeping so peacefully, I didn't want to wake you."

"Why are you so nice to me?"

"Would you like me to be mean?"

He pushed her good leg off his lap. It fell to the ground with a thump. He raised his eyebrows at her. It was so random, it took her off guard. Unable to help herself, she started to laugh. He laughed too.

"C'mon, dinner's ready." He held out his hand to her.

She placed her hand in his and they went inside.

≈

"ALYSSA, NOW THAT you're doing better, I think it's time for a tour, so you know where everything is," Alex said the next day as she lay on the couch resting her leg.

"Does that mean I have to get up?" she asked, feeling petulant.

"Yes, young lady . . ."

"Young? How young do you think I am?"

"I've been trying to figure that out. You're one of those lucky women who will look nineteen forever."

"I'm twenty-seven," she said with a small smile. "Thanks all the same. And you?"

"Thirty-nine, the big four-o is just around the corner."

Twelve years.

There were twelve years between them. Alyssa shook her head as she sat up. What did his age matter to her? "Okay, let's do this tour," she said with no enthusiasm whatsoever.

First, Alex took her to the supply room, which was attached to the cabin. It was as big as the main part of the cabin and was filled with shelves and supplies.

Attached to the supply room was a door that led to a long covered corridor. It spanned the length of the cabin. It was halfway full of firewood. Alex told her it needed to be completely full in time for winter. Having this easy access to the firewood was imperative during the winter. It also kept it dry.

In one corner of the supply room, Alex had his own dressing area. In another corner, there was a wood burning stove to heat the room in the winter. Alyssa gave it a passing glance, feeling uninterested.

Then Alex showed her another door off the main cabin. Inside this door was a small shower stall. It was tiled on the inside and had a drain just like a normal shower, only the drainpipe simply led to the outside of the cabin. Alex heated the water in pots on the stove and poured it into a large basin that sat on top of the shower. He could get to the basin by a ladder which sat next to the door. The basin had a spigot attached to it with a showerhead. You simply pulled the chain and out came the water. The basin held about ten gallons of water. Enough for a fairly enjoyable shower if you wet yourself, soaped up dry, and then rinsed. It was ingenious.

In the far right corner of the cabin there was a bathtub. It also drained outside of the cabin. Alex had long ago placed drapes around the area to form a square. This was now Alyssa's "space" when she needed privacy to change. He also moved a dresser into the area to allow her a place to put the clothes he'd given her to wear. The bathtub was also filled by heating water and pouring it into the tub. Alyssa couldn't get the wood on her splint wet, so Alex filled it and allowed her to sponge bathe next to the bathtub.

In the kitchen was an old fashioned stove, with an oven beneath it. Cabinets lined the wall of the kitchen, giving him storage space, so he didn't have to walk to and from the supply room twenty times a day.

He also had another wood burning stove in the main cabin that helped greatly in the winter with heating.

The kitchen sink was the only place you could get running water. Alex hired a surveyor to come and make sure he could tap into a well to have running water on the property. Everything was in place by the time he arrived and he built around it. The water was pumped from a well into a fifty-five gallon drum sitting in a corner of the cabin, mimicking a small water tower. This provided water pressure. The pipes were well insulated to prevent freezing in the winter.

"The walls of the cabin are also well insulated, keeping it surprisingly warm in the winter," Alex told her. "In the summer, I simply open the windows and let the breeze blow through the cabin." No need for air conditioning, it was refreshing.

Over the concrete slab—that was poured before he ever arrived—he'd installed a beautiful hardwood floor. It was stained in a shiny cherry wood finish and it gleamed in the sunlight.

In the end, Alyssa couldn't feign indifference, she found his cabin amazing, he'd thought of everything and she told him so.

"If you only knew. The first year I forgot screens for the windows. As you can imagine the bugs were terrible. I also forgot a clock. My watch died during the year and it drove me crazy to not know what time it was. The second year, I realized I hated the smell of oil lanterns. Now I have only battery operated lighting which is so much easier. The third year, I realized I needed some way of exercising during the winter. I had major cabin fever. Hence, the treadmill, which I only bring out of the supply room during the winter. It was the little things I didn't think about, things that made a big difference in my comfort level, however."

Next he took her outside to show her the workshop. The workshop was a large, one room building with a dirt floor. It housed stacks of lumber and his tools and supplies for building. He also had shelves filled with different color stains and paints.

He had several projects he was working on—additional shelving for the supply room, extra shelves for the cabin to hold all of his books, another dresser to replace the one he'd given to her, and more outdoor furniture.

"I love coming out here and working on whatever project I feel like on that particular day. I always have several going at once. It relieves boredom. I have a lot of future plans for the cabin. There's always something more to build."

They walked back to the cabin and Alyssa lay back down and elevated her leg. She'd enjoyed seeing how he lived and survived up here. It was obvious Alex wanted to show her more details, but she just didn't feel like it. She didn't feel like doing anything.

So she didn't.

≈

ALYSSA WANTED TO sit outside again the next day when Alex was ready to leave. This time he was also going to work in his workshop. He was glad she showed an interest in being out, but he was worried about her safety.

"All right," he told her, "On one condition."

"What?"

"If you're going to be outside alone, I want you to be armed at all times. It's not enough to just know where the gun is anymore."

Alyssa seemed to contemplate the idea. "Will you teach me how to use it?"

Alex felt pleased with her response. He'd wondered if she would refuse, having seen too much violence recently. She'd been showing a lot of interest lately in the things around her. It was a good sign and told him she was coming out of her shell. Of course, he'd also caught her watching him on occasion. On the day he'd been chopping wood, he swore he'd seen her blush from where he stood. Interesting. It made him wonder what she was thinking about . . . if her thoughts had wandered to the same place as his. He could think of little else.

"Do you remember how to load and unload?"

"Yes, I think I've got that down."

He stood behind her, teaching her how to aim and shoot. The close proximity felt good. They practiced for over an hour until she felt very comfortable handling the gun.

"You're a good shot, Alyssa. You'll be fine."

"Alex," she said, "If Adam comes back, I will use this on him."

Alex nodded, "I'm counting on it, Alyssa."

-11-

THE NEXT WEEK passed uneventfully as they settled into a routine. They always had their meals together. By day, Alyssa sat outside while Alex worked in the workshop. Every once in a while she enjoyed sitting in the workshop, watching Alex work. For exercise, other than the occasional excursion to the outhouse, she walked around the inside of the cabin everyday and at night they sat by the fire and talked. A quiet friendship had developed between them.

It was a late July morning when Alyssa sat outside of the cabin enjoying the beauty and the fresh air. The sounds of Alex working in the workshop always made her feel safe. It meant he was close by. And she liked him close, she admitted to herself. She wasn't sure she'd be able to sleep at night without him. When he'd taught her how to shoot, with his cheek pressed to her cheek and his arms wrapped around her, she'd felt that flutter in her stomach again.

She ignored it.

Time was passing and she was healing. Only one more week and the splint would be removed. It was very uncomfortable and she felt as if she was simply biding her time, waiting for the six week point and then she would be free again. Alyssa couldn't wait. She was sick of the crutches too. They were absolutely the worst part of a leg injury, she decided. Her armpits hurt more than anything.

Suddenly, a deer walked into the clearing. And right behind it was a small fawn with little white spots on its coat. A mother and her baby. She held very still as they walked around sniffing and foraging the ground beneath them. It broke her heart to see them together.

I want my baby.

The fawn stayed close to the mother, moving whenever its mother moved, stopping whenever its mother stopped. The mother deer would occasionally snuggle with her fawn, nudging her nose towards her baby, the baby responding in kind.

Alyssa watched them together, mesmerized. As they started to leave the clearing, she slowly stood and began to follow them. They moved lazily through the trees and didn't seem to notice her. She followed them a short while till the sound of one of her crutches hitting a small branch made a loud snapping noise and they ran away in a graceful prance.

She smiled as they made their escape.

Good mother, keep your baby safe.

Her smile faded. She hadn't been able to keep her baby safe. Her heart heavy, Alyssa retreated to the safe confines of the cabin.

≈

AS THE FIRST week of August was upon them, it was finally time for the splint to come off. As far as Alyssa was concerned, it couldn't come too soon, she was very ready to be rid of it. Alex had her lay on the bed.

"Are you ready for this, Alyssa?"

"Yes."

"I know it will be a relief to have this thing off. I think you need to realize the muscles in your leg are going to be somewhat atrophied. The new tissue around the wound sight is somewhat different from normal tissue. It has to relearn how to function. Of course there's going to be some scar tissue that we're dealing with also. Now is when the real work comes in."

"I'm ready."

He slowly removed the splint. Her leg felt ten times lighter.

"First, I'm going to massage the muscles—warm them up—and then we'll try to start bending it."

The muscles were very tender. At first the massage felt good. The muscles were tight and she could feel the tension slowly slip away. But then her muscles began to scream at her in rebellion. Several moments were excruciatingly painful, like having bruises massaged. She winced and he slowed down a bit.

"Are you okay? Do you want me to stop?"

"No, keep going," she said through clenched teeth. She concentrated on his face. His blue eyes were intense as he worked. He was so good to her. And as she watched him, she had to admit, he was an inordinately handsome man. The kind of man that makes your heart skip a beat when you see him on the street. She'd always known this, she simply hadn't wanted to acknowledge the fact. She still missed Sam. But Alex was dear to her. He was the man who had saved her, who took care of her, watched over her, and protected her. He was, unmistakably, a good man and she loved the person he was on the inside. Still, he was darn good looking on the outside, she thought with a sigh. Under different circumstances . . .

Her thoughts quickly changed as the massage again turned painful.

She felt a rush of love for Alex. These feelings confused her. She recognized the fact that she loved him for saving her, but she knew there was more to it than that. She decided not to dwell on it. Beads of sweat formed on her forehead and she arched her back. The pain was much more than she'd anticipated. Alex sat down beside her, smoothing the hair out of her face.

"Keep going," she told him.

"Alyssa, it's enough for one day. I don't want to overdo it."

"It hurts a lot more than I thought."

"I'm sorry," he said with a soft caress to her cheek.

"I don't do well with pain."

"Who does?" he added.

"Good point."

"Actually, it's been proven that women have a much higher pain threshold than men."

"You're just trying to make me feel better," she responded.

"True, but don't you realize, if the situation were reversed, I'd be going through the roof right about now?"

They both smiled. He was trying to cheer her up and it worked.

"Shall we try to start bending it? Your knee wasn't injured. It's the muscles we're fighting with."

"Okay."

He slowly began to bend the leg at the knee. Alyssa threw her head back on the pillow and gritted her teeth. He halfway completed the process twice and then took her in his arms and hugged her as if he hated seeing her in pain. She dashed at her tears, wanting to get through this valiantly. It was the only way to begin walking again and she was determined.

"Tomorrow we'll walk. Between walking, massaging, and bending exercises, you'll be almost as good as new. You'll see. Today was the most painful. You're a trooper."

She hugged him back, suddenly not wanting to let go of him.

≈

ALEX FELT ALYSSA holding on tight to him, somewhat fiercely. He closed his eyes and gave in to the feeling. He held her for the first time, not as a man comforting a woman, but as a man who is holding the woman he could so easily fall in love with. As he laid her back down, her eyes looked into his and he knew there was something new between them—something new and unexpected for both of them.

"What now?" she asked.

"What?" He felt as though she was reading his thoughts.

"What do I do now?"

He realized she was, of course, referring to her leg. He stood. Back to business. "Muscle relaxant and a hot bath, doctor's orders."

Alex prepared a steaming hot bath. After only being able to take sponge baths, she was thrilled to be able to take a real bath. "This will help relieve some of the ache in your leg," he said as he handed her his robe. "I'll give you privacy to change." After a few minutes he asked, "Alyssa, are you in yet?"

"No."

"Are you decent?"

"Yes."

He opened the curtains. There she stood, next to the steaming bath, wearing his robe and balancing on the crutches. She looked unsure . . . and absolutely adorable.

"Are you having trouble getting in?"

"I'm scared I'll slip."

Alex hesitated about what to do. "Okay, tell you what, I'll hold out my arm and turn and look the other way. I promise I'll keep my eyes closed. Most of the time."

She shot him an apprehensive look.

He smiled rakishly. She didn't. "Just kidding. But if you slip, all bets are off."

"Okay," she said, sounding hesitant.

He held out his arm and looked away. He heard one crutch fall to the floor, then heard his robe whoosh to the ground. His heart pounded unnaturally in his chest. Her hand grasped his arm tightly, her skin sliding against his, soft and supple. He could feel how nervous she was by her desperate grip. Putting weight on her leg was not something she was used to as yet. He heard the water splash as she slowly lowered herself into the tub.

"Okay, I'm in. That wasn't so bad."

"My hand says otherwise."

"Sorry."

"I'll survive." Alex closed the drapes behind him.

"This is wonderful, Alex. It feels so good . . ."

Alex closed his eyes and let out a breath. This scenario was wreaking havoc on his emotions. He hurried to the sink and splashed cold water on his face, giving himself a pep talk. "She needs someone to help her and take care of her, not some lonely man who hasn't seen anyone for three years making advances on her and scaring her to death. She trusts you and you will not betray that trust."

"Alex, did you say something?"

"No, sweetheart. Must have been the wind." Then he started to worry about her. "Alyssa, don't fall asleep in there."

"I'm not."

"When you're done, drain the water, put on the robe, and let me help you out, okay?"

"Okay."

"You sound sleepy, are you sleepy?"

"Alex, I'm fine."

"Sorry."

Every five minutes of her thirty-minute bath, Alex checked to make sure she was okay. He couldn't seem to calm his worry over her safety and he felt like a doting father.

Or husband.

She didn't seem to be bothered by his attention. Quite the opposite, she seemed to like it.

"Okay, I'm ready," he heard her say.

Alex stood outside of the drapes. *Heaven help me.* When he walked in, her face was flushed from the heat of the water and she looked relaxed and happy. She still sat in the tub, the water drained, and his robe wrapped around her. She was a truly beautiful woman, both inside and out. He knew he was falling in love with her, deeper and deeper every day that they spent together. He swallowed and tried to act casual.

"My leg feels so much better. That was wonderful."

He helped her out of the tub. Her skin was pink, warm, and moist. He got out of there quick and let her change.

"I forgot something in the workshop," he lied. "I'll be right back." Alex took a brisk walk in the cool, early evening air. What he really needed was an ice cold shower.

It was just a little too steamy in the cabin.

≈

"ALEX, IT'S BEAUTIFUL," Alyssa breathed as Alex presented her with a hand carved cane.

The last few days had consisted of taking walks around the inside of the cabin, massaging her leg, bending exercises, and hot baths, just as Alex had said. He kept her on the muscle relaxant, which also helped with the pain. It was as if she had her very own private doctor—and she kinda liked it.

While in the bath, Alyssa found herself fantasizing about Alex washing her hair, his fingers massaging her scalp instead of her own. He'd been the one washing her hair since she'd shown up on his doorstep. It always reminded her of the night she'd first arrived and the way Alex had taken care of her.

I'll never forget that night.

"It's not what I expected at all," Alyssa told him, feeling speechless. On the cane, he'd carved out different scenes—pine trees, mountain ranges, the cabin, and even her name. It was a work of art. He'd stained it with a high gloss stain and it shined brightly. Tears formed in her eyes at the sight. Alyssa was so sick of the crutches, she could hardly wait to learn to walk with the cane.

As their eyes met, Alyssa noticed there was something in his eyes she hadn't seen there before. "Thank you, Alex. I'll always treasure this," she said warmly.

"Are you ready to tackle a longer, outdoor walk?"

With excitement, she responded, "Yes."

The excitement was gone a little later as she tried to walk with the cane. It was much harder than she'd thought.

For the next week, Alex had her walk everyday in the area surrounding the cabin. She was ridiculously slow at first, but by the end of the week, she had mastered it and was doing great. Her muscles were adjusting to walking again.

≈

"HOW ABOUT A long walk and a picnic today?" Alex asked her at breakfast.

Although she was doing well, she knew she'd been a little quiet lately. Alex was pushing her, knowing it kept her from dwelling on her sorrows for too long. She appreciated the effort. He wouldn't allow her to wallow in misery.

"All right," she said apprehensively.

"Perhaps you could contain your excitement just a little."

She smiled. "I'm sorry, that sounds wonderful."

Alex quickly packed a picnic lunch and off they went. They walked for about an hour before she'd had enough. They ate their picnic, sitting on a light blanket, surrounded by enormous pine trees that seemed as though they touched the sky.

Alyssa had to admit, the beautiful area she now lived in was a balm to her soul. She examined her surroundings and took a deep breath, understanding why Alex chose to live up here. It was a peaceful existence — until she joined him and marred his serenity.

Her eyes rested on Alex. Sometimes she liked to simply watch him. It wasn't as if she didn't notice him as a man. She did. Yet when those thoughts crossed her mind, she felt guilt sweep over her. She'd just lost Sam. How could she notice someone else so soon? Examining these feelings too closely left her uncomfortable. She simply wasn't ready to face these thoughts as yet.

"Alyssa, what are you thinking about?" Alex interrupted her thoughts.

"Sorry, my mind was wandering." Alyssa looked away, embarrassed at being caught staring at him. Plopping down supine onto the blanket, she let the rays of the sun soak into her skin. *What am I doing here? How can Sam and Clay be gone? How did my life end up this way?* Her mind simply wouldn't wrap around all that had happened. Regardless, she was thankful for this man who sat by her side. Knowing she had feelings for Alex didn't help her understand them. She still mourned her husband.

Her thoughts drifted off as she thought about nighttime. She loved nighttime. It was when she could hold onto Alex and drift into oblivion. For the first time, she wondered how he must feel about them sleeping in the same bed together, with her clinging to him. Alyssa felt herself blush at the thought. She'd been so blind. He must be uncomfortable with it. His priorities had always been her since the day she arrived—her comfort, her rehabilitation, her sadness, and her needs.

Her prayer on a cold lonely night in the woods had been answered sevenfold. Most definitely, she'd been saved. What a twist of fate that she'd gone from being with two brutes, facing utter cruelty in her life and then to Alex, a man who showed her kindness and compassion . . . and love. Yes, love. *I love him and I know, by his actions, he loves me too.* Maybe not in a mind-blowing-crazy-for-you way, but in a soft, I'm-here-for-you way. Alex caught her watching him again and she smiled. He lay down next to her. They both looked up at the sky through the trees, the branches gently wafting about in the soft breeze. Patches of clear blue sky smiled down on them.

"The sun feels good. Thank you for taking me out today."

They lay there in silence, each lost in their own thoughts.

"You're young, Alyssa. You'll never forget what you once had, but you'll find happiness in this life again," he commented randomly.

"Will you, Alex?"

"I've found happiness. I plan to live and die here."

The thought bothered her, but she let it go. "Tell me about your daughters."

She didn't think he was going to answer at first. He'd gone very still at her query. But then he began to speak, almost in a whisper.

"Thank you for asking," he said, seeming pleased. "They were the most beautiful creatures in the world. They amazed me every day. They had my coloring, black hair, blue eyes, but they had their mother's features and her curly hair. To me, they looked like little porcelain dolls. When I came home from work at the end of the day, they squealed with delight, ran to me, hugged me, and kissed me. I loved coming home just for that. I miss it. They talked non-stop and I loved that too. I used to watch them sleep at night. They were so still, so calm, so peaceful. My wife would drag me out of the room telling me, they'll still be there in the morning, come to bed. And then one morning, they weren't there, and it killed me. I moved up here and never looked back."

Alyssa was filled with questions, but she didn't ask them. Instead, she said, "What are their names?"

"Alexis and Anna."

"How old are they?" she asked in present tense, assuming they were still living—but she wasn't so sure. Why else would it be such a painful topic? And if they were alive, wouldn't Alex be with them?

"They were only six and seven when I lost them." He sat up, his back to her. "And, no, I don't want to talk about how I lost them. I'm sorry, I don't ever want to talk about it."

From behind, she wrapped her arms around his waist and rested her head on his back, hugging him tightly. He covered her arms with his own. They stayed that way for a long while, a balm to each other.

≈

WHEN ALYSSA AWOKE the next day, Alex was up, dressed, and making breakfast as usual. He was always up before her, never awakening her as he left the bed. Sitting up, the familiar feeling overwhelmed her. There was a lead weight in her stomach and sadness beset her. No matter how hard she tried, she couldn't shake it. Grabbing her cane, she made her way to the table where she picked at her food and didn't eat much.

"I thought we'd hike to the lake today," Alex offered slowly, interpreting her mood

She didn't respond, having no desire to walk to the lake today or any day for that matter. Alyssa didn't know what she wanted. Alex seemed to sense her 'out of sorts' mood.

"Walking to the lake isn't too long of a walk and it will be good for your leg. Swimming will be good exercise too. I have a t-shirt and gym shorts you can wear as a bathing suit. The height of fashion . . ." Alex said with a smile.

Alyssa couldn't help herself, she smiled back. Her wardrobe consisted of Alex's clothes. Besides her assortment of cut off sweat pants, he'd also given her several pairs of jeans. They rolled up the pant legs and they cinched them at the waist with some nylon cording to make them fit. She wore his button-up shirts with the sleeves rolled up and tied them at the waist. She wore his boxers with a huge safety pin to hold them up. The first time she dressed, Alex told her she looked absolutely darling. She thought she looked silly, but she had nothing else to wear.

"I didn't know there was a lake up here."

"Yeah, there are several small lakes dotting the area. I almost built right next to one, but I decided mosquitoes and I can never be friends."

Alyssa smiled at him once again. Every day, he worked hard to reach in and pull her out of the blackness she was under. If it wasn't for Alex, she'd still be in bed, hiding under the covers. She'd never been a depressed person in her life. As a matter of fact, she was a naturally happy person. But who wouldn't have bad episodes when faced with what she had recently endured? He seemed to understand that perfectly and never gave up on her or lost his patience with her.

He reached across the table and took her hand in his. Alyssa observed their entwined hands, squeezing softly and letting her thumb softly caress his skin. Looking back up at him, she noticed his gaze had turned intense.

"I'll have to check my schedule, but I think I can free up my morning," she said.

He grinned, "Let's go."

It seemed like a long walk, but only because she was slow. However, she now found walking with the cane to be tremendously easier than the crutches.

The lake was breathtaking. It was very small, clear blue, and looked like glass. The mountains in the distance were reflected on the surface. A small waterfall cascaded lazily into the lake from the cliff above. It could've been a picture out of a magazine. The sadness of the morning left and Alyssa felt herself relax.

They sat down on a blanket, Alyssa naturally leaning back onto Alex, her back to his chest. He wrapped his arms around her as if they'd been sitting that way for years together. "I see why you like it here, Alex. It's as if the beauty of the area reaches out and heals you."

"It did exactly that for me. When I arrived here, I can't say I had a death wish, nor was I suicidal. I just didn't care if I lived or died. That's not a good place to be. Living up here, you have to work to survive. Nothing is handed to you. If you want to live, you get up and get to work, you make it happen. I needed that. It was therapeutic. Sooner or later you realize you do want to live and you fight for it."

Alyssa was quiet, letting that sink in. *I'm alive, my life is not over.* She leaned back so she could look up at him. "The other day I followed a mother deer and her fawn into the forest. Do you know why?"

"Why?"

"I was so taken with how the mother watched over her baby."

"I know where you're going with this, Alyssa, please don't . . ."

"It was precious to watch. I should've done something to save my baby. I did nothing but stand there and let it happen."

Alex held her chin. "What could you have done?" he asked fiercely.

"I could have fought. I could have died with them."

"Exactly. You would've died with them. What good would that have done? No good to anyone."

I wouldn't be here with you.

"Now you can go home and tell the story. You can see to it that Adam pays for what he's done. You can go on with life and find happiness."

With you, Alex?

Suddenly, everything changed and she was acutely aware of the fact that she was in his arms, head back, looking up into his blue eyes blazing back at her with emotion. His arms tightened around her. She could imagine kissing him. It would be so easy. All she had to do was lean forward just a little bit . . .

Suddenly, she felt as though she couldn't breathe. She sat up quickly and he let her go easily. Maybe she'd just imagined it. "I know you're right, I guess I just needed to hear it."

"Let's go for a swim. We both need to cool off."

"What do you mean?"

"I mean it's hot out, what did you think I meant?"

"Nothing."

Alyssa was very hesitant to enter the water with a bum leg. Alex took her hands in his and led her in. "The buoyancy of the water will feel good on your leg. You'll be able to exercise with little or no pain."

He was right. Swimming was wonderful and the cool water of the lake was refreshing. He swam backwards, holding her hands in his, slightly pulling her along as she used her legs to propel herself forward. Alyssa felt as if they were the only two people in the world. In many ways, they were.

"It's beautiful here, Alex."

He smiled, "It's one of my favorite spots. I usually come here every day and swim, except in winter, of course."

"It's paradise and you have it all to yourself. No lines to wait in, no traffic, no clock, no deadlines, and no phone. It's as if time stands still."

His gaze turned intense and she wondered what he was thinking. "I'm glad you like it, Alyssa," was all he said.

Suddenly, a sharp pain almost made her double over. They were in the middle of the lake and her leg began to cramp. She panicked and grasped for Alex. The pain was so overwhelming, she could hardly speak.

"Hold onto my shoulders," he told her, staying calm.

Although she felt slightly panicked, she held onto his shoulders as he reached down and massaged her leg till the cramp subsided.

"I think we've found your limit for the day."

They were face to face, only an inch apart. Blue eyes met brown and they held each other's gaze for a long moment, breathing each other in. Then Alex said, "You need a rest."

He had her float on her back and rest her head on his shoulder as they floated around the lake. He occasionally whispered in her ear, "It's all right . . . you're doing great . . . just relax . . . everything's going to be fine."

And for the first time, she knew he was right.

≈

ALEX HELD ALYSSA, letting the water take them where it may. It was utterly relaxing. Alyssa knew something was happening between them, but she couldn't face it yet, that much was obvious. And he wasn't going to push her. It had to come from her. If anything was going to happen between them, she had to be ready. He'd almost kissed her just now. How would she have responded? Before him was a beautiful and charming woman, inches away, and yet miles. He couldn't cross the line between them.

But he wanted to.

He wanted to press his lips to hers and kiss her senseless.

Get a grip, Alex.

-12-

WHEN THEY ARRIVED back at the cabin late that afternoon, Alyssa was lying on the bed resting her leg as Alex started on dinner. "Alex, how do you do your laundry?" The clothes he'd given her were beginning to pile up.

His expression filled with distaste. "A dreadful chore, it's the one thing I hate doing up here."

She laughed. "Oh c'mon, it can't be that bad."

"All right, I give, tomorrow will be laundry day. But I'm warning you, it's pure drudgery. Why do you think I have such a large supply of clothes? Then I can avoid the chore altogether."

"Spoken like a true wealthy man," she mumbled.

That gave him pause. "What makes you think I'm wealthy?"

She cast him an 'are you kidding me?' look. "Oh, I kinda figured it out all on my own."

He didn't respond and he looked upset.

"Alex, how many people could afford to do what you do? You have helicopters delivering supplies in large storage containers. You have every item you could possibly need neatly tucked away in your supply room and a wood burning stove just to keep those supplies warm in the winter, running water you had installed, a workshop filled with wood and every tool known to mankind, and a never ending supply of clothes so you don't have to do laundry Think about it, even I know doctors don't make quite that much."

His expression turned incredulous, then he burst into laughter. "I guess my secrets out."

"Besides, I grew up in Connecticut, remember? The Kendrick name is associated with money."

"Oh, I see, but you figured it out, did you?" He began to walk towards her with a smile on his face.

"Alex, I was just kidding, what are you doing?"

He started to tickle her, his hands roaming up and down the sides of her torso, till she couldn't breathe and finally she yelled, "Okay, I give." He stopped and hovered over her, both of them smiling into each other's eyes.

"Don't worry, you're safe with me. I just want you for your cabin," she teased.

"What!" He started tickling her again mercilessly until she had tears pouring down her face. And still, Alex hovered over her.

"I'll get you back for that."

"I'm waiting on pins and needles . . ." He leaned down close to her then and her heart skipped a beat. She thought he was going to kiss her. He seemed to think better of it and kissed her on the forehead.

Alyssa was quiet at dinner that night. Sensing her anxiety, Alex apologized for tickling her, saying he hadn't meant to touch her inappropriately. She assured him he hadn't offended her.

As a matter of fact, he couldn't be further from the truth. Alyssa kept watching his hands, unable to stop thinking about how they had felt.

All over her.

≈

THE NEXT DAY they arose early to do the laundry. It was the middle of August and the weather was perfect. The rays of the sun soaked into their skin, warming them, and the mountain breeze cooled them. Alyssa realized she'd now been living here with Alex for two months. Life went on whether tragedy had happened in her life or not. She'd mastered walking with the cane, although she was slow. And just as Alex had predicted, she limped, simply because she could not put her full weight on her leg, it was too painful. She was thankful to be able to walk though.

Alyssa felt especially thankful for Alex. He had definitely pushed her and at times she'd felt as though he was a veritable taskmaster, but because of him she was walking. And alive.

As trite as it sounded, she felt as though he was her best friend. Perhaps the best friend she'd ever had in her life. She didn't say it out loud, knowing she would sound like a second grader, and to be honest she didn't know how he would respond.

The creek was about a five-minute walk from the cabin and she held tightly to his hand as they walked. Alex had already carried out buckets of hot water and the clothes to be laundered. They sat in a large pile. She had to admit, it looked a little daunting.

She immediately noticed he already had a large clothesline set up along with various other supplies strewn about the area. Despite his hatred of the chore, he'd clearly done this many times before. He handed her the biodegradable soap and a washboard. It looked like something from a museum.

"Knock yourself out," he said with a roguish grin.

"Really?"

"Really."

"Somehow I thought you'd have some amazing new technology."

"It's next on my list. Scrub or rinse?"

"I'll scrub."

"Here's how it goes. You scrub using the soap and washboard, rinse in the creek, then I'll take it, rinse in hot water, then hang it on the clothesline."

Alyssa walked to the middle of the creek, tossed her cane back on the shore, sat herself down in the water, and started scrubbing.

Alex laughed at the sight. "I hate this chore with a passion. But today, with you sitting in the middle of the creek, I suddenly find it incredibly entertaining."

"This isn't so bad, Alex. It's kinda fun."

He merely raised his eyebrows and mumbled, "Whatever."

But she could see the sparkle in his blue eyes. They worked at their chore for the next couple of hours. She'd just finished washing a small towel, when she yelled, "Hey, Kendrick!" He turned around and she threw the towel at him. It hit him smack-dab on the face. Hard. He looked stunned. A giggle escaped as her hand covered the smile on her face. "Alex, I'm sorry. I didn't mean to throw it that hard."

He picked up a small bucket, a huge smile on his face. "You asked for it, Fontaine."

"Alex?" she said with a clear question in her voice. He scooped water into the bucket and stood before her. "You wouldn't," she challenged.

He did.

She sat there sputtering as the water washed over her while Alex laughed uproariously.

"I forgot, I can't run."

"Guess you should've thought of that before you declared war."

Alyssa promptly splashed him with her hand. Catching him off guard, he was clearly surprised, but then he splashed her back. Before they knew it, it was all out war as they splashed and kicked the water at each other. Alex tripped on a rock and was sitting in the creek along with her in an instant, which brought on another round of laughter. When it ended, they were both totally and completely soaked and sat there smiling at each other.

"Laundry has never been this much fun," Alex told her.

"This water is cold. I think my fingers and toes are numb."

"Truce?"

"Truce."

But as he got up, she splashed him really good in the face and the whole thing started again. It ended when

Alex grabbed the bucket and held it over her head. "Surrender?"

"Never," she said through chattering teeth.

"Alyssa, you're shivering," he said with concern. He scooped her up in his arms and carried her to dry ground. "You need to sit in the sun for awhile to warm up." He held her gaze as he cupped her hands in his, warming them. He brought her hands to his lips and blew on them to warm them with his breath. And then, with his eyes never leaving hers, he slowly kissed her fingertips, one by one. Hardly able to breathe, Alyssa watched him, feeling stunned. He held her fingers to his lips and let them linger there for a moment.

"I'd better get these clothes hung up," he said, making no move to get up. She nodded and he placed her hands back into her lap.

Alyssa let the sun warm her as she watched Alex work. Her eyebrows furrowed as her thoughts wandered. *What's happening to me? I know there's something between us, I'm just not sure exactly what it is or where it's headed. I'm not sure what he's thinking. His eyes are always so intense. I know one thing for sure, I'm the luckiest woman alive. Here I am stuck in the mountains with a perfectly wonderful man. Life has been hard on me . . . and yet I'm happy with Alex. No one has ever been so good to me in my entire life. I've developed feelings for him, feelings I don't understand.*

≈

ALEX GLANCED AT Alyssa a few times and could tell she was deep in thought. When he looked at her, she didn't look away, but met his gaze with a look he could not interpret. He hoped he hadn't scared her with his impulsive actions. It was getting harder to hide his feelings for her. Did she feel the chemistry between them? He simply wasn't sure. The last thing he wanted to do was scare her away. He'd thought long and hard about a few things, and he knew it was time to make some changes between them. He couldn't go on like this for much longer.

It took him awhile to hang up the clothes. For all of their goofing around, they'd actually gotten a lot done.

≈

AT DINNER THAT night, they were both quiet, lost in their own thoughts.

"How did you learn to cook, Alex?"

"Necessity." He'd made beef stroganoff, and it was delicious.

Silence.

They sat on the couch in front of the fire after dinner.

Silence.

When he reached out and caressed her cheek, she turned her face into his palm, pressing her lips onto his skin, kissing his palm, and looking up at him as she did so. He looked surprised and she was too. She hadn't thought about it, it just happened. It seemed like the natural thing to do. Turning away, she said, "I'm sorry."

"Alyssa, you're alive, it's okay to love again."

"What?" she said with dismay.

"You heard me," he said quietly.

"It hasn't been very long, Alex."

"We're not living under normal circumstances. We're with each other twenty-four-seven, under the same roof, in the same bed. Things happen faster."

She stood, alarmed, "Stop, Alex, don't say those things, please." Her eyes pooled with unshed tears.

He stood and faced her, running his hand through his hair. "I'm sorry. Look, Alyssa, I think I'll start sleeping on the couch. Under the circumstances, it doesn't seem right for me to sleep in the bed anymore."

The idea of sleeping alone terrified her. "Oh . . . of course, okay," she mumbled, staring down at the ground, trying to hide her anxiety. "I'll take the couch."

"Absolutely not. You keep the bed."

"I'm sorry, Alex," she whispered.

"You have nothing to apologize for."

But she did, she felt like she'd rejected him. Confusion engulfed her. She loved him. Didn't she? Yes, she did. Maybe he didn't feel the same. Maybe she was imagining things. What exactly was he implying a minute ago? Maybe he didn't mean what she'd thought. Maybe this was his way of getting out of the situation. Maybe he could see that the poor little girl who'd shown up on his doorstep was falling in love with him and he wanted to let her down easy.

"If you need anything, I'll just be right here."

She nodded, not looking at him, feeling ridiculously vulnerable—weak and fragile—without him. He was her rock, her protector, and she didn't realize till this moment just how much she relied on him. "Goodnight," she muttered as she shuffled into her dressing area and slipped on a pair of Alex's pajamas. A tear fell and she dashed at it.

The big bed felt cold without Alex. It had been a long day, she was tired, and although she was deeply distressed, she fell asleep quickly.

I can't move. I can't breathe. There's a rope around my neck, it's getting tighter as Adam tugs on it viciously. Pa slaps me across the face and laughs hysterically. Adam is suddenly in my face, trying to kiss me. "C'mon, Eve, it's our weddin' night." I turn away and see Sam and Clay standing in the distance. Clay is crying and I try to run to him, but I can't. My feet are like lead. Every step seems slow and unbearably heavy. Adam's sweaty hands grasp at me, pulling me towards him. Run, Alyssa, run, get away! It's too late. Adam tackles me to the ground, he's on top of me . . .

Alyssa screamed at the top of her lungs, over and over she screamed.

"Alyssa, Alyssa . . ."

Alyssa opened her eyes to find Alex holding her in his arms, looking upon her with worry.

"You were having a nightmare."

Feeling utterly frantic, she threw her arms around him and burst into tears. A heartfelt plea tumbled forth, "Please don't leave me, Alex, please. I can't sleep without you, please stay with me. I need you. Please stay with me, please . . ."

He lowered her down onto the bed, his face only inches from hers. "It's okay, Alyssa. I'll stay with you, I'll never leave you, it's okay now . . . shhhh."

He kissed her on the forehead several times and wiped away her tears. After turning off the light, he climbed into bed, and she clung to him as she fell asleep.

≈

LETTING OUT A deep breath, Alex admitted she felt good in his arms. It was an awkward situation to say the least. There was nothing sexual about them sleeping in the same bed. He knew that and would never take advantage of it. Alyssa had been through absolute hell and needed comfort. In his heart, he knew things were changing between them. He thought he was doing the decent thing by making a change in their sleeping arrangements. But if this was what she wanted, he wasn't going to fight it. He loved holding her in his arms at night.

They both slept peacefully till morning.

Alex hoped the smells of breakfast would awaken her, but she never stirred.

"Alyssa, are you coming to breakfast?"

Pulling the covers over her head, she garbled, "I'm not hungry."

Knowing he needed to give her some time alone, he responded, "All right, then. I'm going to the workshop."

By the time he came home for lunch, she was up and dressed. She sat at the table, but didn't look at him directly. He could tell by her swollen eyes she'd been crying.

"Alex, I'm sorry about last night. You don't have to sleep in the bed. I'm not so naïve that I don't realize how uncomfortable this must be for you. I'm sorry. I wasn't thinking about it from your point of view. You've been the perfect gentleman. I've only been thinking about myself and how hard it is to sleep right now. When you're there I can relax and let sleep claim me. I feel safe and . . ."

He placed his hand under her chin and gently tilted her head up till their eyes met. "I know, Alyssa. I know and I understand." He smiled mischievously as he added, "You know what, I like sleeping in the bed, as a matter of fact, I hate the couch. So, I changed my mind, I'll be sleeping in the bed from now on. This is my cabin and my bed and I'm sleeping in it, whether you like it or not."

A huge smile slowly broke out on her face. He'd made it sound as though it was his decision, as if it had nothing to do with her insecurity. "Thank you." He helped her to stand, took her in his arms, and hugged her tight. She hugged back.

"Friends?" he asked her.

"Friends," she agreed.

It was all she could give right now and he accepted it. "I'm making something for you. It will be ready in a few days."

≈

WHILE ALEX WORKED on his project for Alyssa, she lay in bed, staring at the walls, and he worried about her. They didn't miss their walks or their swim at the lake. This was the only time she seemed happy. The rest of the time she was listless and depressed. He felt like he was walking on eggshells, waiting for what, he wasn't quite sure. Waiting for her to be happy again, waiting for her to smile and laugh, waiting for a sparkle in those brown eyes. If he was honest with himself, he knew he was waiting for her . . . to notice him.

That evening he absolutely could not sleep. Alyssa lay in her usual position, with her head on his chest and one arm wrapped around his waist. Her breathing was slow and even and he knew she was fast asleep. She felt good. He may be a perfect gentleman, but his thoughts had turned on him and were most ungentlemanly. He turned on the lantern that looped over the bedpost just behind him, and grabbed the book he was currently reading. It sat on Alyssa's pillow, since she didn't seem to need it, he thought a little sarcastically. Not that he was complaining, mind you. He loved the feel of her head nestled on his chest. She still lay in peaceful slumber in spite of his movements. He read for a while, trying to take his mind off the beautiful woman who lay in his arms.

Although he tried to not disturb her, his actions awoke her. She looked up at him, resting her arms on his chest and propping her chin in her hands.

"Are you okay?" she asked sleepily.

Momentarily distracted by her beauty — and the feel of her in his arms — he didn't immediately answer. He was completely enchanted by her. The fire in the fireplace still burned, casting soft light on her features.

"Alex?"

"I couldn't sleep. I'm sorry the light woke you."

"It didn't. Your heartbeat woke me."

"My heartbeat?"

"Yes, it's always steady and even. The sound lulls me to sleep at night. It was beating faster than usual and it woke me up."

"It must be the book. It's a thriller," he lied.

She studied him for a few minutes and he wondered what she was thinking. Would they ever be on the same page? Would he ever be more to her than a security blanket? He knew he was expecting too much of her, too soon. He ran his fingers through her hair — as he always did as they fell asleep — and she closed her eyes with contentment.

"Mmmmm, I love when you do that, it feels so good. It relaxes me and helps me to fall asleep."

Heaven help me.

She looked up at him again and held his gaze. "Are you sure you're okay?"

Her eyes were heavy. "Yes. Sleep, Alyssa. Everything's fine," he whispered.

She rested her head on his chest again and wrapped her arm around his waist, quickly falling fast asleep. He continued to run his fingers through her long hair gently. She had the most beautiful hair he'd ever seen.

He tried to concentrate on his heartbeat, keeping it slow and steady, thus not awakening her. It was as good as counting sheep and the next thing he knew it was morning.

≈

IT DIDN'T TAKE Alex long to finish his gift for Alyssa. He entered the cabin at lunchtime and found Alyssa laying on the couch, deathly still, her face expressionless. Lately, her favorite pastime was staring at the walls.

He knew it was time for her to take a step forward and this was the way.

"Alyssa, I have something to show you. Will you come with me?"

They walked out behind the cabin through a stand of trees and then into a clearing. In this clearing was a tiny well-groomed fenced graveyard, filled with flowers.

Alyssa stopped dead in her tracks. "What is this?"

Alex led her closer. Alyssa stared at the grave markers with a look of consternation. There were five of them, each of them carved with words . . .

Patricia LeAnn Kendrick, Beloved Wife and Mother
Anna Celeste Kendrick, My Daughter, My Angel
Alexis Catherine Kendrick, My Daughter, My Love

And then next to them,

Samuel Evan Fontaine, Dearly Loved Husband and Father

Clayton Andrew Fontaine, Adored Son, Taken too soon

≈

ALYSSA FELT SPEECHLESS. The grave markers had obviously been hand carved by Alex. Her eyes bright with unshed tears, she asked, "How?"

"Car accident. This is the place where I go to remember them, to talk to them." His voice was rough with emotion. "And now you can do the same."

And with that he walked away. At first, Alyssa didn't want to enter. To do so would make it real. She turned away, angry, not wanting to see Sam and Clay's names there. After several deep breaths, she walked through the gate and entered the graveyard, falling to her knees in front of Sam and Clay's grave markers. Deep, racking sobs consumed her till she lost her breath. She cried till she couldn't cry anymore and then she sat there for most of the afternoon, feeling numb.

When Alex walked into the cabin that night, she hugged him for a long time, softly kissing his cheek, letting her lips linger there a second longer than needed. When the connection was broken, she looked him in the eyes.

He told her, "I don't call it a graveyard or cemetery. Obviously there are no bodies buried there. It's just a place to remember them. I call it the remembrance yard."

"Thank you, Alex."

≈

FOR THE NEXT week, all Alyssa did was sit by the grave markers of her husband and son. When Alex went to check on her, he could see her lips moving as she talked to them. She never forgot to arm herself and he knew she was safe out on her own. He gave her privacy and allowed her the time to say goodbye to them, hoping it was giving her some much needed closure. As he walked between the cabin and his workshop every day, he often detoured to check on her. Even though she was armed, he felt the need to make sure she was okay. He was glad he'd given her a memory of her family.

However, after a week and a half went by and all she did day after day was sit by their gravesides, he felt it was enough. He began to walk by and see her napping out there and he knew it was too much. Her behavior was verging on overboard and he knew he had to do something about it.

Alyssa was still lamenting all day, just in a different location. She had so completely turned into herself, he couldn't reach her. In essence, his plan had backfired.

But he knew this was just part of the grieving process. He knew that all too well. One step forward, two steps backward.

Time to bring her forward again.

Alex briskly walked to the remembrance yard, the late August sun beating down on him. With each step, he could feel his emotions bubbling closer and closer to the surface. He wasn't sure he could hide how he felt about her anymore. Alyssa had only been with him for a little over two months. But they'd spent almost every second together. He knew he was completely and totally in love with her. Stopping short of the small graveyard, he felt aghast at the sight of Alyssa lying in the dirt, her body face down before the grave markers of her husband and son. Her hands clenched and unclenched the dirt, filling her fingernails. It broke his heart to see her this way. She loved her family fiercely. Secretly, as he watched her, he wished someone would love him like that. Actually, he wished *she* would love him like that. He couldn't stand it. He wasn't going to let her wallow like this anymore. For a reason he couldn't explain, he felt angry.

"Alyssa!" It came out harsher than he'd intended.

≈

STARTLED, ALYSSA LOOKED at Alex, unable to read the expression on his face. But she thought he seemed upset. She hadn't heard him approach and felt slightly embarrassed to be caught in such a state. Her face must be smudged with dirt and tears. Sitting up, she brushed the dirt off her hands, looking at him sullenly.

"What are you doing?" he said, almost with disgust in his voice. She didn't respond, but lowered her eyes and turned her back to him. What did he want from her? He walked into the graveyard and knelt down behind her.

"Look, this can't go on, Alyssa. There's a lot to be done around here and I need you to start pulling your weight. I can't wait on you, hand and foot, all day while you sit here and cry. Just to survive up here takes work and we need to be prepared for the winter. I can't do it all myself."

Alyssa said nothing, not understanding his mood at all. Seemingly irritated, he grabbed her from behind and leaned her back over his knee, surprising her. His arms wrapped around her torso, lifting her up slightly and bringing her face close to his, her head dangling backwards. Her sharp intake of breath at his actions didn't stop him. His face was only inches from hers as he said the next words.

"I know you miss your husband and son, that will never change, but you're alive and you must go on with your life. This is as bad as it gets. Nothing you face in this lifetime can be any worse than this. Do you hear me, Alyssa?" His voice was rough with emotion and he was scaring her. "Do you understand what I'm saying to you? It's right in front of you, just waiting for you to grasp it. Great happiness awaits you, Alyssa, can't you see it?"

At those words, Alyssa gasped.

Abruptly, Alex crushed his lips onto hers, kissing her hard on the mouth. It was so unexpected, it took her off guard. The kiss was rough at first, unplanned and done in the heat of the moment. But then it changed and passion exploded between them. Alyssa kissed him back, matching his fervor. Her arms reached around him tightly and the kiss momentarily deepened. The world began to spin for Alyssa. Held in this position, she was completely at his mercy. She didn't fight it, in fact, found she didn't want to. Conscious thought eluded her as Alex kissed her as if their lives depended on it, as if they would both simply vanish into thin air without each other. He felt good, tasted good, smelled good, and she felt herself respond to him in a way that overwhelmed her.

And then as suddenly as it began, it was over. They stared at each other, breathing hard, both taken by surprise at the intensity of the kiss.

Guilt gripped Alyssa and washed over her. Roughly, she pushed Alex away and struggled to her feet. Alex slowly stood. They faced each other, and Alyssa found herself filled with emotions that stunned her.

Not wanting to face the sudden onslaught of emotions, she said with disdain, "Go on with my life? You mean like *you*? What kind of life is this? You're not living, you're hiding," she scoffed. Then, with ice in her voice, she said, "I . . . wish . . . you . . . had . . . let . . . me . . . die!" The last word—die— erupted as a vehement scream.

His face a mask of anguish, Alex turned and left.

Staggered at the sudden exchange, Alyssa couldn't catch her breath as she collapsed rather than sat on the ground. She wanted to scream, "Come back, I'm sorry. I didn't mean that." What just happened? It was so fast, so intense. She thought back on every word, every touch, and every expression on his face. Feeling horrible for the things she'd said, she knew she had to apologize. Grabbing her cane, she made her way back to the cabin. Alex wasn't there. She trudged to the workshop. He wasn't there either.

Suddenly, as she walked outside, she felt scared and alone. It felt as if there was someone hiding behind every tree—and they all had Adam's face. Realization hit that Alex had left.

He'd never left her alone.

"Alex . . . Alex . . ." she yelled, but received no answer.

Desperately trying to calm down, she limped back to the cabin. She waited and waited, staring out the window for a long time. After a few hours, it began to get dark and her fear increased. What if something had happened to Alex? As she looked around the cabin, the words Alex had spoken came back to her. He was right, she wasn't pulling her weight. She'd been no help to him whatsoever, only a burden. All she did was sit around and let him wait on her. Besides, she didn't know how to do anything. She couldn't work the stove, and she'd never started a fire in a fireplace in her entire life. She didn't know where anything was, she'd never bothered to go any further than the very entrance to the supply room. Alyssa really didn't know anything about how he actually survived up here or the work it took.

Pathetic.

Panic arose at the thought of nighttime, of being alone in the dark. Dusk had fallen and she couldn't see very well already. In an attempt to make the cabin come to life, she turned on several of the lights.

It didn't work.

Normally it was warm and cozy. The fire blazed and Alex was always there to talk to. He always had some wonderful dish cooking that made the cabin smell fantastic.

Without him, the cabin was cold and lonely.

Shadows seemed to be everywhere. Each and every sound made her jump. Huddling on the couch, scared and alone, she began to cry and once she started, she couldn't stop. For the first time in a long time, she wasn't crying for herself, she was crying because she was worried about Alex. Where was he? Was he okay? She'd hurt him after all of the kindness he'd shown her. She felt horrible and missed his presence keenly.

Her last waking thought was, *"Great happiness awaits you . . ."*

Alex said the exact words Sam had said to her in her

dream. Sam was gone and Alex was her happiness now.

With that thought written on her heart, she fell into an exhausted sleep, her dreams filled with thoughts of Alex.

≈

IT WAS VERY late by the time Alex made it back to the cabin. In his anger, he'd hiked much further than he'd intended, till the anger he felt had dissipated. Now the only anger he had left was directed at himself. He was angry at himself for the words he'd spoken, for handling Alyssa so roughly, and most of all he was angry at the way he'd kissed her. When he'd realized it was getting dark, he felt great worry and knew he shouldn't have left Alyssa alone this long.

The walk back gave him plenty of time to think. He felt horrible and knew he owed Alyssa an apology. What had he been thinking? She wasn't ready to think about someone new in her life. After all she'd been through, he was expecting too much. He peeked into the window of the cabin. Alyssa was asleep on the couch, huddled into a fetal position, and he knew being alone must've been a frightening experience. All of the lights were on—every single light he owned. A sigh of relief escaped as he berated himself for leaving her alone. It was foolish, anything could've happened and it would have been his fault. After quietly entering the cabin, he watched her sleep for a few minutes. Her face was tear stained, making him feel even worse. He covered her with a blanket and went to bed.

Alex awoke very early the next morning and found he couldn't sleep another wink. Embarrassment at his behavior swept over him. Unwilling to face Alyssa as yet, he decided to head for the workshop. He left the bed unmade so she would know he'd been home.

-13-

LIGHT STREAMING IN from the window awoke Alyssa. The lanterns were turned off and the bed had been slept in. It was left unmade. Alex had come home. A blanket had been placed on her and the thought warmed her heart. She felt herself blush as she realized she'd dreamt of Alex all night. She couldn't get that kiss off her mind—the way he'd held her, the passion between them, the way he'd looked at her. It had been there all along, she just hadn't recognized it for what it was. Touching her lips with her fingers, she remembered the feel of his lips on hers. He'd been waiting for her. She knew that now. Alyssa wanted to talk to him and apologize. He'd been so kind to her since the day she'd unexpectedly entered his life. He didn't deserve the way she'd spoken to him. Surely he must be angry with her. He never left the cabin in the morning without the two of them having breakfast together. Alyssa knew what she needed to do.

First, she dressed, then walked to the remembrance yard. Kneeling before the grave markers, she said, "Goodbye Sam, goodbye Clay. I love you and I'll never forget you. Sam, there's one thing I've learned from all of this and that is, life is short, life is tender. It can be taken away in the blink of an eye. When you find love, you grasp it, never let it go, and enjoy each day you've been given to the fullest. And that is what I intend to do. Please forgive me. I'll always love you."

The comforting sounds of Alex working in his workshop met her ears, making her feel safe. Next she returned to the cabin and decided to get to work. First, she went into the supply room to have a good look at what was in there. She couldn't believe her eyes. Alex had thought of everything. He was very prepared. There was enough food in there to last much longer than a year. Mostly canned goods, but there was also crackers, flour, powdered milk, boxed mixes, cereals, assorted pasta, peanut butter, and small packets of condiments, to name a few. It was like walking into a grocery store. Alyssa walked between the shelves filled with batteries, battery operated lanterns, stacks of material, sewing supplies, assorted sodas, bottled water, toiletries, medicines, paper goods—you name it and it was there—and she marveled at the amount of supplies. Alex's dressing area made her grin. It was meticulous, with stacks of clothing folded neatly on shelves. There was even a row of various kinds of slippers.

She'd never given the supply room more than a passing glance, self-absorbed as she'd been. After searching out a broom and some dusting spray, she got to work, cleaning and organizing for the next couple of hours. After rearranging some of the furniture, she was pleased with the results. She discovered brand new throw rugs in the supply room and wondered why they weren't being used. Placing them around the room added a lot to the coziness of the cabin. Wandering outside, she picked wildflowers and placed them in a vase on the kitchen table. It was now getting close to lunch and she knew Alex would be back soon. Having no idea how to use the monstrosity he called a stove, she picked out some canned fruits to toss together as a fruit salad. Then she mixed canned chicken, mayo, and relish to make a chicken salad to spread on top of crackers. She chose a piece of material and placed it on the table as a tablecloth. Then she neatly set the table.

Just as she finished placing the food on the table, Alex walked into the cabin. Their eyes met and held. Alex broke the gaze first and his eyes fell to the neatly set table with lunch laid out. Then his eyes wandered around the room, taking in everything. Alyssa was apprehensive and wondered if she'd gone too far.

"I did some cleaning and rearranging. I hope you don't mind. I can put it back the way it was if you don't like it."

His eyes came back to her and he said, "The cabin has never looked so good. Thank you, Alyssa." He washed his hands at the sink. "Lunch looks delicious."

They made fast work of the lunch. Neither of them had eaten dinner the night before or breakfast that morning.

"I didn't realize how much this place needed a woman's touch," Alex said to her. He smiled, but the smile didn't reach his eyes. He went on, "Alyssa, about yesterday, I didn't mean I want you to wait on me, you don't have to do all this. Don't get me wrong, I appreciate what you've done but, what I'm trying to say is . . ."

"Alex . . ." she interrupted, "I know what you meant, and you were right. I need to help out. I've let you wait on me long enough and I won't do that anymore. I need to have something to do." Pausing, she took a deep breath, feeling awkward as several tense moments passed. "Actually, if you don't mind, I'm gonna lie down for a while. I need to rest my leg, it's aching." She'd never felt nervous in his presence and suddenly she felt tongue tied and couldn't remember what she wanted to say to him. The expression on his face was unreadable and it made her uncomfortable. He looked so solemn. There was so much she wanted to say to him. Everything was coming out stilted and nothing was what they really wanted to talk about. "If it's okay, I'll clean this up later."

"Don't worry about it," Alex responded. Neither of them moved from the table and they avoided each other's gaze. "I guess I'll . . . go back to the workshop."

She hated this. There was a change between them — a barrier, a wall, a great divide. Alyssa limped over to the bed, her heart heavy. Alex walked to the door, and placed his hand on the door handle. Alyssa knew she had to say something. She couldn't let another minute go by without saying it.

"Alex?"

He stopped and turned to face her. "Yes?"

Their eyes locked for a long moment till she hesitantly said, "Thank you . . . for saving my life." It was a form of an apology for what she'd said to him yesterday and yet not what she wanted to say at all. He nodded and turned to go. Alyssa plopped down onto the bed and let out her breath, hating the distance between them. An ache gnawed in her belly.

He turned back to her. "Alyssa?"

She stood. It was her turn to say hopefully, "Yes?"

"I apologize for yesterday. I'm sorry for the things I said and did. It was wrong of me." He paused and then with a decisive tone said, "It won't happen again." And with that he turned and placed his hand on the door handle once again, ready to walk out.

It would never happen again? A sick feeling arose in her. She was losing him. He was leaving and it was settled, they would be friends. All morning the only thing Alyssa had thought about was the way he had held her, the look in his eyes, the emotion in his voice, the passion in him, and the feel of his lips on hers. The latter had been her prevailing thought. It was as if her eyes had been opened and she saw what was before her.

It was great happiness.

Not wanting him to leave, not wanting it to never happen again, she blurted out the first thing that came to her mind. Without thinking she said, "Why not?"

Alex went completely still. He slowly turned and looked at her, his gaze as intense as always. His voice was almost a whisper as he said in disbelief, "What?"

Alyssa's heart beat so fast she thought she would faint. They stared from across the room into each other's eyes. She couldn't back out now. This was the defining moment in their relationship. Everything would be different from here on out.

She felt ready for it.

Swallowing the lump in her throat, she said again,

louder and with more conviction, "Why not?"

Alex let out his breath as if he'd been holding it. She met his eyes and would not break contact, even though she felt so unsure of him. What would he do now?

He didn't move.

Then, suddenly, he was across the room in two seconds. He wrapped his arms around her and kissed her like she'd never been kissed before. The kiss was hard and fast, out of control and wild, as if suddenly they couldn't get enough of each other. She responded in kind. Without realizing it, she'd wanted this for so long. And now she knew he had too. They'd both been unsure of the other. At last they had found each other. Her lips parted as the kiss became more intimate. Intoxicated by the taste of him, the feel of him, she held onto him tightly, feeling as though she would collapse as he overwhelmed her with his ardor. He supported her full body weight in his arms as she gave herself to him with no resistance. She had no idea his feelings for her had reached the depth of emotion evident in his kiss.

When it was over, he stood before her, their faces only inches apart. He took her breath away. Alyssa never would've guessed that the tender and kind man who'd cared for her all this time had such intense passion in him. It surprised and pleased her. They were both breathing raggedly as they stared into each other's eyes.

In a whisper, he asked, "Are you sure? Is it too soon?"

Alyssa shook her head. "The day I walked through your cabin door was the day my fate changed forever. It's the best thing that could've happened to me." And then, hesitantly, "Alex, about yesterday, I'm so sorry. I didn't mean what I said."

Alex covered her lips with his fingertips. "Shhhh, we both said things we shouldn't have." He placed his hands on either side of her face.

"Alex . . ." His name escaped in a whisper from Alyssa's lips as he brought his lips down onto hers again.

This time the kiss was soft, tender, and oh-so-sweet. His arms held her close as the kiss deepened and their mouths opened to each other, their tongues swaying together in perfect rhythm for the next several moments.

Alyssa plunged her fingers into his hair. "I love you, Alex. I love everything about you," she whispered.

He stilled and looked into her eyes. "I've longed to hear those words from your lips. I've loved you from the moment you entered my life. The moment our eyes met." He brought his lips down onto hers again.

Alyssa felt happy and at peace for the first time in a very long time and she told him so. He looked upon her with all of his emotions written on his face and she wondered why she hadn't noticed it before.

"I'm so in love with you, Alyssa."

"I've been so blind."

"You needed time. I knew I had to wait. I was waiting for something, I don't know what, any sign that maybe you felt the same."

"The night you said you didn't think we should sleep in the same bed, I don't know why, but I thought you were trying to get away from me, trying to let me down easy. I thought I had foolishly mistaken your kindness for love. I thought you could see right through me and knew I had fallen in love with you and felt sorry for me. I've depended on you so much, for everything, my very life even. I can't imagine my life without you."

He stopped her words by bringing his mouth down onto hers in a crushing kiss. Their mouths immediately opened to one another, letting their tongues intertwine. He held her as close as he could, as close as two bodies can be, enjoying the freedom to do what they had both wanted for so long. He finally, reluctantly, ended the kiss.

"Alyssa, we need to talk," he said and then kissed her again as if he couldn't stop. "I live in the middle of nowhere and I like it that way. I plan to live my life here. Before this goes any further, you need to know, I don't plan on ever leaving."

"Can I live here with you?" Alyssa said simply.

He seemed surprised at her answer, but it was undoubtedly what he wanted to hear. "I should've known better than to worry about it. You surprise me, Alyssa, every moment of every day. Very few people surprise me. You're a breath of fresh air. I love you." He kissed her softly. "Yesterday, I was rough with you. I'm sorry . . ."

"Alex, it was our first kiss, I'll never forget that moment. You weren't rough, you were emotional. It opened my eyes, the passion in you, the way you looked at me . . ." she paused. "I loved it," she whispered.

He kissed her again with that same driving passion. Alyssa reveled in the fact that he wanted this, that he liked it. He kissed her in a manner that amazed her. They'd both been hiding their feelings.

Later that night, they ate dinner in front of a roaring fire and talked deep into the night.

This time when Alex said they couldn't sleep in the same bed, she agreed wholeheartedly. And as they lay falling asleep in the dark cabin with only the dying fire illuminating the walls, Alyssa in the bed and Alex on the couch, she said, "I miss you."

"I miss you too."

≈

THE NEXT MORNING Alyssa awoke to the sound of Alex in the shower. She lay in bed and listened as he moved about, dressing for the day — the sounds of living with someone. It was comforting in a way she couldn't explain. He approached the bed, freshly shaven, and his hair still wet from the shower. He was dressed but his feet were still bare. A towel hung about his shoulders.

"Morning," he said.

"Hi," she smiled and held out her arms.

He leaned down and their lips met in a soft and tender kiss. He smelled of shampoo and tasted of minty mouthwash. Her fingers wandered through his hair as he continued to lower himself down till his full body weight was on top of her. The kiss quickly became heated. The feel of their bodies intimately pressed together sparked a sudden burst of emotion between them she wasn't prepared to deal with as yet. His lips broke away from hers and he backed up a little to simply look into her eyes.

She wanted more, she wanted to drown in him, to hold on and never let go, to spend her life kissing him. The depth of her emotions scared her just a little and she knew he felt the same as he rolled onto his side and they lay facing each other, both a little wide-eyed.

"What do you want to do today?" he asked.

"I don't care as long as I'm with you. How about the lake?"

"Deal. Get ready."

≈

AS ALEX PREPARED breakfast, his thoughts whirled. He was surprised at Alyssa's affectionate nature. Surprised, but pleased. It was something only a boyfriend or husband would know. They'd been affectionate with each other since day one. Then it was under the guise of comfort. Now it was something else altogether. He had to admit, he liked it. He loved the way she just melted into him with no resistance. He'd never experienced that before. He'd never kissed anyone in his life the way he'd kissed her yesterday — deeply, uncontrollably. Their emotions were running high, he knew that. Still, she looked at him with trust in her eyes.

He would not betray that trust.

From behind him, her arms wrapped around his waist and held him tight. Her hands wandered, massaging his chest. He closed his eyes and enjoyed the feeling of being loved by her. It'd been a long time since he'd had love in his life. He'd been prepared to live his life without it. Not anymore. Not ever again. He turned, took her in his arms and kissed her. She kissed him back with a fervor that thrilled him.

He liked it. He liked it a lot.

"Let's go." If they didn't leave now, they'd never leave the cabin.

≈

AT THE LAKE, they swam together for a long time, stopping to kiss every few minutes. Alyssa felt as if she were dreaming as she gave herself up to loving Alex. He was easy to love.

When they got out, they lay on a blanket, letting the sun warm them. Alyssa worried about her out-of-control feelings for Alex. She knew there was an element of hero worship in her thoughts. Still, she adored him. His passion surprised her. He was an intense man and the feeling was conveyed in his touch.

"Alyssa, what's wrong?" he asked perceptively. "Is this too soon?"

He'd asked the same thing yesterday. He was clearly worried about it and she owed him an answer. "Honestly, the depth of my feelings for you scares me. I've never felt this way in my life. I feel out of control, like I'll die without you. I don't know how to explain it. It's like I've tasted the bitter, and now the sweet is so overwhelmingly good, I just want to bask in it."

He rolled over onto her and kissed her ever so slowly. Tears ran down her face and he wiped them away. They both gasped for air and then kissed some more, completely intoxicated with each other.

"Alyssa, no one has ever said anything like that to me in my life, no one."

Isolated as they were, it was as if they were the only two people who existed and it only intensified their heightened emotions.

Alex held her cheeks and said fiercely, "I feel the same way about you, Alyssa. I've been so scared to say it. I thought I would frighten you. I thought you would think—here's this lonely man who would've fallen for any woman who walked into his cabin. I love you with an intensity that scares even me."

He kissed her again, wild, out of control kisses that left her overwhelmed and breathless.

Life had taken another unexpected turn.

≈

"ALEX," SHE SAID the next morning, "Would you please show me how to use your stove? Actually, I feel like I don't know how to do anything. I don't even know how to start a fire in a fireplace. How exactly do you survive up here? Will you show me?"

He seemed pleased that she wanted to know. "Sure, it's not as hard as you might think." First, he took her to the supply room and they went through all of his supplies together. The amount of items he had in there amazed her. He showed her where he kept the list of new supplies he wanted to have delivered in June.

"If there's something you want, add it to the list."

She could think of a lot of things.

"What's that?" she asked, pointing to what looked like a small trap door on one wall of the cabin. She hadn't noticed it before.

Alex retrieved a folding latrine from the corner of the supply room and set it up. "That, my dear, is how we answer the call of nature during the winter. We won't be able to use the outhouse, we'll be snowed in."

"So, what's the trap door for?" she asked, even though she thought she knew the answer.

"That is where we dispose of the waste. It's similar to a laundry chute. It leads several feet underground to a large container filled with chemicals, similar to the outhouse. Both it and the outhouse containers are changed out every year when the helicopter comes."

Incredulous, she said, "Are you telling me I could have

been conveniently using this instead of walking, excuse me, limping out to the outhouse all this time?"

He smiled at her. "No, actually. I only use this in the winter. It's not meant for long term use. Trust me on this."

"Say no more. I've got it. But I have to admit, you thought of everything."

"Some issues can't be ignored."

They both laughed and quickly changed the subject. Once she felt like she had a handle on where everything was located, they moved on.

Next he showed her how to build and start a fire in the fireplace. First, he had her place tightly crumpled paper in a small circle. Then she topped the paper with old dry pine needles, which he called kindling.

"Don't be stingy with the kindling, it has to burn and get hot enough to be able to ignite your logs," he told her. Then he showed her the best way to place the logs. "Place three logs, horizontally, allowing for space between them so air can get to them."

Alyssa was extremely pleased with herself when a roaring fire ensued. "You make it seem easy. It probably only works when you're here," she joked.

"Believe me, living here, you'll have it down in no time. C'mon, let's tackle the stove."

Alyssa approached the stove with trepidation. "The same principle applies here," Alex told her. "The first thing you have to do is start a fire. Once the fire is going and heats up the stove, it will stay hot for hours. So be careful, by the way. The first year I burned myself more times than I care to admit."

The stove was made of cast iron. It had six burner plates that were easily removable, so the pots could sit directly over the heat for faster cooking. The oven had a thermometer on the outside and a damper to control the temperature inside. "It takes some practice to cook on this, but once you get the hang of it, you'll love it."

Alyssa wasn't so sure, but she was willing to try. "This

is something my great, great, great grandmother would have cooked on. I can't believe it, how did you get this?"

"It's actually the real thing, not a reproduction. The company that makes them only went out of business in the 1980s. I was able to get this one from an antique dealer. It'd never been used."

"I can't wait to try it out . . . I think."

"It's like learning to cook all over again. Once you get used to the temperature, especially in the oven, you'll get a feel for how long something should bake."

Next he took her over to the wood-burning stove. "This one is the same as the one in the supply room. In the winter, the stove in the kitchen does provide a good deal of heat, but not enough. The fireplace is great, but again, it doesn't provide enough heat. I found these at the same place where I bought the stove. They were made by the same company and are considered antiques. They were used to heat parlors, as they called them back then, and they work well. I could've gone with a more modern version, but I liked the old fashion look of these."

The wood burning stove did look like something out of a home in the 1900s. The cast iron legs curved like a claw foot tub and it added to the ambience of the cabin.

"These keep the cabin well heated in the winter. You'll be surprised. Again, starting the fire is the most important principle in dealing with any of these appliances."

"Where do you get all of your wood?"

"I admit I have a huge portion delivered. The rest I collect and use is mostly dead wood, either standing or fallen. It's been three years and I don't seem to have a problem with supply and demand. Eventually, I will need to cut down trees. I'll need to plant seedlings to replace what I cut. There's a whole science to it, so you don't 'run out of trees' as some people would have us believe. Properly managed, our forests would constantly be renewing themselves."

"What else do I need to know?" Alyssa said as she

wrapped her arms around him and kissed him.

"The man of the house needs to be kissed at least twenty times a day in order to survive."

"We'd better get busy then."

≈

THAT NIGHT THEY lazed by the fire Alyssa had started, and ate dinner she cooked. She used rice, canned chicken, spice mix, canned peas and carrots, and soy sauce to make chicken fried rice. She even added scrambled eggs made from powdered eggs. Alex loved it and was glad to have someone else's cooking for a change.

"Alex, what happens when the helicopter comes next June?"

"You're thinking ahead."

"All the talk about supplies being delivered got me thinking about it."

"I think you should go back for awhile. You have some unfinished business."

She agreed. "My father will be wondering where I am, he'll be worried. I know he's probably hounding the police. He's a rather . . . let's see, how do I describe my father? Perhaps, a *rather overbearing man* fits the bill." Alyssa smiled to herself, thinking of some of her father's antics. "I'll need to talk to the police, tell them what happened. Maybe they won't even have found them by then. We were in the middle of nowhere . . ." She stared into the fire, brooding over the events of her life. He pulled her close and she snuggled up to him.

"Alyssa, we'll work it out. Just promise you'll come back to me."

He rested his head on the back of the couch. Alyssa climbed onto his lap, straddling him, and ran her fingers over the contours of his face and through his hair. They didn't speak, just took each other in, holding each other's gaze. She brought her lips down onto his and kissed him.

"I love you, Alex. Nothing could keep me away from

you. Absolutely nothing." And she meant it.

≈

"IT'S TEN A.M. I never sleep in," Alex said as they lazily arose the next morning.

"Do you need to be somewhere?" Alyssa asked, grinning.

"No, Miss Smart Alec, but if we're going to survive winter, I do have things to do," he said as he kissed her good morning. "The problem is, right now, I just want to be with you and I don't even want to think about anything else."

"I can't think about anything else," she murmured as they continued to kiss.

Alex taught her how to make pancakes on the dreaded stove and she ended up making them better than him.

"I knew there was a reason why I wanted to keep you here," he teased and she playfully hit at him with the spatula.

They lingered over breakfast, still in their pajamas. "Let's not get dressed today," she said with a mischievous smile.

They high-fived over the table.

They lay on the couch all afternoon, arms around each other, legs entwined, and read a book together. She loved when he read to her. It reminded her of her early days here, when she was recovering from her injuries and she would awaken to the sound of his voice. It was so comforting. Even then she knew he was a special man. He'd doted over her.

He read to her from Wuthering Heights. She hadn't gotten very far the day he'd given it to her to read. By the time it was dusk, they were only halfway through the book.

"How about a picnic in the dark?" he asked, with a raise of his eyebrows.

"I've never heard of a picnic in the dark," she

countered.

"Neither have I, but it sounds romantic, doesn't it?"

"Are you asking me out on a date, Alex Kendrick?"

"Why, yes I am, Alyssa Fontaine. Are you going to say yes or break my heart?"

"Hmmmm, let me think about it. You are kind of cute and I have to admit, I am mesmerized by your blue eyes and . . ." He stopped her with a kiss and refused to stop kissing her till she said yes. They giggled like two kids and it took her awhile to say yes.

They prepared dinner together, grabbed a blanket, and set off. They found a pretty spot illuminated by the light of a huge moon, perched in the night sky as though it sat right next to them.

"I thought I'd never feel happiness again. I was wrong. I've never been this happy in my life," Alyssa told him.

Alex studied her thoughtfully. "Do you believe in coincidence?"

Alyssa let that whirl in her thoughts for a few minutes. She thought she knew where he was going with this line of questioning. "No, I don't think I do. Not when it comes to the important things that occur in our lives."

"Neither do I." He looked at her intently. "I don't know why I felt a pressing need to get away and live here. I know I needed it in my life, I still do. But now I know there was another reason for me to live up here, another purpose. To save you, to find you, to have you in my life. These things don't happen by chance. I don't believe that for a moment."

Alyssa thought of her prayers and knew he was right. She didn't speak of it, like Mary of old, she kept all of these things in her heart. She nodded at him, suddenly feeling too choked up to speak. Sam was right, great happiness had been awaiting her in life. It was Alex.

When they finished dinner, he leaned over and held her face in his hands. "I love you, Alyssa," he whispered. Then he kissed her, slow and soft. They gradually lowered down onto the blanket and he kissed her with the light of the moon smiling down on them. Alex slowly made his way down to her neck and ran his lips along her tender skin. She threw her head back and enjoyed the soft caress of his lips, the feel of being loved by Alex. Alyssa opened her eyes and stared up at the night sky, bright with stars that gleamed and glittered. Her heart was full. Silently, she thanked God in His heaven for sending Alex into her life.

-14-

THE NEXT MORNING they slept in again. Alyssa woke up with a smile on her face, wondering what new and wonderful things the day had in store for her. It was the first time in quite awhile she'd awoken feeling this way—excited for life. Everyday just seemed to get better. Alyssa made brunch and they lingered at the table again. As Alex spoke, she stared at him and thought about the night before. A smile crept across her face as she looked upon him dreamily. Butterflies fluttered in her stomach.

"What?" he said. "Why are you looking at me like that?"

"I was thinking about last night."

He smiled the same dreamy smile.

"It was the most romantic night I've ever had," she told him.

He reached across the table and held her hand. "It's only the beginning, Alyssa."

They began to clean up and Alyssa asked him where to put the garbage. "You see, there are still things I don't know."

"Let's go for a walk and I'll show you."

She hugged him. "So, let me get this straight, we're going from the most romantic night ever to . . . garbage."

Alex laughed aloud. "You have a point there. But it is a beautiful walk in an area you haven't seen before and I'll make it worth your while." He kissed her.

"Promise?"

"Promise."

They set out on their hike. Alex explained, "The helicopter had to have a large open area to land in, so we chose this meadow. It's about a mile from the cabin. It was a real pain to move things from the meadow to where I wanted to build, but I wanted the cabin to be in a heavily wooded area."

"I love where you chose to put the cabin, it's perfect."

"Thank you. Remember when I told you about the large storage containers, like what a semi-truck would carry, only smaller?"

"Yes."

"That's where we're going."

They came into a huge meadow. It was covered with tall brush blowing gently in the wind. Right in the middle sat five large containers, looking like something out of a sci-fi movie.

"They mar the beauty of the area, I know," Alex commented. As they approached, Alex opened one of them. Inside were several metal containers where he put his garbage.

"I don't generate a lot of garbage, but I was worried about animals getting into it. This seemed the logical solution."

Alyssa had to admit, she was impressed. He'd thought of everything.

"Can you walk a little further?" Alex asked. "You're slowing down, is your leg aching?"

"I'm okay. Where to?"

"The part that will make it worth the while."

"I'm game."

They walked through a thickly forested area, then came out into a smaller meadow literally covered with wildflowers of every color. Alyssa gasped when she saw it. It was the most beautiful thing she'd ever seen. A small creek ran right through the meadow. They walked along it so as not to trample the flowers.

"I've wanted to bring you here for awhile, but I feared it was too long of a walk for you."

"I'm willing to walk for this. It's beautiful, Alex, thank you."

They sat by the creek, surrounded by the fragrance

emanating from the flowers, took their shoes off, and soaked their feet in the water. Alyssa lay down, gazing up at the blue sky. Alex joined her. White puffy clouds interrupted the huge expanse.

"I could stay here forever," she said sleepily.

"Promise?"

She turned her head and looked at him. "I promise I'll stay with you forever."

He returned her gaze as he clasped their hands together. "That's good enough for me," he said as he gave her hand a squeeze. They lay that way for a long time, lazily drifting in and out of sleep.

Alyssa's thoughts wandered. Alex could be intense and very serious sometimes. He was so unlike Sam who was always joking and laughing, a huge smile pasted on his face. Alex had a great sense of humor, but underneath it all, he was filled with intense emotions and passion. She found him intriguing and a little enigmatic, which she knew added to his allure.

"Alyssa?"

"Hmmmm . . ."

"What do you want out of life? What are your hopes, your dreams?"

The familiar sadness washed over her. She'd just lost her dream. That part of her life was over. Alex was her future, he was everything to her. Her dreams lie with him now.

"Everything I want out of life revolves around you. Without you I wouldn't have a dream." She paused, deep in thought for a few moments. Then she told him, "I want to live someplace beautiful. I want to go outside everyday and let the beauty of the area seep into my soul and make me happy to be alive. I want my home to be there. I want a huge, rambling house and I want to design and decorate every room. I want that house to be filled with life, with children, with laughter. Without that, I don't want the house, it would be meaningless. I want a bunch of kids, two dogs, two cats, and a goldfish. I don't want a quiet house. I want children running through that house and jumping on the beds if they feel like it. I want a husband, a companion, who is my best friend, who I love, adore, and respect . . ." she turned and rested her eyes on him. "That would be you," she whispered and then added, "Am I scaring you?"

"Not in the least," he answered in all seriousness.

Alyssa gazed upon the August sky again, feeling the warmth of the sun beating down on her and continued, "I want to have family dinner every night with all of us together, no matter how busy we are. I don't want it to last five minutes, I want it to last at least thirty minutes. I want it to be the time when we all tell each other about our day, every detail, good and bad. I want to look over at my husband, sitting at the head of the table, and I want him to look at me with a smoldering look and then share a secret smile with him. At night, after we have put all the children to bed and the house is quiet, I want to retire to our bedroom and I want him to take me in his arms and . . ." she turned and looked at him. "Did I say that out loud?"

There was a sparkle in his eyes as he said, "Yeah, you did."

"I'm sorry, I was rambling."

"I thought it was just getting good." They both smiled.

"Is that too much to ask for?"

"No, Alyssa, it's not too much to ask for. I used to ask that question or a form of it to my patients. In particular, to the ones who were at high risk, the ones who knew they could die on the operating table. I wanted to know if they were happy with their lives and if they died, would they die in peace? To my surprise, the answers were greatly varied and were rarely what you just described. Many wished they'd fulfilled dreams of adventure. For example, climb Mount Everest, bungee jump, or sky dive. Some had dreams of travel. They wanted to see the Eiffel Tower or the Great Wall of China. Some, who had what you just talked about, wished they had done something more with their lives, as if that wasn't good enough. Their answers never impressed me, Alyssa, but yours does. Many people search their entire lives trying to find happiness. It would seem to be elusive and fleeting. But what you just described, that's where you find happiness in this life. I know that."

"And you, Alex, what is your dream?" she asked softly.

"My dream is your dream, Alyssa. Nothing in life would make me happier." He moved till he was on top of her and held her face in his hands. "Only I'm going to finish that dream for you," he said quietly, in his intense manner. "At the end of the day I'm going to take my beautiful wife into my arms—that would be you—am I scaring you?"

"No," she whispered. His thumb wiped away a tear trickling down her cheek.

"And I'm going to make love to her all night long and I'll never stop telling her I love her." He pressed his lips to hers tenderly. "We'll have that dream one day, Alyssa, we'll make it happen . . ." He kissed her again, not the wild kisses that so often overtook them, but sweet, gentle, slow kisses, leaving her with the knowledge that life could be exquisite once again. With this man at her side, she could go on and life would be worth living.

"All night?" she whispered.

"That okay with you?"

"Oh my, yes."

His kiss changed, turning fervent.

"Alex?"

"Hmmm?"

"I can't feel my feet." The water in the creek was cold.

They both laughed as they sat up and Alex massaged her feet to warm them. Then he sat back and touched his feet to hers, rubbing their feet together in an oddly intimate manner. She looked up to find him watching her intently.

"So, just how many children are we talking about, Alyssa?"

"I think six is a good round number. Am I scaring you?"

"No, I might even have said more than that. I hated being an only child but, six is good." He slowly caressed her feet with his.

They shared a long look between them as Alyssa thought of all he meant to her, of all they would share if their dreams came true, of intimacies yet unshared.

"Alex, you're smoldering."

Alex burst into laughter and quickly got to his feet, pulling her up with him. He held her hands as he looked into her eyes and said, "My dear Alyssa, I hate to tell you this, but so are you." She felt herself blush and as they embraced their laughter echoed through the meadow.

≈

AS LATE SEPTEMBER approached, Fall was upon them and there was a definite chill in the air. The leaves had changed to vibrant colors of orange and yellow, making Alyssa gasp at the beauty surrounding her.

The last month had been incredible, their time together, pure magic. At first, Alex didn't step foot in the workshop, nor did he worry about all of the other chores demanding his attention. Instead, they spent every second together.

Life seemed sweeter than usual, everything seemed more precious, every moment, cherished. It had to do with experiencing loss. Alyssa looked at life so very differently now. Alex expressed similar emotions.

They went back to work with great reluctance. Alex had projects to finish before winter arrived, so Alyssa busied herself with projects too. First, she made hand sewn drapes for the windows. Alex loved them and the coziness they added to the feel of the cabin. Alyssa spent most of her time experimenting with new recipes. She practiced and practiced till she came up with a delicious homemade bread that turned out fabulous in the oven. It took many tries and several failed attempts to figure out how long to bake it.

"I'm glad you and the stove are now friends," Alex commented.

"Actually, we're not friends yet, but we're definitely acquaintances."

Alex laughed heartily at that.

One late afternoon, Alyssa trudged to the workshop, her cane gripped tightly in her hand. Alex had been working all day, determined to finish several projects before winter. He was working himself ragged, but Alyssa had learned he was unwavering when he had a goal in mind.

It was a good quality and one she admired him for, so she didn't complain. He already had the woodshed filled with firewood and this eased his worry. Since their lives literally depended upon that wood during the winter, she understood his anxiety.

"Hey handsome, how about stopping for lunch?"

Alex looked up with a distracted smile. He'd been completely absorbed in his work. As a matter of fact, he'd been spending all of his time out here lately. If she didn't know better, she'd think he was avoiding her.

"I didn't realize how late it was," he said. "Thank you, Alyssa. That was sweet of you."

They wandered outside, laid out a blanket and sat down to eat the lunch Alyssa had packed for them.

"How long till the first snow?"

"Probably a month. Sometimes it's earlier, sometimes it's later."

"Are we ready?"

"Survival wise, yes. I'm working on a few surprises for you."

"For me?"

"Yep. A few Christmas surprises."

"But I don't have anything to give to you." She hadn't even thought about Christmas. He was thinking way ahead of her.

"Wrap a ribbon around yourself, that's all I need," he said with a wink.

Alyssa simply smiled at him, her mind whirling with ideas. *Christmas present for Alex – what to do, what to do.*

There was one shelf in the supply room filled with all kinds of fabrics and sewing supplies. Alex didn't use much of it. When asked, he'd explained that he'd simply contacted a fabric store and asked for a supply of materials and 'fix-it' items they thought he would need for living in a remote area without easy access to civilization. They'd obviously assumed there would be a lady of the house. They'd sent him three huge boxes filled to the brim.

"Crochet hooks, they sent me crochet hooks," he'd commented with a grimace. "Guess I should've mentioned I'd be living alone."

As Alyssa had dug through the shelf, she'd found a decent supply of yarn too. She'd laughed to herself at the thought that Alex would ever sit in his cabin and crochet.

Presently, however, it gave her an idea for a perfect present. While he finished his projects in the workshop, she would secretly get to work on a Christmas gift for him.

Alex lazily spread out on the blanket, his hands behind his head, and Alyssa cuddled up to him. Leaves fell from the trees and rustled around them. She slowly unbuttoned his shirt, and covered his chest with kisses. "I missed you today."

"Mmmmm . . ." was his only response as he lay there very still—never even opening his eyes—and let her do as she pleased.

≈

ALEX LET OUT a deep breath. He knew Alyssa was just a little innocent of exactly what she was doing to him. She didn't seem to realize the effect she had. After awhile, she buttoned his shirt and lay on her side, facing him. He rolled over onto his side to face her. They didn't say anything, just observed each other, thoughts whirling. Alex knew in his heart things were again changing between them. It was the very reason he stayed out in the workshop for such long hours. If he stayed in her presence for too long, 'things' were going to happen between them and he wasn't sure she was ready. What was the right thing to do in this situation? Her emotions were still so raw. He didn't want to take advantage of her. He gently cupped her cheek.

"Your heart's beating very fast," she whispered.

So she did know. Slowly, she moved his hand from her cheek down to her neck till his fingers rested on her pulse. It was racing.

She felt it too.

His fingers traced the length of her arm and their hands clasped together tightly. He didn't say anything more, but he knew there was a subtle change between them.

He wanted more out of this relationship and it weighed on his mind. It would appear she felt the same. Their relationship had reached a breaking point, something he hadn't seen coming.

What now?

Alex returned to the workshop, his heart heavy. Lately, Alyssa spent her days cooking, relishing in making dinners he loved. She'd completely embraced her new life and seemed happy. And he was too. Ecstatic, actually.

Just the other day, he'd returned from the workshop to find homemade bread cooling on the counter, and a pot of something Alyssa had cooked up simmering on the stovetop. The cabin was immaculately clean and a fire roared in the fireplace. He strolled to the door of the supply room to find Alyssa humming to herself with her beautiful voice. Seeing her so completely happy and content thrilled him to no end. She was busy organizing the supplies in the supply room—*according to their expiration date*. She'd also made an inventory list which she kept up meticulously. Alyssa kept the supply room so much more organized than he ever had. She wasn't kidding when she'd said she was an obsessive organizer.

He leaned against the doorframe and watched her for several minutes unnoticed. It struck him how incredibly wonderful it was to come home to her. She made the cabin come to life in a way it never had before. He'd spent three years alone. He wondered how he'd ever survived it. Alyssa noticed him standing there and a huge smile broke out on her face.

This was the best part of all—the greeting he received upon entering the cabin. It was the same whether he'd been out at the workshop for an hour or for five hours. He stood still and waited for it. She dropped what she was doing and walked over to him immediately. She wrapped her arms around him and kissed him as if she hadn't seen him in a long while.

"Have I mentioned that I'm madly in love with you?"

"Not in the last three hours. I was beginning to wonder," she murmured as they continued to kiss and she ran her fingers through his hair.

It was the best part of the day.

Yes, things were good between them. However, after their afternoon liaison today, the next step of their relationship weighed heavily upon him. Was Alyssa really ready for such a step? By the time he walked into the cabin, he still had no answers. They ate dinner and settled themselves on the couch as usual. Alex grabbed a book and began to read out loud as they sometimes did. Alyssa snuggled up to him, wrapping her arms around him. As he read, she buried her lips in his neck, kissing him over and over, while running her fingers through his hair, deliberately trying to distract him.

It worked.

Still, he knew he surprised her when he suddenly

slammed the book closed, threw it on the floor, and kissed her hard on the lips. She lay back on the couch and he followed until he was fully on top of her, the kisses becoming more and more heated. They couldn't get enough of each other. There was urgency in their kisses. He was wildly in love with her and he knew she felt the same.

There was a fierceness, an intensity to their love. Loss had a way of heightening your emotions. They both knew it could end — suddenly, painfully.

Alex tore his lips away, his eyes burning into hers. His hands held her cheeks as he tried to catch his breath. Her ragged breathing matched his. He lowered his forehead to hers. There was a line they hadn't crossed in their intimacy with each other.

They were dangerously close to crossing it tonight.

He looked deep into her glazed eyes — she was soft and warm, overcome in the heat of the moment, all her defenses down — she was completely his for the taking and he knew it.

"Alyssa . . ."

His fingers moved from her cheek to caress her lips. She kissed his fingers and he lost all control. He crushed his lips to hers again, kissing her deeply, ravenously, their tongues swirling together with urgency. They'd both been somewhat guarded in their intimacy, allowing themselves time to grow in their love for one another. Tonight was the passageway to another world, another dimension. The room began to spin as he took her to dizzying heights and rapturous cliffs . . . he stood on the edge wanting to jump.

Instead he descended back to earth, knowing they were reaching the point of no return.

Abruptly, Alex arose, tearing himself away. He paced back and forth, then walked to the cabin door as if to leave, but then thought better of it and slammed the door. He ran his hand through his hair several times. Walking back to the fireplace, he stood with his back to Alyssa, staring into the fire, his hands resting on the mantle. This was crazy, utterly crazy.

Madness.

≈

ALYSSA REMAINED ON the couch, watching Alex, wondering if she'd done something wrong. "Alex, what is it?" He seemed angry and she mentally reviewed her actions of the afternoon and evening. She knew she was guilty of, perhaps, coming on a little too strong.

He didn't answer, just continued to stare into the fire. Letting out a deep breath, he sat back down on the couch, elbows on his knees, and his head in his hands.

"I can't do this, Alyssa. I can't do this anymore."

"What do you mean?" His words frightened her.

He turned to her. "Are you even ready for this?"

"I . . . I . . ."

"Exactly."

"I love you. I know that without a doubt."

"If I hadn't stopped things just now, what would've happened? What? Were you prepared to follow through?" he asked quietly.

Several tension filled moments passed wherein they simply stared hard at one another. When she said nothing, he said quietly, "You're not ready for this and I won't take advantage of your fragile state. I can't do it."

"I'm ready for us, Alex. It's not what you think. You don't understand. Please let me explain." He was right. In the end, she would've held back, but not for the reasons he thought.

"Explain what?"

She held his hands and looked in his eyes to gauge his reaction. "I want you to know, I've never been with anyone but my husband. We waited for our wedding night. That's important to me. Despite my behavior of a few minutes ago," she added, trying to lighten the mood.

It didn't work. He closed his eyes and nodded. When

he looked at her again, his expression was grave.

It was her turn to stand up and face the fireplace, deep in thought. Finally, she faced him and said, "I'm sorry. I owe you an apology. I know I cling to you a little too strongly. It wasn't my intention to lead you on and then tell you no." A tear fell. "I can't explain my behavior other than to say that I recently faced cruelty in my life. I faced unwanted advances and the constant fear of being raped. I faced death and losing the people I love. Now that I'm with you, I realize just how good it is to love, to feel love, to be loved, to kiss you, to hold you. It feels like a precious gift I've been given. I love you, Alex. This is the good part of life and I want to embrace it, to experience it. I want to feel good, I want to live, I want to feel happiness again and you bring that to me. You bring laughter, love, and companionship back into my life. You erase all of the bad and make everything good again . . ."

He stood and faced her, the fire roaring next to them. He put his fingers to her lips, "Alyssa, you misunderstand me. Please don't apologize. I'm not angry with you and I certainly don't feel led on by you. I was worried about taking advantage of your rather delicate mental state. That's all. Don't get me wrong, I love your affectionate nature. You won't hear any complaints from me. Everything that's happened between us has been mutual, there's nothing one sided about it." He took a step closer and stared into her eyes, his lips a whisper away from hers, "And it's good between us, like I've never experienced before."

Her heart skipped a beat.

His eyes glittered as he went on, "I've only ever been with my wife and we, also, waited for our wedding night. I have a great deal of respect for that. I don't want a casual affair. I've never wanted that in my life." They embraced tightly. Taking her by the hands, he helped her back down onto the couch. They both now knew where the other stood and found they were on common ground.

Alex went on. "Do you realize winter is coming? We're going to be alone in this cabin for four months. I know we're alone now, but in the winter the snow will be so deep we won't be able to go outside. Just us. Alone. Here in this cabin. Me and you. Twenty-four-seven. No break."

Alyssa stared down at her hands, her cheeks on fire. "I know."

"I have a lot of respect for you, but . . ."

He didn't finish his sentence. He didn't have to.

He knelt before her and held her hands. "If we were in civilization right now, I would whisk you away, right now, tonight, this very minute. I'd marry you in a red hot second."

Tears filled her eyes. "And I'd say yes."

He kissed her, their arms wrapping around each other, lips parting, tongues tangling, hearts racing . . . then he moved away rather abruptly. "That always gets us into trouble." He stood and stared into the fire again.

He was practicing restraint. It struck her that he was, as usual, thinking of her first.

"This leaves us in an impossible situation. We're in the middle of nowhere. You're in no position to walk out of here and I won't leave you here alone. We have several more months—completely alone—before the copter comes." He faced her. "I love you, Alyssa. I think it's obvious to both of us that we've come to a point in our relationship where we both want more. Much more." He paused. "What do we do?"

They were both silent for several minutes as they contemplated their situation.

"What did Pioneers do? What did the Indians do? People who didn't live in civilization, what did they do?" Alyssa wondered out loud, simply voicing her thoughts.

"They make up their own ceremony and marry themselves, I guess," he answered casually, distracted.

And then their eyes met.

Thoughts whirled wildly through her mind. Several

seconds passed. He raised his eyebrows and threw her a questioning look, clearly thinking the same thing as she was.

"We couldn't . . . could we?" Alyssa said with disbelief.

"Why not?" He knelt in front of her again.

"It wouldn't be legal."

"A marriage is a promise to be faithful to one another, a promise to love each other forever, a promise to stay together through the trials of life. I can promise you that."

Tenderly, Alyssa placed her hands on his cheeks. He was looking at her with such intensity, as was his manner. She was touched by what he'd said, much more than he knew. "I can promise you that too." It came out as a whisper and they kissed again, collapsing back down onto the couch, kissing with unrestrained passion for several minutes.

Alex ended the embrace, stood quickly, and sat on the hearth. "It's safer over here."

They sat very still, lost in contemplation. "Alex, are you serious?" she asked him quietly.

"This is crazy. I don't know if I am or not. Think about it, Alyssa, just think about it."

-15-

PRIVATE INVESTIGATOR DOUGLAS Rayburn felt discouraged. It was time he let his client know that unfortunately, in this case, the police were right. There were no leads. It was as if his daughter had disappeared into thin air. No one had seen anything. He'd taken his time retracing their steps through Tahoe.

Apparently, they had a wonderful family vacation. From there, all they knew is that they were driving through the pass to get to Sacramento and somewhere along the line, foul play occurred. Mr. Fontaine and their son were left for dead. Mrs. Fontaine and their car were missing. It was telling that even though bulletins had been sent out nationwide on the car, no sightings had been reported. It was all very odd and curious. His instincts told him there was more to this case than met the eye. He'd swear by it.

Forensics estimated the father and son had been there for about fourteen hours before they were found. That's a lot of time to get away. No one was even looking for her during those first critical hours. She could be anywhere, really, even across the country by now. Even out of the country for that matter.

But he didn't think so. He would bet she was still close. The trail was just a little too cold, too neat and clean. If whoever took her had been traveling, there would've been someone, somewhere who saw something. They would've found some sort of evidence by now.

No, he'd lay odds she was still in the area. Of course, within this great mountain range you could be lost forever. Surely these mountains held many secrets.

Douglas had one other idea he decided to give a try. There were several small little communities dotting the area. He was going to spend some time in each of them posing as a retiree looking for real estate. He would spend his nights in the local hangouts. He would sit and listen. That was what he was good at. Maybe a clue would turn up. Criminals often brag about their exploits, especially when they've been drinking. It was a shot in the dark, but worth a try. He'd spent twenty-five years as a cop. The one thing he loved about his job now was he could spend two weeks on one lead if he so desired. The police just couldn't put that much time into one case.

He dialed Mr. McCall to let him know of his plans.

-16-

FOR THE NEXT week, Alex and Alyssa busied themselves with the work of surviving. They didn't talk about marriage again, but Alex knew it was exactly what was on both of their minds. As a matter of fact, it was all he could think about. Once the idea was formed, once he contemplated it, wrapped his mind around it, the idea didn't seem so ludicrous anymore. At least, not when the circumstances they were in were considered.

In the meantime, Alex presented Alyssa with two nightstands to flank either side of the bed. Alyssa told him she was impressed with his craftsmanship. He had hand carved designs on the front of them and stained them with a cherry stain. They placed battery operated lanterns and the book they were each currently reading on them. The nightstands gave the cabin an even homier feel and added to their comfort. Alyssa's overjoyed reaction pleased him immensely.

Alyssa was also very surprised when a large blanket covered mass appeared in the supply room.

"What is this, Alex?" she'd asked with curiosity.

"Promise me you won't peek. It's a Christmas surprise. Do you really think anything else would've taken me away from you? I wanted to finish before the snow hit."

Alyssa had thrown her arms around him with gratitude and he loved being loved by her.

As far as the marriage decision went, it was already made in his mind. He was positive it was the right thing to do. Now all he had to do was propose.

"Will you go on a walk with me?" he asked, trying to appear casual. "There's something I want to talk to you about." She agreed with a glimmer in her eye. It seemed clear that Alyssa knew the significance of this moment. They walked in an unusual silence. "Sorry, I know this area is a bit overgrown. Keep going, we'll be rewarded, I promise," Alex told her.

"Where exactly are we going?" she asked.

"You'll see." He led her into a beautiful grove of trees with a small clearing in the middle. The sun poured in through the branches of the trees, making the light appear in strips and giving the area an ethereal look and feel. It was as if time stood still. A few butterflies floated about softly and there was a feeling of complete and utter peace.

"Alex . . ." she whispered. "This is so beautiful."

"Do you like it?"

"It's amazing. It's not something you can find easily. It's like a hidden paradise."

Alex led her to the middle of the grove, pleased with her response. He faced her, taking both of her hands in his. "The first time I saw this grove was when I came up here backpacking, simply stumbling across it. I was a broken man. I felt like my life was over. Instead, I found peace here. This spot was where I came up with the idea that I was going to live and die up here. I knew I wanted the cabin to be close to it." He hesitated, considering his words carefully. "And now I've found love here, something I didn't expect." Alex fell to his knees in front of her, his eyes never leaving her face.

"Alex?" she said, taken aback. He'd surprised her after all.

"Alyssa, I've thought this through, hear me out. I love you, I adore you, I worship the ground you walk on. I want to spend the rest of my life with you," he said slowly, annunciating every word. He retrieved the ring from his pocket. "This ring belonged to my mother. I'm sorry, it's all I have to give you." He began to remove her wedding ring. "May I?"

She nodded while a tear rolled down her cheek. He moved the ring to her right hand and slipped his on her left hand. It was a perfect fit.

"Marry me, Alyssa," he whispered.

Visibly overcome with emotion, she lowered to her knees in front of him "Yes, Alex, yes." She pressed her lips to his ever so softly.

All at once, everything seemed right with the world.

"This is a beautiful ring. I love it even more because it belonged to your mother. I couldn't ask for anything better than this. I love it."

Alex was touched at her sentimentality. The ring was a silver band, studded with diamonds circling the entire circumference.

Then she voiced the issue weighing on both of their minds. "When, Alex?"

"It's all I've thought of for the last few days. I don't want to wait till we're back in civilization. I don't want to wait that long. I want to make love to you," he said in a rough whisper and then kissed her hard on the mouth. "I want you as my wife now." A tension filled pause ensued.

"How?" she asked, wide-eyed.

He helped her to her feet. "I'm going to build a gazebo right here in the middle of this grove and this is where we'll marry. We'll write our vows together. We'll have them say exactly what we want. We'll hold our own ceremony." He took her face in his hands. "We'll marry right here before God. He'll be our witness." The astonishment on her face was blatant. "Is this crazy?" he asked.

"Yes," she answered, her expression slightly incredulous. Alex felt his jaw clench with tension. "Let's do it anyway. I can't think of anything I want more in my life."

Alex picked her up and twirled her around in a circle. "You won't regret this, I promise."

The decision was made.

≈

ALEX DIDN'T TAKE what they were preparing to do lightly. Alyssa loved him for it. They both knew they were on shaky ground. But they'd thought it through and, given their circumstances, it seemed like the logical solution.

The only solution.

The next few weeks were a frenzy of activity as they made wedding preparations. Alex was busy building his gazebo and he absolutely would not let her come and see it. They spent several evenings sitting at the kitchen table until the wee hours of the morning, firstly, writing the vows they would each say to one another. They kept their thoughts secret, saving their innermost expressions for their wedding day. Secondly, they agonized over exactly what their marriage document should say. Alex dug out an old typewriter from the supply room to type out the document and make it look official, to include a place for each of them to sign. They wanted to make this as legal as they could, under the circumstances.

They agreed on keeping the document in a lockbox for safekeeping.

They agreed they would use the document to one day make their marriage legal.

"Alyssa, if I could marry you properly, I would. You know that, right?"

"Yes, I know that, Alex. I'm with you one hundred percent on this. We're in this together," she assured him.

Alyssa spent time with a needle and thread and some white fabric she found in the supply room. She made a very simple flowing white dress for herself.

At last, the agreed upon day arrived. As the sun rose that morning, Alex prepared a bath and helped her in. He sat outside of the drapes as she bathed and they talked quietly. He always worried about her being in the tub and still refused to let her get in and out herself.

"Alex, can I ask you something?" she said from behind her wall of drapes. After tonight, there'd be no need for barriers.

"Sure."

"All those nights I slept in your arms, was it hard for you? What I mean is, there were many nights I was so distraught and I clung to you. What stopped you from, I mean, you probably could've done anything and I would've welcomed your kind touch. You could've taken complete advantage of me and I'm not sure I would have objected. What stopped you?" she finally finished.

She heard him expel his breath as if he'd been holding it.

"I'm sorry, I know that's a loaded question."

He didn't answer immediately. Finally, he said, "I've always known anything could happen between us. After the experience you'd been through, I knew you craved loving physical contact. I also knew that intimacy, although it was probably mine for the taking, was not what you really wanted. I knew you would've regretted it and it would've put a wedge between us. There were many nights I knew it wouldn't take much for things to happen between us. Honestly, Alyssa, I didn't want you like that. Don't get me wrong, I wanted you. You always call me a perfect gentleman, but my thoughts are not very gentlemanly, I admit. It was a great temptation to me. But I wanted it to be for all the right reasons. It wasn't just intimacy I wanted from you. I wanted your love also. When we make love, I want you to know who you are making love with." He paused, letting that sink in and then the next words came out in a rush and yet with conviction. "I wanted it to be a conscious decision, not a heat of the moment mistake. I didn't want to take advantage of you in a weak moment, which would've ruined everything. I wanted you to love me for who I am. I wanted a commitment between us. I wanted you to fall in love with me. I wanted it all."

Silence greeted him and Alyssa sat in the tub completely still, slightly breathless. His words stunned her.

"Alyssa?"

She knew he'd come in if she didn't answer quickly. "Alex Kendrick . . ." she said effusively "You are a good man, the best."

≈

ALEX CLOSED HIS eyes. She had no idea what those words could possibly mean to him. There was so much he'd never told her. He didn't want to tell her. He didn't want her opinion of him to change. After the series of events that led to his decision to live up here, he'd never realized how much he needed for someone to say those words to him. "Alyssa, there's so much you don't know about me." There. He'd said it. Now she knew.

"I know, Alex. A man doesn't go and live in the middle of nowhere, all alone, unless he's running from something. I trust you. I know you'll tell me when you're good and ready. I accept that. I know what kind of man you are. I've thought this through. You've already proven yourself to me and nothing can change how I feel about you." It was Alyssa's turn to be greeted by silence. "I'm ready to get out now."

Alex opened the curtain and there she sat in the drained tub with his robe wrapped around her tightly. He helped her out, apprehensive over their recent words. It was something they never spoke of. "Thank you, Alyssa. Thank you for being so understanding."

They embraced. "Till tonight then. For all the right reasons," she told him. They kissed longingly and went their separate ways to prepare for their wedding.

≈

ALYSSA BAKED AND decorated a cake, writing their names across it with frosting. Alex set up a dressing room for her in his workshop. She wasn't allowed in the cabin for the few hours before the wedding. He had even more surprises in there. She passed the time making a garland of flowers for her hair and a bouquet of flowers, tied with a ribbon, to carry.

Finally, it was time. It was a late October evening and the brisk chill in the air reminded her winter was nearly upon them. It felt fresh and invigorating, rather than cold and uncomfortable. It felt appropriate for new beginnings.

Alex wanted the wedding to be at dusk and when she walked into the grove, she knew why. Candles were placed in varying spots around the grove and lined the railing of the gazebo. It was still light, but during the ceremony, the sun would set and they would be surrounded by the illuminated candles.

The gazebo was charming. Stained a natural wood color, it blended into its environment. Shaped like an octagon, it stood in the middle of the grove, commanding attention. Lattice work covered the bottom half and Alyssa was surprised at the amount of detail Alex had put into it.

Alex stood in the gazebo waiting for her. When their eyes met, memories filled her mind. The dramatic way in which they'd met, how he'd saved her, and the way he'd taken care of her. All of it had led to this. She would never forget this moment.

He wore jeans and a simple white cotton dress shirt, untucked, with his sleeves rolled up. His blue eyes sparkled as she walked towards him. His demeanor surprised her just a little. She'd wondered if they'd take one look at each other and burst into laughter, feeling silly at their actions. But Alex was completely serious, almost solemn. The same feeling rested upon her as she approached him. Life had not been kind to either of them. That was about to change. They were taking matters into their own hands, taking control of their lives, and giving themselves another chance at happiness. As she held his gaze, she knew she wanted this more than anything else in the world.

≈

ALEX WATCHED ALYSSA approach, looking beautiful in the simple white gown she'd made, holding flowers in one hand and her cane in the other. She looked soft, sweet, and vulnerable. His feelings for her were tender and precious. Slowly, she walked towards him, her limp pronounced, but her head held high. She was lovely, utterly charming, and he felt his heart melt at the sight of her. Her long hair blew slightly in the breeze. He knew what they were doing was just a little crazy, yet he'd never been so serious about anything in his life. He'd done everything in his power to make it special and meaningful to both of them. This wasn't a rash act, it had been well thought out. He saw trust in her eyes and suddenly felt very calm as she joined him in the gazebo.

≈

THERE WERE THREE steps leading up to Alex. She left her cane at the bottom as Alex helped her up. With a shared smile, they joined hands, and Alyssa knew they were doing the right thing.

"You are absolutely exquisite," Alex said simply, his voice rough with emotion. "Today, we marry and join our lives together," he said softly, befitting the significance of the ceremony they were about to embark upon. He nodded to her. They'd decided she would go first.

It took her a few moments to gather her thoughts. There was so much she wanted to say to him.

"Alex, I tried to think of when it was that I knew I was in love with you. I thought about the past few months and couldn't pinpoint a time when I knew, because there was no such time. There are many kinds of love and I realized it was the moment I walked into your cabin . . ." She had to pause, take a breath, and regain control of her emotions. "The moment my eyes met yours, I was in love with you. That love grew over the next several months, but that was the beginning. You were my savior, my protector, my hero, my knight in shining armor, all rolled into one. You saved me from an unthinkable fate, then you saved me from death, and then you saved me from myself. And now, you save me with your love. I loved you the moment I saw you and that love has only grown stronger. I love your kindness, your tenderness, your compassion. When I see you, my heart skips a beat, when you kiss me, I think I'll die of happiness. Without you, I know I would not be alive today. I don't know why I've been so blessed to have you in my life immediately after facing such tragedy. I don't know why I've been so blessed to find love again so soon, but I'm thankful for it and I'm going to take it, grasp it, and hold onto it forever and never let go. Alex, I've never in my life loved anyone—ever—like I love you. Do you understand what I'm saying to you?"

He closed his eyes and took a deep breath. He nodded and she continued.

"We both lost the people we loved most on this earth. I know our love is . . . intense because of that. I wouldn't have it any other way. Nothing short of miraculous could've made me love again. I've never felt this way before. I want to hold onto you and never let go. I feel pain when we're not together, actual physical pain. I long for you, a look, a touch, a glance. We both know your life can be taken from you in a blink of an eye. But what has happened here between us can never be taken away from us. Never. The memory of this time will always be with us. I don't think we've fully realized the magnitude of what has just happened. It's beyond anything I've ever experienced—absolutely dreamlike and yet stark reality. I arrived desolate and yet I found pure bliss with you. I spent nights in these mountains feeling complete, total, and utter despair. Never had I felt so small, so helpless, so *not* in control of my life. Yet, here I am, wildly, crazily, and completely out of control in love with you. And yet, I feel calm, peaceful, and happiness fills my soul at a simple look from your eyes, the sound of your voice, the sound of your laugh, the touch of your hand, a kiss of your lips, the feel of your arms around me. I love you, Alex."

≈

ALEX LISTENED RAPTLY to every word she said. These were things he'd never heard her say. He loved her more with every word. Tears filled his eyes and he was completely taken aback, suddenly looking upon her with new eyes. He knew she loved him, but he didn't completely understand the depth of her emotion until now. After all he'd been through in his life, she had no idea what those words meant to him. It was his turn and he didn't think he could speak. She reached up, wiped his eyes, and ever so gently kissed him on the lips.

To his surprise, the first few gentle snowflakes of winter began to waft about, adding to the beauty of the grove.

Alyssa gasped. "It's so beautiful."

It was perfect, as if someone had cued Mother Nature.

"Alyssa . . ." It came out in a whisper. He hesitated, taking several deep breaths. When he was ready, he continued. He moved closer to her so their faces were only an inch apart, his eyes riveted to hers as he spoke. In a rough whisper, he said the things he'd always wanted to say to her, "You walked into my life so unexpectedly, I didn't know what hit me. You were broken and bruised and I had to wait for you to heal. Physically and mentally. But as I sat and watched you sleep, willing you to live, I knew my life had just taken a turn. I knew nothing would ever be the same again. I also knew I loved you the moment our eyes met. I felt an immediate connection between us. I felt as though I could hear your thoughts. They would've had to kill me to take you away from me that night—my feelings for you were that strong. That night, taking care of you, erasing your wounds, I saw trust in your eyes and I loved you for it. The way you let me take care of you that first night, the way you looked at me, I think of that moment in time as sacred. I feel blessed to have been the person who dressed your wounds and eased your pain. Now as I look in your eyes, I see utter devotion and I love you even more for it." He gently pressed his lips to hers. "The loss you had suffered was so great and I knew it was right and proper to bide my time. I would've waited forever for you. I respect the love you have for your husband and son. It's one of the things that made me fall in love with you. I observed how much you loved your family and I longed for you to love me like that. Now that I have that love, I hardly feel deserving of it. A man who hides from society, what kind of life is that? Hardly a life at all. I've had loss in my life and the thought of losing you scares me to death. But the thought of not loving you, of not having this time we've been granted, of not taking advantage of every moment we've been given, scares me even more." He paused, getting a grip on his emotions. "You are my life, my very breath. I love everything about you, Alyssa, the way you think, your courage under impossible circumstances, the way you love, fiercely and unconditionally. I'm completely captivated by you. I love my eyes upon you, just to behold you—your hair, your hands, your eyes, your lips." He kissed her again, a feather touch of a kiss that sent a chill up his spine. "I've never experienced all consuming, passionate love until now, the kind of love you know in your heart comes only once in a lifetime. Without you a part of me would die, I would die. I want to have children with you, live our lives together through ups and downs, grow old with you and die with you by my side. I want it all. I want a deep, abiding love that lasts forever. I want forever with you." He kissed her again, this time wrapping his arms around her. They quickly became absorbed in one another.

"I don't think we're supposed to kiss till the end," she said through her tears. They both laughed and wiped the tears from each other's faces. He decided it was simply one of the quirks of a private wedding. They could do whatever they wanted.

"Too late," Alex said quietly.

≈

ALYSSA WAS TOUCHED beyond words at what he'd said. His voice was so strong with emotion, his vehemence, surprising her. His words were profound, eloquent even, leaving her in awe of him.

"Let's make this official," Alex said. They stood apart from each other only connected by their hands. "Are you ready?"

"Yes."

They'd written the next part of their vows together, following the usual pattern.

"I, Alyssa Janae Fontaine, take thee Alexander James Kendrick to be my husband for now and for always, through whatever trials in life we may face, through happiness and sadness, through sickness and health, through good times and bad. With God as our witness, I pledge my love, devotion, and fidelity to you, Alex, for as long as we both shall live."

Alex moved close to her again, with his face only inches from hers. Again, he whispered his vows, emphasizing each word, "I, Alexander James Kendrick, take thee Alyssa Janae to be my wife for now and for always, through whatever trials in life we may face, through happiness and sadness, through sickness and health, through good times and bad. With God as our witness, I pledge my love, devotion, and fidelity to you, Alyssa, for as long as we both shall live."

They smiled at each other.

"Mr. and Mrs. Alexander Kendrick," he said softly.

"*Now* you may kiss the bride."

With their hands clasped, and their bodies close together, Alex kissed her, a long, slow and tender kiss. The kiss deepened as they became immersed only in each other. They savored the moment as darkness fell and they were surrounded by tiny pinpoints of light emanating from the candles. A light flurry of snowflakes still gently wafted about. It was magnificent.

"I love you, Alyssa, I love you," he whispered.

She whispered back, "Alex, *this* is our wedding. I can't imagine anything more wonderful than this. I don't ever want to re-do it in civilization and make a mockery of this night. Thank you for everything you've done to make this night special." They kissed again and the kiss quickly became passionate, almost fierce.

Alex whispered, "Let's sign our papers and go back to the cabin or our wedding night will take place right here in this gazebo."

They each, in turn, signed their names on the marriage document. Alex locked it in the lockbox and placed it in a small hidden cabinet in the bottom of the gazebo.

"There, it's official. If we ever have to prove it, here is our proof. We'll make it legal one day, Alyssa."

Alex had another surprise. He'd carved a beautiful sign that read:

Alex and Alyssa
Married in this grove
October 20th
With God as our witness

Alyssa had tears in her eyes as she looked at it. "I don't know what to say. You've left me speechless, Alex."

He smiled, extremely pleased she liked it. He hung it up in the gazebo. They blew out the candles and walked back to the cabin, arms around each other. Above the cabin door, he'd hung another hand carved sign that read, *'Honeymoon Cabin.'* Alyssa smiled incredulously when she saw it and he winked at her.

"Wait here for just a moment. I have a few finishing touches to take care of." She couldn't imagine what more he had in store for her.

Alyssa looked up as a break in the clouds revealed a

midnight-blue sky filled with stars. Was it her imagination or did they seem to sparkle even brighter than usual tonight? She remembered a night not long ago when she looked up at the stars and begged God in His Heaven to help her. Now she thanked Him for sending Alex into her life. "Thank you, thank you," she repeated over and over. The world was beautiful again. The clouds closed and snowflakes drifted down, landing on her hair and nose. She stuck out her tongue and caught a few while laughing aloud.

Alex came out of the cabin. "Mrs. Kendrick, your wedding night awaits." He picked her up and carried her over the threshold. "Our dream awaits," he added softly.

When he set her down, she couldn't believe her eyes. The cabin was transformed, alight with candles. Sheer white material was draped from the ceiling to the floor around the bed. Soft music played from the CD player. The table was set with a white tablecloth, candles, and a light dinner. The cake elegantly graced the middle of the table. Alex watched her as she was mesmerized by the sight.

"Alex, it's so beautiful. You're a romantic," she accused, surprised, but pleased.

"Guilty."

"You didn't have to do all this," she commented. "But I love it."

"My dear Mrs. Kendrick, this is not a seduction scene," he said with his face close to hers. "It's our wedding night, that's a given . . ."

She acted shocked and playfully hit him on the shoulder. "Oh, really?!"

He kissed her and she melted into him, engrossed.

"Really," he said with a wink.

"Touché."

They smiled at each other and then his smile faded. "In all seriousness, I wanted this night to be different from all other nights. I wanted it to be special, a night you or I will never forget."

"You've done that, Alex. I'll never forget this night."

"This is only the beginning."

He led her over to the table and they ate the light dinner he'd prepared. They cut the cake and fed each other a piece, with none of the usual frosting mess on each other's faces.

And then, dinner was finished, cake was finished. It was time. They sat at the table looking at each other through the candlelight. Alyssa suddenly felt very nervous and her heart pounded painfully in her chest. They'd waited for this moment for a long time. The room seemed to be filled with electricity. Alex approached and held out his hand, "Dance with me, Alyssa." She looked up at him and then down at his hand. She watched her hand join in his and looked back up at him.

"Leave the cane, I'll support you." His blue eyes were hot and fiery. She succumbed totally.

This was no fumbling schoolboy, this was Alex and he knew exactly what to do. They danced for a while, clinging to each other. Soon they began to kiss. The kiss deepened and soon became more and more demanding. Suddenly, Alex's hands moved to her shoulders and he turned her around, surprising her. He was now behind her, wrapping his arms around her waist. Alyssa tilted her head back and their lips joined again in a searing kiss. She buried her fingers in his hair as his hands moved up her body, agonizingly slow, to the top button of her wedding dress and he unbuttoned only the top two buttons. His hands stilled as he kissed her deeply and pulled her even closer to him.

Alyssa—wanting to add something to her dress to adorn it—had cut a long slit down the front, hand hemmed it, and painstakingly made buttonholes. She then added ten buttons down the front of her dress. She'd thought about this moment, anticipated it, and yet never realized how the simple act of unbuttoning her dress would affect her. Alex did everything with finesse and lovemaking was no exception. There was no stumbling, no groping. He moved as if this was a carefully choreographed dance. Her heart continued to race and her breathing quickened. The rise and fall of her chest was exaggerated as his lips left hers and slowly moved down to her neck. He unbuttoned the third button. They were both quickly becoming carried away.

Her eyebrows furrowed as she realized there was something bothering her and she suddenly knew what it was. It was something he'd said that morning while she was in the bath. She had to clear the air before things went any further.

"Alex . . ." she whispered, not really wanting him to stop but knowing she needed to say this to him.

"Hmmmmm . . ." was his only response as he continued to shower her with kisses and he unbuttoned the fourth and fifth buttons of her dress. In a minute, she would be powerless to stop him. Their lips met again as his hands wandered the length of her. She needed to say something to him, it was important to her. She hadn't spoken of it in her wedding vows.

"Alex . . . wait . . . please . . ." she said, almost imperceptibly, caught in the moment, her actions betraying her words.

≈

ALEX HEARD HER softly spoken plea and his hands stilled. He turned her to face him, their hands clasped together. He feared she simply wasn't ready for this step in their relationship and mentally prepared himself for it.

"What is it?" he questioned. "Is something wrong?" Her face was flushed and her eyes were the brownest he'd ever seen them, like molten chocolate.

She smiled at him, "No, everything is absolutely perfect. But there's something I want to say to you, something that's weighing on my mind."

He nodded, feeling apprehensive. "Go on."

She took a step closer to him and said firmly, with absolute certainty, "I love *you*, Alex Kendrick." There was great emphasis on the word *you*. "I know where I am, I know who I am, I know why I'm here, I know how I got here, and I know what I lost on my way here." She paused a moment to swallow the sudden lump in her throat. "I'm not confused, I'm not distraught, and I'm not on the rebound. My mind is clear. I'm not filled with conflict and my reality is not distorted. Do not misinterpret my anguish over my losses for bewilderment. I know what I'm doing. I know who I'm making love with . . . you, Alex . . . only you. I love *you*." She stepped even closer to him, her lips almost touching his and whispered seductively, "Make me your wife."

Alex let out his breath, but didn't move. His eyebrows rose slightly. He'd underestimated her. She'd been through hell and he did worry she clung to him because of it. Now the lingering doubts hidden in the deep recesses of his mind vanished. Her wedding vows had been more than he'd anticipated. But these words were what he needed to hear at this moment. She knew what she was doing with clarity and it left him astounded. It changed everything for him. He didn't realize how much it had bothered him until this moment.

Looking up at him expectantly with lips parted, she tipped her head back, ready to meet his kiss. She was waiting for him to make love to her. He wasn't going to make her wait any longer.

"Thank you," was all he said before everything changed between them. Suddenly, they both let go of all their inhibitions as he took her in his arms once again and this time there was nothing to stop them as without constraint, they urgently, demandingly, became one in every sense of the word, holding nothing back from each other.

≈

LATE THAT NIGHT found them wrapped in each other's embrace, burrowed under the patchwork quilt. Alyssa felt a certain euphoria she'd thought was gone from her life forever.

Alyssa had looked forward to experiencing the feel of Alex letting go and making love to her with unrestrained passion. He did not disappoint. Alex had an intense personality and she had often wondered if it would carry over into his intimate life.

It did.

"I want to stay right here forever in this moment, just like this, safe in your arms," she whispered with a catch in her voice.

"You got it," he told her as he trailed kisses over her creamy skin.

Alyssa knew it was back on again.

The rest of the night was exquisitely slow and tender, with moments of their earlier wild abandon repeated.

Throughout the sleepless night they were both brought to tears — tears of happiness.

-17-

"HELLO, STERLING McCALL here."

"Mr. McCall, this is Douglas Rayburn."

"It's about time I heard from you. I thought you'd fallen off the end of the earth. On my dime too. Do you have news for me?"

"As a matter of fact I do. I've already contacted Detective Pitaro and he agrees we may be on to something."

"Well, what is it, man?"

"As you know, I've been spending time in some of the local bars in the area. It has proven fruitful. A man came in the other night, bragging about how he was going to go back and kill some mountain man who'd stolen his woman and killed his Pa. When asked about his woman, he said she was real pretty and he wanted her, so he up and took her. Get this, he said he had to kill her husband and son first. He was drunk and he was laughing as he talked about it. It may be nothing or he may be able to lead us right to Alyssa, if it's her. It may just be the ramblings of a drunken man, but it seems too much of a coincidence. The kid goes by the name of Adam, but I doubt it's his real name. We're having him checked out."

"It has to be her. Do you know where he is? Are we following him?"

"We have him under surveillance. There's just one problem."

"What?"

"Winter in the mountains is harsh. He's not planning on going up to 'steal his woman back,' as he puts it, until spring."

"Can't we make him go now? Let's bring him in, make him take us to Alyssa."

"It's too risky. We can't tip our hand and let him know we're on to him. We may have no chance of ever finding her if we do. He kidnapped her and committed murder. He's not gonna admit to it. He would have nothing to gain and everything to lose. We need to bide our time and follow him. Hopefully, he'll lead us right to her."

Sterling slammed down the phone. His daughter was stuck in the woods with some mountain man for the winter — who was a known killer — and they want to wait?

It was too unbearable to think about.

-18-

ALEX AWOKE WITH Alyssa in his arms, feeling warm and sated. They'd hardly slept and yet he didn't feel tired, only happy. He looked upon her face and could see the contentment on her features even in quiet slumber.

Alex covered her face with kisses and she smiled, her eyes still closed.

"I'm sorry, did I wake you?" Alex asked innocently.

"No, you didn't wake me. I'm sure I'm still dreaming," she replied, stretching like a cat that was very pleased with life.

"Then we're in the same dream. There's just one problem," he told her as he continued to shower her with kisses.

Alyssa opened her eyes and with a quizzical look asked him, "There's a problem?"

"Yeah, a big one," he said as he took her face in his hands. "I never, in my wildest imagination, could've dreamt what happened between us last night."

They shared a secret smile before he covered her mouth with his and so the morning went. Absorbed in each other as they were, they hardly noticed the passing of time, till they realized they were both starving. Alex arose, made brunch and they ate in bed.

The ground outside was covered with the first layer of fresh snow. They went on a long walk together and then hurried back to the cabin to be in each other's arms again.

That evening they sat by a roaring fire, sipping hot chocolate, only to find themselves too distracted with each other to even feel much like doing something as bothersome as eating and dinner was forgotten that night.

For the next week, the days were more of the same. While the snow fell with a vengeance, they honeymooned and thought only of each other.

≈

ONCE THE SNOW started, it never seemed to stop. It was a sight to behold. Enchanted, Alyssa spent a lot of time looking out the windows watching the snow fall. After about three days, the snow reached the bottom of the windows in the cabin. They couldn't go out the door without digging themselves out. They were ready for winter in their isolated bliss and even welcomed it. They would be stuck in the cabin together for approximately the next four months and Alex called it their four-month honeymoon.

She smiled to herself and felt the heat of a blush cover her face, even though no one was around to see it. She loved the way he made love to her—softly, tenderly, explosively, wildly. Life didn't get better than this. She knew it and savored it.

Alex joked with her one morning as they lay in bed, "How 'bout I whisk you away to a cabin in the mountains for the winter? I know this great place. Outside will be a winter wonderland, while we'll be warm and toasty inside with nothing to do but make love with each other all day and night. How does that sound for our honeymoon, Mrs. Kendrick?"

Alyssa smiled a lazy smile at him from beneath the covers of the patchwork quilt. She felt relaxed, happy, and totally at peace. "Sounds heavenly, take me away. Wherever you go, I'll follow." They laughed as they embraced, kissing and cuddling the morning away.

They soon had a routine going. They would arise in the morning and take turns on the treadmill. Alyssa was slow, but found the exercise helped her leg immensely. Then they would bathe, dress, and breakfast together. They spent most of their time on the rug or the couch in front of the fire, talking or reading, but mostly in each other's arms, kissing and making love. They both kept the fires stoked and Alex was right, the cabin was surprisingly warm. Alyssa had no cabin fever whatsoever. She was content to simply be with Alex.

One of their favorite traditions was filling the bathtub with steaming hot water and taking a bath together with the drapes open to behold the wintery scene outside. Lying in the hot bath, intertwined with Alex, always made her feel absolutely relaxed. Secretly, Alyssa battled with the feeling that she was living on borrowed time. She comforted herself with the thought that she'd paid her dues and this was her reward. Maybe she'd died and this was her heaven.

They were both lightly dozing in the tub one day, with their heads slumped against the opposite sides of the porcelain. Alex's big toe tapped her chin and she couldn't hide the smile that took over her face. He was making sure she wasn't falling asleep. She suddenly bit at his toe, snapping her teeth like an angry animal. His reaction was immediate as he pulled his foot away, splashing water all over the floor. He threw his head back and laughed out loud. She loved when she made him laugh like that. They sat there smiling silly smiles at one another.

"Are you happy, Alyssa?"

"The happiest I've ever been in my life."

"Me too."

The days passed far too quickly and before Alyssa knew it, Thanksgiving was upon them. They prepared a feast, knowing they would never be able to eat it all, but they would have fun trying.

"Shall we both say what we're thankful for?" Alex asked her. "It was always a tradition at our house to go around the table and let everyone have a turn to express their thankfulness."

Alyssa sat at the table feeling utterly content, surrounded by warmth from the fire, a feast of delicious foods in front of her, a view of pure white outside the windows, with snowflakes drifting softly about, and Alex across from her, looking handsome in a Henley sweater. Soft music played over the CD player and the soft lighting in the cabin made the atmosphere warm and inviting. She looked at him through the glittering candlelight on the table and smiled.

"That's easy. You. I'm thankful for you, Alex."

He winked at her. "And I'm thankful for you, Alyssa."

He smiled, his eyes bright with happiness and she wondered if the same look was reflected in her own eyes. She didn't doubt it. Alex arose, was at her chair in two short strides and took her into his arms. He carried her to the bed and it was a long while later that they went back to their Thanksgiving feast.

Alyssa found Alex to be an extremely passionate man and all of that passion and love and emotion was directed at her. She basked in it, literally flowering under the light of his love. Alyssa became a different person during this time. She was blissfully happy and Alex often said it showed on her face. There was no stress, no worry, and even no tears. Alex saw a completely relaxed and happy Alyssa.

"I love the way you're always smiling serenely at me, like you have some sort of secret for happiness."

"I do."

"And what might that be?"

"You, of course."

They found themselves to be completely compatible in every way.

As they prepared for Christmas, Alex donned snowshoes and climbed out a window to go cut a branch off a pine tree. They used this as their Christmas tree. They decorated it by tying red ribbons all over it. Alex owned a few Christmas CD's and this added to the Christmas spirit.

One evening in mid-December as they lay by the fire wrapped in each other's arms, Alyssa told him, "The curiosity is killing me. I want to know what is under that blanket in the supply room."

Alex laughed, enjoying the suspense. "As your doctor, I promise, it's a myth, you won't die of curiosity."

"Can I die of happiness?"

"If you can, then we're both terminally ill," he whispered as he kissed her. They melted into each other with only the firelight, a witness to their love.

They spent Christmas Eve sitting by their small Christmas tree, singing Christmas carols together, dissolving into laughter when they couldn't remember all the words.

When Christmas morning finally arrived, Alex made her close her eyes as he moved his surprises into the main cabin.

"Okay, open your eyes."

Alyssa didn't know what she'd expected, but what she saw left her completely stunned. She stared, open-mouthed, at the two objects before her and tears immediately poured down her cheeks.

"Alex . . ." she whispered. He left her speechless. Sitting before her was a beautiful rocking chair and a small cradle. She knelt before the cradle and ran her hands over it.

He knelt beside her. "I still have a few finishing touches to add to the cradle. And I need to stain it. But I wanted you to pick the color."

She was completely overwhelmed with his gift. It meant the world to her and he knew it.

He helped her up. "Try out the rocking chair." She sat down and, with her eyes closed, slowly rocked for a few minutes.

Suddenly, she was out of the chair and in his arms in an instant. She hugged him tightly. "I love you, Alex, I love you." She began to kiss him and when she showed no sign of ending the kiss, he knew exactly what she wanted. He carried her over to the bed where they spent the morning making love.

"Thank you, Alex. I love them. I hope I'll be pregnant soon." She'd actually felt disappointed when she wasn't pregnant the last two months. A honeymoon baby would've been nice.

"It will happen in time, Alyssa. I know it will. Meanwhile, I want to enjoy our time together. Don't be in too much of a hurry."

She smiled at him. He made her so happy.

They had breakfast together to the sound of Christmas carols.

"Oh, I have something for you, Alex. I almost forgot."

"I already had my present . . ." he teased and she blushed as she hurried to the supply room where she'd hidden his present on a shelf, wrapped in tissue paper. He was clearly surprised by the gift. He opened it and immediately put it on. It was a crocheted scarf and hat. The scarf looked great on him, but the sight of the hat on him made her dissolve into laughter. He didn't care. He loved it and wore both the scarf and hat the entire day, even though they were inside.

"Thank you, Alyssa." He seemed touched by her efforts to make him something. "I'll always treasure these. This is, by far, the best Christmas I've ever had."

Alyssa had to agree.

A few mornings later at breakfast, Alyssa asked Alex, "How exactly are we going to raise children up here?" It had been on her mind lately and she worried a little over it.

"I've been thinking about that actually," he told her. "We're going to need *a lot* more supplies. And we'll need a two way radio. In an emergency, I want to be able to call for the copter immediately. I'm not taking any chances with you or our children. Don't worry, we'll work it out. We have plenty of time," he answered with a smile.

She let it go, trusting Alex.

January and February passed much too quickly. Truly, their time together was magical. It was four months of pure bliss. No one gets to have a four-month honeymoon and they enjoyed every minute. There was simply nothing to take away their attention from one another.

No cell phones, no pagers, no computer, no e-mail, no deadlines, no jobs, no pressures. It was heaven.

One morning in late February, Alex was getting ready to open the cabin door for the first time since early November. The snow had melted enough to open the door, after a little digging out.

"Are you ready for this?" he asked. "I'm not sure I want this time to be over."

"I don't either. Once you open the door, I feel like a period in our lives will be over forever. I don't want this time to end." She hugged him tightly. "Let's not open it today," she said as she kissed him aggressively.

"Okay, you convinced me."

They didn't open it till a few days later.

Alex looked outside. "I can see patches of earth. I've never stayed in the cabin this late in the season. Usually I'm anxious to get outside." He took her in his arms. "Everything is different this year."

"Yes, it is."

They clung to each other. "Nothing's over, Alyssa. It's just the beginning. But what a beginning it has been . . ." he teased and they laughed.

"I'll stay trapped with you in a cabin any time," she murmured as he kissed her.

"How 'bout next November?" he asked.

"It's a date."

"Promise?"

"Of course."

They opened the cabin door together and realized they had no remorse.

"Let's start our new life together," he said softly.

Hand in hand, they walked out and did just that.

As March arrived, signs of spring, of new life, could be seen everywhere. Alyssa worked with Alex on several projects they'd talked about all winter. Alex added a front porch onto the cabin and then built furniture for it, to include a porch swing. Alyssa loved the idea of being able to sit outside together on warm summer nights. Alex also built a small fence around the front of the cabin, making a front yard with a rock lined walkway and a gate. Together, they planted flower seeds in the front yard, and started a garden to the side of the cabin. They planted all kinds of vegetables and looked forward to harvesting them. They worked together, side by side, and Alyssa enjoyed every minute of it.

Life was good. They were happy together.

They briefly discussed what would happen in June when the helicopter arrived. Alyssa was secretly dreading the interruption to their private world. She knew Alex was right, she needed to go back, see her father, let him know she was okay, talk to the police and tell her story. It was something she needed to do.

But then, she'd be back.

The decision had been made long ago to live up here with Alex. Alex also wanted her to have the corrective surgery done on her leg. She dreaded it and wasn't sure when she would do it. The idea of a long separation between them left her filled with apprehension. She didn't know if he would go back with her or not. It wasn't a subject she wanted to broach, she wanted to live in the moment and not think about ever leaving him.

The thought of being apart from him made her chest constrict tightly and a cold sweat cover her body.

He was everything to her.

Absolutely everything.

-19-

APRIL PASSED IN wedded bliss. By mid-May, Alyssa was spending more and more time out working in the garden, trying to beat the inevitable weeds. The front of the cabin was now blessed with a mass of wildflowers and it looked incredible. Alex was busy in the workshop and she loved the sounds of him working, reminding her he was close by.

Alyssa smiled secretly to herself as she tugged on a stubborn thistle. She wasn't positive as of yet, but she suspected she was pregnant. Wanting to be sure first, she hadn't told Alex yet. They had both hoped she would be pregnant by now, but it simply hadn't happened yet. It certainly wasn't due to a lack of trying. A day didn't go by without intimacy between them. Their relationship was fierce, a little intense, and they both loved it that way. Life was at last good for them and they were holding onto it with tightly gripped fists.

Still, they were both ready for a child of their own. However, they agreed it was good to have some time for themselves as a couple first. But now she was ready. Alyssa wanted to give Alex a baby. His children had meant the world to him and she knew how happy it would make him. As for herself, she still missed Clay horribly and always would. She accepted that. But she knew she was ready to give her love to another child without feeling as if she was replacing Clay. No one could ever replace Clay in her heart.

Alyssa proudly scanned the garden. Everything they'd planted had started to grow. She was excited to be able to eat fresh vegetables, instead of canned. They had planted carrots, corn, potatoes, green beans, watermelon, cantaloupe, lettuce, zucchini, and pumpkins. It was something Alex had wanted to do from the beginning. He'd just never gotten around to it. A shadow fell into her vision and she looked up with a smile, prepared to see Alex.

The smile died on her face.

Her entire body went cold and her eyes widened in shock.

There before her was . . . Adam.

Her worst fear. Alyssa blinked, thinking maybe she'd just had too much sun and was seeing things. Her life with Alex passed before her eyes like a movie. She was back at square one. Her life had reached full circle. She'd evaded her fate and now it was back to claim her. Her time was up. She really had been living on borrowed time.

"Hello, Eve. I've come back fur ya."

That voice, it sent a chill up her spine. She thought she'd never hear it again in her life. A scream stuck in her throat, her heartbeat rapidly increased, and her hand immediately went to her hip where she normally carried her gun in a hip holster.

The gun wasn't there. She'd opted to leave it off while she worked today, thinking this would never happen. Alex made her feel safe and she'd become complacent. Their life together was idyllic. It simply didn't include tragedy, they'd already seen their fair share. They'd both paid their dues, it was their turn for happiness.

This can't be happening.

That pause was all he needed. He came at her quickly, tackling her to the ground and covering her mouth with his hand. Alyssa struggled like she'd never struggled before. This man was not going to take her life from her again. They rolled on the ground, arms flailing, he, trying to get a good grip and, she, trying to get away from his grasp. Without the leash attached to her neck, she could give as good as he could. She fought like a wildcat, getting a few good hits in. Frustration and anger gave her the strength she needed. His nose was bleeding. Her lip was bleeding. She wanted to scream to Alex, warn him, and yell for help. But the effort to get away from Adam took all of her strength. It was a windy day. Would Alex hear her from the workshop? Probably not. They rolled through the garden, trampling the plants. They rolled right into the fence and knocked it over. He had the upper hand and then she did. And so it went.

Alyssa put up a good fight. It was a noble effort.

Finally, he was atop her and slapped her hard across the face, causing her head to snap to one side. The blow stunned her and the few seconds it took to recover were all Adam needed to gain control. He pulled out a knife and held it at her throat.

"Scream and yur dead," he said through clenched teeth. The wild look in his eyes scared her and she knew he meant it. "That was kinda fun, Eve. I like a woman with spunk."

That voice was so eerily familiar. A sob escaped. She wanted Alex. Their time couldn't be over. It had been much too short.

He pulled a coiled rope out of his pocket and dangled it before her eyes. "Remember this? I've been saving it for you."

Her heart sunk. There before her eyes was presumably another 'leash.' Panic overwhelmed her. "No, please don't put that on me, please . . ."

Adam laughed cockily. None too gently, he rolled her over onto her stomach, his knee pushing painfully into her back. He slipped the rope over her head and she struggled as he tied it around her neck. She held the rope with her hands desperately trying to keep it from strangling her. He pulled it tight and she could only breathe by pulling at the rope with her fingers, which were now trapped between her throat and the rope. Adam meant business this time, she could feel his anger as if it was a living, breathing thing. She didn't remember him being this violent—this out of control—before.

Why hadn't she listened to Alex? She never should've gone outside without being armed. There was nothing more for her to do. She thought of Alex working in the workshop, oblivious to what was going on. He'll return to the cabin and find her gone. But he'll know what happened, he'll figure it out quickly. He'll follow and he'll find her, just as he had in the past. He'll save her and Adam will be sorry he ever crossed Alex's path.

Adam forcefully yanked her to her feet. It was an all too familiar feeling—one Alyssa thought she'd never face again. She and Alex had let their guard down. Now that they were so happy together, it didn't seem possible Adam would show up on their doorstep again. Alyssa longed for Alex and his loving arms around her.

"Now let's pay a little visit to the mountain man."

She didn't move. Cold, hard fear washed over her. She couldn't live if he took Alex from her. "Please, just take me, I'll go with you. Don't hurt Alex."

"Ain't that sweet." He tugged on her leash, bringing her face close to his. His face had turned red with anger and a vein in his neck protruded angrily. "I don't think so. He's gonna pay fur what he's done."

She should've known that offering herself never saved the people she loved. With one hand on the leash and the other hand holding the blade of the knife at her neck, Adam pushed her forward towards the workshop.

He was in complete control.

Adam knew exactly where Alex was. He'd obviously been watching them. She wondered how long he'd been watching and just how much he'd seen. The thought sent another chill tingling up and down her spine.

I can't lose Alex. I won't survive it. Dear God, please don't take Alex from me.

They walked into the workshop, slowly approaching Alex. He was working on sanding a piece he'd just built and didn't look up. Alyssa struggled to try and warn him. With the rope tied tightly about her neck, she could barely say his name.

"Alex . . ."

≈

ALYSSA ONLY HAD to whisper his name and he knew. He went deathly still. He knew by the tone of her voice, the pleading sound, the anxiety he could hear in that one single word. Slowly he stood and faced his worst nightmare.

Fear for Alyssa's life made him hesitate at immediate action. The sight that met him was not one he would soon forget. In the next few seconds, several things registered. There Alyssa stood, her breath coming in gasps, blood trickled from her lip, dirt smudged her face, and her hair was a tangled mess. Adam stood almost directly behind her — giving himself cover — holding a rope tied tightly to her neck. His other hand held a knife to her throat. It was immediately obvious to Alex they had struggled. She'd put up a good fight. Adam's nose was bleeding.

She was having trouble breathing. Her fingers pulled at the rope in a desperate attempt for air. A single tear dripped down her face. At the sight of her being held in such a manner, red hot anger washed over him. Her eyes met his.

Our life together isn't over. I won't let it be over.

His eyes narrowed. The first time he'd been faced with Adam, he'd wanted to save the beautiful young woman so obviously there against her will. There was so much more at stake now. Alyssa was his life, his love, all he lived for. Only seconds passed before Adam acted.

"I've come back fur my woman. Eve is mine!" Adam shouted at him in a snarl. With no hesitation whatsoever, Adam released the leash — his other hand still holding the knife at Alyssa's throat — and brandished a gun, immediately aiming it at Alex. Just as he pulled the trigger, Alyssa — using the only weapon available — elbowed his arm. The bullet hit Alex high in his left shoulder, knocking him to the ground, a burning pain enveloping him. He was shocked at Adam's quick actions. He was determined this time around, no more fumbling around or listening to Pa's orders. The kid had more grit than he'd given him credit for.

Alex felt stunned as he lay there, holding his shoulder, warm blood seeping between his fingers. His head was starting to spin, and he fought to stay conscious. Alyssa needed him. Ignoring the searing pain in his shoulder, his eyes sought out Alyssa. The panic in her expression was blatant as she struggled in Adam's arms. He'd holstered his gun and was tightening the rope around her neck, punishment for ruining his aim. Just when Alex thought she was going to pass out, Adam loosened the rope and she sucked in air in deep gasps, her eyes slightly wild.

It was imperative he stay calm. He took in the situation. Adam thought he'd already won. *Not while I still have breath in me. I'll never let you have her. Never. Even if I have to die to do it, I'll see to it you never lay your filthy hands on her again.*

It may very well be the only thing he could do for her, he thought desperately. At least she would have a life without the fear of Adam always lurking in the background. He lay very still, waiting for the right moment.

"I'm back, mountain man. Me and her have some unfinished business." He licked Alyssa's cheek, slowly, from jawbone to eyebrow and laughed a crazed laugh.

Alex could see the shudder that passed through Alyssa from where he lay. Alex was ready to rip Adam to shreds with his bare hands. *He doesn't realize what he's dealing with.*

"Yur a dead man!" Adam yelled.

All at once, Adam plunged the knife towards Alyssa's abdomen, stopping only an inch away from contact. Alex flinched, every muscle in his body tense and on edge.

Adam laughed loudly. "Am I makin' ya nervous,

Doc?" He waved the knife around in the air. "If there be a baby in here, I'll cut it out and throw it away." He slowly ran the knife across Alyssa's stomach. "You stole her from me." He moved the knife up her body until it rested on her throat again. He laughed his cruel laugh. "I don't like anyone touchin' my property. Have you been touchin' her? I know you have. Never again, mountain man, never again."

It was then Adam noticed the freshly stained cradle, sitting just to his right. He went wild. He pulled Alyssa with him close to the cradle and stomped on it. After five or six stomps the cradle lay in pieces on the floor. All the while, he was screaming like a crazed man. His eyes were wild and darted about the room.

With the knife at Alyssa's throat, Alex didn't move as he glared at Adam.

≈

ALYSSA FELT FROZEN as she watched Alex struggle between pain and wanting to get up and fight.

Please live, Alex, I need you to live. Don't leave me. I can't live without you, I don't want to live without you. Adam had already stolen her life from her once. She couldn't let it happen again.

The anger in Alex's face was unconcealed. His eyes narrowed, the rise and fall of his chest was pronounced, and his hands clenched into fists. He was about to explode.

She knew at that moment, Adam was not going to leave here alive. He was about to face the wrath of Alex. Adam underestimated Alex and the depth of emotion that had developed between them. He had no idea what they'd become to one another. Adam could never understand the kind of love they shared. He didn't know he was dealing with two desperate people who would do anything for each other.

Adam focused on Alex once again and yelled,

"You stole my woman and killed my Pa. Now yur goin' ta pay fur what you done." Once again, he released the leash, produced his gun, and aimed it directly at Alex. Clearly, this time he planned on making the shot fatal. Knowing he would anticipate her actions, Alyssa immediately elbowed his arm again with all the force she could muster and this time he lost his grip and the gun flew from his hand, landing on the ground.

Alex didn't hesitate, shifting his weight, he drew his gun, cocked it, and aimed at Adam's head. "Not this time," Alex said with steel in his voice.

Seeing Alex's gun, Adam crouched behind Alyssa like the coward he was.

"Go ahead, shoot. It'll have ta go through hur first," replied Adam.

Alex did not back down. "Let her go."

Adam pressed the blade of the knife against Alyssa's neck. Blood trickled down her throat, making her gasp as Alex paled.

"Put down the gun or she dies." They glared at each other for a few moments. They were at an impasse.

"You won't kill her. You want her," Alex said icily.

≈

MEANWHILE, STERLING, DETECTIVE Pitaro, Douglas Rayburn, and two other officers assigned to the case were about a mile behind Adam. They followed the GPS tracking system hidden in Adam's backpack. Detective Pitaro had refused Sterling's presence for the operation, but the man had raised such a fit, he finally gave in. The man wanted to be there to see his daughter. He tried to remind him it may not even be Alyssa, but Sterling was convinced it was her. He had to admit, in the same circumstances, he would do the same. Nothing would be able to keep him away. So, he told Sterling he was with them at his own risk. But the man had kept up well. Complained a lot, but kept up. He hoped Adam was not leading them on a wild goose chase.

"He's been stopped for about an hour now. I think we'd better move. We need to see what he's up to," Detective Pitaro said to the others.

They picked up their pace, moving as quietly as they could. It was when they came upon a grove of trees with a gazebo in it that they stopped.

"What is this?" They all looked around in awe at the beautiful surroundings.

When Sterling saw the sign in the gazebo, all hell broke loose. "She's here, close by, that's her . . . he forced her to marry him . . ." he sputtered.

Sudden gunfire disturbed the serene atmosphere. The policemen were suddenly all business. "Radio the helicopter, tell them to come now."

"Stay back," they yelled at Sterling. Weapons drawn, they ran towards the sound of the gun shot.

≈

"YOU WON'T KILL her. You want her," Alex repeated. Alyssa's eyes widened at Alex's taunt.

"W-What?" Adam stuttered.

Everything happened very fast, but to Alex it seemed as if in slow motion. Alex shot Adam just below the knee. It was the best shot he could get without hitting Alyssa. Adam shrieked like a wounded animal. With distorted features, he tossed Alex a triumphant look as he took the knife at Alyssa's neck and thrust it down clumsily, stabbing it into Alyssa's side.

A yell escaped from Alex, "NO!"

The deed done, Adam fell backwards onto the ground writhing in pain.

Alyssa was finally able to free her fingers from the rope around her neck. She fell to her knees, clutching her side, a look of sheer horror on her precious features.

Alex's vision began to blur, darkness creeping in from the edges. He couldn't lose Alyssa. He knew he didn't have much time. He looked for another piece of Adam to shoot, but he couldn't see clearly enough to take another shot.

Suddenly, Alyssa's head violently jerked back. Adam had found the end of the leash. A filthy hand groped at Alyssa, he was searching for the knife. If he pulled it out, she would certainly bleed to death.

An adrenalin rush gave Alex renewed strength as he got to his feet and threw himself on Adam.

≈

ALYSSA FELL TO the ground while gingerly holding her side. She watched in horror as Alex and Adam were a tumbling mass of arms and legs, hitting at each other. Adam had the use of both arms, while Alex could only use his right arm, his left being disabled by the gunshot. Alex was visibly weakening.

Adam was going to win.

She had to do something. She knew enough to know she couldn't pull the knife out. Fighting to stay conscious, she dragged herself along the ground till she reached the destroyed cradle. She grabbed a broken piece of the cradle. It was splintered and looked sharp at one end. Alex and Adam were still struggling to gain control over the other. Alex momentarily had the advantage as he sat atop Adam, straddling him. Their arms struggled in a wrestling match with each other.

When both of Adam's hands had a stronghold on Alex's right arm, Alyssa knew she had to act fast. Crawling closer, she saw her chance and took it. In the struggle, Adam's shirt had come untucked. She plunged the piece of wood into Adam's exposed mid-section.

Doesn't feel too good, does it?

He howled in pain, releasing Alex's hand. Alex immediately grasped Adam's throat and began to squeeze the life out of him, but his strength continued to wane. At first, Adam grasped Alex's wrist with both hands, then noticing Alex's diminishing strength, he let go with his right hand and reached behind his head, desperately groping the ground, knowing his gun was close.

Alyssa panicked as she watched Adam struggle and then find his gun. She felt helpless as she watched his fingers slowly curl around the barrel. In a moment, he would have control of it and Alex would be dead. She remembered the knife Alex kept sheathed to his ankle. With shaking hands, she pulled up Alex's pant leg.

≈

ALEX COULD SEE Adam had recovered his gun. He knew he was too weak to take it from him.

But he was not about to give up. He'd never let this man lay a hand on Alyssa again. Another burst of strength shot through his body at the thought.

At the same time, Adam smiled a cruel smile, sure of his victory.

"Alex," he heard Alyssa whisper. He felt her soft touch on his arm as she crawled closer. He turned his head to look at her for a split second. In that one glance, a myriad of thoughts went through his mind—how much happiness she had given him, and how much he wanted a life with her by his side.

She handed him his knife as he thought of the moment he'd handed her this very knife the last time they'd fought Adam. He took it and turned his attention back to Adam. He still fumbled with the gun, going into shock from his injuries. His hands were not working correctly. Adam saw the knife and tried to speak, but couldn't form a single word.

Alex lowered his face close to his, and said slowly, through gritted teeth, "Damn . . . you . . . to . . . hell." Then with the last bit of strength he had, Alex stabbed Adam in the heart.

He wasn't sorry.

Alex struggled to his feet, feeling sapped of energy.

Regardless, he grabbed Alyssa by the hands, and pulled her gently away from Adam. A soft moan escaped from her lips. He didn't want to cause her pain, but he also didn't want her anywhere near Adam. He knelt down next to her. She immediately clutched her side and blood covered her hands. He loosened the rope and removed it from her neck.

"Alyssa, Alyssa, you're going to be all right."

"Alex . . . love you."

Alex collapsed next to her. If he could just rest for a moment, then he'd tend to Alyssa . . .

Suddenly, the area was crawling with people, yelling and screaming orders to each other. A helicopter sounded in the distance. Alex turned and looked at Alyssa. Her shocked expression matched his. Who were all of these people? Where did they come from? They shared a worried look between them. He knew this was the end of a chapter, an end to a part of their life he didn't want to be over.

Alex stretched his hand out towards Alyssa and she stretched hers towards him.

And that was the way they found them.

≈

A POLICEMAN APPROACHED and knelt down by Alyssa. "Alyssa Fontaine?"

"Yes."

"It's her, I've found her. She's hurt," he yelled.

Alyssa heard a helicopter land, knowing it was close by.

"We've been following Adam. We thought he would lead us right to you and he did."

Paramedics from the helicopter approached. They began to tend to her and to Alex. She heard someone yell, "This one's dead." Great relief washed over her. She didn't have to live in fear of Adam anymore. Unexpectedly, her father appeared before her eyes and she wondered if she was seeing things. "Dad?"

"Yes, Alyssa, I'm here and everything is going to be okay now. Just hold on a little longer."

She'd never seen her father look so worried, so upset. It was good to see his face. She'd longed for his presence and now, here he was, as if she'd conjured him up out of her imagination. They gave her something for the pain and she felt herself losing consciousness. Seeking out Alex, she saw the paramedics placing him in a bed for transport to the hospital, just as they'd done to her. From a distance, it seemed, she could hear them reading Alex his rights as they handcuffed his uninjured arm to the bed. Alyssa was alarmed. This wasn't right. She tried to sit up. He looked over at her. He, too, was almost out of it.

"No . . . what are you doing? Alex . . . no . . . Alex . . ."

Everything went black.

-20-

ALYSSA AWOKE IN a hospital bed, tucked into the covers so tightly, she felt like a human burrito. Her tongue felt like cotton and her head was heavy. She could hear whispering around her.

"It's very common for a victim to fall in love with her kidnapper."

"He made her marry him. I hate to think what she's been through."

"She keeps mumbling his name."

"No!" she wanted to scream. "No!" She couldn't speak and her eyelids felt weighty. Everything went black again.

≈

"ALYSSA, ALYSSA, CAN you hear me?"

It was her father's voice. She peeled her eyes open, feeling unbearably exhausted. There were several people surrounding her bed, looking at her sympathetically.

"You have five minutes, Detective, that's all," the doctor said.

Her memory slowly returned. "Alex, Alex," she mumbled, her throat feeling like sandpaper. Her neck was bandaged where Adam had cut her, restricting her movement.

"Alyssa, sweetheart, you're going to be fine. The stab wound missed your major organs. It was only about an inch from the side of your torso. You were very lucky. You lost a lot of blood. That's why you feel so weak. You're in a hospital in Reno. Honey, the detective wants to speak to you. He needs to ask you some questions. Can you do that?"

"Water," she begged. They propped her up and helped her drink a few sips of water. Alyssa observed her father, bestowing him with a small smile as he held her hand.

"Dad."

"Mrs. Fontaine, can you tell us what happened?"

She couldn't start at the beginning, not when they had arrested Alex. "Alex . . ."

"Don't worry, he won't be bothering you. He's handcuffed and his door is being guarded by police even as we speak. We won't let him near you."

"No, you don't understand. Alex saved me, he saved me from my kidnappers. He saved my life. I love him. Without him I would've died. Please don't treat him like this." Her voice was hoarse and she could barely croak out the words, but she had to make them understand.

"Are you telling me Alex Kendrick was not holding you there against your will?"

"No, he wasn't. My kidnappers were Adam and his father, I only knew him as Pa. It was pure luck when we stumbled upon the cabin where Alex lives. Alex saved me. He killed Pa in self-defense. Adam shot me in the leg. Alex took care of me. I would've died, please, I want to see Alex, where is he? Is he okay? Please let me see him. I want Alex." Alyssa could feel the panic rising in her, the need to see him, a raw ache in her belly.

The doctor intervened. "That's enough. She needs her rest. You can talk to her more later. Mrs. Fontaine, Mr. Kendrick is fine. He's asking for you too. You'll be able to see each other soon. Rest now." And then to the detective he said, "Alex Kendrick is a well known surgeon. I don't believe for a moment that he kidnapped anyone and I think Mrs. Fontaine has just confirmed that fact."

≈

DETECTIVE PITARO IMMEDIATELY went to the hospital room of Alex Kendrick. He'd done his research on him. He had quite a history, some of it a little suspicious, but nothing had ever been proven. He was a wealthy man, known for his advanced surgical techniques and handsome good looks. He didn't need to kidnap a woman. Women would've fallen at his feet to be with him. If what Mrs. Fontaine said was true, then he was a hero, not a criminal.

≈

ALEX LAY IN bed with his shoulder well bandaged and his arm in a sling. No one would talk to him and tell him how Alyssa was or where she was. He was handcuffed to the bed, angry as hell, and in pain. When the detective walked in, Alex did not smile or even acknowledge him.

"Mr. Kendrick, may I ask you a few questions?"

"All right, but only if I can ask a few questions back. Where is Alyssa? Is she okay?"

"She's here and she's going to be fine. Will you explain to me what happened? How did Mrs. Fontaine come to be with you?"

"Finally, someone wants to know my side of the story. May I ask why I'm being held like this? Why am I being treated like a common criminal? Adam attacked us, it was self defense."

"I apologize. But I can't do anything about it till I hear your side of the story. Go on, I'm listening."

"She was kidnapped by two bumbling idiots. They were terrifying nonetheless. They murdered without remorse. They burst into my cabin one night and held us at gunpoint. They had treated her abominably. She was bruised and beaten. When the opportunity came, we fought back. I shot one of them. He's buried about a mile from my cabin. I can tell you the location. Adam was the other one. He was injured in the scuffle, but he escaped. We feared he would return."

"Why did you hold her at your cabin?"

Alex took a deep breath. "I did not *hold* her at my cabin. She'd been shot in the leg by Adam. She could barely walk for the first two months. There was no way she could walk out of there and I wouldn't leave her alone. We feared Adam would return. I have no communication with the outside world. We decided to wait until the helicopter came to deliver my supplies. It only comes once a year."

"Did you force her to marry you?"

Alex looked the detective in the eyes.

"We found the gazebo . . . the sign . . ."

Alex wondered how to explain this to him. "We had a lot of time together, things happened between us. We fell in love. I love her. As crazy as it sounds, yes, we married ourselves. She was not forced to do anything."

≈

DETECTIVE PITARO KNEW what he was saying held the ring of truth. He liked this man. He'd saved Alyssa. He loved her and it was obvious Alyssa loved him too. He took out his keys and unlocked the handcuffs.

"I'm so sorry, Mr. Kendrick. Your story matches what Mrs. Fontaine told us. We had to be sure. Don't worry, Alyssa set us straight. All we knew was Adam planned to go up into the mountains to take out his revenge on some mountain man who had stolen his woman and killed his father. He bragged about killing the husband and son. We were sure it was Alyssa. We were under the impression that the mountain man had now, in turn, kidnapped Alyssa. We were wrong. She was lucky to have walked into your cabin. Thank you for saving her."

"How is she? When can I see her?"

"She's going to be fine. She wants to see you too. I don't think the doctors will be able to keep you two apart for much longer. At least, I wouldn't want to be the person who tells Alyssa she can't see you." He chuckled, thinking of Alyssa's insistence that she see Alex immediately. "She's rather upset at the separation." Alex Kendrick was a lucky man indeed. "That's quite a story. You two have been through a lot. Darned romantic, if you ask me. This is one case with a happy ending. When you're both well enough, we'll need the whole story. We'll give you a couple of days to recover first. Thanks again, Mr. Kendrick."

≈

THE NEXT DAY Alyssa was beside herself. She looked the nurse in the eye and said icily, "Do not give me another shot. I don't want to sleep anymore, I want to see Alex. Where is he?"

"Alyssa, honey, you'll see each other soon," her father tried to soothe her. "Take your shot for the pain."

"No, I want Alex. I want to see him now. I WANT ALEX." She'd had enough and she wasn't backing down for anything.

The nurse and her father exchanged a glance. She was starting to get hysterical. The doctor entered the room, taking in the situation.

"There's no harm in it, she'll heal better when she can rest. Mr. Kendrick is doing quite well. I'll have him sent down."

Alyssa lay back down and relaxed. They'd been apart for two nights. They'd never been separated for nearly a year and Alyssa felt like she would die without him. She needed to see him and see that he was all right. She wanted to hold him, to touch him, to feel him.

Two hours later, Alyssa was lightly dozing when she felt someone sit on her bed. Her eyes flew open.

"Hello, sleeping beauty."

Alex was before her, his arm in a sling and heavily bandaged, but he was okay. When she immediately started to cry at his presence, he lowered his head till their foreheads were touching. "Shhhhhhh," he soothed.

Being careful of his shoulder, she hugged him tightly. His good hand gently smoothed her brow.

"Everything's okay now. It's all right, we made it through." He kissed her and once they started, they couldn't stop. They spoke in between kisses.

"They wouldn't let me see you," Alex murmured.

"I was so worried," Alyssa whispered.

"No one would tell me anything."

"They thought you kidnapped me."

"I love you," he said with his lips on hers.

"Don't leave me."

"I hate being apart."

"How's your shoulder?" she asked.

"Hurts like hell."

"No more Adam."

"I'm so glad."

"I was so scared."

"Everything's fine now," Alex reassured her.

They kissed, they cried, Alyssa held his face in her hands and she ran her fingers through his hair, thankful that Adam had not taken Alex away from her.

≈

STERLING STOOD IN the doorway, a witness to their reunion. He had a grudging respect for Alex Kendrick. He'd had him checked out. He was a wealthy man and a renowned surgeon. Why he lived in the middle of nowhere by himself, he didn't understand. It was ridiculous if you asked him. He had lost several members of his family, but Sterling didn't understand why that would make anyone live up in the woods roughing it. Especially when he had the kind of money he did. He was thankful for him nonetheless, he had saved his daughter. They were going to have a little talk about this marriage business though. Sterling heard giggling behind him and turned to see three nurses peeking into the room. They had tears in their eyes and they mumbled the word 'romantic' several times. He rolled his eyes, turning his attention back to Alex and Alyssa. They were still kissing and whispering to each other. He heard Alex tell Alyssa everything was going to be all right. He wondered if it would be. There was still so much they didn't know. Sterling cleared his throat, making his presence known. It was enough already.

One of the older, no-nonsense nurses entered the room. "All right, young lady, you've seen your young man. I insist upon your pain shot now."

Alyssa agreed to it and fell asleep with Alex sitting by her side.

≈

THE NEXT DAY, the detective wanted to hear Alyssa's full story for his report. Her father arrived, acting uneasy, making Alyssa anxious. A nurse wheeled Alex into her room whereupon he went straight to her. They embraced and kissed, exchanged how are yous and I love yous as if no one else was in the room. Detective Pitaro watched with a smile, but her father seemed annoyed and interrupted with, "All right, let's get this going."

Alex sat in the wheelchair, close to Alyssa's bed, and held her hand. Her father and the detective each pulled up a chair. Detective Pitaro pulled out a notebook, prepared to take notes.

"All right, we have several reasons for calling this meeting today. Firstly, I would appreciate a full account of exactly what happened to you, Mrs. Fontaine. Can you start at the beginning? Leave nothing out, even if you think it's unimportant."

Alyssa began to tell her story to the detective. Tears fell when she talked about Sam and Clay. Anger washed over her when she talked about Pa and Adam. Alex held her hand through it all and took over telling the story when she got to her arrival at the cabin. They listened intently.

When they were done telling their story, Detective Pitaro remarked, "Wow, that's some story. I don't think I need to remind you of how lucky you were to walk into Mr. Kendrick's cabin, but, I do have one more question. You can tell me to mind my own business on this one, if you so choose." He cleared his throat. "You consider yourselves to be married?"

"That's preposterous," her father sputtered.

Alex and Alyssa exchanged glances. "Yes, we do," Alyssa said as she looked her father in the eye. "It was a decision we made. Winter was coming and we loved each other and had we been at home we would've married, but we couldn't. We had our own ceremony . . ." Alyssa faltered, and looked to Alex for help.

Alex took over. "We have the documentation. We tried to make it as legal as possible. I'm sure when the circumstances we were in are considered, we can have it declared legal." With his eyes on Alyssa he said, "We are committed to each other and as far as I'm concerned, yes, we're married." She smiled at him and he kissed her.

Sterling was quiet, so the detective went on. "I guess congratulations are in order then," he said as he shook Alex's hand. "I commend you for sticking to your moral principles in a difficult situation." Her father cast the detective a nasty look, as if to say, *whose side are you on?* Detective Pitaro continued, ignoring Sterling's glare.

"Okay then, let's move on. There are several things you need to know," he hesitated, "Brace yourselves, some of this may be unpleasant for you to hear. Have you told them anything, Mr. McCall?"

"No, I thought it best to wait."

Alex exchanged a worried glance with Alyssa. "What is it?" Alyssa asked apprehensively.

"I guess it's best to just get this all out in the open. First of all, we thought you'd be interested to know, we've done some research on Pa and Adam. Pa's real name is LeRoy Abernathy. His record shows four accounts of sexual assault on minor boys and two attempted abductions of minor boys. Adam is another story. Of course, his real name is not Adam. His record shows one account of attempted sexual assault on a woman. The woman did not press charges for his failed attempt and he was released.

He was going by the name of Bobby Abernathy, however further investigation has shown he is actually not Mr. Abernathy's son at all. He is Allan Browning, reported missing by his parents when he was only four years old. He was taken from his front yard while outside playing. He was presumed dead. His body was never found and the case was cold. It would appear he was kidnapped by Mr. Abernathy at a very tender age and probably had little or no memory of his former life."

Shocked at this revelation, Alyssa gasped. Adam was as much a victim of Pa as she had been. She felt sorry for the little boy, but not for the grown man.

"Mrs. Fontaine, are you okay? Shall I go on?"

"You mean there's more?" What else could they possibly have to tell her?

"If you'd like to do this another day . . ."

She looked to Alex once again and he nodded at her, squeezing her hand, giving her comfort and reassurance. "No, go on," she told them.

The detective and Sterling swapped nervous glances.

"What? What are you not telling me?" Alyssa asked, beginning to feel alarmed. Alex was quiet, but his eyebrows furrowed, showing his concern.

"Please forgive me for bringing back painful memories, but we feel it's important for you to know the whole story. I apologize in advance for the graphic nature of the details. As you know, and as we figured out by the evidence, Mr. Fontaine was holding your son, Clay. They were standing at the edge of the lake. The bullet hit Clay in the arm. It went through his arm and lodged next to Mr. Fontaine's heart, giving him literally seconds of life left. The fatal shot severed his artery. The forensic evidence shows that Mr. Fontaine, with super human effort, used his last seconds of life to help Clay. The force of the gunshot and the ensuing fall to the ground caused Clay to fall, face down, into the shallow, rocky water on the shore of the lake. We believe Clay was unconscious after hitting his head on a rock. Sam crawled over to Clay and pulled him out of the water, crawled back to dry land and positioned Clay, cradled close to his own body. Their bodies were found that way the next morning by a hunter. Sam's body protected Clay's from the elements."

Tears streamed down Alyssa's face and her chest rose and fell quickly. "What are you saying?" She sat up in the bed.

"We're saying that Sam, under absolutely impossible circumstances, it's completely unexplainable, used strength he did not have to save the life of your son, Clayton."

"What?"

"He's saying that Clay is alive, Alyssa. Clay is alive!" her father shouted at her.

Alyssa looked at Alex, who was just as shocked as she was.

"Clay is alive. Clay is alive," she repeated over and over as everything went black and she collapsed onto the bed as Alex caught her with his good arm.

-21-

ALYSSA HEARD ALEX calling her name as if from a great distance away, dear, sweet, and familiar.

"Alyssa . . . Alyssa . . ."

As she slowly came to her senses, her eyes fluttered open. Cradled in Alex's good arm, her head nestled close to his chest, her eyes wandered around the room, taking in the doctor, a few nurses, Detective Pitaro, and her father, all surrounding her bed, looking upon her with concern.

The doctor checked her vital signs. "She's all right now, let's give her some air. She just fainted, that's all." The doctor cleared the room. Her head was dizzy, her hands felt numb, her feet tingled, and yet happiness soared in her.

"Clay is alive?"

"Yes, Alyssa. We wanted you to recover from your injuries before we told you. We thought you were strong enough. I'm sorry, I know this is a shock. Alyssa, he's in a coma. He's never come out of it. We're all hoping that hearing your voice and feeling your touch will bring him out of it. There's nothing physically wrong with him. The doctors don't know why he stays in the coma. His life support was removed months ago. He's fine, he just won't wake up." Her father smiled at her, pleased to tell her the news of her son, his grandson.

Tears of joy washed down her cheeks. "Clay, Clay," she mumbled repeatedly. Alex held her close as their eyes met. "Alex," she whispered. What did this mean for them? It was too much to take in at once.

"We'll leave the two of you alone for a bit. Congratulations, Mrs. Fontaine." They left and closed the door behind them.

Their eyes had not left each other's, their expressions

suddenly tentative. Alyssa knew what Alex was thinking, he didn't have to say it. This news changed things between them, but neither one of them acknowledged it.

Alex smiled at her. "It's the best news we could've possibly heard. It's a miracle. I'm so happy for you, Alyssa." He kissed her, slow and tender.

Sterling entered the room again. "I've talked to the doctors. They've given the okay for both of you to be moved to the hospital in Connecticut where Clay is. If I can make the arrangements we can make the move tomorrow."

≈

"WHICH HOSPITAL?" ALEX asked.

"Connecticut Memorial, in Ashbury."

Alex should've known. Alyssa had grown up only forty-five minutes away from Ashbury, where he'd grown up. Connecticut Memorial was the best hospital in the area. It was only natural that Clay was there. Still, Alex wasn't thrilled about being back on his home turf, the very hospital where he'd worked for years. Not by a long shot.

"Alex, are you okay?" Alyssa whispered.

His trepidation must have shown on his face. "Yes." He nodded to Sterling. "I'll make all of the arrangements." He grabbed the cell phone he'd had delivered to him that morning and placed a call to Curtis, his estate manager. When he'd called that morning, Curtis was very surprised to hear from him. All contact had been through Jerry for the past three years. He'd explained his situation and requested a cell phone.

"Hello, Curtis, It's Alex. . . . yes, thank you . . . it's good to be back in town, thanks. No, no, I'm fine. Listen, I need to have some arrangements made. I want a private jet at the Reno Airport tomorrow morning at ten a.m. sharp. We'll be going to Connecticut National Airport. We need a nurse on board and a light lunch will be sufficient. I want a suite in a hotel as close to the Connecticut

Memorial Hospital as you can find, reserved in my name. Have one of my cars delivered to the hospital . . . no, I don't care which one . . . no, don't have the house opened, I won't be going there. Also, I would like you to contact Connecticut Memorial Hospital and see about Clayton Fontaine, a pediatric patient. See that he has everything he is in need of. I want absolutely none of this leaked to the media, understood? Yes, all right, thank you."

He ended the phone call and noticed the small smile on Alyssa's face as she looked at him with new eyes. She raised her eyebrows and said, "Are you kidding me?"

He smiled and winked. "Welcome to my world."

$$\approx$$

STERLING OBSERVED ALEX and Alyssa, wondering at their relationship. Their flight to the east coast was luxurious and comfortable. A nurse fretted over them and they were well cared for. Alyssa cuddled up to Alex and fell fast asleep.

"Thank you, Mr. Kendrick, for all you've done for us."

"Alex, call me Alex, please."

Sterling had to admit, he was a little bent out of shape when Alex took over. Sterling had worked hard all of his life to provide a prominent lifestyle for his family. It was important to him. He was not a rich man, but he lived well. And he still wasn't happy about this whole marriage business. He felt he could see the future and he didn't see how things could possibly work out for these two. He planned to talk to Alex about it at the first opportunity. In the meantime, he decided to accept what Alex could do for them.

When they arrived at the hospital, Alex and Alyssa were settled into their rooms. They ran some tests, took some blood, and gave them both the once over. The doctors said they were both doing well and would be able to leave in a day or two. They said Alyssa could go down and see Clay that evening. Sterling felt relieved that

Alyssa was going to be okay and looked forward to witnessing the reunion with her son.

≈

CLAY'S DOCTOR CAME to see Alyssa late that afternoon. She and Alex were talking quietly when he entered and introduced himself. He explained he wanted to speak to her about Clay's medical condition.

"Mrs. Fontaine, I'm so glad to meet you. I hear you're recovering well from your injuries . . ." he began when Alex interrupted him with, "Kendrick, it's Mrs. Kendrick." This was said with his eyes on her. He looked upset about it and she was too. She knew without him saying it exactly what he was thinking—she was thinking it too. If people knew their story, no one would recognize them as being married.

The doctor began again, "Mrs. Kendrick, I know you're anxious to see Clay, but I wanted to visit with you first. There's no way to prepare yourself for the sight of a loved one in a coma, but talking about it beforehand helps. Unfortunately, a doctor carries the burden of being the bearer of bad news at times. I apologize if this seems callous, but I'm going to be frank. I want you to know what we're dealing with. After Clay was shot in the arm, he landed in the shallow water of the lake face down, hitting his forehead on a rock. He was unconscious and he aspirated a great deal of water. After his father pulled him to dry land, Clay somehow coughed up most of the water and began to breathe again on his own. The trouble is, we don't know just how long it was that he wasn't breathing. We don't know the exact amount of time his brain was deprived of oxygen. We really don't know the extent of brain damage he may have sustained. The good news is that his brain waves appear to be normal. The puzzling news is that he persists on staying in a comatose condition. The brain is still somewhat of an enigma to medical science, even with all the incredible advances we've made.

The outcome of this case can go either way. Either Clay will stay in a comatose condition for an indeterminate amount of time or he will awaken and make a complete recovery, after extensive rehabilitation that is. You, being here with him, could make all the difference in the world, in fact, we're all counting on it." He finished with a smile.

Alyssa half-heartedly thanked him for his time and when he left she turned to Alex. "Is this good news or bad news? I can't tell."

"That was good news, brilliantly disguised as bad news, with a little 'we just plain don't have a clue' sprinkled on top. It's what we doctors are good at." At least that made her smile. "Don't be discouraged, Alyssa. Clay is alive — he still lives — and while he still lives there is always hope. Don't give up on him." He climbed onto the bed with her, wrapped his good arm around her and they dozed together, clinging to one another. They gave no thought to someone walking in on them. They were so used to doing whatever they pleased and old habits die hard. Besides, they didn't want to change their ways for even a second.

Finally, and it couldn't come too soon for Alyssa, she and Alex went together to go see Clay. Clay was in a different wing of the hospital, one meant for long term patients. Because of her leg injury, combined with her recent injuries, the hospital made her sit in a wheelchair. Because of his injured shoulder, Alex couldn't push the chair. His arm would be in a sling for another couple of weeks and he wasn't supposed to use it. Hence, an attendant rolled her down the long maze of corridors that smelled strongly of antiseptic and Alex walked beside her. They ran into several staff members Alex knew from his time spent working in the hospital. He stopped to say hello and introduced Alyssa as his wife, which made her beam.

Underneath it all, Alyssa was a nervous wreck, yet thankful to have Alex at her side. It was a miracle Clay was alive. She had Alex and now she had Clay too. She couldn't be happier. Her life had taken another new and unexpected turn. When she arrived in the room, her father was already there, reading to Clay. It was a beautiful, cheery room any two-year old would love. Teddy bears and toy trucks lined the windowsill. She was sure they'd all been bought by her father. By his bedside sat a family picture of herself, Sam, and Clay. She took all of this in after a matter of seconds and then her eyes rested on Clay.

≈

ALEX WATCHED AS Alyssa went to her son's bedside. She held his hand and began to silently weep. Alex stood over her, one hand gently massaging her shoulder, giving her strength. At the sight of the reunion of mother and son, there wasn't a dry eye in the room. She caressed his cheek and ran her hands through his soft curls. She spoke to him softly, saying his name over and over, telling him she loved him. Alex was envious. He would give anything to find out one of his daughters was still alive.

Clay was a beautiful child. He had a head of bleach blond hair and rosy cheeks. Other than the fact that there were a few tubes and a heart monitor attached to him, he looked perfect, like he was just taking a nap.

Alex couldn't stop his eyes from resting on the picture on the bedside table. It was a picture of Sam, Clay, and Alyssa. They were walking in a park. Clay was in the middle, holding the hands of his parents. Sam, who was as blond as Clay, had an easy, natural smile. He had the look of someone who was always pleasant, almost happy-go-lucky. A stab of jealousy shot through him.

He ignored it.

It was the picture of Alyssa that caught his attention. She looked so beautiful, so radiantly happy, a huge smile on her face. It was an Alyssa he didn't know, before tragedy had struck in her life.

Alex caught Sterling's eye. His thoughts were written all over his face and he knew it. His life was spiraling out of control and he didn't like it, not one bit. Alex knew this was a happy occasion. He was thrilled for Alyssa. Absolutely.

But he couldn't help feeling as if he'd just lost something.

≈

ALEX STAYED AT Alyssa's side every second of every day as—for the next few days—Alyssa spent all of her time at her son's bedside. She talked to him non-stop and cradled him in her arms. They taught her how to exercise his legs and arms to keep his muscles and joints healthy. Alex helped wherever he could. It was heartwarming to watch her with her son. It made him realize what a good mother she would be and he longed for a child of their own.

Alex was released from the hospital and went to stay in the suite. Alyssa stayed so she could be with Clay and because they wanted to watch over her for a few more days. She tired easily and felt faint quite often. Dizziness and nausea overwhelmed her at times. The nurses sent her back to her own bed on several occasions. She wasn't thinking about herself, only Clay. They were sure she was just over extending herself, but wanted to be sure all the same.

Alex found himself worrying over her, but Alyssa seemed oblivious to her own health concerns. All of her strength went towards caring for Clay. One night as Alyssa sat by Clay's bed, Alex slowly entered the room. He'd left for the afternoon to tend to some business with his attorneys.

He walked up behind her, wrapped his good arm around her and whispered in her ear, "Mrs. Kendrick, have you eaten or slept at all this afternoon?"

≈

ALYSSA FELT RELIEF at his presence. She stood, faced him and let herself be wrapped up in his warmth. In truth, she wasn't feeling well, but she hadn't wanted to leave Clay. They stood that way for awhile, feeling the comfort they could give to one another as if it was tangible. Finally, she looked at him and said, "Guilty." He took her by the hand.

"Come with me."

He somehow managed to push her wheelchair back up to her room even though Alyssa protested. He insisted he was fine. He opened the door to her hospital room and there before her eyes was a table set with a white tablecloth, candles, romantic music, and a five-course dinner. She got to her feet and was in his arms in seconds, kissing him—a long and sweet kiss. He kicked the door closed, giving them privacy.

"That was all I needed," Alyssa told him.

"I need you to be well. I hate being at the suite by myself. I can't sleep without you, the bed feels so cold and empty." They continued to kiss. "I know you want to be with Clay, but I need you to take care of yourself too, okay? Promise me."

In between kisses she mumbled, "Promise."

"Eat some dinner. You'll feel better," he coaxed.

Alex doted on her and she had to admit, she loved it. As they ate, the conversation turned to recent events.

"I was so scared. I didn't expect to see Adam."

"You were very brave. I could tell you'd given him hell."

"I wasn't about to let him ruin my life again."

"It's over, we made it through the ordeal and you needn't live in fear of Adam any longer."

"Thank you, Alex, for protecting me from Adam. Again."

"I told you there was a reason why I needed to live at

the cabin. It was to save you."

Alyssa didn't know what to say to that. Her heart was full. Without Alex, her life would've taken a very different turn. She reached across the table and held his hand.

"Clay is a beautiful child, Alyssa. I'm envious."

She wanted to say, *he's our child now, Alex*. But she didn't. It wouldn't ease his pain over his daughters.

Alex then told her about a few coma cases that had ended happily and explained what to expect when Clay woke up. She listened intently until she could hardly keep her eyes open.

"You need your sleep," he said.

"I wish we were back at the cabin," she whispered. They smiled at each other, knowing what they'd do next if they were. "I miss you."

"Me too," he said softly. "I miss being able to do whatever we want, whenever we want."

"Stay with me till I fall asleep?" she asked.

"Of course."

As she drifted off she said, "I love you, Alex."

"I love you, Alyssa."

≈

THE NEXT MORNING, Alyssa woke up to Alex arriving with croissants, fresh fruit, and orange juice for breakfast.

"Thought you could use a break from hospital food."

"I knew there was a reason why I love you so much."

He smiled, but there was something different in his eyes. He looked upset, even though he tried to hide it.

"Alex, is everything okay?"

He joined her on the bed and she sat up to meet him, kissing him tenderly.

"I'm fine now," he whispered.

"I missed you. I hate being apart," she whispered back.

"Can't sleep, need you," he mumbled with his lips on hers.

They were interrupted by the sound of someone clearing their throat rather loudly from the doorway.

"Jerry," Alex said warmly.

The two men hugged and patted each other on the back, clearly happy to see each other. Alyssa noticed the way Jerry's eyes watered, but he tried to hide it.

"Alyssa, this is Jerry Nelson, my good friend and colleague and the man who ensures we have the supplies we need up at the cabin."

Jerry was a big teddy bear of a man. He had a huge smile that seemed to envelop his whole face. He had a full head of gray hair and lively eyes, as if he'd just heard a horribly funny joke. Jerry's eyes rested on Alyssa, his huge smile ever-present. She liked him immediately.

"The woman of the hour. It's a great pleasure to meet you, Alyssa." He leaned over and kissed her forehead.

"I've heard a lot about you, Jerry." She smiled up at him. Despite the difference in their ages, Jerry and Alex had become fast friends during their time in medical school. Jerry had made the decision to pursue medical school late in life.

Jerry studied her intently for a moment, looking into her eyes. "Alex, she's a beauty."

"Inside and out," Alex told him.

"You lucky son of a gun," Jerry added with a raise of his silver eyebrows.

"Don't I know it," Alex said.

Alyssa suddenly felt awkward. They were both staring at her with smiles on their faces and making comments to each other. She felt flustered.

"Hey, I'm in the room, guys."

They all laughed then and Alex and Jerry began to catch up with each other. Jerry and his wife, Teresa, were high school sweethearts and had married just after graduation. They had five daughters, two in college.

"I would've been here sooner, but we were picking the girls up from college. I heard about you on the news. I came as quick as I could."

He obviously cared for Alex very much. She knew Alex had a lot of respect for Jerry and trusted him. Alyssa found herself watching Alex as he spoke animatedly with Jerry. It was a side of him she'd never seen. Alex caught Alyssa's gaze, and paused mid-sentence, smiling at her and completely losing his train of thought.

Jerry chuckled. "Earth to Alex," he joked. "I can see you two are smitten with each other."

"Guilty," Alex said. "And I'm not apologizing for it."

≈

THAT AFTERNOON ALEX and Jerry had lunch together while Alyssa spent time with Clay.

"What happened, Alex? I didn't want to ask in front of your young lady. I'm sure the news didn't get it right."

"Not a chance in hell," Alex responded bitterly.

"She's gorgeous, quite stunning," Jerry remarked. "Leave it to you, Alex. How'd you manage to find yourself a young lady in the middle of nowhere?"

"It surprised the heck out of me."

Then, in all seriousness, Jerry asked, "What happened?"

Alex told him everything from the beginning. Jerry was mortified by the details. "I can't imagine that happening to one of my daughters. The thought of it actually happening to Alyssa is quite disturbing."

"They damn near killed her, Jerry. We lived in fear of Adam returning. Then when he did, neither one of us were expecting it . . . or our world to come tumbling down."

"You're a hero, Alex," Jerry said with a raise of his bushy eyebrows.

"And I won the princess too," Alex responded with a smile.

"You're really in love with her, aren't you? This girl got under your skin. I could swear your eyes are sparkling," he ribbed.

Alex chuckled lightly. "I'm not surprised. She's . . . everything to me."

"One look at how she looks at you and I'd say she feels the same."

Alex sobered. "If you could've seen her when she arrived at my cabin, she was dead on her feet. The way she looked at me, it was as if I could hear her thoughts. I knew I wasn't going to let them take her. I knew I loved her even then. I could only hope she could love me. And then, when it finally happened . . ." Alex was lost in thought for a moment, then added, "It was the happiest time of my life."

"I'm happy for you, Alex. Heaven knows you deserve it."

"I thought Adam was going to kill her. I thought our time together was over." He paused for a moment. "I loved Trish and Alyssa loved her husband, Sam. But we lost them. Do you know what it's like to find love again after losing it? It's completely different. It's intense, every emotion is heightened, you appreciate every second, you take nothing for granted. Each moment counts. Most of us live our lives so caught up in trivial, everyday matters, never really stopping to think, what if I lost the people closest to me? How would I live today differently if I knew it was coming? Did you know we had four months together — alone in the cabin — during the winter? We were completely snowed in. It was like a dream. We spent most of the time in each other's arms. And that's the polite way to put it." Jerry smiled broadly. "I'll never forget that time." Alex stopped, realizing how he must sound. "I'm sorry, Jerry, I'm rambling. I sound like an idiot."

Jerry guffawed loudly, patting him on the shoulder several times. "You sound like you're in love and I'm not complaining. I'm hanging on every word and reading between the lines."

Alex scoffed. "Shut up." But his huge grin betrayed

him. The conversation lagged for a moment. Now was the time to tell Jerry Alyssa was his wife. Now was the time to tell the story of their private wedding.

But he didn't. He'd told people she was his wife, but they didn't know the nature of their circumstances. Jerry did. He'd catch on immediately. He couldn't face being questioned about it by his good friend. He wasn't sure he would understand. Only Alyssa's father and the detective knew the true story and Alex wanted to keep it that way for the time being. The media was already plastering what they knew of their story all over the news. If the details of their marriage leaked, he could just imagine what the headlines would look like. He'd be massacred.

≈

JERRY COULDN'T WAIT to get home and tell Teresa about Alex and Alyssa. They always shared everything that happened during the day with each other as they got ready for bed. She sobbed like a baby at the story of Alyssa's plight.

"Alex saved her?" she repeated in awe. "That's so romantic."

Jerry rolled his eyes in response. His wife had her head in the clouds. She was a sucker for a good romance, always cried at movies too.

"I'm worried about him though."

"What do you mean?"

"I'm not sure, just a feeling. Something's bothering him. I'm wondering if he wants to go back to the cabin. He was tense at lunch, and a bit preoccupied."

"But he'd have to leave Alyssa."

"Exactly."

-22-

THAT EVENING ALEX sat at Alyssa's bedside, deep in thought, watching her sleep. He sat deathly still as he brooded over his circumstances. Alyssa looked beautiful, calm, and at peace. But she wasn't recovering as fast as she should be and it worried him. She seemed to have no strength and what she did have all went towards Clay. He loved her and he loved her son. But loving them meant he would have to stay here. He was in turmoil. He felt a burning desire to be back at the cabin. The media was driving him crazy and the urge to flee was strong. Sterling suddenly entered the hospital room with a determined expression, interrupting his troubled thoughts.

"Alex, can I speak with you?" he whispered.

"Of course." They retreated to the hallway.

"What is it?" Alex asked.

"Not here, let's go down to the cafeteria."

Alex cast him a long look, wondering what he wanted. They strolled down to the cafeteria, chose their meals, and settled at a table by a window. They exchanged pleasantries for a few moments. Then Sterling got down to business.

"Alex, I don't think I've thanked you for all you've done. Thank you for saving my daughter. She means the world to me."

Alex wasn't sure how, but he knew there was a 'but' coming. "She means the world to me too," was all he said in response.

"Look, your story has been all over the news lately. I'm sorry you've been through so much in your life and I know only half of what the media says is fact, but . . ."

Oh yes, there it was.

". . . quite frankly, I don't want my daughter's

name associated with you . . . Dr. Death," he added for effect and Alex flinched. "She has enough on her plate as it is."

Alex looked Sterling in the eye. His given name suited him. The name Sterling brought on an image of cold, hard steel into his mind. "Don't you think that's for Alyssa to decide?"

Sterling didn't miss a beat. On the immediate heels of Alex's words, he began his tirade. "She's been through hell. I don't think she can make a rational decision right now, nor do I think she's made a rational decision for the past year. Have you ever thought that maybe her love for you is a form of hero worship? She was on the rebound. She loved Sam, heaven only knows why. You're a handsome man, you rescue her, take care of her, I'll bet she practically fell into your arms."

That comment was designed to cut to the very bone and Alex knew it, but he also knew better. Sterling went on.

"Do you plan on living at your cabin again?"

Now he was getting to touchy territory. "Yes, as a matter of fact I do. I plan to live out my life there."

"Why?"

"Why?" Alex repeated.

"Yes, why. Let me answer for you. I'll tell you why, because you can't face reality. You couldn't face it three years ago and you can't face it now," Sterling added cruelly.

"You know nothing about me," Alex said quietly. He vaguely remembered Alyssa saying her father was an overbearing man. *An understatement.*

Sterling had struck a chord and he knew it. He continued. "The reality is . . ." he added as if Alex had not said a word, ". . . you're tearing her apart. She loves you, I'll give you that. But she loves her son more than life itself and he needs her right now, all of her. Once he does wake up, he will need months of rehabilitation. He'll be a full time job. Have you thought about that?"

He'd thought of nothing but that.

"He can't go and live in the middle of nowhere. Not now and not any time in the future. He may not even wake up for who knows how long. It could be today, tomorrow, it could be next week, next month or even next year. Are you prepared to stand by Alyssa's side through that?"

That wasn't the issue and Sterling knew it. He was grasping with that last comment.

Without giving Alex a chance to respond he continued, "This relationship is doomed, can't you see that? Every time she looks at you, she'll be reminded of a truly horrific experience, something no human being should ever have to go through, a time in her life she's better off putting behind her. She'll never be able to do that with you by her side. It will eventually destroy your relationship. Mark my words, I can see it coming."

Alex let that sink in. In all truthfulness, he'd already considered that thought months ago. He'd also dismissed it almost immediately. He knew Alyssa associated him with a happy time in her life. She thought of the two events separately in her mind and he loved her for being so reasonable. The events she'd lived through had not affected her mental balance. She was completely stable. He wished her father would acknowledge that fact.

"Alyssa knows what she's doing. I have faith in her." The words she'd said to him on their wedding night filtered through his mind and he longed for that moment.

Sterling again continued as if Alex hadn't said anything, moving on to his next point, almost as if he was worried he would forget each point he wanted to make and had to get it out fast before he lost it. "I can see it in your eyes. You're ready to get the hell out of here. The media hounds you night and day. Ghosts from your past haunt you. You don't want to be here and I don't want you here."

Alex sat very still, but his eyes flashed and his jaw clenched at Sterling's words. Alex couldn't believe this man was Alyssa's father. She was nothing like him.

"Look, what I'm saying to you is this: Alyssa's life is here now. She can't play house with you anymore in your secret hideaway. Her responsibility is with Clay. If you love her, truly love her, you'll let her go. It will tear her apart to not be with you, even I can see that. Therefore, I think a clean break is best. I don't really care what you say to her, just end it and make it believable. Heaven knows the marriage is a joke, surely you must know that. You need to leave her alone and let her go on with her life. She'll cry and be sad, but she'll get over it. She'll be able to dedicate her life to her son. She won't be expending her energy to pine after you. You'll be doing her a huge favor. Go and do what makes you happy—run back to your cabin and hide. After all, it's what you're good at."

Alex stood quickly, bumping the table. A glass fell to the floor with a loud crash. People stared. There were a lot of things he wanted to say, none of them very nice, but out of respect to Alyssa, he didn't say them.

"You don't know your daughter very well, Mr. Fontaine."

Alex angrily walked out, ran out of the hospital, and jumped into his car. He drove for a long time, Sterling's words echoing in his ears. He couldn't believe a father could be so callous to his daughter's feelings. So much of what he'd said was way off base. And yet, some of it was exactly what had been ruminating in his mind already. It just hadn't formed into conscious thought yet. Alex drove for quite a while—something he wasn't really supposed to be doing—till his shoulder ached from even this small amount of use. He had no destination in mind and his thoughts churned viciously. He finally made his way to a park, positioned his car to provide a lakeside view, and pondered his options.

Firstly, could he stay? An immediate, 'no' washed over

him. He didn't want to stay, he longed to be back at his cabin and have his solitude.

Secondly, could he leave Alyssa? No, even the thought sent a shudder through him. He loved her. He longed to be with her.

He couldn't have both. He was at an impasse.

What it really came down to was, simply, that he couldn't live here. He wasn't willing to change that fact. It was out of the question for him. He hated being here. He hated the memories, he hated the whispers and stares, and he hated the stories that were flying out of control.

Alyssa has to stay here with her son. She can't leave. She can't come with me.

He knew what that meant.

It was over for them.

It had been the only thing Sterling had said that made any sense. The thought rummaged around his brain, desperately trying to take hold. He couldn't imagine life without Alyssa. It was against some unknown law of nature for them to be separated. But he knew it was the only answer.

Of one thing he knew for sure, it wouldn't be permanent. Someday he'd be back for her. Things change, children grow up. One day she would be free to be with him again.

When he arrived back at the hospital, his decision was reinforced. The ever present newshounds waited at the doors of the hospital.

"Mr. Kendrick, the car crash that killed your family has never been fully explained. What do you have to say about that?"

"Is it true the police considered you guilty of foul play?"

"Do you miss your daughters?"

"Were you and Mrs. Fontaine having an affair even back then?"

"Did you kill your family to be with her?"

Alex walked past them, deliberately ignoring their questions, even though their words hit him with the force of a blow. He'd had it. His decision was made.

I'm outta here.

He looked down on Alyssa in her hospital bed, sleeping soundly. He kissed her on the cheek. "I love you," he whispered. He left a note for her, the coward's way out and he knew it. He couldn't even begin to try and pretend he was leaving because he wanted to end things with her, as Sterling had suggested. He knew Alyssa would see right through such an explanation. She knew how much he loved her. He'd never hidden his feelings for her. But he did make it clear this was goodbye, for now anyway.

Alex returned to his suite, and didn't sleep at all that night. He paced the room, wearing a path in the carpet. He ran what he was doing over and over in his mind. He thought it and then re-thought it.

And in the morning, he was gone.

≈

ALYSSA AWOKE TO find a note by her bedside, along with her hand carved cane. It was from Alex. She opened it eagerly, only to wish she'd never laid eyes on it. It stated, simply,

My darling Alyssa,
I had the cane delivered. I wanted you to have it.
I'm so happy for you that Clay is alive.
I will always love you and cherish the time we had
together.
I'm sorry, I can't stay any longer.
You're safe now. Be happy and know that I love you.
Goodbye,
Alex

She started to cry and then she started to scream, uncontrollably. She was hysterical. The nurses rushed in. None of them knew what was wrong till they saw the note lying on the floor. They quickly gave her a shot to calm her.

It was much later in the day when the doctor came in to check on her. She lay in bed staring sullenly. Her eyes were red and swollen.

"I understand you had some bad news today."

"Yes," was all she said.

"Look, I don't know if this helps any, but I know Doctor Kendrick. We worked together years ago. He's had a rough go of it. Give him some time, he'll come around. He's a good man."

She didn't respond.

He cleared his throat. "This probably isn't the time, but I'm going to take a chance. As you know, we did several tests to check up on you. It seems Doctor Kendrick was worried you weren't recovering well and we agreed with him. Of course, it has been convenient for you to be here with your son and all, but that wasn't the reason we had you stay. At any rate, we know the reason for your constant fatigue. It's good news, at least I hope it is. I can't believe this has been overlooked. It should've been caught right away. It's a miracle, really, after all you've been through. You're pregnant, Alyssa. I would say about six weeks along. Congratulations. It explains all of the symptoms you've been having. Perfectly normal, under the circumstances. If you promise to get plenty of rest and take good care of yourself, we'll release you in the morning."

The only response he got was a tear sliding down her cheek.

-23-

WHEN ALEX ARRIVED back at the cabin, he was unprepared for the rush of memories that overtook him. Everything reminded him of Alyssa. He couldn't escape her, missing her terribly. He went to work, cleaning, organizing, and trying to expunge her touch from the cabin. It was no use.

He went out for a long walk and still he could find no peace. The garden was dead without Alyssa to care for it. He found he didn't care and covered it with dirt, erasing any evidence it had existed.

Everything was how it had been left after Adam's little rampage. The fence around the front yard—closest to the garden—was broken. She'd been working in the garden that day. It must've been where Adam attacked. He assumed the broken fence happened during the struggle between Alyssa and Adam. He was proud of her. She had fought well. He wished he'd been there to protect her earlier.

With joy in his heart, Alex removed the grave marker for Clay in the remembrance yard. As he entered the workshop, memories of that fateful day played through his mind. There was no way he would've let Adam take Alyssa from him.

And yet here he was without her. How did things get so complicated? He knelt down by the destroyed cradle and picked up the pieces. He would build a new one. Someday he and Alyssa would be back together. Someday they would have a child. He wasn't giving up on their dream. He put the workshop back together, thinking of that day and how he would've died to save Alyssa. He wondered how she was. How had she reacted to the letter, to his leaving? It killed him to think about it.

He couldn't sleep in the bed that night, too many memories of Alyssa. He ached fiercely for her. He slept on the couch, not sleeping well, tossing and turning. Mostly, he stared into the fire and wondered how she was.

≈

ALYSSA WAS STUNNED. She'd lain in bed last night, sleepless, with silent tears rolling down her face. Presently, she sat in the hospital bed feeling utterly numb. She hadn't spoken a word since the earth-shattering letter. Tears wouldn't even fall anymore, she was all cried out. Alex loved her and she knew it. How could he leave? After all they'd been through, she just didn't understand how he could end it so abruptly. Did he really expect her to say, "Oh, okay, see ya. It was nice while it lasted." Placing her hand on her stomach, she stared at the television lifelessly, knowing she had a part of Alex with her no matter what. The thought sent a thrill of happiness through her. This news would make Alex so happy. This baby wanted to be born, to live. It was a miracle baby. How else could it have survived the trauma her body had suffered?

Suddenly, she was riveted to the news. Clay had taken all of her attention lately. As she watched the images fly across the screen she realized with a frown, she'd been blind to what Alex had been going through. Painfully unaware.

Oblivious even.

"Dr. Death strikes again. Multi-millionaire, Alex Kendrick, has made another appearance in town. It would seem he was involved in the disappearance of Alyssa Fontaine, wife of the late Samuel Fontaine. If you remember the story, the family of three had been vacationing in Tahoe. The bodies of Mr. Fontaine and his son were found in the Sierra Nevada Mountains last year. Mr. Fontaine was found dead and the son, Clayton Fontaine, was left for dead. He remains in a comatose condition. No one knew what had happened to Mrs.

Fontaine. She was presumed dead. However, an ongoing investigation into her disappearance has led to her whereabouts. Evidently, Mr. Kendrick has been living in a highly confidential, extremely remote location in the mountains and for the last year Mrs. Fontaine has been with him."

"Lucky lady," one of the female newscasters remarked. Laughter erupted in the studio.

"That's a matter of opinion. Alex Kendrick, otherwise known as Dr. Death — because he has seen his fair share of it — has not had a lucky life. Death seems to follow the people he is closest to. As a child of twelve he saw his mother hit by a car. She died while the young Alex held his mother's head in his lap."

A picture of a very young Alex holding his mother appeared on the screen.

"I bet whoever got that shot made a pretty penny." Again, the studio callously erupted in laughter.

"At age fifteen, his father was stricken with pancreatic cancer. The fatal cancer hit very suddenly. It took him sixteen days to die, and the young Alex absolutely refused to leave his bedside. Reportedly, he died with Alex holding his hand. Years later, as Alex was home from college on Christmas break, his grandfather had a heart attack and died with Alex at his side in the ambulance, reportedly begging him not to leave him. The grim reaper wasn't finished with him yet. Alex married Patricia Garret, a young lady he met in college. They had two daughters together. Alex was driving the car that mysteriously spun out of control, killing his wife and daughters. Alex walked away literally unharmed. The police found the crime scene suspicious, though no charges were ever placed against the young doctor."

Pictures of the wreckage filled the screen. The car was so twisted and mangled, it was a miracle he'd survived at all. Shock set in as she stared incredulously at the screen.

Alex was driving the car. Why didn't he tell me?

Footage of Alex appeared on the screen. The media surrounded him, firing questions as fast as the words could leave their lips.

"Is it true that you crashed the car on purpose?"

"Was your wife planning on leaving you, Doctor Kendrick?"

"Is it true you never wanted to be a father?"

"Did your wife marry you for your money?"

"Why is it that everyone around you dies?"

Alex pushed through the crowd, not answering a single question, his face a mask.

"The devastated Doctor Kendrick insisted on going back to work. Known for his revolutionary surgical techniques, he made a name for himself in the medical field early in his career and was considered quite brilliant. The hospital allowed him to return without question. Two of his patients died on the operating table within a month. The families took Doctor Kendrick to court claiming they were textbook cases and he had no right to be operating in his mental condition. The cases were both thrown out of court, but the young doctor's excellent reputation was now tarnished. Rumors of cash settlements were flying but have never been confirmed. Alex took a leave of absence from the hospital, but then disappeared and for the past three years no one has been able to find his whereabouts, till a few days ago."

A video of Alex walking into the hospital played across the screen.

"Is it true you kidnapped Mrs. Fontaine?"

"Were you involved in the attempt on her husband and son's lives?"

"Will she be the new Mrs. Kendrick?"

"Are you in love with her?"

Alex ignored them, but she saw the look on his face. She knew how upset he was by their questions. Tears glided down Alyssa's cheeks. She wished he had trusted her enough to tell her everything. She understood so much now. She knew why he lived the way he did. She even understood why he'd left. Detecting movement, Alyssa turned to see Jerry standing in the doorway.

"I'm sorry you had to hear that, Alyssa."

"I had no idea."

"He didn't tell you?"

"He told me some of it, but he left out a lot of key details. Was all of that true?"

"Basically. Alex never spoke of it. I'm his best friend and he never spoke to me once about any of it. I tried. I thought it would help him to talk about it. He's an emotionally handicapped man, with good reason. It does something to a man when he faces so much loss in his life. It changed him. Then he had this hare-brained idea to live in the mountains alone and I couldn't talk him out of it. You know the rest."

"I didn't know he was driving the car." He'd always said he didn't want to talk about it, so she'd never pressured him. She understood now why he didn't want to speak of it. The media had insinuated horrible thoughts. Perhaps he thought she would jump to the same conclusions.

"He has never talked about what happened that night. The guilt at being the only survivor was eating him alive. The police were constantly questioning him. It was killing him. People stared, they whispered and gossiped. He hated it. But in the end, it was the cruel things the media insinuated that put him over the edge, that and being called Dr. Death. Do you know how many lives he has saved over the years? Thousands. Two of his patients die and suddenly he's labeled incompetent. Those patients died of complications, not anything Alex did, just so you know. I was on the board that investigated the cause of the deaths. He is one of the best surgeons I've ever worked with, as well as one of the best men I've ever known. He has a heart of gold. It's a crying shame, what he's been through."

Tears slipped down her cheeks unchecked. "I don't understand, stories die, breaking news happens. They'll forget about him."

"I know that and you know that, but Alex can't see it. He was born into a wealthy family. The media has been fascinated by him his entire life. He's a private man and he's always hated the way his life is paraded on the television. A handsome, wealthy heir—they can't get enough of him. He hates the media, but he can live with it, he has all of his life. It was when the news started to say the things he was already thinking and beating himself up over, that's what got him. He couldn't live with the guilt." He stopped for a moment, studying her. Then he went on, "You're the best thing that has ever happened to him, young Alyssa. Don't let him get away." He winked at her.

"He's gone. He left me. He didn't want to stay, he said he couldn't stay. I don't understand how he could just leave," she said sadly.

"Keep in mind, it's not that he *won't* stay, he *can't* stay. I don't think he has it in him. The emotional scars are just too deep. To be honest, I was very much against this idea of his to live alone in the mountains. But now I can see this is just his way of coping with his lot in life. What he's faced would've gotten the best of most men. It would've been so easy to become an angry and bitter man. Instead, he found happiness and peace. He's still not ready to face real life. But something tells me with you by his side, he can do it. Besides, we have the upper hand, my dear."

"How?"

Jerry smiled mischievously. "I know the location of the cabin and I arrange the helicopter deliveries, remember?"

Alyssa smiled back. Hope surged inside of her. She liked Jerry. He encouraged her to look ahead and not give up on Alex. She thought of something he'd said earlier. "Jerry, I don't believe he's emotionally handicapped. He has a great capacity to love. I know, I was loved by him."

"Point taken."

"It was the happiest time of my life."

"He told me the exact same thing. Listen, Alyssa, I've known Alex since our college days and I have to admit, I've never seen him so smitten. His eyes follow you wherever you go. When he sees you, his eyes light up and damn near sparkle. That man loves you, of that I'm certain. I couldn't be happier for him, it's just what he needed in his life." Jerry paused and she could tell he was mulling something over in his mind. "Alyssa, is it true you married yourselves?"

"Who told you?"

"Hospital grapevine. Gossip travels like wildfire."

She hesitated. "We haven't told anyone, they must've overheard somehow. Yes, it's true. There was no other way. It's not something we're announcing to the world. We know people won't understand, we know it was a crazy thing to do." Alyssa looked away, at a loss for words.

"He didn't tell me about it, although, I can understand why. The fact that he was willing to do such a thing says a lot about how he feels about you. Alex would never do something like that, not unless he meant it. Women throw themselves at him, always have. Handsome *and* wealthy, a true aphrodisiac. He never took advantage of it. He was never a womanizer. College buddies use to really rib him about it."

After spending so much time with Alex, she felt she already knew this about him, instinctively. She changed the subject. "I'm leaving today, they're releasing me."

"That was actually what I came here to talk to you about. I know this is a hard time for you right now and I don't think you should be alone. Teresa and I would like to invite you to come and live with us for as long as you need to. Before you answer, there's something you need to know. Alex has provided for you. He's paid for a suite in a nearby hotel, in advance, for the next six months. I have strict instructions for that to be extended if need be. He's left you one of his cars, to be at your disposal. All medical bills have been taken care of, to include everything on Clay, even his future medical care. An account has been opened in your name with a hefty sum of money in it for whatever you may need. I have all of the paperwork at home."

Alyssa was speechless. Everything was taken care of. No worries.

"I'm going to be frank. Alex asked me to watch over you and to make sure you had everything you needed. Truthfully, he didn't want you to have to rely on your father. His words. But that's not why I'm offering you a place in my home. I'm doing it because I want to and for no other reason than that."

Alyssa was slightly taken aback at Jerry's forthrightness. Yet she appreciated it all the same. "I wasn't sure where I was going to go, actually. Thank you. Just until I figure out what I'm going to do, of course. My father lives forty-five minutes away but, I don't want to be that far from Clay. Are you sure I won't be putting you out?"

"Not at all. We'd love to have you. My wife, Teresa, already has the guest room prepared. She can't wait to meet the woman who stole Alex's heart."

Touched at their thoughtfulness, she accepted his offer. Jerry left and she pondered on everything he'd said. She was thankful to Alex for taking care of her financial worries. But she didn't want his money, she wanted him. She ached for him.

Her next visitor of the day was her father. "I don't understand, Alyssa, why can't you stay with me?"

"Dad, please try to understand. It's forty-five minutes away, even longer in traffic. I don't want to be that far from Clay."

"I want to take care of you, Alyssa. It's the least I can do after Alex walked out on you."

"Don't say that."

"Why not? It's true, isn't it? I knew he wouldn't stay. The man has issues. You're better off without him. Death follows whoever he's closest to. It's as if he's cursed. Do you really want to be exposed to him?"

Alyssa felt the blood drain from her face. "Don't ever say that again. Alex brought life to me, he saved me. Don't repeat the cruel things the media has fabricated. I won't hear of it."

"Okay, okay, I got it. But it doesn't change the fact that he left you. I knew he didn't have it in him to stick it out."

Alyssa let that sink in for a minute. Her dad always liked to be in control. "What do you mean by that? Dad, did you say something to him?"

"What makes you say that?'

"Why aren't you denying it?"

"We had a talk, but the man makes his own decisions."

Alyssa could only imagine what her father had said during their 'talk.' She knew him too well. Sam always told her the outrageous things her father told him he should be doing with his life. They even learned to laugh at it. But it wasn't funny now. Not at all. Her unstable emotions left her unwilling to argue with him.

"Look, there are things I need to know. What happened to our home and our belongings?"

"The home was sold. Your other car was sold. The money was put into trust for Clay. The household items were cleaned out and what was thought to be sentimental is in storage in Arizona, just in case you were still alive. I never gave up hope, you know."

She was still reeling from the knowledge that almost everything from her former life was gone. "I know, thank you, Dad. But I need to know, where do I stand financially?"

"Your bank account has been left untouched. The life insurance money from Sam was placed in a trust fund for Clayton. I take it Mr. Kendrick could not be bothered to provide for his *wife*?"

"As a matter of fact, he has provided for me. And he's covered all of Clay's care, present and future," she said quietly.

"Isn't there something you're forgetting?"

"What?" she said tiredly.

"Wouldn't you like to know where your *husband* is buried? Perhaps you could pay him a visit," he said cruelly.

Her father meant well, but sometimes he simply didn't think before he spoke. Needless to say, by the time he left, she felt frazzled. But the day wasn't over yet.

Her next visit was over the phone. It was an extremely emotionally exhausting phone call with Sam's parents. Through their tears they told her how happy they were she had returned home safely. They invited her to come and live with them and she loved them for their kindness. She explained that she didn't want to move Clay and they understood. They'd been to see him a few times and they believed he would wake up now that she was at his side. They had hoped to have Clay at a hospital in Arizona, but Sterling had insisted on him staying in Connecticut. It was a draining phone call to say the least. They still mourned their son keenly. Alyssa couldn't face them no matter how much she loved them and wanted to see them.

How could she face them carrying another man's child?

≈

LATE THAT AFTERNOON, Jerry picked her up and the drive to his home was swift. She would be as close as possible to Clay. As they pulled in front of Jerry's home, she saw a red Honda CRV in the driveway.

"It's yours," Jerry informed her. "Of all of his cars, it was between the Honda or his black BMW. It's a convertible and he thought this suited you better."

She didn't respond. *Of all of his cars? Just how many cars does he have?* She was beginning to feel like a mistress, tucked away and paid off. She knew Alex didn't mean it that way. But she felt it all the same.

Jerry and Teresa lived in a large ranch style home in a quiet neighborhood only five minutes from the hospital. It was not overly pretentious, but was a nice and well cared for home.

Alyssa ate dinner with the family. She was quiet most of the time. As she observed them, happy and talking together, she longed to have a family of her own with Alex. Jerry and Teresa had five daughters. Christa, Carolyn, Clare, Caitlyn, and the baby of the family, Casey. She was six and still wanted to spend her time talking to her mom and dad. They were all polite and friendly girls. Casey stared at the bandage she still wore around her neck, but didn't say anything about it. She had obviously been told not to. It was a surface wound and was almost completely healed, but looked rather horrific, so she still wore the bandage.

Alyssa had to admit, sitting there with a normal, happy family, she felt like a soldier returning from war with all the battle scars to show for it, physical and emotional. Everything that had happened to her in the last year seemed surreal. Her time with Adam and Pa seemed a distant nightmare, something that only happened to other people and you read about it in the newspaper. Her time with Alex—she pondered on that for a moment—was like a dream you never want to wake up from. She wished she could huddle under the covers, go back to sleep, and awaken in the cabin with him next to her.

She liked Teresa immediately finding her to be one of the nicest ladies she'd ever met. She was tall, with blond hair that fell just passed her shoulders. Jerry talked only when he could get a word in edge-wise while Teresa talked almost non-stop, the words pouring out of her mouth.

Teresa helped her get settled that night. The guest room was cheerful, painted bright yellow, with cream colored carpet and a red bedspread. Red tulips filled a vase on the dresser. An overstuffed red chair sat next to the bed.

Teresa's next words to her spilled forth, "This is our guest room. I hope you'll be comfortable here, Alyssa. I want you to relax and recover from your injuries. These things take time, you know. I told Jerry, don't you let her stay by herself in some fancy, cold hotel room. That just won't do. I hope you don't mind, Alex told Jerry your story and Jerry told me and I have to tell you, I cried like a baby. It has to be one of the most romantic stories I've ever heard. I'm so proud of Alex for saving you. You know you'll be safe here. We'll watch over you." Without missing a beat, she went on. "Towels are in the connecting bathroom and extra blankets are in the closet. I'm glad we don't have stairs, they'd be hard for you to master with your cane. I hope you like breakfast, we always have big family breakfasts in the summer. I guess you'll be having corrective surgery soon. I dare say Alex did an excellent job on your leg. It's amazing you can even walk."

Teresa barely took a breath in between her words. Alyssa smiled. Either she'd stop talking or pass out any minute now. She stopped talking.

"Teresa, thank you so much." Maybe Teresa talked non-stop, but she also listened intently when you spoke. "There's something I'd better tell you—Alex doesn't know yet—I just found out yesterday. I'm pregnant, about six weeks." She was about to explain that she couldn't have the surgery because of the pregnancy, but Teresa let out a huge holler, jumped up and down, and was so excited that Alyssa couldn't help but beam. Teresa asked if they could tell Jerry. Alyssa nodded. She called Jerry into the room and excitedly told him the news. Jerry congratulated her, smiled, but then his look turned solemn and they all fell silent.

Alyssa couldn't help it, feeling embarrassed, she started to cry. Teresa held her while she cried and Jerry rubbed her back.

"There, there, now, you just let it out and don't you worry about anything. We're going to get Alex back, mark my words, Alyssa, we'll think of a way. We women have our ways, now don't we? A baby! Oh my, he'll be so happy. A baby changes everything, you know."

Alyssa smiled through her tears, knowing she had a friend in Teresa. After they left, she changed into a nightgown Teresa let her borrow. She winced as the movement brought on pain from the sight of her stab wound. That day seemed so long ago now.

She desperately needed to shop for clothing. Jerry had brought her clothing belonging to Christa to wear home from the hospital. She appreciated their kindness and wondered what she would've done without them.

The paperwork from Alex sat on the dresser. Alyssa opened the bank book and saw the 'hefty sum' of money he'd left her for 'whatever she may need.'

Five-hundred-thousand dollars. Half-a-million.

Oh my.

≈

THE NEXT EVEVING Alyssa approached Jerry—absorbed in paperwork—in his study.

"Come on in, Alyssa, I'm about finished here. I've completed the arrangements for the delivery of Alex's supplies this year. This will be the first time I haven't gone up there and overseen the delivery. They've got it down to clockwork. I'm sure everything will be fine. With all that's happened, I feel I'm needed here right now. Not to mention the fact that I'm still a little peeved with Alex for leaving."

This news sent a shiver of regret through Alyssa. She'd helped Alex write the list for this year's deliveries. She should be there with him, poring over their new supplies and organizing them into the supply room. She thought about all of the things they'd looked forward to receiving and longed to be with Alex at the cabin. She didn't understand how he could've left her.

Sitting in a chair across from Jerry's desk, she didn't waste any time getting right to the point. "When can you take me to see Alex?"

Jerry sat back in his office chair and studied her. "Honestly, Alyssa, I think we need to give Alex a little time to miss you before we go traipsing up there."

"How long?"

"A month," he suggested.

Despair washed over her, surprising in its strength.

"I also think you need time to get your health back. You have the baby to think of now. I'll make you a deal. You concentrate on your health. Eat well, get plenty of exercise, start on your vitamins, and see the doctor. In exchange, I'll make all of the arrangements to go and see Alex exactly one month from today. Deal?"

She didn't want to wait a month. But she saw the logic and the wisdom in his thinking.

"Spoken like a true doctor. Okay, deal." Alyssa turned to leave.

"Alyssa, may I ask, what will you do when you see him?"

She stared into space. "I don't know. Tell him about the baby. Tell him how much I love him. Beg him not to leave me." She glanced at Jerry, embarrassed by her words. "I'm sorry."

"Don't apologize. I want to see the two of you together and happy again."

≈

ALYSSA LOWERED HER eyes as a look of sadness shadowed her features. Jerry was concerned about her, much more than he let on. He loved Alex like a brother and he thought Alyssa was perfect for him. She obviously loved him deeply. And Alex was obviously besotted with her. He would do anything to help these two work things out. They'd been through so much together. Teresa planned on keeping her busy and it would be the best thing for her.

"Everything will work out, Alyssa. I know it will."

"Thank you, Jerry," she whispered and left the room.

-24-

ALYSSA DID EXACTLY what they'd talked about. She set out to be the healthiest pregnant woman alive. Her days were spent at Clay's bedside, willing him to wake up, all the while taking good care of herself and her unborn baby. While she was thrilled Clay was alive, she knew the fact that he was in a coma hadn't really registered as yet. How could she feel sadness when her son still lived? She yearned for him to awaken. It was like being teased by happiness or having it dangled out in front of you and then having it snatched away just as your fingers grasped it. Regardless, it was a miracle he was alive and for that, she was thankful.

On the opposite end of the spectrum, she longed for the day when she could see Alex again and tell him the news of their baby. Surprisingly, the month went by quickly. Teresa took her shopping and out to lunch on several occasions. She was slowly building up a decent wardrobe, but with maternity clothes just around the corner, she didn't want to buy too much. Secretly, she missed Alex's clothes.

True to his word, Jerry took her to see Alex exactly one month later. As they sat aboard the helicopter, she was a bundle of nerves, having no idea what she would say to Alex or how he would respond to her showing up. In her mind, she imagined him taking her in his arms and kissing her. Then he'd say, "Let's never be apart again, ever." She was a little over two months pregnant, but not showing yet. Having lost so much weight during her recovery, she'd just barely regained her normal weight.

Teresa helped her pick an outfit that befit the location and yet, in her words, would 'knock him dead.' She wore a pair of slim fitting jeans and a dark brown square necked t-shirt with a jade blue necklace. She bought a pair of comfortable brown boots that were easy for her to walk in. He'd never seen her in real clothes, but he'd always wanted to. A small overnight bag sat in the helicopter. She hoped Alex would want her to stay. *He'll be so happy when he learns of the baby. I'm sure of it.* Still, as they landed in the clearing, her heartbeat fluttered and her hands clenched together nervously.

I'm back, I'm finally back.

"Everything's going to be okay, Alyssa," Jerry said reassuringly. "Go get your man."

Alyssa nodded. *Please be happy to see me, Alex, please.*

She made her way through the trees to the cabin. It was nearly the end of June. It was only a year ago that she'd arrived at the cabin. It seemed like such a long time ago now. When she walked into the clearing, Alex was already outside, waiting to see who'd entered his sanctuary. The sound of a helicopter was his doorbell.

When they saw each other, they both stopped dead in their tracks and took each other in.

The sight of Alex, after not seeing him for a month, made her heartbeat flutter. Taking a deep breath, she walked closer, very slowly, limping more than usual and still using the cane he'd made for her. Without him as 'taskmaster,' she wasn't walking nearly as well.

He hadn't shaved in a couple of days, she noticed. She didn't remember him ever not shaving in the morning when he arose, even during their winter months together. His hair was overly long and disheveled as if he'd just gotten out of bed. In all of their time together, she'd never seen him like this. She had to admit, she liked it. He looked ruggedly handsome. He wore his jeans, a white t-shirt and a men's button up dress shirt. The shirt was unbuttoned down the front and at the cuffs, untucked, slightly wrinkled and looked as if he'd hastily thrown it on. He wore his slippers. She remembered thinking they were loafers when she'd met him.

"Hi." She smiled at him.

"Hi." He did not smile back.

Her smile faded and her heart sank. Disappointment crept in and she desperately tried to hold it at bay. It wasn't the reunion she'd anticipated.

"You look good, Alyssa. Are you well?"

"Yes, I'm better." And then, "How's your shoulder?"

He shrugged. "As well as can be expected."

They continued to study each other. It had been a long month apart.

"You didn't have the corrective surgery?"

"No, not yet, they wanted me to wait till I was stronger." It wasn't the time to blurt out the fact that she was pregnant and couldn't have the surgery as yet. Perhaps it would now seem a desperate act, a way to hold onto him.

"Clay?" he inquired hopefully.

"Still has not woken up," she responded, hating the disappointment in his features. *Problem not solved. I still can't live here with you.*

Silence.

They continued to get their fill of each other with their eyes. Snippets of memories paraded through her thoughts: the first time their eyes met, eating a piece of cornbread at his gentle hands, the look they'd shared as Adam attacked and he'd slid the knife to her and she caught it perfectly by the handle, waking up to find him sitting by her bed as she recovered, their water fight on laundry day, their first emotional kiss in the remembrance yard, kissing in the moonlight during their picnic in the dark, the vision of him falling to his knees and asking her to marry him, the look on his face as he said his wedding vows to her, his lips only an inch away from hers, and making love with him next to a roaring fire in a snowbound cabin. Her stomach clenched at the feelings these memories evoked.

Alyssa wanted to throw her arms around him, but somehow didn't think he would welcome it. A pain in her chest overwhelmed her. She swallowed and tried to remain calm.

Please love me, Alex.

She wondered if she'd made a mistake in coming. Her eyes wandered around the area. The garden was gone. It was just a pile of dirt. All of the flowers they'd planted in front of the cabin were dead. Alex had let those things go. The fence she and Adam had knocked over had been repaired. The thought of that day made her shudder. Her gaze returned to Alex. They had to talk, they couldn't leave things dangling the way they were. She searched his face, probing for any signs of softness and finding none.

"Can we talk?" she finally said, simply.

"Let's go inside."

Entering the cabin again was like walking back in time. It was filled with so many memories. Alyssa closed her eyes and wished for it to be another time—the time when she was so happy here. It was the condition of the cabin, however, that gave her pause. Alex was always so meticulously neat and clean. Shock registered on her face as her eyes took everything in. Dishes were on the table and scattered on the kitchen counter along with opened cans of food that had yet to be thrown in the garbage. The curtains she'd made were nowhere to be seen. The bed was unmade and the blankets were a tangled mess. The patchwork quilt sat in a heap on the floor. Her side of the bed was stacked with books. Her nightstand had been removed. His clothing was strewn about as if he'd taken off the item of clothing, thrown it down, and wherever it landed was its new home. The throw rugs—to include the rug that normally sat in front of the fireplace—were gone. They'd spent countless hours on that rug locked in each other's arms. It saddened her that it was missing. She felt her confidence slip. The rocker he'd made her for Christmas was also gone and she wondered what he'd done with it. Her eyes wandered around the cabin and then flew to him, "Are you okay?"

He shrugged again. "Never been better," he said, his face deadpan. "I'm still recovering from my shoulder injury. I haven't felt like doing much lately."

Oh yeah, his shoulder. For a minute there she'd thought he was depressed without her. So much for wishful thinking. If she didn't know better she would say Alex had given up on life. But then, maybe she didn't know him as well as she thought she did. She noticed he'd cut out a picture of her from the newspaper. It was taped to a kitchen cupboard. A couple of years ago, Sam wanted a nice picture of her and she'd gone to a portrait studio to have it done. She'd given one to her father, also. It was the picture that ended up getting plastered in the newspaper when she was missing and then, again, when she was found. She stared at it, remembering she'd been thinking of Sam when the picture was taken. She turned and faced Alex. It was Alex she was thinking about now. She realized—apart from the grainy newspaper photo—all evidence of her had been removed from the cabin. He had erased her from his life. Even the crocheted hat and scarf she'd made him no longer sat on a hook by the door. She suddenly felt very unsure of him and the feeling overwhelmed her.

≈

"I DIDN'T HEAR the helicopter leave." Alex wanted so much to take her in his arms and kiss her. He missed her so much. He thought of her every waking moment. She filled his dreams at night. He let only his eyes feast upon her. He knew she was shocked at the condition of the cabin. He didn't feel like doing anything lately. So he didn't. He knew he was mourning the loss of her from his life and he'd let himself fall into an indifference about everything he knew wasn't healthy. But, he didn't care.

"It hasn't left. They're waiting to see what I want them to do."

She wants to stay. I want you to stay too, Alyssa, more than anything. But it can't be. Alex knew this was the time he had to end it once and for all, for both of their sakes. He thought about what would happen if they tried to keep a long distance relationship going. He didn't want to constantly have someone begging him to come back. It wouldn't happen at first, but eventually it would. Bitterness would settle in. It would ultimately destroy them. What kind of relationship would that be?

The thought of going back was abhorrent to Alex. It was out of the question. He was absolutely not willing to live in civilization again. And she can't live here anymore. It's best to end this once and for all. Someday when Clay is better, he'd be back for her, if she'd have him. But for right now, Sterling was right. Clay needed her, all of her. He had to let her go. He had to make her go. It was the decent thing to do. They couldn't be together anymore. He knew Alyssa would hang onto their relationship and it would kill her. It was all or nothing. She'd never let go of him unless she believed he didn't want her anymore. It was time for her to go on with her life without him. *I have to make her believe I don't want her anymore.*

This wasn't going to be easy.

"I've missed you, Alex. It came as a shock to me when you left."

He didn't respond and he didn't look her in the eyes.

"What do we do now?"

Alex turned his back on her. He couldn't look at her while he said things he didn't mean. "I think we both know it's over, Alyssa."

There was a long silence.

He went on, "We met at a time when we both needed companionship and it was good for awhile. I think we both knew it couldn't last." He winced inside. When he was met with silence again, he turned to look at her.

Her eyes were wide and unblinking, her mouth slightly parted in surprise. When his eyes met hers, she lowered her eyes to the floor and her fingers turned white as she clenched her cane with a death grip. Her other hand covered her stomach and he wondered if she was going to be sick. It was obvious she hadn't expected him to say such things. Why would she? He wondered if she would see right through him.

"We're married, Alex. It's not over," she said softly.

He turned his back on her once again. He rested his hands on the fireplace mantle and stared into the fire. "There's not a court in the country that would consider our marriage legal. You know it and I know it. We married ourselves, we can unmarry ourselves. I release you from our marriage. I release you from our promises to each other."

His words hung in the air between them. He closed his eyes. He'd meant every word he said to her that day. In his mind, they were married and always would be.

"Alex," she whispered. "How can you say that?"

Indeed, how could he?

This wasn't going well. Alyssa approached, placing one hand on his shoulder. "I love you, Alex, please . . ."

He shrugged her hand off his shoulder and stepped away from her. Alex knew if he held her he would never be able to follow through with this. She stood so close, he could feel her breath on his face. Anger at their situation got the best of him. Alex looked her in the eyes and through gritted teeth said, "What do you want from me? You want money, is that it? What I left you with wasn't enough?"

She froze and her eyebrows knit. "What?" she whispered, almost inaudibly. "Is that what you think?"

Alex took several steps away from her, let out his breath and ran his fingers through his hair. He faced her with a safe distance between them and said, "No, that's not what I think. I'm sorry, that was uncalled for." He didn't know why he said it. He absolutely knew Alyssa loved him for himself. Money was most definitely the one thing that did not stand between them. He wanted this confrontation to be over and it was the first thing that came to his mind, knowing it would hurt her. He found he couldn't let her believe he thought that of her.

"I don't want anything from you. I just want to be with you," she whispered, softly, pleadingly, her voice thick with emotion, confusion in her eyes.

He was touched at her words and took one step towards her, hardly able to control himself. Their eyes met and held and for those few moments Alex almost gave in. He imagined picking her up, pressing his lips to hers, carrying her to the bed and . . .

Aggravated, he swiftly turned his back to her again.

≈

ALYSSA WONDERED WHY he wouldn't face her. She'd seen his look soften at her words, was sure she saw the love in his eyes, but then his face hardened and the moment was gone in an instant. Had she imagined it? A feeling of panic arose. He didn't want her to touch him, he didn't even want to be near her.

"Look, it was fun while it lasted, but it's over. I release you. Now I'm asking you to leave, please go."

Fun? Is that really what he thought of their time together? "You don't mean that."

"Try me."

"Then say it to my face," she challenged and then immediately wished she could take it back.

Alex whirled around, took a step closer and yelled, "It's over, Alyssa, how many times are you going to make me say it before it sinks in? It's over, our marriage is over. I do not want you here anymore, do you understand? I want to be alone in my cabin, without you. I'm politely asking you to, please, turn around and leave. Go home."

≈

ALYSSA FLINCHED AT his words and took a step backwards as if she'd been physically hit. The look on her face was one of utter devastation. Alex watched as her face drained of color. He knew in his heart his words had come out much harsher than planned.

"I . . ." She continued to look at him in stunned disbelief. Her eyes blinked ever so slowly as if her eyelids were very heavy. "But . . ." Her eyes filled with tears. Several tense moments passed.

"Oh . . ." Understanding dawned. She lowered her eyes as she slowly backed up till she ran into one of the kitchen chairs and sat down.

Alex watched as she brought a shaking hand up to move the hair out of her eyes. A sob escaped. She placed her hand over her mouth to quiet the sobs. He watched as she literally crumpled in front of him. He turned his back to her again. He couldn't watch. He was about to take her in his arms and say, *You're right, I don't mean it. I love you, I'll love you forever.*

Too late, the deed was done. She was free. Free to be with Clay, free to go on with her life, and not worry about him anymore. Suddenly, he couldn't remember why that was so important. Was it really worth all of this? *I'm sorry, Alyssa. This is the way it has to be. It's for the best.*

≈

IT DIDN'T GET any clearer than that. Alyssa finally got it. He didn't want her. He'd already said goodbye. It was over for him. It was foolish of her to come. She didn't know what she'd expected, but this wasn't it. Alyssa couldn't control her tears and she didn't want Alex to hear or see her like this. An idea had formed in her mind. It was something he'd said earlier and suddenly she knew what she was going to do.

"This isn't o-over, Alex."

She tried to sound firm, but the words came out in between sobs and the effect was lost. Alyssa walked out, slamming the door as hard as she could. The 'Honeymoon Cabin' sign above the door fell at her feet, lying on the ground, broken in two. Somehow this was significant. The sign was broken and so were their lives. Falling to her knees, she picked up the pieces and held them to her heart, wanting to save them, something to remember happier times by.

Alyssa knew what she had to do. She made her way to the grove where they'd married, sobbing all the way, her tears blurring her vision. When she arrived in their grove she went straight to the gazebo, the sight making her chest constrict tightly. Once, she had experienced happiness beyond her wildest dreams there. But not today, perhaps never again. She opened the compartment under the gazebo and pulled out the lockbox, hugging it to herself as she cried.

Alex didn't want her anymore.

-25-

AFTER ALYSSA LEFT the cabin, Alex slowly moved to the table and sat down. He held his head in his hands. *What have I done?*

He'd just let go of the person he loved most in his life. He knew he had to let her go. There was no other way. He half expected her to yell and fight, but that wasn't Alyssa. It would've been easier if she had raged at him. Instead, her reaction had been heart wrenching.

Something began to nag at him. Suddenly, he knew what Alyssa was doing, where she was going, and what she was getting. He was out the door in seconds, knowing he couldn't allow her to do it. In record time, he was in the grove. Just as he thought, there she was, holding the lockbox. She held it to her heart and leaned heavily on the gazebo, sobbing. It broke his heart to see her this way but, he couldn't let her take those papers.

"That's my property, Alyssa. Give it to me, I can't allow you to take it," he said tersely. He was burning mad that this was happening. This wasn't the way it was supposed to be.

≈

STARTLED, ALYSSA LOOKED up at Alex. She'd never heard that tone of voice from him or seen him look so angry. That this was happening seemed incomprehensible. This isn't what she'd come here for. Alyssa didn't want to fight with him. Although she didn't feel it inside, she said to him in an unwavering tone, "I'm taking it, Alex."

She hugged the lockbox and the pieces of the sign to her chest with one hand, while the other hand held her cane. She turned and started walking away from him. He ran after her. Even though she picked up her step, he caught up in no time, standing in front of her, blocking the way.

They faced each other and she saw steely determination in his eyes. They'd pledged their love to one another in this very spot and now, here they were, at odds with one another. For the first time since she'd met him, she felt fear course through her and wondered how far he would go to not let her take their marriage papers.

But she wasn't giving up either.

Alyssa tried to go around, he blocked the way. She tried another way, he blocked the way. After the third time, their eyes met and they faced each other, breathing hard.

"Give it to me, Alyssa. It belongs to me," he said icily.

"No!" she screamed at him.

≈

ALYSSA COULD HARDLY speak through her tears. Alex had never seen her cry like that. He'd never seen anyone cry like that.

"Let me pass!" she yelled.

"No," he said coldly, knowing those papers could crucify him in the media. He saw the fear in her eyes and hated himself for it. He grabbed for the lockbox as she dropped her cane and held on with both hands. They struggled, each pulling on the lockbox. She was no match for him, but she wasn't going to give in. Alyssa yanked the box away from him and turned.

Alex came to his senses. *What am I doing?* Not wanting to hurt her, he let go.

She wasn't expecting him to let go. The momentum of yanking the box away as she tried to turn and walk the other way caused her to fall to the ground face first with a thud.

Alyssa did not let go of the lockbox.

The pieces of the 'honeymoon cabin' sign lay scattered,

mocking them. Alyssa lay on the ground, crying, and didn't immediately get up.

Alex closed his eyes. *How did it get to this? How did I let things get this far, this out of control?* His anger left him. "Alyssa, I'm sorry. Are you okay? Let me help you up." He reached out to help her.

"Don't touch me!" she screamed as she struggled to her feet. She recovered the pieces of the sign. Alex held the cane for her.

"Can I have my cane or do you want to keep that too?" she raged.

He handed her the cane. "I'm so sorry," he said. He didn't want things to end like this and yet he knew the words he'd just said to her had hurt her deeply.

All at once, she threw the cane at his feet. She took the pieces of the 'honeymoon cabin' sign and threw them at his feet too.

"I . . . don't . . . *want* . . . them!" she shrieked the word, want, as loud as she could.

Alyssa was so worked up, her breath came in gasps. She turned and began to walk with a wobbly limp towards the helicopter, nearly losing her balance several times.

"Alyssa, wait. Don't leave like this."

He stood in front of her again, blocking her way. They faced each other, both breathing raggedly, torn at what was happening between them.

"Don't leave like this? Like what?" she cried with great agitation. "You asked me to leave, remember?"

The words, 'hell hath no fury' passed through his mind as he looked at her sorrowfully.

≈

SEEING THE REMORSE in Alex's eyes, Alyssa took several deep breaths and lowered her eyes to the ground, feeling humiliated, as if she was behaving like a madwoman. Desperately, she tried to regain her composure and retain some dignity, while wondering if she could die of a broken heart.

"I came here because I love you. What do you want from me?" she asked through her tears, laying her heart out in front of him, only to have him stomp on it.

"I don't want it to end like this," he told her.

So, this is the end. "I'll pay you back every dime, it will take me some time, but I'll pay it all back to you," she said, her breath coming in gasps. It was suddenly very important for him to know that.

"No, Alyssa, no," he said tenderly. "I want you to have it. I want you and Clay to be happy and comfortable. If you need anything, it's yours. I'd give you anything." He touched her cheek and then quickly dropped his hand to his side. "I don't want you to pay anything back to me. I didn't mean what I said."

"Then why say it?" She could barely speak through her tears. In anger people often said what was bothering them deep inside and now she knew how he really felt.

"I was angry, I'm sorry."

"I don't understand. Why are you angry with me?" she said in her brutally honest fashion. Tears rolled down her face and she didn't try to hide them, even though she hated herself for breaking down in front of Alex. She'd never felt so humiliated in her life. While she loved him intensely, he'd completely turned her down. It hurt so much she could barely breathe.

≈

ALYSSA HAD A point. He'd been grasping at anything to say to make her leave before he gave in and took her in his arms and kissed her. Indeed, why would he be angry with her when she'd traveled a great distance to come and tell him she loved him? He was angry at their circumstances, he was angry at himself for saying things he didn't mean, but she didn't know that. All she knew was he'd suddenly turned on her. He could see the confusion in her eyes as he sent mixed messages. He needed to be firm.

Alex looked her directly in the eyes and said resolutely, "I'm angry that it's over. But it's the way I want it to be." He hesitated at saying the next words, but knew he had to say it, "It's over for me."

She stared right back into his eyes for several seconds as if she was trying to read his thoughts. The words he'd uttered finally registered in her befuddled brain. He swore a light turned off in her eyes at that moment.

Alyssa lowered her gaze and let her head hang down. The lockbox was still held tightly to her chest. Her right hand reached over to her left hand and began to remove her wedding ring.

Alex quickly covered her hands with his. "Keep it, please keep it. I want you to have it," he whispered.

They stood that way for a few precious moments, her hands in his, until she broke the contact. He hated the feel of her pulling away from him, something he'd never once experienced.

Her voice became very quiet as she said softly, "Please let me leave."

He realized he was still blocking her way, preventing her from leaving. He moved out of the way and said again, "I'm so sorry."

Alyssa kept walking, with difficulty without her cane. He followed, not really wanting her to leave. She didn't try to hide the fact that she was crying, that she was devastated. All thoughts of pride had left her. He'd once longed for Alyssa to love him fiercely. He knew now that she did and he was throwing it all away. After going through so much, he hated doing this to her. She didn't deserve this treatment. He knew he'd confused her with his words when the look in his eyes must've spoken volumes. They'd shared so much and he knew she was completely taken aback. Deep in her heart, she knew he loved her, didn't she?

When he saw Jerry standing by the helicopter, he froze. Jerry looked from Alyssa to Alex.

"Go, let's go. Hurry!" she yelled. That she thought he was going to try to take the lockbox again was obvious. Briefly, he wondered whose side Jerry would be on.

"Alyssa, wait . . ."

She turned to him one last time, holding onto the lockbox for dear life. Even then he could see a semblance of hope in her eyes. He paused, momentarily taken aback at the sight of her. Even with her tears, she looked so absolutely beautiful, perhaps even more so because of the emotion and vulnerability apparent on her face.

"I . . ." What? What could he possibly say to make everything okay? "I'm so sorry," he said again, hating the look of defeat on her face.

≈

JERRY DIDN'T UNDERSTAND what was going on. Alyssa was crying uncontrollably and Alex looked stricken. Alyssa boarded the helicopter with Jerry's help. Jerry then approached Alex.

"What the hell were you thinking, Alex? Marrying yourselves?"

"What would you have done?" Alex fired back.

Jerry studied his old friend. He loved him like a brother, but he didn't understand his actions. "I don't know," he answered him, subdued. But then he added, "Have an affair. The rest of the world does it without blinking an eye."

"I couldn't do that and neither could Alyssa. And I know you, Jerry, neither could you," Alex said very quietly.

Jerry let it go, knowing his friend spoke the truth. Maybe in their circumstances he would have done the same, but he couldn't imagine even coming up with the crazy idea. "What's going on?"

Alex avoided the question. "Don't forget to send the

helicopter for me in two months," he reminded. "And please take care of her, Jerry. If she needs *anything*, it's hers." And with that, he turned and went back to the cabin.

Jerry couldn't get Alyssa to speak the entire trip home. During the helicopter ride she cried like a baby. She hugged a metal box to her and wouldn't part with it. Once back in Reno, they caught a commercial flight home and although Alyssa had stopped sobbing, the tears never stopped rolling down her cheeks.

≈

ALEX HEARD THE helicopter leave. As if in a trance, he went to his workshop, working for the next two hours at repairing the 'honeymoon cabin' sign. It suddenly seemed so important to him that it be fixed. When it was fixed to his satisfaction, he hung it up over the door in its rightful position. He placed Alyssa's cane on his mantle. He stoked the fire in the fireplace and sat down on the couch. His shoulder ached. It was healed and he could use it. But it would never be the same. He and Alyssa both had battle scars given to them by Adam. They were an actual, physical, constant reminder that their time together wasn't a dream, it was real.

He wondered what she would do with those papers. *Please don't do anything rash, Alyssa, please.* Those papers would put the final nail in his coffin if the media got wind of it. Still, in the end, he couldn't take them from her. He wasn't about to fight her for them, he didn't want to hurt her. He wasn't proud of his behavior today. He couldn't believe he let things get so out of hand. He didn't want this to be a memory, especially in the grove where they'd married.

What have I done? The irony was he didn't want to ruin their relationship by trying to keep up a long distance romance. And yet he'd done exactly that and he'd broken her heart in the process. He didn't know how he'd expected her to react, but somehow he hadn't realized how heart wrenching it would be. The sight of her crying for him had broken *his* heart. "I'm sorry, Alyssa." He didn't see any other way. If he'd told her the truth, he knew she wouldn't have accepted it.

I just want to be with you.

More than anything else, those words spoken so plainly, so simply, so honestly, haunted him. He'd seen the overwhelming love in her eyes. She'd looked so good, so beautiful. She'd had so much hope in her eyes. He'd seen it, he'd felt it.

He'd squashed any and all hope she harbored.

He buried his face in his hands and cried for the first time in years.

≈

"COME IN," ALYSSA said after Jerry knocked on her door early the next morning.

Jerry entered, dressed in scrubs, and ready for work. After studying Alyssa for a moment, he took note of her puffy eyes and defeated demeanor. The metal box was now sitting on the nightstand, opened.

"Can I speak with you?"

"Yes."

Jerry sat on the chair next to the bed while Alyssa watched him listlessly, as if there was no life left in her. "May I ask what happened?"

"He doesn't want me anymore. He said we married ourselves, so we can unmarry ourselves. He releases me from our promises to each other. He doesn't want me to be at the cabin with him. He *politely* asked me to leave."

It was the way she said it that alarmed Jerry the most. She spoke matter of factly, in a soft tone, as if repeating a memorized verse. There were no more tears. She was eerily calm.

"Did you tell him about the baby?"

"No."

"I see."

"He told me he didn't want me anymore. All thought of the baby left me. I don't want him to be with me only for the baby."

"He has a right to know."

"Does he?" she said defensively and then immediately deflated. "I know he does." They sat in silence for a few moments.

"Alyssa, I have one question for you. Please forgive me for asking. Do you love him or do you love him for saving your life?"

A fleeting look of anguish crossed her features. "At first, I admit to a feeling of hero worship. He seemed larger than life. I was grasping for any lifeline and he was there. You can't imagine the despair I was in when I arrived at his cabin. He was my only hope. I loved him even then. My love for him grew every day I was there." She looked him in the eyes. "Yes, I love him, more than I've ever loved anyone in my life—as a woman loves a man."

"I'm sorry, I had to ask. Now tell me this, do you believe he loves you?"

She was quiet for several moments, contemplating the question. Then she looked him directly in the eyes again and said, "I know he loves me. I have no doubt of it. Even after yesterday's fiasco, which I haven't come to terms with as yet."

Jerry smiled at her, but still no smile crossed her lovely features. "I've known Alex a long time. I know he loves you too. I know by the way he looks at you, I know by the way he speaks of you, I know by the way he wants to take care of you. So, we have to ask ourselves a question. Why is Alex doing this? What is his motivation?"

He saw a flash of hope in her eyes as the thought whirled in her mind. "What are you saying?"

"Think, Alyssa, why would Alex do this?"

"He wants to be alone. He can't face his life here, he

wants to live at the cabin. And I can't leave . . ." She trailed off.

"Why can't you leave?"

"Because . . . I need to be with Clay."

"It would appear we have a problem, now wouldn't it?"

"That makes no sense. I know he wants to live and die at the cabin. But surely we can work something out that suits us both, it doesn't mean we can't ever be together. I respect his wishes to live up there, he knows that. But I can't now and . . . do you really think that's why he's ending things with me?"

"I think he realizes the impossibility of the two of you staying together. I think he loves you enough to let you go." Jerry didn't mention Alex's trip home in two months. He'd let that remain a surprise.

"But not enough to stay here with me," she countered. When he started to respond, she held her hand up. "Don't answer that, I know why he can't stay here, I even understand, I really do. I just miss him so much." She thought for a moment. "Why didn't he talk with me about it? We could've worked something out."

"Would you really have accepted that, Alyssa?"

≈

ALYSSA PAUSED. "YES, of course I would have . . ." She thought about living here by herself with their new baby and with Clay. All of the responsibility would be on her. "I don't know . . ." She thought about only seeing Alex on the weekends if even that. She would have to do all of the traveling. It wasn't a short trip. It would be hard on small children. Would Clay ever be able to make such a trip? It would be an impossible situation. "No, I guess not."

"Look, please don't take it personally that Alex wants to be at his cabin. He was gone for three years and the minute he comes back the media is all over him once again. It's not you he's running from. Besides, I'm not sure our Alex will last long at the cabin this time around. Give him some time. I think we may find he comes back here before long. And when he does, look out, he'll be coming for you."

"Do you really think so?"

"Yes, I do. Now, how about solving my curiosity about this metal box. What on earth is in this?"

"Take a look."

Jerry studied its contents for several minutes.

"He fought me for it. He didn't want me to take the papers. In the end, he let me have them." Tears filled her eyes at the thought of the way they had fought in their grove. She'd never seen him so angry before, at least, not directed at her.

"And what will you do with them, Alyssa?"

"I'm going to have our marriage declared legal. It was something we planned on doing." Her voice cracked, her composure slipped. The tears rolled down her face and she wiped them away.

"Alyssa, are you sure you want to do that? Do you realize what will happen? It means a court appearance and media attention. It means Alex will have to come back. He'll hate that. Do you really want to do that to him?"

"No, I don't," she sighed. "Now that I've had time to think it over, I can't do it. The media attention would destroy him. I realize that now."

"Just go down to the county courthouse, sign some papers and your marriage will be legal."

"It takes two. And he wants out."

Jerry glanced at his watch. "I've gotta go in a minute. But I want you to think about this, Alyssa. I believe Alex has already thought this through. I believe he saw no other option than to end things. He believes he's doing the right thing because he knows you wouldn't have accepted it any other way. He believes there's no way for the two of you to be together. I don't believe for a moment he doesn't want you anymore." He let his words register. "And I don't believe he wants out of your marriage."

Alyssa longed for it to be true. She was still stunned at his words.

All at once, Jerry took one of her hands in both of his, surprising her, and said with great emotion, "Don't give up on him, Alyssa, he needs you. He was devastated at the loss of his family. He's still not over it, as much as he'd like to think he is. That's why he can't come back yet. I beg you to not give up on him. He loves you, he needs you."

Alyssa nodded, too choked up to speak. After Jerry left, she mulled over what he'd said. Could Jerry be right?

"It's over for me."

The look on his face as he said those final words would haunt her for a long time to come. Although sadness gripped her, she got herself up and went about her day, knowing Clay needed her, knowing the life growing inside of her was depending on her, and knowing in her heart how happy Alex would be when he learned of it.

It was the only thing that kept her going.

≈

ALYSSA HAD A nightmare that night. She was in the cabin. Adam and Pa were there. They were tying the ropes onto her neck and wrists. They were laughing and taunting her. Alex stood there watching and he didn't do anything to help. He said, "Go ahead and take her. She's too much trouble." He turned and left. She pleaded for help, screaming at him, *please save me, please don't leave me, come back, please come back!*

Alyssa came to her senses in a panic and saw a worried Jerry and Teresa looking in on her, the other children trailing in behind them. Tears were pouring down her face and her nightgown was moist with sweat. With confusion she took in her surroundings.

"Alyssa, you were screaming. Are you okay?" Teresa asked with concern.

"I'm sorry, I'm fine, really. It was just a nightmare. Go back to bed, I'm sorry I bothered you." Embarrassed to have awoken the household, Alyssa tried to hide her shaking hands.

They left reluctantly. Teresa reminded her she was just down the hallway if she needed anything and closed the door.

Alyssa collapsed onto her bed. There was no Alex to hold her and comfort her. There was no Alex to wipe away her tears or cool her down with a cold washcloth on her forehead. She couldn't lay her head on his chest and fall asleep to the sound of his heartbeat or the feel of his fingers running through her hair. And for that, she cried herself back to sleep.

≈

OUTSIDE IN THE hallway, Jerry and Teresa could hear her softly crying. They exchanged worried glances. They had awoken to her screaming for Alex. She obviously hadn't realized she'd been screaming his name.

"All right, back to bed. Let's give her some space," Jerry said tiredly.

-26-

OVER THE NEXT couple of months, Alex tried to tell himself he was happy. He went about his chores and worked in the workshop. He found himself listening for the sound of a helicopter every day. He went to bed at night feeling disappointed Alyssa hadn't come to see him again. But then, why would she? He'd sent her away. He'd told her they were over.

Somehow, the cabin didn't have the appeal it once had. To his surprise, he found himself missing so many things. He longed to drive his car, fast, with the top down, and the wind in his face. He thought about going out to a movie and eating a tub of buttery, salty popcorn. He wanted to spread out on the couch and watch pay-per-view movies all day long. He wanted to ride a roller coaster till he was sick. He wanted to stay in a fancy hotel and order room service whenever he felt like eating and not have to get up and cook it himself. He wanted a bathroom with running water and an endless supply of hot water for a long, hot shower. He wanted to have a Saturday afternoon barbeque and invite the neighbors. He wanted to watch TV and see who was the next *American Idol* or the latest *Survivor*. He wanted to watch the news and debate about the latest hot topic.

And, most importantly, he wanted to do all of these things with Alyssa at his side.

Suddenly, he felt like he was missing out on something. Life was happening all around him and he was stagnating. Life simply stood still here and he didn't want to stand still anymore, he wanted to participate. He wanted to work in the medical field again. He wanted a huge, rambling house filled with children, laughing and playing and, yes, even jumping on the beds if they felt like it.

He wanted those children to be his and Alyssa's children.

He wanted to come home everyday to her. He wanted to see her face light up like it did when he walked into the cabin after having been out in the workshop. He longed for the greeting he always received from her when he walked in the door.

Life was worth living just for that.

He wanted to spend his nights with Alyssa in his arms, making love with her whenever he felt like it.

And if the media wanted to call him Dr. Death, then he'd go home and laugh about it with Alyssa. As long as he had her, he didn't really care what the hell they said. None of it seemed to matter much anymore.

Memories of their winter together permeated his thoughts. It had truly been a four month honeymoon and was the happiest he ever remembered being in his life. The thought of it made the days seem never ending and the nights, pure torture. As the long days passed, he made a decision. It was a life changing decision, but one he felt at peace about. He had to go to Alyssa and beg her forgiveness. He didn't want to be apart from her ever again, not even for one night.

For the rest of his life.

≈

ALYSSA CONTINUED TO spend her days at Clay's bedside. She was now just over four months along, and the weight gain gave her a glow of health. She still didn't look pregnant, but she felt good. Nevertheless, life without Alex was gray and dreary. As she sat next to Clay, day after day, she knew in her heart she could go on with her life if he would just wake up. She longed to see his precious smile and hold him in her arms and feel his little arms holding her back. Every day she silently thanked Sam for saving their son. She'd found great happiness with Alex. But Clay was a huge part of that great happiness too. And soon she would have Alex's baby. Her future did hold great happiness. She hadn't been able to see it when she was with Adam and Pa. Sam had been there for her even in death, letting her know she still had something to live for. Regardless, Alyssa knew she was simply going through the motions of life, simply existing.

Waiting for life to happen.

Consequently, it took her by great surprise when Teresa let slip that Alex was due in town the next day. Evidently, while he was in town the last time, he'd promised the hospital he'd speak at a benefit. This was news to Alyssa, yet she was pleased to hear Alex was willing to leave the cabin. It was huge progress. Jerry had purposely not told her he was coming. She approached him in his office that night.

"Alex will be in town this weekend?"

Jerry ran his hands over his face tiredly. "Teresa told you."

"Yes."

"He's never done this, Alyssa. I'm not sure what to make of it. I didn't want you to get your hopes up. I think, no, I *know* his willingness to come is because of you, not because he feels obligated to help the hospital. I think he wants to check up on you."

Alyssa nodded, but said nothing. Jerry hadn't heard his words on that awful day. He didn't know how firmly Alex had told her it was over. To be honest, it hurt that Alex would come back for a hospital benefit, but not for her.

Alyssa felt a great deal of trepidation at the thought of facing Alex, although she had no idea if she would even see him. The next day seemed interminable as she sat at Clay's bedside wondering if he would come waltzing through the hospital door at any moment.

He didn't.

It was early September and the lingering Indian summer had left her feeling hot, sticky, and sapped of energy. She looked forward to a shower and collapsing into bed. She entered the house as Casey came running to her, taking her by the hand.

"Alyssa, we have company, c'mon."

Alyssa smiled as Casey pulled her into the living room. When she looked up to see Alex, her smile died instantly, something that was clearly not lost on Alex.

"Hello, Alyssa," he said quietly.

Alyssa avoided his eyes as Teresa spoke.

"Now that Alex is in town, we thought it would be nice to have dinner together tonight. He just arrived and . . ." Teresa rambled on and Alyssa stopped listening.

"I already ate at the hospital," Alyssa blurted. She hadn't, but she wanted out of this obligation and it was the first thing that came to her mind. She didn't think she could sit through a dinner with Alex as if nothing was between them.

"Alyssa, you need to keep up your strength and hospital food won't do. You need a delicious home cooked meal," Teresa responded.

Alyssa felt like a child. There was nothing for it. She was trapped. "I'll just get cleaned up. Excuse me."

Alex looked puzzled. "Haven't you been living in the suite?" he asked.

"Oh, heavens no, Alex. We have her living right here with us in our guest room. We didn't want her to be alone," Teresa explained.

"That was good of you, Teresa. Thank you," Alex said with his eyes on her.

Alyssa said nothing as she turned and slowly made her way down the hall to her room, her heart heavy. Closing herself into her connecting bathroom, she leaned against the wall and stared at her reflection. Her cheeks were flushed. Her eyes looked wide, even to her. Her back slid down the wall till she was sitting. She curled her legs up close to her chest, resting her head on the wall and closing her eyes, willing herself to calm down.

I can't do this. I can't face him, not with how things are between us. She sat that way for a long time, till she could hear Teresa calling everyone to dinner. She had to go. They were waiting for her.

"Alyssa, are you okay?" Alex asked as she entered the dining room.

Of course, I'm not okay. Did you really think I would be? She didn't answer. They were interrupted by Casey, who begged Alex to sit by her.

He gave Casey a kiss on the cheek and told her she was his favorite girl. Teresa had told her Casey was the same age as his youngest daughter, Anna, would have been. It must be bittersweet for him. Casey clearly adored him. Alyssa could see a glimpse of the kind of father he'd been. Teresa served dinner and Alex continued to laugh and joke with Casey. He listened intently to everything she said, a captive audience to her ten year old thoughts.

Alyssa didn't feel like eating. Instead, she pushed her food around her plate with her fork, lost in thought. An overwhelming sadness came over her. Alex had the right to know about their baby. She supposed she could just blurt it out right now in front of everybody. His reaction ought to make for a rather riveting dinner.

But she didn't want to do that. The moment should be special. How did it come to this? Here they were sitting at a dinner table, miles apart. She loved him. She wanted to be with him. She wanted to touch him. She wanted him to look at her the way he used to.

Instead, it was as if they were both guests at a dinner party. Strangers, at that.

≈

ALEX NOTICED ALYSSA'S melancholy, but was distracted by her simple presence. He'd forgotten how beautiful her hair was. He loved it, he missed running his fingers through it, he missed washing it for her, he missed combing through it—anything to be able to simply touch her. But there was a stillness about her as if she was in another world, almost a dreamlike state. She looked unbearably sad. Her hands moved slowly and she stared at nothing in particular. She hadn't taken a bite of her dinner. He exchanged worried glances with Jerry and Teresa.

≈

"OUR MARRIAGE IS over, Alyssa." Alex's words echoed in her mind. That was the worst day of her life. Then she thought of all that had happened in the last year and corrected herself. *That was the second worst day of my life. How can so many bad things happen to one person? I must be cursed. Alex was the only good thing in my life. He washed away all the bad and made my life good. Now that he's gone, I have nothing.* Filled with self pity, her thoughts continued on in this vain, never once allowing herself to dwell on Clay or the baby growing inside of her. Instead, she thought only of the man across from her and how he didn't want her anymore.

"I want to be alone in my cabin, without you." How could he say that after all they'd shared? How could he sit here at this table with her and not feel anything?

"Alyssa?"

Taken out of her reverie, she mumbled, "What?" Everyone was looking at her. Her eyes rested on Alex.

"You were miles away," he commented casually, as if conversing socially with a stranger.

He was most definitely not a stranger to her. Memories of their time together played through her mind—the feel of her body beneath his, their bodies tangled together . . .

"I was wondering if you were eating all of the things you were craving while at the cabin. Let's see, if I remember correctly, it was pizza you missed the most."

He was trying to make conversation, and grasping at that. "Yeah . . ." she said distractedly. "I don't think . . . no, I guess I haven't had any pizza since I've been back." She lowered her eyes again. Feeling edgy, her hand began to fold and unfold the corner of her napkin.

All of the girls burst into conversation about what their favorite kind of pizza was and how they could never live without it for a year. They weren't leaving her out. They tried to include her in the conversation. But she felt left out all the same. Suddenly, she knew she didn't belong. She felt like an intruder. They were Alex's friends and she wondered what the heck she was doing here. Alyssa observed Alex talking animatedly, watching him while she brooded. They all laughed at what he said. He looked happy with a big smile on his face. He caught her looking at him and his smile slowly died. Averting her eyes, her thumb absentmindedly stroked the handle of her fork as she thought and continued to stare at nothing in particular.

Alex used to smile at her. His eyes used to sparkle when he looked at her.

"Alyssa, are you enjoying wearing real clothes?" To everyone else, he clarified with a chuckle, "She spent nearly a year with only my clothes to wear."

Her eyes locked with his. Memories flooded her thoughts—his gentle touch as he washed her face when she'd first arrived, the feel of him when he held her close after a nightmare, carrying her back to the cabin on the day she'd decided to try and leave, floating in the lake while he held her and whispered soft words in her ear, that first wild kiss when she'd challenged him with the words, 'why not?'

He was waiting for an answer.

"I've had so much fun taking her shopping," Teresa exclaimed.

"I'm sure the two of you have a great time together."

Memories continued to play like a movie in her head—the time he'd tickled her and she liked the feel of his hands on her, lying in the flower-filled meadow with their feet soaking in the creek, telling each other of their dreams and finding they had the same one, the way he'd kissed her the night they came up with the idea to marry themselves. The thought made her heartbeat rapidly increase. He'd kissed her with a passion that only hinted at what was to come between them, a passion left unfulfilled until their wedding night. Quickly, Alyssa brought herself back to the present. She was only causing herself pain to dwell on what once was.

Alex was waiting for her to say something. "Yeah . . . it's . . . nice," she told him unenthusiastically. Maybe if he hadn't dumped her, things would be different right now, she thought bitterly. The conversation around her continued. It registered, but she wasn't listening.

"Turn around and leave. Go home." The memory of his words would never leave her. She remembered the day he'd first kissed her in the remembrance yard, filled with such emotion. He had passion for her then. He'd said this was as bad as it gets, meaning life didn't get any worse. He was wrong. Sam couldn't be with her. The choice was taken from him. Alex had a choice and chose to not be with her. This was as bad as it gets. Tears were imminent.

"How is your father, Alyssa?" Alex asked.

"What?" She was in her own world of sorrow. He repeated the question.

"He often comes to see Clay," she answered, curtly. Avoiding his eyes, she arose, feeling unable to take anymore.

"If you'll excuse me, I have to go and . . . do some errands," she said quietly, casting one last glance at Alex as she limped pathetically out to her car. Even that wasn't hers. *What am I doing here? I have nothing. Adam took everything from me. Everything.*

"Alyssa, wait."

It was Alex, he was coming after her. She turned around to face him.

"Where are you going?" he asked with a frown, searching her face for answers.

The tears were about to fall. She had to leave. "Anywhere but here," she said in a whisper, climbing into her car — no *his* car — and driving off.

"Alyssa, wait, please . . ." she heard him plead.

She ignored him.

≈

ALEX WATCHED HER leave as his jaw clenched with tension. Sterling was wrong. He, himself, was wrong also. He hadn't freed her to go on with her life or simplified her life in any way. He'd hurt her beyond repair. He could see it in her eyes, he could feel her sadness as if it was a living, breathing thing.

"*I just want to be with you.*" Those words haunted him again as he walked back into the house. Everyone still sat at the table, only no one was talking or smiling anymore. They all looked like someone had just died. As Alex joined them, they sat in total silence for a few moments.

"Where will she go?" Alex asked. It was nine o' clock at night.

"I don't know. She never goes anywhere, except to see Clay," Jerry informed him.

Alex felt even worse. He'd left her when she needed him the most.

"Alyssa has nightmares," Casey said to Alex. "Sometimes she screams your name. It wakes me up at night."

He took a deep breath and ran his hand through his hair. It was time for him to leave. "Thank you for dinner, Teresa."

All night he wondered where Alyssa was and if she was okay. He knew in his heart she wasn't.

It was time to make amends.

Look out, Alyssa, I'm coming for you.

-27-

ALYSSA AWOKE THE next morning with a heavy heart. A soft knock sounded on her door. The clock read seven a.m. "Come in."

Jerry and Teresa were up, fully dressed and ready for the day. She wondered what was going on.

"Alyssa, get up, I'm taking you shopping," Teresa declared.

"Shopping?" She really didn't feel much like shopping.

"I think we'd better explain first," Jerry said to Teresa.

"What's going on?" she asked, sitting up quickly. "Is everything okay?"

"Everything's fine, relax."

Alyssa propped up her pillows and lay back down on her bed. Jerry closed the door to her room.

"We have a plan and we hope you'll go along with it," Jerry told her.

"A plan?"

Teresa took over. "Alex has agreed to attend a hospital benefit tonight. His family has always contributed a large sum of money every year to the Pediatric Cancer Center at the hospital. It was something that was important to his grandfather and he has carried on the tradition. When they found out he was in town last time, they asked him if he would speak at the benefit. I'm going to whisk you away and we're going shopping for a dress to knock his socks off. We'll spend a couple of hours at the salon and he won't know what has hit him when he sees you tonight."

"You want me to go to the benefit? He hasn't invited me."

"We have. We'll be there with you. The dress is black tie. It will be quite fancy. When Alex sees you dressed to the nines, he won't be able to contain himself. Let's just say it's a little push in the right direction," Teresa said excitedly.

They both stood there with silly smiles on their faces.

Alyssa was dumbfounded by their plan. Were they really serious? "He doesn't want me anymore," she stated quietly.

Jerry frowned, "Come now, Alyssa, we both know that's not true."

"C'mon, this is your chance, Alyssa. He won't be able to resist you, I guarantee it," Teresa coaxed.

Why not? It was worth a try. She wanted to see him, she couldn't deny it. Even though she feared rejection, she said, "Okay." After all, she had nothing to lose.

It was already over.

≈

THAT EVENING SHE was a bundle of nerves, however. Alex had made his feelings clear. What was she doing? Setting herself up for heartbreak? As it turned out, Casey became ill with the stomach flu and Teresa decided to stay home with her. Jerry was her escort for the evening. But if their plan worked, she would end up with Alex. The question was, would he want her?

To her surprise, Alex had stopped by the house three times during the day to see her. He'd also left her hand carved cane for her. Alyssa had to admit, she was glad to have it instead of the awful faux wood replacement cane Jerry had picked up for her. By late afternoon, Jerry's cell phone had sixteen missed calls, all from Alex.

He was trying to reach her.

The thought gave her a dash of hope. Alyssa worried over ignoring his attempts and expressed this to Jerry. He responded that he felt Alex needed to feel a little anxiety. He felt it was his turn to come after Alyssa. Maybe if he felt he was losing her, it might wake him up a little. Alyssa worried about that line of thinking. She didn't want to cause Alex anxiety. She felt he'd been through quite enough in his life. At any rate, she went along with it and just hoped it didn't backfire in her face.

Alyssa stood in the ballroom of the swanky hotel with her arm linked to Jerry and her stomach in knots. She wore a sparkling gold dress that cascaded down to her feet. It fit her figure perfectly. Extra waves had been added to her hair and it was pulled up to one side. The other side framed her face. She'd had a manicure and a pedicure. Light make-up was all she'd needed to top off the look. A simple gold necklace was her only jewelry. Elegant gold flat sandals adorned her feet. Heels were out of the question with her injured leg. Teresa and Christa had jumped up and down with delight when they saw her.

"Alex is going to be stunned and speechless and falling all over himself to be with you," Teresa exaggerated.

Alex wasn't the fumbling type. Alyssa knew that all too well. Still, she hoped Teresa was partially right. Her eyes scanned the room, hoping to see Alex. She didn't feel like she belonged here, but she held her head up high and tried to appear confident. The women were dressed in their fanciest gowns and the men, all in tuxedos. The room was beyond elegant. Chandeliers graced the ceiling, illuminating the area. It seemed the whole room, including the occupants, sparkled and shimmered. Jerry told her the couples attending had paid five-hundred dollars a plate for their dinners. The proceeds benefited the Pediatric Cancer Center at the hospital. Softly lit tables surrounded a dance floor where couples were swaying to the soft sounds from the live orchestra. Waiters dressed in tuxedos walked around with platters of unrecognizable culinary creations.

She saw Alex first when he finally made an entrance. He made his way through the room, stopping to shake hands and talk with various people. He may not like living in society, but he was in his element. He moved through the room with apparent ease and confidence, looking devastatingly handsome in his tux. Her eyes took in every inch of him. This was a side of him she didn't know. He was coming closer to where she stood. When he finally saw her, he did a double take. He froze, his eyes widened and he slowly looked her up and down. Their eyes met and she knew he liked what he saw.

At that moment, a woman attached herself to his arm, pulling him out to the dance floor. With her body pushed up against his, she began to slow dance with him. He didn't decline, Alyssa noticed. His eyes, however, were glued to Alyssa and she knew she'd taken him by surprise. Not knowing what else to do, she looked up at Jerry with worried eyes. Jerry softly patted her hand reassuringly, escorted her to a table, and they sat down.

"I can't do this. Please take me home," she begged.

"He can't keep his eyes off you. Give him some time."

Alyssa felt the weight of his stare. Thoughts of their wedding vows entered her mind. *I love my eyes upon you, just to behold you, your hair, your hands, your eyes, your lips.* Did he still feel that way about her? "I can't watch him with someone else. It kills me." It hadn't occurred to any of them that Alex might already have a date for this function.

Huge oversight.

"I know her. She's always flirting with Alex. He's not interested, don't worry about it. He's just being polite."

≈

ALEX LISTENED AS Michelle talked and flirted, while pressing herself up against him, his mind elsewhere. He had no idea Alyssa was going to be here. Shocked, he was still reeling from the sight of her. He'd never seen her look so stunning. She was an absolute beauty. He'd wanted to speak to her all day, there was so much he needed to say to her. Last night had been eye opening and he was desperately worried about her. They were both pining for the other and, quite frankly, he was miserable. It would appear she was too.

Clearly, she'd spent the day getting ready to surprise him. And surprise him she had. He'd wanted to ask her to attend with him tonight, a peace offering of sorts. And a chance to be alone with her and explain himself. He hated these functions. But this was an event that was important to his family, so he had agreed. At the time—in the back of his mind—he'd known it would be another chance to see Alyssa. He watched Jerry escort Alyssa through the crowd and settle at a table, actually feeling a pang of jealousy that Jerry had Alyssa at his side. He wanted Alyssa at *his* side, feeling her arm linked tightly through his. Michelle started to run her fingers through his hair and he finally asked himself what he was doing here, being polite to this viper of a woman, when his beautiful bride was waiting for him. He caught Alyssa staring at him and the look she gave him was so sad, it broke his heart. Alex was done being polite. *To hell with this, I want Alyssa.* He peeled Michelle off him and said, "Thanks, but I'm going to dance with my wife now." He left her standing there in the middle of the dance floor looking bewildered.

≈

ALYSSA COULD FEEL the tears coming.

It's over for me.

She was such a fool. "This was a mistake. Please take me home."

Jerry handed her his handkerchief. "Dry your eyes, Alyssa. Alex is on his way over here now and he's coming for you. About time too."

Alyssa gaped at Jerry with wide eyes. "Are you sure?"

"Yep."

She took a deep breath, scared to look. Suddenly she felt very, very nervous. Ridiculously so. Frozen with fear.

"Dance with me, Alyssa."

Her eyes closed of their own volition. She'd heard those words before. Slowly, her eyes rose to his.

"Please," he said, his eyes beseeching. He held his hand out to her. She looked down at his hand, watched her hand join with his and looked back up at him. Their eyes held each other's gaze.

"Leave the cane, I'll support you."

It was the exact words from their wedding night. She stood and faced him. He slowly brought her hand up to his lips and without breaking eye contact he kissed her hand tenderly, caressing her skin with his lips. Alyssa swallowed the lump in her throat. Then, hands entwined, they made their way to the dance floor.

Their arms wrapped around each other with ease. There was no awkwardness, they melted into each other. Alyssa rested her head on his chest and they danced that way for the next while.

≈

JERRY CALLED TERESA on his cell. He'd promised to update her on what was going on. "They're dancing . . . yes, very close . . . no, he hasn't kissed her yet . . . yes, they make a stunning couple. They've been dancing for awhile now. Yes, I'll keep you posted." He hung up. She wanted to know all of the details and had rapidly fired questions at him.

≈

ALEX HADN'T SPOKEN to her yet, just held her close. He felt so good. The smell of his aftershave sent ripples of desire through her. Finally, she dared to look up at him, their lips only an inch apart.

"You look absolutely stunning," he said softly.

"Thank you."

He lowered his forehead to hers. "Thank you for coming tonight, for taking a chance on me."

"I'd already lost you. I felt I didn't have anything to lose."

"You never lost me, Alyssa, never," he whispered as he

kissed her forehead and let his lips linger there. "Let's get some air," he suggested.

They discovered a dimly lit balcony, overlooking a beautiful garden. It was a balmy September evening and the fresh air felt good. As they faced each other, Alyssa kept one hand on the railing to balance herself. Alex stood with his hands in his pockets, seemingly a little hesitant.

"I tried to reach you all day today."

Alyssa nodded. "I know."

"There's so much I want to say to you," he said quietly. "But I'm utterly distracted. Have I mentioned you look absolutely gorgeous tonight?"

"Yes, you have. Thank you."

"I just want to stand here and look at you." His eyes traveled the length of her. "And I'm strangely content."

She would have to tell Teresa her plan worked. "Are you wearing socks?"

"What?" he asked with a puzzled expression.

"I wondered if I could tell Teresa that we knocked them off."

Alex chuckled, and answered with a sparkle in his eyes, "I can feel them slipping even as I speak. I swear it."

Just then, the same woman as earlier came out onto the balcony and wrapped her arms through Alex's arm.

"May I have another dance, Alex?" she asked with a pout.

Dismayed, Alyssa deflated, staring at the ground. Would he leave her? Was this all the time she'd have with him?

Alex didn't move an inch. Surprised, she discovered his eyes locked on hers as he said, "Michelle, I'd like you to meet my wife."

Alyssa couldn't hide her astonishment. Alex was telling her he still considered them to be married. She slowly smiled at him and he returned the smile. The Alex she knew was back. Extending her hand to Michelle, she announced, "Hi, I'm Alyssa Kendrick."

Michelle did not take her hand. Gradually, Alyssa let her hand drop to her side.

"Aren't you a cripple? Didn't I see you with a cane earlier?" Michelle questioned her nastily.

Alyssa's smile died on her face, but as she glanced back at Alex, she saw that his eyes had still never left hers. A flash of anger crossed his features as his eyes narrowed and his jaw clenched. Michelle couldn't know of the bond between them her leg injury had helped create. She'd just made a major faux pas and Alyssa knew she was now on Alex's bad side.

Too bad for her.

Alex shook his head in the negative ever so slightly, the communication meant only for her. "No," he started thoughtfully. "I don't *think* she's a cripple," he said ever so slowly, "but . . . when I go home and make love to her tonight . . . and kiss every inch of her creamy skin," he paused for effect, "I'll check. And I'll let you know." A small smile played on his lips as he winked at her. Alyssa smiled tenderly at him. "Oh and I forgot to mention, I'm saving all my dances tonight for my wife," he told Michelle unhurriedly, his eyes still never leaving Alyssa's.

Michelle made a scoffing sound and stormed off without saying another word. As she left the balcony, she slammed the door as hard as she could.

They dissolved into laughter like two kids.

As their laughter faded and they sobered, Alex told her, "It's not over, Alyssa, it will never be over. Please forgive me."

Those were the words she needed to hear. She simply nodded.

"You're too far away," he said, still standing with his hands in his pockets. He stood casually, but Alyssa could see the fire in his eyes and she knew that look. She took a step closer to him. Their bodies stood close, but not touching. Their lips were only an inch away from each other.

"Is this better?" she asked.

"It's getting better every minute."

They stood that way for a few seconds savoring the anticipation of what would happen next. She could see the desire in his eyes.

"Are you going to kiss me?" he whispered.

"Do you want to be kissed?" she whispered back.

"You know I do. Only ever by you."

Ever so slowly she placed her lips onto his in a soft, sweet touch of a kiss. It was feather light. Her lips softly caressed his in a slow, tender manner. It was their first kiss since they'd been separated.

It was worth the wait.

She backed away a little and looked into his eyes. A tear escaped and ran down her cheek. He took his hands out of his pockets and cradled her face. His thumbs gently brushed away her tears.

"No tears tonight, Alyssa." He crushed his lips down onto hers and their arms wrapped around each other. It was a kiss filled with the passion they shared for each other.

≈

UNBEKNOWNST TO ALEX and Alyssa, Jerry watched unabashedly from the window looking out onto the balcony. He called Teresa. "They're kissing."

He could hear squealing and giggling in the background as she told Christa. "What kind of a kiss?"

"What kind of a question is that?" He rolled his eyes.

"Jerry, you know what I mean."

He did. "It's an arms wrapped tightly around each other, not coming up for air, bodies pressed together, all out passionate kiss." Other than in the movies, he'd never really seen anyone kiss the way they were kissing right now. He started feeling a little hot under the collar.

"Is it over yet?"

"Nope."

"Jerry, are you sitting there watching?"

"Yep."

"Turn away, shame on you. Have they stopped yet?"

"Well, what do you want me to do, watch or turn away?" And then he added, "It's not over yet." He watched as the kiss became even more passionate. He smiled. It was about time. Lately, this had been way too much drama in his life. He couldn't take it anymore. He was happy for Alex. It was about time those two found happiness in their lives.

"What are they doing now?"

"Still kissing."

He could hear Christa exclaim that it had been three minutes. Oh my gosh, she was timing it. But then, maybe they were all a little obsessed with Alex and Alyssa. After all, here he was staring at them during a private moment.

And he wasn't about to look away either.

-28-

WHEN THE KISS ended, Alex whispered, "Stay with me tonight, Alyssa. Please."

She whispered back, "Yes."

"I have to stay for the speech, but then we can sneak out of here. Wait for me?"

She nodded and he glanced at his watch. "It's almost time now. Let's go in."

Placing her arm in his, he escorted her inside just as they were about to start the ceremony. A man approached and asked Alex to join him up front.

Alex turned to her, "Don't leave."

"Not a chance." As he started to go she said, "Wait, Alex, I need my cane."

"I'm sorry. I'll get it for you."

He went back to the table where she'd been sitting, found her cane, and then brought it to her. He held her face in his hands and kissed her, right there in front of everybody. It wasn't a quick kiss, it was a passionate kiss that left her breathless. People stared, but he didn't seem to care or notice and Alyssa liked the public display of affection towards her.

"Please don't go away. There's so much I want to say to you," he said again and she nodded. He walked to the front to await his turn for his speech. Alyssa watched him till he disappeared in the crowd. A thrill of anticipation ran through her as she thought of telling him about the baby tonight. She maneuvered through the crowd till she found a spot where she would be able to have a good view of Alex.

"Does he always kiss you like that?"

Alyssa looked to her side to see Michelle standing next to her. "Excuse me?"

"I said, does he always kiss you like that?"

Alyssa wondered if she was being serious or sarcastic. She couldn't tell. Michelle was a pretty woman, but the sour look on her face made her look as though she'd just eaten a lemon.

Whole.

She wasn't sure which kiss Michelle was referring to. It didn't matter. "Yes, he does," Alyssa told her honestly. Michelle scoffed and walked away. Alyssa felt just a little sorry for her. She knew what it was like to be obsessed with Alex.

The ceremony began, stealing the focus of her thoughts. When it was Alex's turn, she was impressed with his public speaking ability.

"When my grandfather was only ten, he watched his six year old sister suffer and lose her life from the degenerating effects of cancer. He grew up to become a great doctor. He never wanted to see another person suffer the way she had. He founded the Pediatric Cancer Center at Connecticut Memorial. It was his life's work. He supported it monetarily. My father continued to support it and I will continue to support it as long as there is breath left in me. My grandfather was an ever present example to me in my life. Thank you for honoring him here tonight. He was an inspiration to me and to us all." Alex's eyes searched the crowd until his eyes rested on her. "And thank you to my beautiful wife, Alyssa, who is now the inspiration in my life. Thank you."

Alyssa wiped away a tear as she listened to Alex. When he acknowledged her as his wife, her heart was full. Something had changed. Everything was going to work out. She was sure of it. When he found her in the crowd, he said, "Let's get outta here."

"I need to tell Jerry I'm leaving with you."

"He knows, I just told him. He said I was stealing his date."

"Don't let him fool you. That was the plan all along."

"Hmmmm . . . how very devious," he said with a smile.

They strolled through the parking lot till they reached his black BMW. The car was luxurious inside and still had a leathery, brand new smell to it.

Sitting in the close confines of the car, she couldn't keep her eyes off him. "I've never driven with you before, Alex. I have to admit, with you dressed in a tux, driving a fancy car . . . heady stuff."

"Don't let the trappings seduce you, Alyssa," he said with a wink.

"You know me, I'm easy. If I meet a man who owns a cabin *and* an outhouse, I'm his forever. It's the outhouse that particularly impresses me."

Alex laughed aloud and she loved the sound of his laugh — the sound of happiness.

The rest of the drive was quiet as they drove to Alex's suite, a somber mood suddenly resting upon them. The suite was on the fifth floor and Alyssa had never been in anything so fancy. The room was done in a muted cream color, from the carpet to the upholstered furniture and on to the draperies and even the linens that covered the bed. It was fresh and inviting. Alex dimmed the lights and turned on the gas fireplace with the flick of a light switch. They shared a look, not saying a word, but both knowing what it meant. The ease of starting a fire with the flick of a light switch seemed a great luxury to both of them.

The atmosphere suddenly changed as they faced each other solemnly. He took her hands in his and it was the first time she'd ever seen Alex behave as if he was nervous. He swallowed, "Alyssa, I owe you an explanation and an apology." He let out his breath. "I hope you can find it in your heart to forgive me. Nothing I said that day was the truth, absolutely nothing. It was a foolish thing for me to do. I thought I was doing the right thing, the decent thing. I couldn't see how we could be together anymore. I thought letting you go was the best solution. It wasn't. I only hurt you. I meant none of it. I thought if you felt I didn't want you anymore, it would be easier on you to stay with Clay. It was the dumbest thing I've ever done. I regret that day and wish I could take it back every day of my life. Please forgive me."

In response, a tear slipped down her cheek.

"I'll never forget our time together at the cabin," he said softly. "I love the mountains, I love the cabin. I thought I wanted to spend my life there. In the beginning, it was a sanctuary, a place for me to heal. When you arrived it became an absolute paradise, the happiest time of my life. But now, without you . . . it's absolute hell. I want to be with *you*. I don't want to be alone anymore. Please forgive me for taking so long to realize this. I'm alive and I want to live, with you, with Clay, with our children. I want our dream. My life is with you now. I'm coming home and I don't ever want to be without you again, not even for one night. Will you forgive me?"

She kissed him then, a kiss filled with all the emotion she felt for him. Alex took a step away from her rather suddenly as he pulled a folded up paper out of the breast pocket of his tux.

"I had the papers drawn up, Alyssa. They're waiting for your signature and our marriage will be legal."

Stunned, tears dripped down her face as she signed with a shaking hand.

When she was done, he kicked off his shoes and removed his socks. "It's official, they're knocked off, Mrs. Kendrick."

Then with his eyes never leaving hers, he slowly removed his tux jacket. He unbuckled his belt and tossed it to one side. He took off his tie, untucked and unbuttoned his shirt. He took her hand and held it to his chest. His heart pounded wildly. "You do that to me."

She took his hand and held it to her chest. Her heartbeat matched his.

"I love you, Alyssa." He pressed his lips to hers. The

kiss started slow and sweet and quickly turned passionate.

He picked her up then and carried her to the bed, their lips never parting. They slowly lowered down, he on top of her. They made love deep into the night, both secure in the knowledge that nothing was over between them.

≈

IT WAS NEARLY three a.m. when Alex and Alyssa lay facing each other in the large bed, talking quietly. They left the drapes open so the light from the stars and the moon illuminated the room. Neither one of them felt like sleeping. They spoke to one another in barely audible whispers.

"Do you know how much I love you, Alyssa?"

"I think I do, Alex, because I feel the same."

"Thank you for being so forgiving."

"May I ask you something?"

"Anything."

"Will you tell me about the night of the car accident?"

He closed his eyes for a second. "I'm sorry I didn't tell you. I just couldn't bring myself to talk about it. I thought you might look at me differently."

"I've seen the news reports. I know you, Alex. I know what they say isn't true. I've seen how you act in a crisis. You act honorably. Nothing could change my opinion of you."

"Thank you." He was quiet for a minute and then he began his story of that fateful night, his voice remaining a quiet whisper.

"I'd worked a twelve hour shift at the hospital. I was exhausted. When I returned home it was late afternoon. The girls and Trish wanted to go for a drive to a nearby lake and have dinner together. I hadn't spent any quality time with them in a couple of days and I missed them. I needed to unwind after my busy day. I couldn't have just fallen asleep anyway. We had dinner in a restaurant, overlooking a lake, about an hour away from home. Then we walked along the shore together. The girls frolicked in the water. They danced about and splashed each other. I loved seeing them so happy, so free. Then we stopped for ice cream and climbed back into the car to head home. The girls sang songs in the backseat and we laughed at their antics. Soon, they fell asleep. It was a school day and they had been up since early that morning. It was late and they needed to be up early the next day. Trish and I talked for a while. She asked me if I was okay driving. I told her I was. I knew I could drive without falling asleep. She offered to drive, but I declined. I was still unwinding, thinking about the day. I knew I would soon be home and have a good night's sleep. Trish fell asleep also. The car was quiet and peaceful. I thought about waking them and making them put on their seatbelts. They'd unbuckled them to get into comfortable sleeping positions. I thought to myself, just this once, I won't worry about it. Let them sleep. That was a mistake. One I'll have to live with for the rest of my life. I was driving on a curvy mountain road. I was alert and I did *not* fall asleep for even an instant. Suddenly headlights were coming straight for us. They were in my lane. I swerved to avoid them. They swerved also. I had to get out of their way a second time. I lost control of the car then and we went off the road. Everything happened so fast. It was about a twenty foot drop. I was the only one with a seatbelt on." Alex paused, collecting his thoughts.

"I awoke in the hospital asking for my family. They didn't want to tell me right away. I knew by the look on their faces the worst had transpired. I was told they died upon impact. At least I know they didn't suffer. The news said I was literally unharmed. I was covered with bruises and small cuts and I had a severe concussion. Guilt gripped me at being the only survivor. I wished I had died with them. The police questioned me. They thought I had fallen asleep at the wheel. After all, I had just worked a twelve hour shift. They told me I had no business driving that night, as if unaware of the fact that I'd just lost my family. Nothing they said could've made me feel worse. I told them about the other car, which incidentally had not stopped. There were no skid marks. The police said there was no evidence of another car. It was the way they began to question me that bothered me the most. It was as if they were looking for foul play. The news got wind of it and played it for all it was worth. I had just lost my family, my life. It killed me. I didn't understand how they could speak so callously of it." They were silent for the next few minutes.

"I'm at peace about it now, but I'll never forgive myself. It's not something you ever get over. I've accepted that."

"Anyone who knows you knows the truth. It was just a freak accident. It wasn't your fault. There was nothing you could've done to change what happened. Seatbelts or not. I've seen the picture of the wreckage. I can't believe they have the audacity to show it. But it's a miracle you lived through it. You do know that, don't you?"

"I do now."

She reached out and caressed his cheek. "I'm glad you lived. I need you in my life. Thank you for telling me. I wanted to hear it from you." She paused. "There's one more thing I want to know, to hear in your own words."

"What is it?"

"The court case."

Alex let out a deep breath. "It was a fiasco from the start. The families of my two patients were so overcome with grief, I knew how they felt. I could hardly bare to listen to them speak. During the days we spent in court, I wasn't even questioned about the patient's medical conditions. They questioned me about my past. They implied people around me died, that it was no coincidence. It was a circus. Everything they said was overruled, but the damage was done." He closed his eyes. "You know what they called me?"

"Yes, don't say it. It's beyond cruel. It doesn't bear

repeating," she whispered, knowing he was speaking of the name the media called him, Dr. Death.

"I went back to work too soon, I knew that. I buried myself in my work and it was therapeutic for me, but it was too soon. They died of complications that couldn't have been foreseen. It happens sometimes. My attorneys were confident we would win the case. I hadn't done anything wrong. The hospital supported me. My colleagues supported me. In the end, I couldn't face the raw grief felt by the families. I couldn't face the whispers and insinuations being made. It was just too painful. The judge was threatening to throw the cases out of his courtroom. I couldn't wait for that decision. I settled out of court with a cash settlement. I just wanted it to be over. My attorneys were angry with me and advised me not to do it. My actions screamed guilt. I didn't care. The media was having a heyday with me and quite frankly, for the first time in my life, I absolutely couldn't handle the things they were saying. It was too much. That was when I took a leave of absence and got the hell out of there. I found a spot in the mountains that reached out and became a balm to my soul. I've never looked back or regretted my decision."

"I know what a wonderful doctor you are, you took care of me, you saved my life. You brought life to me, made me want to live again. I'll never forget that. The things the media said would've killed a lesser man. You did the right thing. Thank you for telling me. I know it's hard to speak of."

"I love you," he said quietly.

As morning approached and they dozed in each other's arms, Alyssa knew it was time. She whispered in his ear, "Alex, there's something I have to tell you."

His eyes opened lazily. "What is it, sweetheart?"

"Promise you won't be angry with me," she said, filled with apprehension.

"Is something wrong?"

"Not exactly."

"I don't like the look on your face. You look scared. What is it?"

"Just hear me out. Please."

"Whatever it is, it doesn't matter. I love you. Stop looking at me as if it's the end of the world." He smiled at her. When she didn't smile back, he said, "Alyssa?"

"Let me explain before you say anything. Promise."

"You're serious?"

"Yes."

"Okay, I promise, but you're scaring me, what is it?"

A few tense moments ensued. "I'm pregnant. About four months along," she blurted.

Alex was speechless for a full minute, his eyes staring into hers. "How?"

She wanted to smile at him and say, 'the usual way,' but she didn't. It wasn't the time for humor. "Shortly before Adam came back, I suspected. I wasn't sure yet and I didn't want to get our hopes up. After the attack, it never occurred to me a baby could've survived. He lived through the stabbing. The doctors don't know how, other than he had a great will to live."

"You had no energy, no appetite. I was worried about you. I never suspected pregnancy, not after everything you'd been through."

"It was a miracle he survived it. I found out the day you left. It explained all of the symptoms I was having."

"He?"

Alyssa nodded. "It's a boy."

"A son, I have a son," he mumbled, seemingly overcome. He kissed her softly. Then his eyebrows knit. "I don't understand. Why didn't you tell me?"

"I went to the cabin to tell you. But that day didn't end up quite the way I thought it would."

He closed his eyes as if in pain at the thought of that fateful day. "After the things I said to you, you could hardly have blurted out, *by the way, I'm pregnant.* I don't blame you."

"I wasn't trying to keep it from you, Alex, I swear to you, I would never do that. It was just the way things happened. I thought you didn't want me anymore. I thought . . ."

He reached up with one hand and covered her lips with his fingers, stopping her words. "I know, Alyssa, I know. I've made a mess of things. I'm sorry I've put you through so much. Everything will be different from here on out, I promise. I love you." His hand cradled her face and he kissed her, slowly trailing down to her stomach. And then to her belly, he said, "Have I got a story for you . . . wait till you hear how I met your mother . . ."

-29-

WHEN SHE NEXT awoke, it was late morning. Alex was up, showered, dressed, and on the phone ordering breakfast. He'd let her sleep in.

"You were sleeping so peacefully, mama. I couldn't disturb the two of you." They smiled at each other. He joined her on the bed and kissed her. He was freshly shaven, his hair still wet from the shower and he smelled of aftershave. "I thought we'd have breakfast on the terrace." He murmured against her lips, his hands wandering the length of her.

"Okay." Alyssa showered, then came out in a robe. "Alex, it would seem I'm in a familiar predicament. No clothes."

"And that would be a problem because . . ." he said mock seriously.

"Alex Kendrick, you're in trouble now," she said as she walked towards him with a firm look, a small smile betraying her. He grabbed her and took her in his arms. They collapsed onto the bed, laughing.

"I'm waiting for my punishment," he mumbled. She ignored him and held him to her tightly, covering his face with kisses.

"Mmmm . . . I think I'll get in trouble more often," he said under his breath. A knock on the door interrupted them. It was room service with their meal.

As Alex went to answer the door he said to her, "I guess wearing my clothes won't go over so well now that we're living in a *cultured environment.*"

After their meal was beautifully placed out on the terrace and the waiter left, Alex took one look at the expression on Alyssa's face and laughed.

"No clothes, what a dilemma. This does seem to be a

problem whenever you're with me," he teased and then added, "We'll go straight to Jerry's and get some clothes, okay?"

"Okay."

Alex turned on his cell phone then and as he studied it, a frown appeared on his face. "Your father has been trying to reach me, Alyssa. Several times, in fact. Jerry, also . . . and the hospital." He looked up at her with a concerned expression. Alyssa felt the blood leave her face as she collapsed onto the edge of the bed. Alex dialed her father's number.

"Sterling, it's Alex."

Alyssa could hear her father's voice boom over the airwaves, but she couldn't make out what he was saying.

"Yes, Alyssa's here with me," Alex slowly responded. Then, "No, I'm at a different suite, not the one I reserved for Alyssa."

Evidently her father had tried to call the suite that Alex had held for Alyssa. Alex had not stayed there, thinking Alyssa was using it, and when he arrived things were not such that he could've stayed there with her.

"I'm sorry you couldn't reach us. Yes, I know, and I'm sorry you were worried." Alex suddenly looked at Alyssa. Shock at whatever her father was saying to him registered on his face. "Yes, okay, I'll bring her over immediately," he said as he snapped his phone shut. He knelt down in front of her.

"What is it?" she asked with trepidation.

"Alyssa," Alex said tenderly, running his hands through her hair. "It's Clay."

Her heart skipped a beat.

"He's woken up. He's come out of the coma. He awoke in the night and they've been trying to reach us." Alyssa closed her eyes and took several deep breaths. For a minute, she'd thought the worst. They embraced and she clung to him.

"I'll take you to the hospital. Let's go."

Alyssa threw on her evening dress and they hurriedly left. They drove to Jerry's and she quickly donned jeans and a blouse. Alex drove quickly, but deftly, and got her to the hospital in record time.

He kissed her tenderly. "Let's go see *our* son," he said with a smile and she smiled back at him mistily through her tears, thankful he included Clay as his son.

Alyssa and Alex walked into the hospital hand in hand. They went straight to Clay's room. When Alyssa walked in and Clay saw her, he started to cry, held out his arms towards her, and said, "Mama."

Alyssa gently picked up her son and held an awake Clay in her arms for the first time in so long. It was something she thought she'd never be able to do again. He wrapped his little arms around her and held her tight. She slowly rocked him as she wept.

≈

ALEX FELT TEARS slide down his face at the sight and even Sterling was quietly weeping. When Clay calmed down and Alyssa cradled him in her arms, Alex took a closer look. He was surprised to see that although Clay had Sam's coloring, he had Alyssa's eyes. Two huge brown eyes stared back at him.

"He's beautiful, Alyssa."

Alex wrapped his arms around Alyssa, Clay, and their unborn son.

He had a family again.

lancaster house

Zoe Grayson needs a change. So, she moves to another state, purchases an old, dilapidated 1920s Victorian Mansion, and sets out to restore it to its former glory. As she begins the restoration, she finds herself falling in love with the old house . . . not to mention its illustrious builder, Mr. Lancaster. Zoe becomes obsessed with the house as she discovers its secrets; hidden rooms, secret passageways . . . and a mysterious man who seems to think the house is his. Who is he? More importantly, how does he live in her home unseen and unheard? The unexpected answers leave her reeling—and questioning everything she's ever known. To her dismay, Zoe's actions land her in the local psychiatric hospital, scheming for ways to return to Lancaster House . . . and the love of her life.

Watch for these titles:
coming soon at www.taylordeanbooks.com

i have people

Holly Sinclair is happily married to the love of her life, Gabriel. Young and in love, Holly hopes to have their first child soon. Of course, Gabriel wants to wait till Holly's health is restored, much to Holly's dismay. She feels perfectly fine. So what if she just woke up from an eight-month coma? So what if some of her memories are missing? She remembers Gabe and that's all that matters, right? That is, until HE enters her life again . . . she forgot about HIM.

the middle aisle
a sequel to lancaster house

Zoe Grayson is back in Lancaster House, ordered to bed rest for the duration of her unexpected pregnancy. Doctor Wade Channing, her overzealous psychiatrist, is living in Lancaster House, taking care of her, waiting on her, and tending to her every need. It seems to be the perfect arrangement. There's just one catch. She has to tell him her story—everything that has happened in her life since the moment she escaped from Serenity Hills. It's been quite an adventure to include renovating another home and a walk down the middle aisle. But, that's all over now. Nothing is real. It never was. How did she end up in this miserable situation?

21919495R00197

Made in the USA
Lexington, KY
04 April 2013